The Shotgun Arcana

The Shotgun Arcana

R. S. BELCHER

TOR®

A TOM DOHERTY ASSOCIATES BOOK

NEW YORK

THE SHOTGUN ARCANA

Copyright © 2014 by Rod Belcher

All rights reserved.

Map by George Skoch

A Tor Book
Published by Tom Doherty Associates, LLC
175 Fifth Avenue
New York, NY 10010

www.tor-forge.com

Tor® is a registered trademark of Tom Doherty Associates, LLC.

The Library of Congress cataloging-in-publication data is available on request.

ISBN 978-0-7653-7458-5 (hardcover)
ISBN 978-1-4668-4273-1 (e-book)

Tor books may be purchased for educational, business, or promotional use. For information on bulk purchases, please contact Macmillan Corporate and Premium Sales Department at 1-800-221-7945, extension 5442, or write specialmarkets@macmillan.com.

First Edition: October 2014

Printed in the United States of America

0 9 8 7 6 5 4 3 2 1

Dedication

To my children, Emily, Jonathan, and Stephanie: Write your tales, never allow them to be written for you. Find your voice and make it a strong one. I can't wait to hear the stories you live. Have fun creating them—that's the best part! Nothing will ever make me as happy or proud as being your father. I love you.

To my sweet mom, who endured Vulcans, Timelords, and Jedi; Micronauts, superheroes, uncharted dungeons, scary monsters, Alice Cooper, and the KISS Army. Thank you for loving me enough to let me be me, and for the typewriter when I was thirteen. Thank you for being my friend, and my wise council, for letting me find my own truths, my own ways, and for supporting me on whatever path I was walking. I love you, Mom.

To the memories of Ken Witt, Pam Bardoner, Reggie Haney, Jeff Barger, and Jeff Franco. Your lives were full of service to others and you made the world a better, brighter place with your presence. Rest.

To the memory of Torri Lyn Saunders. You touched so many lives in your lifetime, made so many of them more than they would have been without you. I am honored and fortunate beyond the cage of words for our time. You are remembered with smiles and laughter and, most of all, love. Go play now, the moon is waiting.

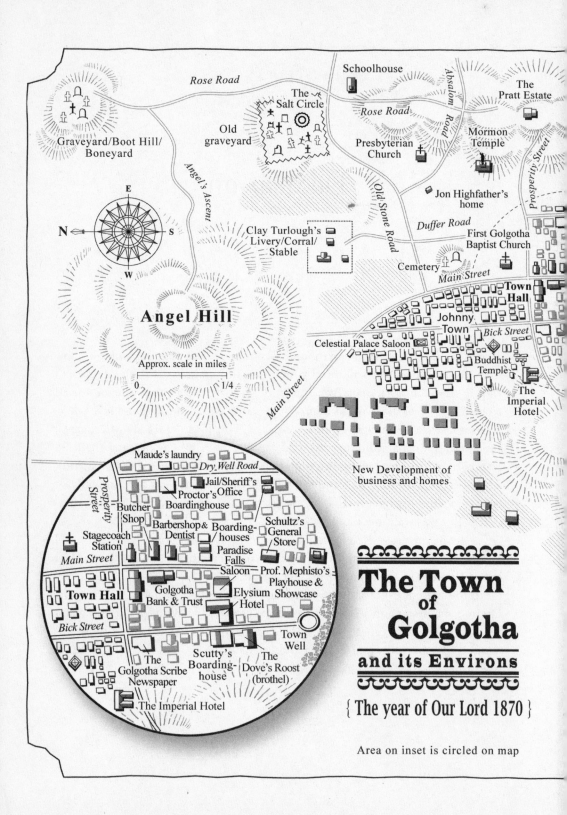

Schoolhouse

Rose Road

Rose Road

The
Pratt Estate

Absalom Road

The
Salt Circle

Old
graveyard

Presbyterian
Church

Mormon
Temple

Graveyard/Boot Hill/
Boneyard

Jon Highfather's
home

Angel's Ascent

Duffer Road

First Golgotha
Baptist Church

E

Clay Turlough's
Livery/Corral/
Stable

Old Stone Road

Cemetery

N   S

Main Street

**Town
Hall**

W

Johnny
Town

Bick Street

Angel Hill

Celestial Palace Saloon

Buddhist
Temple

Approx. scale in miles

The
Imperial
Hotel

0   1/4

Main Street

New Development of
business and homes

Maude's laundry

Dry Well Road

Prosperity Street

Jail/Sheriff's
Office

Proctor's
Boardinghouse

Butcher
Shop

Barbershop &
Dentist

Boarding-
houses

Schultz's
General
Store

Stagecoach
Station

Paradise
Falls
Saloon

Prof. Mephisto's
Playhouse &
Showcase

Main Street

Golgotha
Bank & Trust

Elysium
Hotel

Town Hall

Bick Street

Town
Well

The
Golgotha Scribe
Newspaper

Scutty's
Boarding-
house

The
Dove's Roost
(brothel)

The Imperial Hotel

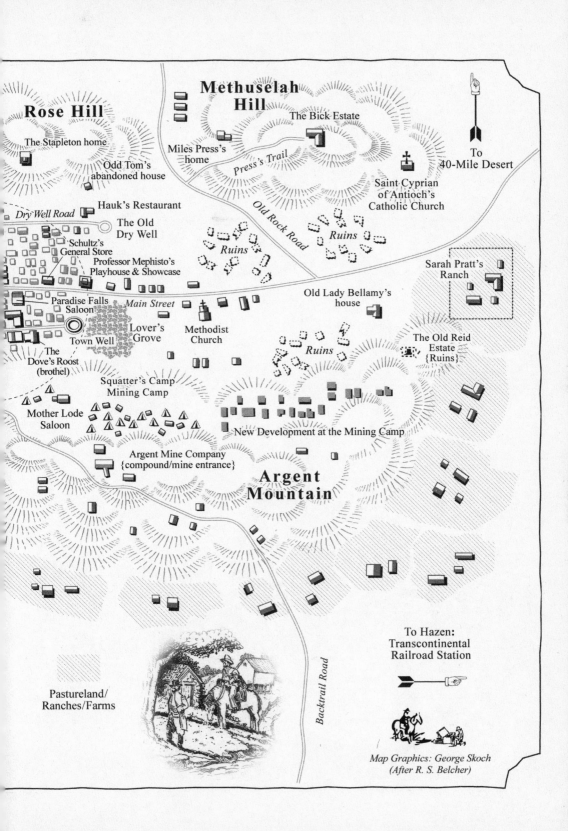

Rose Hill

The Stapleton home

Odd Tom's abandoned house

Methuselah Hill

Miles Press's home

The Bick Estate

Press's Trail

Saint Cyprian of Antioch's Catholic Church

To 40-Mile Desert

Hauk's Restaurant

Dry Well Road

The Old Dry Well

Schultz's General Store

Professor Mephisto's Playhouse & Showcase

Old Rock Road

Ruins

Ruins

Sarah Pratt's Ranch

Paradise Falls Saloon

Main Street

Lover's Grove

Methodist Church

Old Lady Bellamy's house

Ruins

The Old Reid Estate {Ruins}

Town Well

The Dove's Roost (brothel)

Squatter's Camp Mining Camp

Mother Lode Saloon

New Development at the Mining Camp

Argent Mine Company {compound/mine entrance}

Argent Mountain

To Hazen: Transcontinental Railroad Station

Backtrail Road

Pastureland/ Ranches/Farms

Map Graphics: George Skoch (After R. S. Belcher)

The
Shotgun
Arcana

Temperance (Reversed)

February 18, 1847
California

Bloody footprints in the snow greeted the rescue party from Bear Valley. They approached the camp from the direction of frozen Truckee Lake. The stained tracks veered, looped and crossed themselves—a drunken, demonic scrawl, an artist signing an infernal work in crimson. They ended at a mound of snow and ice roughly the size of a man.

"John, go check out that drift," Reason Tucker said to one of the Rhoads brothers. Tucker was a big man, broad, with a plain face and kind eyes. He wrapped his exhausted horse's reins around a low-hanging tree branch, trembling with fresh snow, and patted her shivering neck. "Rest of y'all start making a noise, call out. See if anyone is alive."

Mr. Eddy had told them where they would find the cabins, but all Tucker could see were misshapen hills of snow. So much snow, like the Almighty had grown tired of creating and had just decided to white it all out.

On the way up the Sierra Nevada Mountains, Ned Coffeemeyer had opined over their puny campfire, likening the snow and the violence of the blizzards to the Great Flood of Noah's time, swallowing up the wicked.

"That's a myth," the dark stranger said as he rolled a cigarette. The stranger had joined the party after they set out from Fort Sutter. Knowing what dire and ugly work was likely afoot once they reached the camp, if they reached the camp, the remaining seven members of the rescue party had taken the stranger up on his offer to join them.

They had lost so many men. Some dead, due to the weather and the treachery of the climb, others deserting due to fear of certain death. The somber-garbed stranger's appearance, with his black hair, goatee and mustache, his fine ebony horse and his eyes the color of sin, stark against the snow, had seemed like providence. "The flood wasn't God's doing," the stranger said.

"You don't believe in the holy word of the Lord, sir, the Bible?" Daniel Rhoads said across the campfire, rising slightly in agitation at what he perceived as blasphemy. The stranger narrowed his eyes and regarded Rhoads. The gaze was enough to knock all the righteous anger and the surly irritation of the trail out of Rhoads and freeze him in his tracks. His brother, John, took his arm and pulled him back to his seat on the fallen log.

"Let him be, Danny," John said softly. "Sumbitch got eyes like a rattler. Nothing good gonna come from riling him."

"To answer your question, sir," the stranger said, and then licked his rolling paper. "I do believe in the Almighty, more than most, I'd wager. I just don't believe everything I read."

"You have some queer views on the Good Book, Mr. . . . ," Septimous Moutrey said, sipping his cold, bitter black coffee.

"Bick," the dark stranger said, lighting his quirley. "Malachi Bick."

Now, seeing the massive mountains of snow where the cabins should be, Tucker had visions of women and children, still, cold, buried in tombs of ice. Frozen, dried up, like the pharaohs of old, some leaning with blood-caked fingernails against doors sealed by tons of snow and ice. Unmoving in the frozen darkness.

Joseph Sels's shout, frantic and muffled by the eerie, silent weight of the winter tableau, snapped Tucker back to his senses.

"Captain Tucker! Up here! It's bodies, sir!"

Tucker and the others shuffled-waddled-ran as best they could to avoid the sudden trap of falling into a thirty-foot snowdrift, which didn't support their weight. All of the party were shouting now, hollering out greetings and calls for any survivors to come into the washed-out daylight. Sels had climbed a narrow path behind one of the drifts that should have concealed a cabin. Tucker and John and Daniel Rhoads joined him. Daniel was still ill from the rarity of the air this high up in the Sierra, fighting for each breath.

Piled obscenely, like firewood, were human bodies: dozens of bodies, all frozen stiff and partly clothed. They were covered by a few inches of newly fallen snow. Near the bodies was a wide, low tree stump with a rusted axe, its blade buried in the wood. Blood had seeped into the wood grain of the frozen stump

"Children," Sels said in a whisper. "So many children. They're so tiny . . ."

Sels was a coarse man. He had been a sailor; he had lived a harsh life on and off the sea, and was only a few steps ahead of a deserter's noose. He had seen much ugliness in this world, but the tiny stiff forms, the sunken faces, brought him to his knees. He crossed himself and muttered the Lord's Prayer to the cold children.

"Most of the adults were lost when Graves' party tried to make it to Bear Valley," Tucker said, putting his hand on the former sailor's shoulder. "Say your peace, but be quick. It's getting dark, and we need to keep looking."

There were more shouts from the other men of the party, but Tucker didn't hear Bick's powerful, controlled baritone among them. Looking at the bodies, Tucker allowed a grim fantasy to cross his weary mind—that Bick, the stranger, garbed in black and astride a stallion the color of coal, was Death himself, come for an accounting.

"You were right about that drift with the bloody tracks, Captain," John Rhoads said. "Dead man. Been that way a long time—almost looks like some kind of a ghoul. He didn't have any shoes, but he was dragging a leg bone; looked the right size to be a man's too."

"Lord preserve us, the stories are true; they've degraded to man-eaters, cannibals," Sel said, rising off the snow and fumbling for his pistol under his coats and cloak.

"Steady," Tucker said. "We have nothing but scandalous rumor, gents. Let's not fly off the—"

"Captain!" It was the teamster, Sept Moutrey, shouting. "Look, they are coming out of the ground! The dead rising!"

In the feeble, struggling twilight, Tucker and the others began to see sections of the large and small snow mounds shudder and the snow fall away. Figures—skeletal, dirty, and pale—began to crawl, to rise, from the drifts. For a second, even Tucker felt fear clutch his stomach and balls. It was as if the snow itself had given up its corpses and animated them with a cruel mockery of life.

Bick appeared from a tangle of trees off to the left of the cluster of buried cabins. He walked quickly toward a shriveled, dark-haired creature that may have once been a human. She had appeared out of a hole in a drift near the center of the camp, and even in her pathetic state, she moved as if she were in charge. There was a nobility, a scrap of will in her that had not been devoured in the long frozen horror.

She stood and regarded Bick, while the other rescuers struggled to approach her as well. One of her small hands covered her mouth, the other hung limply at her side. She looked at the dark stranger with the last of the tears she could muster from the well of her soul. "Are you men from California, or do you come from Heaven?" the woman asked. Her voice was a dry rasp.

Tucker and the others had arrived now. Tucker noticed the rescue party was looking at the woman with revulsion and more than a little fear. She was like a bleached corpse, still moving, barely. Her face was a skull with pale, blotchy skin pulled too tight over it, like a drum. Tucker was surprised at how Bick regarded the woman, though. It was the first time since Tucker had met him that Bick had compassion in his eyes.

"These men are from California," Bick said. "They have come to help you, take you home."

"I'm Levianh Murphy," the woman said. She faltered, her eyes rolling back as she began to fall. Tucker and several of the men rushed forward to catch her, but Mrs. Murphy regained herself and stayed on her feet.

"Thank you, gentlemen," Mrs. Murphy said. "The Lord God has sent you to us, as providence. I'm sorry we can't offer you better hospitality."

Tucker heard Bick mutter under his breath as more of the cadaverous survivors crawled from their holes and gathered around Mrs. Murphy and the rescue party. "Remarkable," Bick said softly. "You people never cease to amaze me."

Darkness fell over Truckee Lake and the razor wind howled through the survivor camp, vicious and brazen, ripping into the makeshift shelters and rattling the collapsing cabins the survivors and rescuers huddled in. The full moon, bright and accusing like a vengeful queen, burned cold, silent light onto the camp.

The man out in the snow with the human leg bone was identified by Mrs. Murphy as a Mr. Wolfinger. She implied that he had met his fate at the hands of another member of the party. When Tucker inquired about the leg bone, a queer look crossed Mrs. Murphy's face.

"It makes my soul sick," she said. "No one can sit in judgment of us, though, save the Good Lord above. That's what Leanna told us."

"Leanna?" Tucker said.

"Leanna Donner," Murphy said. "George's little girl."

"Why in God's name are you people listening to a child?" Tucker asked.

"Because it talks to her," Mrs. Murphy said. "She is its High Priestess."

"The little girl?" Tucker said. "Whose high priestess?"

"The God," Mrs. Murphy said, her eyes glazing over. "The God in the Pot."

She would speak no more and went to her bed, turned to face the wall like an errant child, and hummed herself to sleep.

Many of the children, despite their lethargic condition from starvation and the life-sapping cold, were too excited by the prospect of rescue to sleep. A little girl named Naomi, who was about two years old, fidgeted in Tucker's lap, under the horse blanket he had with him.

"You intendin' to settle on a spot, Little Miss?" Tucker said. The girl's face was scabbed with patches of frostbite and dark from soot. Her cracked lips spread into a big smile.

"'Ventually . . . ," Naomi muttered.

"Well you better hurry that process up, directly," Tucker said gruffly, although there was a smile in his tired eyes. "The cot you're jumping on intends to get a spot of shut-eye. You hear me?"

The little girl giggled and hugged Tucker's arm. Her laugh was the best sound Reason Tucker had ever heard. Children were a mystery to him still. He hoped to have a mess of them someday. Children could endure disasters, madness, and evil far better than grown men. Perhaps, he thought as he was drifting off, it was because the world had not yet fully beaten out of them the notion that anything was possible, that people were good, and that God answered prayers. Tucker was so tired, even with the numbing, painful cold, the stench of death and the constantly squirming, occasionally kicking, little bundle of life on his lap; he fell into a hard, dreamless sleep.

There was noise in the darkness, a blast of sub-zero wind. Tucker awoke with a start, raising his rifle to protect the slumbering charges all around him. It was Ned Coffeemeyer, opening the door to the Murphy cabin and stepping inside.

"Colder than a witch's tit, Captain," Ned said as he shook the snow and ice off him. Several of the sleeping forms on the floor groaned. In the darkness, a child coughed.

"Mind your language," Tucker said. "Got children in here."

Tucker blinked a few times as Coffeemeyer adjusted the wick and the hood on the lantern the rescue party had brought with them and held his hands near the lamp to warm them. Tucker looked around the room.

"Where's Bick?" Tucker asked. Coffeemeyer shrugged as he laid his blanket down on the cold, damp, earthen floor of the cabin. He used his pack as a pillow.

"Blazes, far as I'm concerned," Ned said. "I relieved him couple hours ago."

Tucker carefully lifted the little girl and covered her under his still-warm blanket as he stood. He buckled on his gun belt and picked his rifle up again.

"He ain't here," Tucker said, "and I'll wager that mudsill is up to no good somewhere."

"Well," Coffeemeyer said as he dimmed the lantern and pulled his hat over his eyes. "He's got to be over in the Breen family cabin, next door, Captain. No-body's fool enough to walk miles to get to the cabin the Graves and Reed fami-lies are supposed to be holed up in, and Mrs. Murphy said it's about seven miles down to the Donner family camp."

Tucker stepped carefully over the sleeping forms to reach the cabin door.

"I'm checking the cabins," Tucker said. "All of them."

"Want me to come with you?" Ned asked, sitting up and pushing his hat back.

"Nah," Tucker said. "You get a few winks. If I'm not back by the time you wake up, come looking. If you can't find me and Bick shows up, you restrain him or shoot him. Understand?"

"Will do, Captain." Coffeemeyer said. "Be careful. I don't trust that sumbitch."

Tucker picked up one of the torches they had made from oiled cloth and tree branches. Once outside, he turned his back to the screeching wind and used his body to cover the match as he lit it and then the torch. The flame shot up the oiled rags and crackled and fluttered like a banner in the relentless maelstrom. He trudged toward the drift that held the cabin the Breen family had staked claim to when the party of pioneers had been forced to ford here at Truckee Lake for the winter. It took a few minutes of checking with Aquilla Glover, the current sentry on third watch, to ascertain that Bick was not in the Breen cabin.

"Why not wait to morning, Captain?" Glover asked. "Sun will be up, it will be warmer. We were headed out there anyway."

"Not waiting," Tucker said. "I'm not sure who or what Malachi Bick is, but he's up to no good and I can't wait to see what he's about. These people are al-ready crazier than a pack of dogs in the sun; can't blame the poor bastards. Bick might take advantage of them. You gather a crew and follow me out in the morning. You hear a racket tonight, you shake a leg and come on out quick as you can."

Taking a few extra torches and a spare flask of oil, Tucker set out on the nar-row walking path worn into the frozen packed snow. It was a little over a mile to the Graves family's cabin, and then about six more miles to the tents and shel-ters the Donners had quickly assembled to hold about twenty people near the bank of Adler Creek.

The torchlight jumped and shifted. Making a feeble, faltering circle of light in the dark, skeletal wood. Tucker's boots crunched and slid on the packed snow and ice every few steps, making him lurch and stagger like an infant learning to walk. The woods and the snow ate the noise of his passing, his panting breath, making him feel claustrophobic and watched. He clutched his rifle tightly, wait-ing for shrieking, pallid cannibals to spill from the dead woods to rip and bite his flesh. Tucker was not a religious man, but he quietly began to mutter the Lord's Prayer as he struggled through the all-devouring darkness.

As he neared the Graves' buried cabin, he began to imagine knocking on the cabin door, it flying open and dozens of scab-covered, talon-like hands tearing at him and pulling him into the putrid-smelling shadows of the cabin interior. He imagined being forced to participate in alien rituals to ravenous, inhuman gods. He imagined the sensation of teeth sinking into his flesh everywhere, a bloody morsel of impure meat being forced between his lips as obscene chants and prayers drummed into his brain.

Tucker had no desire to knock on that door and no idea what waited on the other side. If it were daylight, with his fellow rescuers at his back, he knew that the buried cabin held starving men women and children. But here and now, alone on the stage of his fears and imagination, he saw only snapping, stained teeth and madness.

A fear settled into him like the cold, turning his bones to frozen stone. And as many men do he began to attempt to rationalize a way to avoid his fear. Near the Graves settlement, he had spotted some horse tracks, which he took for Bick's black stallion's. Now, searching as quietly as he could near the cabin, he saw that the tracks went past the cabin and continued toward the Donner camp-site, five or six miles distant. He decided to avoid the Graves and whatever waited within. Tucker trudged on, his fear spurring him to put more distance between himself and the cabin door.

He neared the Donner camp after long hours of struggling, of near exhaustion at the efforts to navigate the jagged scar of a trail, to avoid falling asleep in the warm, narcotic slumber of the life-stealing cold.

Dawn was near, a purple bruise across the throat of the east. Somewhere, crows cried out, laughing at his struggle in the ash-colored predawn. Tucker heard the choked gurgle of the creek mostly frozen but still fighting to escape.

He saw a fire jumping, dancing in the smaller of the two tent shelters. He saw shadows moving about the fire, and he saw Bick's horse waiting patiently outside the shelter. He cocked his rifle and made his way down, trying to shake the weariness, the dizzy fear and the numbing cold out of him.

"I understand, Leanna, this was not your doing," the voice said as Tucker approached the flaps to the shelter. The fire stood watch outside the roughly constructed tent. It was a fresh fire, newly made and set on a wooden base, like the campfires they had made during their ascent to Truckee Lake. The voice was warm oil, rubbed into leather—Bick.

"But now we have to make this right, and I have come to help you with that,"

Bick said. The voice paused. "Please, Captain Tucker, you must be cold from your trek. Come inside."

Tucker stepped around the campfire, dropping his torch into the fire. He pushed the rotting blanket aside, stepping into the shelter. There were dozens of people in the dirt-floored tent; most were too weak from hunger or exhaustion to stand. Near death, their eyes were already seeing into the lands of shade. They looked at Tucker with glassy, bulging orbs, but they were seeing things he could not. Some of them looked at Bick and mouthed words silently. One feebly crossed herself and smiled at him with rotted, stained teeth. Bick, seemingly untouched by the cold, the ice, the stench or the plight of the survivors, stood next to a little girl, maybe ten, perhaps twelve. It was hard to determine through the starvation and the neglect. She was wearing a filthy, torn nightshirt covered with dirt, shit and blood. Her hair was brown, long and matted. Tiny bones and black feathers were tied in her hair like ribbons. Her brown eyes were wide and sad.

"Leanna, this nice man is Captain Tucker. He's in charge of the rescue party I was telling you about. Captain Tucker, this is Leanna Donner."

"Bick," Tucker said, leveling his rifle at the man in black, "what are you up to out here?"

"Put the gun away, Tucker," Bick said. "I'm here to help you and them." Something in the timbre of his voice filled Tucker with an overwhelming desire to kneel, to bow his head to this man. The jumping light from the lantern in the tent cast Bick's shadow larger, almost inhuman, like some great bird, on the rotting canvas. Tucker lowered the rifle.

"Now, Leanna, please tell Mr. Tucker what you told me about how this all started."

Leanna looked at the ground, shyly, as if she had been caught in a naughty act. "It sang so pretty to me at first," she said softly, with a bit of a lisp. "When we stopped at the end of the desert for water, I heard it singing to me, and I walked away from the others to go find where it was coming from. Momma would be very mad at me, but it sounded so pretty and so alone."

Tucker looked from the girl to Bick in bewilderment. "Bick, what is she talking about?"

"Go on, Leanna," Bick said, placing a hand on the child's head.

"I found it in a cave," she said. "It asked if it could come to our new home with us and I said yes. It hated the cave and it couldn't leave on its own. The songs of old men and angels kept it there. I hid it in my blankets. It was quiet except at night. It talked to me when I slept and sometimes it was in my dreams."

Tucker knelt so that he was looking into the girl's eyes. She was crying a little bit, but her voice remained almost a monotone.

"Did this man put all this fool nonsense into your head, darlin'?" Tucker asked.

"Let her finish, Tucker," Bick said. "This is important. Go on, Leanna."

"Everyone was really mad at each other a lot, and after I found it and brought it with us, things got worse," she said. "Mr. Reed and Mr. Snyder, they fought. Mr. Reed killed Mr. Snyder, but folks said Mr. Snyder tried to kill Mr. Reed first. They made Mr. Reed go away on his own. Everyone kept getting angrier and breaking up into little gangs and groups. And it was whispering to them, in their dreams and behind their eyeballs. Then we were here, and Pa . . . Pa said we had to stay here until after the snow, and it got worse. It all got worse. We didn't have much food and we ate shoes and rugs after the horses were all gone. But it told me what we needed to do to make everything better. It talked through me sometimes to everyone, and sometimes it told me the words to say."

Tucker looked at this small child who spoke so well . . . too well. It was hard to breathe. He felt like he was a few steps away from dizzy madness in his mind and a tight terror in his chest he would be helpless before, but what choice did he have in any of this? The little girl didn't appear insane. She didn't appear to be lying either. The eerie words of Mrs. Murphy came back to him. Murphy had said this sweet, disheveled child was the high priestess of a god.

"Leanna, honey," Tucker said. "You keep saying 'it.' What is it?"

"I'll show you," she said with a joyless smile. "Come here. You, too, Mr. Bick, come."

She shuffled back into the shadows of the tent. The other occupants writhed on the floor, in the dirt, like maggots in a hot skillet. They moved to make a path for their priestess and the two pilgrims. Many of them began to whisper a chant through dried, aching throats. Bick and Tucker followed the little girl. Tucker clutched his rifle and tried to bury his fears from earlier in the night, but he was becoming drunk with terror. The horrible, ridiculous fantasies he had summoned alone in the woods were coming to life now. This was no dream, no nightmare. This was the waking world and nothing seemed sure anymore.

"Meat," the broken, starving faithful hissed, "meat, meat, meat . . ."

At the back of the tent was a large black iron cook pot. The rancid stench was much stronger in the shelter here. Tucker gagged.

"Meat, meat, meat," the starving chanted.

"Sweet Lord, save our souls," he muttered, realizing he was praying like a child, terrified and seeking any protection he could find. He and Bick peered over the lip of the cauldron.

Inside were the scabbed-on remains of old meals baked to the iron walls. There was a viscous liquid with islands of white grease and blue-green mold near the bottom of the pot. Jutting out of the rancid broth were human long bones—arms, legs—boiled clean and brittle from being cooked over and over again. Smaller finger and knuckle bones, dozens of them, clustered like colonies of pale grubs in the remains of the liquid. More bones crisscrossed near the base of the pot, and resting in the nest of bones was a human skull.

"Meat, meat, meat," the chanting grew louder, more insistent.

The skull was yellow from age, obviously not the same as the other bleached and brittle bones in the pot. A thin spider web of hairline cracks radiated outward from the left brow, just above the dark, hollow orbits where eyes had once been. From the crown, and slightly back, was a several-inch-long fissure in the bone. It looked like a jack-o'-lantern's smile. The mandible and the maxima were intact, but the sockets for the teeth were all cracked and empty.

"No," Bick said. "No, damn it! This is all wrong."

"Yeah, no kidding," Tucker said. "These folks are eating each other, and it looks like they are worshiping a skull, a dammed skull!"

"Damned," Bick said. "Truer words were never spoken."

"Meat, meat, meat!" the weak and the dying snarled, thrashing on the dirt floor like snakes.

"Stop!" Bick said softly, but his voice held thunder like a cannon. Everyone in the shelter heard it. A blast of frigid wind howled through the tent. The candles were snuffed out, and the lanterns guttered. The chanting stopped.

Bick knelt by the girl. "Leanna, is this the way it was when you found it in the cave?" The little girl looked down again; she shuffled a little under the dark man's gaze. "I promise you are in no trouble, Leanna, but I must know."

"Bick, leave her be," Tucker said.

"Mr. Tucker," Bick said, "I like you, I see you have a kind soul. Please don't interrupt me again." Bick gently lifted Leanna's chin until she was looking at him again. "Leanna?"

"The teeth," Leanna muttered. "It told me to pull all the teeth out."

"What did you do with them, Leanna?" Bick asked.

"I . . . It . . . told me to scatter them outside, at dawn. The birds came and took them."

"Birds?" Tucker said. Leanna nodded.

"Crows," she said. "I've never seen so many crows. They made the sky dark again. They swooped on down and took them all, like bread crumbs. Then they flew off in every direction."

"When, Leanna?" Bick asked, standing.

"Yesterday morning," she said. "It told me you were coming."

Tucker looked at the dark rider. Bick ignored the captain's gaze. He cupped the little girl's face as she looked up at him. She was crying.

"I'm sorry," she said. "I did bad. I'm sorry."

"No, Leanna," Bick said, his voice softened. "You just did what you were told. It's all right. I want you to help Captain Tucker in any way you can. He is going to take you and your family home. You understand?"

"Yes, sir," she said.

Bick removed his duster and carefully wrapped it around the skull in the pot. He took the bundle and placed it under his arm. Tucker noticed for the first time since he met Malachi Bick that the man's breath didn't stream out of his mouth and nose in a cloud of condensation like everyone else's in the soul-numbing cold.

"Leanna, you are going to forget about this," Bick said. "All of this, in time. You all will. Life is a dream you wake from. Don't let this nightmare ruin the rest of your dream. Good-bye, Leanna. You were very brave. Thank you, bless you."

Bick touched the girl gently on the head, nodded to Tucker, and made his way out of the shelter with the skull under his arm.

Tucker followed him out into the gray light of morning. "One dammed minute, Bick! What is all this, some of the Devil's work? Are you in league with ol' Scratch?"

Bick had placed the skull in one of his saddlebags and was climbing onto his horse, a beautiful Arabian the color of coal. His name was Pecado.

"I only wish this was the Devil's work," Bick said. "It would make this much easier. This is far worse. And, no, like I told you, I'm here to help you. This isn't my responsibility. I'm cleaning up someone else's mess."

"Can you tell me what the hell is going on here?" Tucker said.

Bick sighed, and then looked down at Reason Tucker. "You really want to know, don't you? Very well. These people passed through my home on their way west. The little girl took the skull into her possession, unknown to me, or anyone else. The skull exuded certain . . . influence over these people, and this is the result—all this madness, murder, death, all this terrible hunger and rage."

"These were decent, normal, God-fearing people," Tucker said. "What the hell did that skull do to them?"

"Nothing that wasn't already there," Bick said. "I'm taking it back home and securing it. Unfortunately, now pieces of it have literally been scattered to the four winds. It wants to be loose in the world, it always has, and it seems to have found a way for fragments of it to be so."

"How did you know all this?" Tucker asked. "Why are you taking it? Are you some kind of expert in all this witchery? You wander around collecting cursed things?"

"Actually, I'm more of a homebody," Bick said. "Like I said, I'm cleaning up some other jackass's mess. But I do seem to collect interesting . . . trinkets. Good luck, Captain Tucker. Safe journey to you and yours. I doubt we will meet again. I'd prefer you speak as little about all this as possible."

Tucker scratched his head. "I wouldn't even know what to say. Careful heading down, and headed home, Mr. Bick. I can't imagine a place with things like that skull, a body could ever truly call home."

"It's as close to home as folks like me ever get," Bick said as Pecado began to trot toward the frozen creek. The dark rider and his obscene prize rode away into the blinding, bitter white of the Sierra dawn. Overhead, the dark shapes of crows mocked him as he began his long decent.

Judgment

The moon was a bullet hole in the sable night, bleeding ghost light across the wasteland of the 40-Mile Desert. The 40-Mile was part of the price you paid for the West. That price was often paid in blood and tears, and yet still they came—headed west, headed just a little ways farther out, away from safety and rules and meaningless lives and anonymous deaths.

Some were lured by promises of gold and silver, others came for the vision of a new world, a new life in a land big enough for everyone to have dreams. Some came hacked and hewn, inside or out, from the war, from the madness and the carnage, because they had nowhere else to go.

They all headed west, where luck and fortune still flowed like milk and honey and where your fate wasn't set in stone. You could be a hero, a villain, a self-made man, or you could vanish without a trace, erasing the person you once were.

But first there was the crossing: there was the 40-Mile and other places just like it. Many met the crucible of the desert and failed. The floor of the wastes was littered with the bleached bones and artifacts of lives lost in the attempt.

A soul would need to be crazier than a snake in the sun to leave behind civilization and kin, home and hearth, to travel for months in a wagon or on horseback to a land still more myth than reality, full of gunslingers and savages, outlaws and madmen, sickness, wild animals and spirit-crushing loneliness.

And still they came. Hope is a powerful drug. The moonlight washed onto the shore of the desolate, murderous land and found at the very edge of the

40-Mile, a town. Huddled in the cradle between two small mountains, the town waited. She waited for those strong enough to endure the initiation of the 40-Mile, she waited for those seeking solace or redemption or anonymity: the blessed and damned.

Golgotha waited with open arms, embracing the night. On the rooftops of Golgotha, two shadows pursued a third across the roof of the Dove's Roost, a house of ill repute tucked away from the sanctity of Main Street behind Golgotha's largest saloon, the Paradise Falls. One of the pursuers began to close the gap and the other shouted out in frustration and redoubled his efforts.

"Mutt! Hey, Mutt!" Jim Negrey shouted, panting as he sprinted as fast as he could across the uneven and partly unstable roof of the cathouse. "Dang it, Mutt, I ain't got no four-legged kin in my blood! Wait for me!"

Jim was sixteen. His sand-colored hair whipped in the desert night's cold wind. His eyes were bright but also old. He had his father's six-gun holstered on his belt and a silver deputy's star pinned to his vest. A small leather pouch, tied by a leather cord around his neck, bumped and jumped against his chest. The pouch held his dead father's jade eye. Jim's boots thudded like hammers as he gave all he could to catch up with his partner. Jim's partner was a blur. Thin as a whip and twice as fast, his hair was longer than Jim's, falling to his shoulders, oily and black. His battered leather Stetson had fallen off his head and jumped against his back, held on by a stampede cord. The man was an Indian, with a thin, pointy nose that showed signs of having been broken a time or two. The thick, black eyebrows above his crooked nose grew together and his narrow face was marred with scars and pockmarks. His teeth were yellow and crooked but his incisors were straight and prominent. He carried a pistol strapped to one thigh and a huge knife strapped to the other and, like Jim, he wore the silver star of a deputy. His people denied him a name. He called himself Mutt.

"C'mon, lazy britches," Mutt shouted back over his shoulder, grinning. "I'm only using two legs, and besides I'm tired of chasing this damn thing all over town. I'm of a mind to catch it tonight!"

The shadowy figure they pursued was small, perhaps four feet tall, and was moving at remarkable speeds with an odd gait, more reminiscent of a penguin's waddle than a man running. The pursued approached the edge of the Dove's Roost's roof, turned back to regard Mutt and Jim with glowing red eyes possessed of pupils of green fire. The thing hissed at the deputies and then leapt, almost flew, across the gap between the Dove's Roost and the roof of the boardinghouse next door, run by Mr. and Mrs. Scutty. The thing spread its arms as it jumped and wing-like membranes under each arm extended to allow it to catch the night wind and glide to the next roof. Its taloned feet hit the roof and it scampered to disappear into the darkness again.

"It's got wings," Jim muttered to himself. "Of course it has wings."

"Like hell I'm letting some flying . . . whatever the hell that is . . . git the better of me!" Mutt yelled.

"Mutt, don't!" Jim shouted, but it was too late. Mutt increased his speed and launched himself across the gap between roofs with a yip and yell that would have put gray-coated rebels to shame. He hit the other roof, rolled, and came up running and laughing.

"Aw, dammit," Jim muttered, as he picked up speed. He reached the edge of the roof, jumping for all he was worth. He landed on the roof of the boarding-house, barely, his feet scraping and slipping on the weathered and cracked wooden shingles, almost falling backward and down three stories to the floor of the narrow alley below. Jim steadied himself.

He saw some movement in the darkness of the alleyway, two figures, cloaked by night, shifting, grappling roughly. He thought he heard a woman cry out for just an instant. Jim paused, peering down into the now-silent alley, struggling to pierce the shadows, straining to hear. He looked up to call out to Mutt, but the deputy and the creature were nearing the edge of the boardinghouse roof, both fully engaged in the pursuit.

The creature had veered toward the southern side of the roof and sprung out again, its weird arm-wings spread. It landed easily on the roof of the Elysium Hotel and scuttled-waddled off at breakneck speed, hissing and growling. Mutt was already preparing to spring after it, his thin legs churning and his arms pistoning as he prepared to leap.

"C'mon, boy! You're gonna miss all the fun!" Mutt shouted, and then howled as he flew through the air. Mutt landed in a crouch, popped up and kept running.

Jim gave one last glimpse into the narrow, seemingly empty alley. All he could hear now was the raucous banter of the Dove's Roost's clients and ladies. The Roost was always noisy at night; most likely nothing to fret over. Still, something tugged at him. He heard Mutt whoop again as he pursued the monster. The alley would have to wait.

Jim sprinted after Mutt and the creature. He tried not to think about the fall and the impact if he slipped or fell short. He wondered how his late pa would have handled this, but that thought was of little use to him now. Pa would have never gotten himself into this kind of fool mess in the first place. Jim laughed at the thought and flung himself into space, chasing after his friend and the thing they both hunted.

———

The trouble had started quiet enough. Trouble in Golgotha usually took its time to make a ruckus. About a month ago, Clancy Gower had come by the jail to report something very disturbing. Clancy's goats were dying, being slaughtered. At first he had suspected his neighbor and cattle rancher, Doug Stack. Doug and Clancy had a long feud over Clancy's goats wandering onto Doug's property and eating up his grazing land and his few meager crops. But this was different, and Clancy said he was pretty sure Doug had nothing to do with the animals dying. The goats had all been drained of blood, but there were no wounds he could find to explain the shriveled carcasses.

Talking to Doug uncovered that he had lost some cows in the exact same way and that his troubles had started about the same time as Clancy's.

"Something sour-smelling," Mutt had said to Jim as they examined the fallen carcass of one of Doug's heifers. "Whatever did this, it ain't a natural predator, not a coyote or such." Jim nodded. Mutt's senses were far more refined than most men's, due to his parentage, and the boy trusted Mutt's nose a sight more than many things in this world.

"Ain't Sheriff Highfather gonna come on out and deal with this proper?" Doug had asked.

"'Fraid you're stuck with us, Doug," Mutt said. "Sheriff's away on business." Sheriff Jon Highfather's "business" involved a trip to New Orleans to properly dispose of a gris-gris bag holding the trapped souls of four dead men. It was the final chapter of a hoodoo war, fought in Golgotha a few months back. Neither Mutt nor Jim saw it necessary to elaborate on the nature of Jon's trip and most folks who lived in Golgotha for a while learned not to ask too many questions if they wanted to sleep at night.

They set several traps for whatever was killing the animals, but it had proven fruitless. It was only when Mutt decided to buy one of Clancy's remaining goats and set the trap with live bait, that they saw results.

"Who's paying me for this goat?" Clancy had asked when Mutt had made the request.

"Send the bill to the mayor's office," Mutt had said with a smile. "Harry will square up with you."

"Mayor Pratt will have your hide," Jim muttered. Mutt's smile just got bigger. They tied the small gray goat kid to one of the trees in the supposedly haunted stand known as Lover's Grove, moved downwind of the kid and waited. Tonight it paid off. The creature had appeared out of the foliage and looked into the kid's eyes with its own glowing orbs. The baby goat suddenly stopped protesting and stood passively, waiting to be drained. The creature remained cloaked mostly in shadow, except for its blazing, pitiless red-and-green eyes, its jutting, elongated jaw and slit of a mouth filled with razor-sharp fangs.

Before the thing could drain the tiny goat dry, Mutt and Jim had jumped out to grab it and secure it in a canvas bag. The thing hissed at them, angry for disturbing its meal, and leapt away, and the chase was on.

Jim landed on the roof of the Elysium Hotel, his boots crunching against the slick slate. He saw Mutt and the creature locked in battle. The thing jumped through the air, bouncing and launching itself again and again, slashing Mutt's face, head and shoulders with its razor-clawed hands. It made a high-pitched shrieking sound each time it attacked. The sound made Jim feel dizzy and nauseous. The deputy was swatting at the small creature the way you might to try to shoo a cloud of gnats from your face as he fumbled to grab his fighting knife.

Jim drew his pistol and advanced, but he dared not fire for fear of hitting Mutt or a stray bullet sailing down to the street. It occurred to Jim that below this roof and a few stories down it was business as usual on Main Street in Golgotha: the cowboys, miners and ranch hands wandering from the saloons to the whorehouses to the hotels unaware of the bizarre battle waging on the rooftops.

"Damn it," Mutt growled. "Hold still so I can gut you, you nasty little goatsucker! Ow, dammit!"

The creature raked Mutt's face and neck, but the deputy was quick enough to avoid the worst of the injuries. Mutt's knife flashed, splitting through the thing's hide of coarse black hair and cutting the creature across its wide torso. The creature howled in pain and leapt-flew toward the roof's edge facing Main Street. It disappeared over the edge.

"Jim! Git it!" Mutt shouted as he wiped the blood from his face. "Anyone sees that thing and half of damned Main Street will open fire. Those soaked jackeroos are more likely to hit themselves than that little bastard!"

Jim reached the roof's edge a few seconds after the creature had jumped. He looked down, leveling his father's old .44 Colt, to see that the beast had lighted on one of the Elysium's terraces on the top floor of the hotel. The thing looked up at Jim with its glowing, unearthly eyes and then smashed through the glass terrace doors into the hotel. Without thought, Jim jumped down lithely and followed the creature inside.

The Elysium had been the finest hotel in Golgotha until its owner had recently opened an even grander hotel, the Imperial. However, the Elysium was still one of the fanciest places Jim had ever seen in his life. The terrace entrance that the creature had crashed through opened into a small private dining room, part of the grand suites on the top floor. The room had engraved black walnut chair rails on the walls and beautiful imported wallpaper with a dark rose pattern print above the rails. The floor was covered by a fine European rug and an oval dark walnut table was the centerpiece of the room. The table was covered with fine china, a linen tablecloth and a beautiful silver candelabra.

The dining room was occupied by a gent Jim recognized as having arrived a few days ago on the stagecoach from Virginia City. Older fella, with tufts of white hair at the fringes of his sun-spotted pate, white muttonchops, and a beard under his chin. Fancy clothes too.

His companion worked at the Dove's Roost; Jim thought her name was Becky. She was a pretty girl, with long brown hair falling below her shoulders and yellow ribbons in it. She wasn't much older than Jim. Jim had seen her around town for quite a while. Becky was screaming at the top of her lungs at the third occupant of the dining room, who had crashed in on the couple's intimate supper.

The creature hissed at the girl and she fell back into the arms of her dining companion. The man pulled her back toward the double doors that led out to a hallway in the hotel, knocking over a silver cart and sending platters of food and pitchers of drinks crashing to the floor in the process.

Jim brought his gun up, steadying it with both hands and aiming at the creature, now fully visible in the gaslight of the opulent dining room. Its elongated head scanned left to right. It looked at Jim and the gun and growled lowly.

"Y'all go on now," Jim said to the old gent and Becky. "We got this covered. Sorry to ruin your fancy vittles."

Becky smiled when she recognized Jim. "Oh thank the Lord you're here, Deputy Jim," she said. "What is that thing?"

Mutt dropped down from the roof onto the terrace, his face bloody but his gun hand steady. He walked in and stood next to Jim, covering the creature.

"What in damnation is the meaning of this?" the old white-haired man said, still edging toward the doors with Becky. Jim noticed the old man was putting the girl between himself and the monster.

"Spell of local trouble," Mutt said. "Nothing we can't handle. Why don't you take your granddaughter on out of here?"

The old man sputtered. His face was getting redder by the moment. "Granddaughter! What the hell kind of town is this where you got some smart-mouth injun and a snot-nosed short britches as the law! I have a mind . . ."

The creature roared, threw back its head and showed all its rows of yellow, bloodstained fangs. The old man ran out into the hallway ahead of the stench of shitting himself when the creature had roared. Becky followed him out, giving Jim a final glance back.

"Thank you," she said. "Please be careful, Deputy Jim." And she was gone.

"Well, ain't that just sweet as peaches," Mutt said, grinning. "'Deputy Jim.'"

Jim got redder and decided he'd rather pay attention to the dagger-fanged creature, pacing and hissing in front of him, than his friend's ribbing right now. It seemed less perilous.

A bald man wearing wire spectacles and a simple gray suit popped his head through the partially open door. Both deputies recognized him as Dex Gould, the manager of the Elysium. Behind him was a wall of muscle covered in tweed—a man with bright red hair, a handlebar mustache, and a derby hat. His name was Gordy Duell. Gordy's brother, Kerry, worked over at the Paradise Falls Saloon. Gordy was the hotel dick. He stood at Dex's shoulder with a lead-filled, leather-covered blackjack in his huge, ham-like hand.

"You fellas all right?" Dex called. "We heard the commotion and Mr. Craytor said that . . . Oh my God, what the fuck is that?"

"Jist a little lizard, came outta the desert," Mutt said. "What say we stick with that story, Dex, okay? Anybody ain't lived here too long should buy it."

The creature snarled at Dex and Gordy. Mutt leveled his gun and whistled to get the thing's attention again.

"Damn," Mutt said. "Not that I am one to judge by appearances, mind you, but that thing is uglier than a bag of white men's assholes. I know why it stays to the dark now."

"It is hard to look at," Jim said, still aiming at the thing. "Like it ain't quite finished baking, if you get my meaning."

The creature grew quiet and began to look intently at Mutt and Jim with its glowing red eyes.

"I think . . . it's trying to . . . hypnotize us, Mutt," Jim said. "I don't think it's working."

"It'd have a damn sight better chance if it wasn't so backside ugly," Mutt said. "Now, vampires, there are some hypnotizers, I'll tell you what. We had those toothy bastards pass through town a few years back and . . ."

The creature snarled and began knocking dishes and trays off the dining table.

"What the hell you call this thing anyway?" Mutt asked. "A goat-sucker? A flying hairy cow pie? Outhouse goblin? I mean what?"

The creature began to give off its high-pitched screech again making the plates on the table jump and shiver. Mutt winced at the sound and Jim felt dizzy and sick.

"Shoot it!" Jim shouted to be heard over the cry. Both deputies aimed at the thing. Its glowing eyes narrowing, it crouched as it prepared to launch itself past the deputies and once more into the night. The shrieking grew louder and then the creature sprung. Jim and Mutt opened fire. The thing jerked and spasmed, then hit the ground a few feet from them and laid still.

"Mutt, your ears are bleeding," Jim said.

"Wonder my damn eyes aren't," Mutt said. "Ears will keep." He pointed down to the dead creature. "Just glad regular lead worked on it. The really bad ones, it always takes something special to put them down."

The deputies, with help from Dex and Gordy, covered the thing's body with the tablecloth and sealed the doors to the dining room.

"Someone go fetch Clay Turlough to dispose of that thing," Mutt said. "He'll have a day at the fair examining it."

"Clay won't come," Jim said. "He'll send out one of his new hands to do it. He don't go out much anymore, since the fire." Jim let the thought trail away. Mutt didn't reply, but he wasn't smiling.

There were crowds in the lobby, folks who had heard the commotion upstairs or had seen something happening on the Elysium's roof or had already been smacked in the ear by the swiftly moving rumors and gossip on Golgotha's streets.

"Faster than a damned telegraph," Mutt said as he and Jim escorted the covered body through the crowd and onto the back of one of Clay's wagon.

"Hey, Mutt, what is it this time?" Judah Stenton called out. "Another one of them boogermen? Those black-eyed children? Like the ones that up and took the Summerton family and only left their shadows behind, moving?"

"Aw, Jude," Mutt said, laughing. "The boogeyman ain't gonna want to git you. He takes a bite of your sorry ass and he'll be pickled for a week! Now git on back to your corn mash and let us be."

Clay's new farmhand, Joe Williams, was thick with muscles. He had a mop of black, curly hair. Joe was from New York, supposedly a war hero, but he didn't talk much about anything—which was the main reason Clay hired him. Joe dumped the covered carcass unceremoniously in the back of the wagon.

"Much obliged, Joe," Mutt said. "Tell Clay that Sheriff Highfather will most likely want to know whatever Clay susses out about this critter and tell him I said to not be a stranger, okay?"

"Okay," Joe said, and started to climb up on the seat of the buckboard. Mutt smiled at Joe.

"Damn, Joe, let a fella get a word in edgewise, why don't ya?"

Williams stared at Mutt, then snapped the reins. The wagon began to rattle and bump its way north down Main Street out to Clay's livery, off Duffer Road. The crowd continued to mutter among themselves.

"Them bat-people again, I bet ya. . . ."

"Hope the buildings ain't coming alive like last June again. . . ."

"Long as it ain't those worm things. I still can't swallow pert near nothing without wanting to upchuck. . . ."

"All right, git!" Mutt shouted to the crowd that still milled around the hotel entrance. "You want a show, there's one over at Professor Mephisto's Playhouse. Now go on, 'fore we run y'all in!"

The crowd slowly scattered back into the still-bustling flow of traffic on the street. Mutt waved to Gordy, who was standing by the entrance to the Elysium. Gordy nodded back. The deputies headed south on Main.

"Well, that was fun," Mutt said. Jim looked at him.

"You git your bell rung?" Jim said. "That was no fun at all."

"Naw it weren't," Mutt said. "Trying to be all positive and whatnot. People like to hear good things sometimes, not always bad things."

"Uh-huh. Widow Stapleton is starting to rub off on you," Jim said with a grin. Mutt scowled. "She back yet from that errand she had to run over to Virginia City? Been about three days."

"Nope," Mutt said. "Back tomorrow, I hope. Been gone long enough."

"Well ain't that just sweet as peaches," Jim said.

"Shut your hole, boy," Mutt said. "Starting to attract flies."

Jim laughed. "Real positive there, Mutt."

They walked toward the entrance to the Paradise Falls. The crowd at the busy saloon was spilling out the doors, socializing on the wide porch. There were a group of cowboys, running a herd down from Rock Creek; a group of Portuguese horse barons headed back East from some business in San Francisco and a few of the local Mormon businessmen trying to have some fun away from the disapproving eyes of the temple elders. The ladies of the saloon moved between the men like sunlight breaking through a bank of storm clouds.

"Seems like more people coming every day," Jim said. "Town is booming again."

"Liked it better when it was bust," Mutt said.

They turned down the narrow, dark alley between the saloon and the hotel, headed back toward the Dove's Roost and Lover's Grove, both on Bick Street.

"What you think Mrs. Proctor will have for makings for Thanksgiving," Jim asked.

"We just shot something that looked like the devil's asshole and you're thinking about Thanksgiving dinner?" Mutt said, shaking his head.

"Not even a week away," Jim said, "and a fella works up a powerful hunger battling evil little flying goat vampires."

A look of longing crossed Mutt's bloody face. "I hope she can git some of those fancy oysters on the half-shell like last year. Damn, they were good."

"Ma used to do up a fine suckling pig too," Jim said, looking down and fiddling with the bag hanging at his chest. Mutt slapped him on the back and ruffled his hair.

"I know it ain't home, but you got family here, Jim. We'll have a Thanksgiving to beat the Dutch." Something scuttled in the dark of the alley, running from the deputies.

Jim laughed. "You gonna go see Doc Tumblety about those scratches?"

"Only if I want them to get worse," Mutt said. "Man could put a hurting on a corpse. Worst sawbones I ever did see. You my momma now, boy, fretting over little cut and bump?"

"Figured a face like that, you need as few additions as you can get," Jim said. Both men chuckled.

"Gives me character," Mutt said, grinning.

"That it does," Jim said.

Jim tugged on Mutt's sleeve to stop as they reached the border between the Dove's Roost and Scutty's boardinghouse. Many of the girls from the Dove were out on the porch or sitting on the windowsills, chatting up prospective clients from the crowd of men milling near the front doors and porch. "Before we go get the goat kid," Jim said. "When we were chasing that thing I thought I heard a commotion and I saw someone messing around in that alley. Check it out?" Mutt shrugged. "Most likely one of Bick's whores doing a little side work, but we'll go double-check. 'Sides, give you an excuse to see if Miss Becky made it home safe and sound."

"Shut up," Jim said, smiling a little and getting a lot red in the face.

"Think I can cook some fatback up on those big old glowing red ears right now," Mutt said, laughing. He stopped laughing when they turned into the alley and saw what was there to greet them.

Near the back of the alley, where the shadows were deepest, was the body of a woman, or at least parts of her body. The woman had been ripped open, from throat to groin, and her insides had been poured out onto the mud- and shit-covered floor of the alley. Several lengths of her guts, radiating out of her split torso, were stretched taut and nailed to the simple wooden fences on either side of the alley. It looked like a dripping spider web made of intestines. The whole alley reeked like a slaughterhouse.

Jim had seen a lot of things in his year in Golgotha, but nothing prepared him for this. He felt horror and nausea swell up in him like a balloon. Jim recognized the woman's face, but he didn't know her name. She was one of the Dove's girls, he knew that. He had seen her numerous times on the street. She'd always smiled at him with that mouth that was now split ear to ear, and she was always nice to him, just 'cause. Always.

Jim staggered back to the entrance of the alleyway. He dropped to his knees, retching.

Mutt stood looking at the hellish exhibition. He was very still. "Jim, you stay up there," he said. "You hear me? I want you go fetch Clay. Not Clay's men— Clay. Tell him I said get his ass out here. Get that jackass Tumblety, too, and go tell Mr. Ladenhiem; he's the manager at the Dove. Tell 'em. Tell 'em all to come quick. Go on, git."

Mutt heard Jim sprint away behind him. He hated the boy had to see this. No one should ever have to hold this in the bone gallery of memory.

"Damn sight uglier than anything else I saw tonight," Mutt said to the atrocity and the darkness. He wanted to spit, but his mouth was dry. "A damn sight."

The Seven of Swords

Maude Stapleton crouched low to the debris-strewn stone floor of the buried temple. The mountain lion was twenty feet away. It knew, as Maude did, that the chase had come to an end. Maude locked her gaze with the big cat's through the miasma of sick, unnatural, yellow light. The cougar was a female and it was beautiful. Nearly three feet tall at the shoulders, almost seven feet long, nose to tail, and at least 175 pounds. Teeth and claws designed to do one thing: kill quickly and effectively. It had eyes like gold, and fur to match. Maude had no desire to kill the beast—it would be like murdering a sunrise—and no desire to be killed by it.

This cougar had mauled and killed a five-year-old boy from one of the ranches that existed in the green belt of pasture and scrubland straddling Golgotha. It hadn't been provoked, and it seemed to be in excellent health, as the deep jagged wound on Maude's upper back attested. If Maude hadn't twisted at the last second, her spine would have been severed and she would be dead: a fine meal for this golden lady.

Something was unsound with the cougar's mind. Maude could tell by its movements, the dilation of its pupils, the beating of its heart, the way it was breathing, that something was wrong with it.

So far everything was happening as Constance's dream had foretold, except for the location. Her daughter's disturbing dreams had started a few months ago. The setting was always the same—an alien city, made of the bones of giants, squatting in the middle of a vast, humid grassland. Even when the dreams involved the local folks of Golgotha, they were always transplanted to a courtyard of sunbaked stones and marrow-yellow portcullises within the bone city. Maude had asked if the city had a name.

"Carcosa," Constance said.

"I saw you fighting a lion there," Constance had said when Maude had calmed the fourteen-year-old, who always awoke from the dreams terrified. Maude brushed the brown hair out of Constance's eyes and caressed her daughter's cheek. "It was very quiet, it snuck up on you."

"Did I win?" Maude asked, smiling. Her beautiful daughter looked up at her with her dead father's soulful brown eyes.

"The lion lives," Constance said, and hugged her mother very tightly.

Maude had picked up the rogue cat's trail at the farm where it killed the little boy, Nathan Diachuk. She had arrived at the Diachuk ranch in the dead of night, dressed in loose black clothing suited to a man, her long auburn hair, shot through with strands of red-gold and silver, tied up into a ponytail, and a neckerchief covering half her face. She'd added to her disguise by employing techniques taught to her that allowed her to alter her posture, body language, even voice. To an observer, she stood, moved and talked like a man, which was exactly what Maude wanted them to see.

Her skills had come after a decade of training under the supervision of her maternal great-great-great-grandmother, an ancient woman she was introduced to at the age of nine as Bonnie Cormac, but who the world knew as the pirate queen, Anne Bonny.

Gran Bonny taught Maude how to live, truly live. She disclosed to her the secret history of the world, the story of Lilith—the first human to rebel against the tyranny of Heaven and declare herself truly free. Anne educated her in the discipline and the doctrine of the Daughters of Lilith, an esoteric order of women who had protected and guided humanity since the dawn of time.

The Daughters' duty was known to them as The Load, and Maude took it up when she drank deep of Lilith's blood on a night long ago, under a bright, swollen moon, like the one that hung silently in the sky tonight. The training, the blood, made her powerful—the better of any foe she had ever faced. She had full control over her own body and mind, an innate understanding of the nature of human physiology and psychology as well as an intuitive mastery of the physical world. The one thing in this world that could lay Maude low was herself, and she did just that.

Maude met a man shortly after Gran Bonny died. She still, to this day, could not understand why she fell in love with Arthur Stapleton; why she had married him. She was thankful for the union, though, for it had given her the joy of her daughter, Constance. Constance was worth it all, even though she had allowed her training to lie fallow for over fifteen years while she was a wife to Arthur, a mother to Constance; even though she had allowed the confines of society to bury the Daughter of Lilith alive.

It took nearly the end of everything in the universe to bring her back to herself: Arthur's murder, Constance's abduction and forced initiation into a murderous cult of nihilists. In the end, Maude had saved her daughter and healed the Earth by using the very last drop of Lilith's blood. Constance would be the last of the Daughters of Lilith.

Maude wondered if Constance's strange dreams were perhaps a byproduct of her taking Lilith's blood last year, to counteract the horrible effects of the blood of the Wurm, forced upon her by the cultists.

It took Maude three days and nights to find the mountain lion. Her tracking skills were rusty and that was exactly the reason she was using them. She knew if she had asked Mutt to accompany her and track the cat, he would. But she had expressly asked him to do none of that.

"Okay, can you please explain this to me again," Mutt had said to her as they stood on the porch of the Golgotha jail a few days ago. Mutt was leaning against the wooden rail of the porch. Behind him, wanted posters tacked to the wooden board next to the door shuddered in the hot, high wind next to pinned sprigs of agrimony, wolfsbane and garlic that the sheriff refreshed regularly. "Can you start with the part where you're going after a crazy man-eatin' mountain lion alone?"

"I think you have the gist of my plan," Maude said.

"Why in the world would you do a fool thing like that, Maude?"

People wandered by, walking down Dry Well Road. Across the street, the new town butcher, Garvey Hatlock, was loading a pair of cured hams on the back of a buggy for Mrs. Higbee, the cooper's wife.

"It killed Alfred and Erna Diachuk's little boy," Maude said. "Isn't that reason enough?"

Mutt tapped the silver star on his coat lapel. "I don't see one of these on you, and this sounds more like work for the law."

"Then deputize me," Maude said with a smile. Mutt laughed, a wide grin crossing his coarse face. Maude loved his laugh, his true laugh, and she loved bringing it out. "I can 'whup,' as you'd put it, the entire Golgotha sheriff's office, if need be."

"Yeah," Mutt nodded, still smiling. "I've seen you with your dander up and I'm pretty damn sure you could at that. But I deputize a woman and all those folks who want to string me up in this town would throw me a first-rate lynchin' and then a right fine party to boot."

Maude laughed.

"They would be majestically huffed about it," he said. "Come to think of it, that's another good reason to do it."

Several folks noticed the widow talking unchaperoned with the half-breed Indian deputy. Maude could read their disdain in the silent language of their movement and posture. Not that she needed those special skills. The majority had their disapproval spilling out of their faces. It was one of the reasons she and Mutt tried to always talk in public, to defuse the whispers of scandal and innuendo. The other reason was that those rumors had a basis in fact, and both Maude and Mutt were skittish about what might happen if they did find themselves together, alone.

"You do cultivate a way with people," Maude said. "That is for sure."

"So, seriously," Mutt said. "Acknowledge the corn, Maude. Why are you bent on tracking this cat?"

"Most men would simply forbid me to do it and be done with it," Maude said. "You are not most men."

"I am a unique desert bloom," Mutt said, lowering his eyes at her compliment. "'Sides, we have already established you could most likely pummel me good and sound, so I don't think me orderin' you to do anything would end too well for me."

She smiled, but then it faded.

"Mutt, I'm going because I need to know. I need to know what I've lost after all these years. The training, the power. I have to test myself and see what I can still do, what I can't do."

"You were a sight to behold in the mine, last year," Mutt said. "You saved my life. You saved Constance. Hell, for all we know you saved the whole damned world, Maude."

"That was different," Maude said. "That was me fighting for the people I love, to keep them alive, keep them safe. It was one part skill to three parts desperation. I need to know what I can do when my mind is clear and my emotions are in check. I need this to find out how much of me, the me I built up so long ago, is still alive."

Mutt started to put his hands on her shoulders but stopped himself, crossing his arms instead. "Thank you for saving my ragged hide and thank you for counting me as someone you . . . care about."

"I do," Maude said taking a step closer to the deputy. "Very much so . . . care about you."

They could both feel the eyes, the hatred, from the passersby. In this breath, neither of them cared. The world was two, only two. The realization of consequence settled back over them and they both took a step back, not for themselves, not for fear for self, but for what taking another step forward might cost the other one.

"Why hunt the mountain lion?" Mutt said. "Particularly."

"Because it has to be done," Maude said. "It killed that little boy and it will do it again, if someone doesn't stop it. You're shorthanded with the sheriff away and so many more people coming into town these days. . . ."

"And the real reason?" Mutt asked.

"Because I don't know if I can stop it, and it frightens me," Maude said. "I was trained to face any human being and know their weaknesses, their soft points, how to kill them. But this . . . this isn't a human being; it doesn't have the same motivations, the same anatomy, the same mind. This will be a test of my ability, my skill and courage. Without my courage, all the skill in the world is useless to me. I'm going after the cougar because the cougar can kill me."

Neither of them said anything for a while. They looked at one another, their eyes speaking.

"I understand," Mutt said after a moment, "what it means to lose your way, lose faith in yourself. All we got in this life that we can count on, birth to bones, is our soul. It's worse than death to be walkin' around and not know who you are. Be careful, Maude. I'll check on Constance for you."

"Gillian Proctor is as well," Maude said. "Thank you, Mutt. You're the only one in my life that could understand."

"Come home quick," the deputy said. "We'll miss you."

Maude took no water, no food, no horse and no weapons with her. Her satchel contained only packets of herbs she could not find in the desert and a small coil of rope. Her excuse for leaving town was to fetch supplies for her new business in Virginia City. After Arthur's death and the settlement of his estate, Maude and Constance were left a sum of money that was enough for them to live comfortably for some time, but not forever. Furthermore, Maude's father, Martin Anderton, had set up the newly married couple's financial affairs so that Arthur, and then Martin, were the custodians of the sizable inheritance that Gran Bonny had left to her, including Anne's estate southwest of Charleston, Grande Folly.

The few correspondences Maude had conducted by mail with her father in the past year had not helped the situation. Martin was resolute that he remain the caretaker of the properties and her money. Given that Maude was a woman, most courts were still inclined to view her as an emotional child, unable to handle her own economic destiny, so she had little in the way of recourse.

Maude decided to do exactly what Gran Bonny had always told her to do—rely on no one but herself for her fortune or her life. She used some of the money her father gave her as an "allowance" to start her own business in Golgotha—a laundry, the town's first.

At first it was just her and Constance doing the work, but as more orders came in and Golgotha continued to grow from the opening of the Argent Mine, Maude needed more laundresses. Gillian Proctor helped as much as she could, given her own jobs of running a boardinghouse and preparing and delivering meals to many of the town's citizens, and her impending marriage to Auggie Shultz.

It was a bit of problem finding women out on the frontier that could work, and wanted to. Most were either wives or prostitutes; both were often forbidden to work outside their respective houses. The solution came when she met and engaged some of the Chinese women of Johnny Town, the sprawling Chinese community that made up the northwestern corner of Golgotha. With primary work on the transcontinental railroad finished, more Chinese were pouring into Golgotha daily, looking for work in the mines or on the proposed doglegs off the main railroad line.

The Chinese women were impressed that Maude spoke some of the Yue dialect that Gran had taught her. After some negotiations, three women, Jiao, Ron and Chuan, agreed to accept positions at the laundry and Maude's business had enough people to keep up with the growing demand.

Maude also found in her late husband Arthur's connections to the floundering Golgotha Bank and Trust a means to secure a position as a bookkeeper for the bank, which was now under the ownership of three gentlemen recently from Kansas City. Once Maude pointed out her discovery that one of the investors was covertly diverting funds, there were only two owners.

Maude approached the bankers, Daniel Bracken and Roger McCredle, with a quiet offer: she would invest her own capital into the bank in exchange for becoming a secret partner of the two men in the venture. After the two men reviewed the numbers and realized how much of an asset Maude had already been to them by uncovering the embezzlement, they agreed, with the implicit understanding she would remain silent about her stake in the bank.

With her immediate economic challenges conquered, Maude's attention returned to the thing that kept her awake at night, the thing that haunted her dreams when she did sleep—nagging fear. Fear of having lost all the things she had worked so hard to obtain, in her flesh and in her heart; seeing how much of her years of training had been buried under almost two decades of neglect. And that led her to the cougar.

She had traveled in the bitter night and rested in the unforgiving day. All the tools Gran had given her to survive began to come back to her. She was surprised how many of them came to her without even conscious thought, simply instinct. She needed them to survive and they were there, waiting: rusty, buried but still there.

On the third night she followed the big cat's trail into a hilly section of the scrubland, and into what at first appeared to be a natural cave, about halfway up the small mountain. There was lots of debris from the mountainside by the entrance, small rocks and even boulders split and shattered as if the whole mountain had undergone some terrible upheaval, struck by a massive hand.

Maude had been traveling by starlight, using a technique to adjust her eyes to allow her to see better in the low light. As she stood at the mouth of the cave, she realized this trick would do her no good more than a few yards in. The darkness was absolute—as dark as what waits for us on the other side of our final breath. She closed her eyes, measured her breathing, and moved the blood within her to the places her mind willed it. Gran had called it Blood Working, but explained that it was discipline and control over one's facilities and body, not supernatural.

"A lot of what you do, they will call magic, girl," Gran had said, long ago, sitting on her driftwood bench on the beach, the crashing Atlantic her classroom.

Anne Bonny, at well over one hundred fifty years of age, was slender, slight even, with a mane of snow white hair, a few stray strands of iron and copper remaining, and was still capable of making a sailor blush or laying any man on the planet low. She cackled and raised a bony finger at young Maude, age thirteen, sitting crossed-legged in the Indian fashion before her great-great-great-grandmother. A wicked intelligence, and a soul thirsty to drink deeply, drunkenly, of life, flashed from the emerald fire in the old woman's eyes. "That's so they can fear you, label you, call you a 'witch' and worse. Like animals afraid of lightning.

"Bah! Magic! 'Tis nothing of the sort!" She spit onto the sand at her feet. "I know magic, girl, seen it all over the world. Different names, different sources—juju, Satanism, Kabala, hoodoo, Kapu and thousand others—and it's all the same. Unpredictable, clumsy at times, relies on gods and spirits and all kinds of nonsense that ain't you, ain't in you, ain't of you. Damnable stuff is less reliable than guns . . . or men. What we practice you can count on, from tit to tail, lass. You respect it, practice it and it will serve you."

"Isn't the blood of Lilith magic?" Maude asked.

"Is the sunset magic? The opening eyes of a babe? Cool water when you've been walking the desert? Love? Is love magic?" Gran reached under her tunic and pulled out the ancient flask that she wore on a crudely wrought iron chain about her neck. The flask was made of iron and yellowed bone with a thin filigree net of silver wrapped over its ancient, pitted surface. The flask was capped with a blood-red ruby the size of a thumbnail. "There are so many things in this life that are wondrous and defy being jammed into a category, hard as we might want them to. The blood is one of those. It doesn't give us our abilities, or our skills. It simply toughens us up a bit, gives us the fortitude, the focus and the strength to endure the training. You can learn this stuff without the blood, lass, most of the abilities were added to by Daughters of Lilith from across the world over the long eons, since the first of us drank The Mother's blood and took up The Load. Who knows, you might add a few tricks of your own to the repertoire."

"But how do Daughters from all over the world, from different ages, learn the knowledge, the skills of another half a world away? Do we all meet from time to time?"

"No," Anne said. "There are a few things that might draw us all together. All of them horrid. Hopefully you won't have that happen in your time. No, it's a property of the blood. We just 'know' things about the others who carry The Load and them about us. It comes in dreams and in the secret parts of your mind that are always at work, always whispering, but that you are mostly unaware of. As knowledge that affects us all is added, we all just sort of become aware of that possibility and then we have to still train and perfect the skills or seek out the full information, but we just . . . know."

"That sounds like magic to me," Maude said, smiling. Gran growled.

"Infuriating little wagtail!" she said. "Let's quiet all those questions with some breath-control exercises! Into the water, now! I want you fully immersed and holding your breath for thirty minutes this time! Go!"

At the entrance to the cave, Maude increased the sensitivity of her hearing and the acuity of her sense of touch. She could feel and "see" the currents of air moving about her, perceive the openings and the obstacles in the darkness of the cavern. Her nose picked up a hint of the heady musk of the mountain lion's scent and even perceived a sourness in it that would indicate a sickness, perhaps a poisoning. She stepped into the darkness and swam with it, in it. She was as silent as smoke. As she moved deeper into the cavern, she discovered it descended, and that a well-worn set of stairs was hewn into the rock. The big cat had gone down the stairs. Maude followed. Continuing downward on the narrow, winding stairs , Maude's closed eyes began to register some kind of light beyond her lids. She opened her eyes and could see, but she couldn't believe what she was seeing.

The stone stairs spiraled down into a cavern, the walls of which were carved in intricate relief; the façades of ionic columns of the Greek fashion circled the circular stone vault. Between the faux pillars were strange murals depicting scenes of monstrous beings crashing to the Earth, thrown by other monsters from on high, beyond the stars. Other murals depicted the creatures, composed of writhing snakes and parts akin to crustaceans, birds and insects, possessing millions of gibbering mouths, being warred upon by women with spears and others wielding flame. The final murals depicted the creatures being dragged down under the sea and into mountains, where, in chains, they slumbered, dreaming. The last panel of bas-relief depicted the stars tumbling down, the mountains shattering and the seas boiling as the horrible things arose from their slumber, and most prominent in the depiction of the destruction was a thing that seemed to possess the qualities of a man and serpent.

The whole cave was bathed in a sick, lemony light that came from a small naturally formed cistern beside the foot of the stairs. As Maude silently neared the foot of the staircase, she noted that the water in the cistern seemed clear and clean, but gave off an unearthly greenish-yellow glow. She couldn't tell if it was the water itself glowing, or if it was a property of something within the natural pool.

The whole place reminded Maude of the well room, deep below the Argent Mine, where she had battled to save her daughter and the world last year. Similar, but this place's architecture seemed to be firmly grounded in the ancient Western world, a temple to some blasphemous pantheon of gods the Greeks feared enough to placate but dared not worship.

The chamber had an intrinsic wrongness to it. The very atmosphere, the feel of the gravity—it all felt wrong, off, to Maude.

She didn't have long to ponder the mystery of an ancient Greek temple buried in the foothills of Nevada as a dark shape dropped upon her with a growl that shredded the silence. Maude twisted her upper body and that instinct alone saved her from the mountain lion's ambush. The great cat had been lounging on a rock shelf above the room and had pounced silently, surprising her. It suddenly occurred to Maude, as she pushed the pain of the gash in her back to a distant place in her mind, that despite her silent movement, the cat had smelled her approach and had been ready for her. She had grown arrogant, thinking her training made her invisible, untouchable.

The cat scrambled to lock its teeth onto her neck, but Maude tumbled backward and landed a powerful kick to the side of the cougar's head. The cat staggered backward and shook its head from the force of the blow. That led to a standoff, the two predators crouched near each other, knowing that only one was going to leave this cave.

Maude felt the wet blood on her back oozing. The wound needed attention, but for now all she could do was slow the flow of the blood and keep the pain contained.

The cougar padded over to the cistern and lapped at the glowing water with its wide tongue. It shuddered, as if it had a seizure, then growled low and turned back to glare at Maude, some mad, alien light now reflected in its beautiful eyes.

"So that's what made you sick, you poor girl," Maude said. "I'm so sorry, this isn't your fault, is it?"

The big cat snarled and began to pace before the cistern, its tail slashing back and forth. Maude stayed low and watched very carefully the fluid ripple of muscles and the twitch of tendons beneath the cougar's golden fur.

This was the reason she had come out here. Her training had taught her how to heal, manipulate, misdirect, kill or incapacitate people. She knew the roadways of nerves and pressure points that crisscrossed the human body. Very little time had been paid to types of animals other than man, but Maude had a vague feeling, like an old memory itching at the back of her mind, that there was . . . something.

She stood and took a clumsy step to the left, slightly turning her back to the cougar. It was a feint and it worked; the cat launched itself at her with a roar. Maude twisted suddenly right and moved her legs to a stable, balanced position. The cat shifted, too, in mid-flight, to compensate for Maude's trick. *Clever girl*, Maude thought. It was the only thought she had time for as she saw fangs and claws barreling down on her. Her response was pure instinct; she dropped to one knee and saw the cougar's belly sail over her, claws flailing wildly at her. From this angle she could strike upward and most likely rupture most of the cat's major organs. Again, by instinct, Maude didn't take the killing blow. Instead, she launched herself from the crouch into a spinning flip that brought her above and behind the cougar as they both sailed toward the cave floor.

Maude slid her arms under one of the cougar's forelegs and behind the great cat's neck as they hit the ground. The two tumbled and rolled. Maude hung on as the cat tried to get around and find purchase to rake Maude with her claws, or shake her loose. Maude held on. Quickly, she slid her free arm under and up around the cat's other foreleg and completed the hold around the mountain lion's neck. The cat raked her arm as she slipped by it, leaving an ugly, gushing wound on her right forearm. The pain was hot, jagged fire up her arm and shoulder. Maude didn't let go.

She now had the mountain lion pinned. She felt the cougar's vertebra as she gripped the cat's neck. Using the spine as her map, Maude was confident that the nerves she sought were there. She applied pressure to the site with her thumbs, the exact amount to affect a human. The cougar snarled and thrashed, fighting to get free. As it felt the pressure on its neck it fought harder. It wasn't working. A thrill of panic ran through Maude, but then she applied more pressure, more. Maude squeezed with all her might and hung on. The cat kicked and clawed as best it could with its rear legs. A stray swipe caught Maude's shin. The stab of pain made her wince and gasp, but she held on. This would work. This had to work.

Time expanded and contracted as the struggle continued. The cougar began to shudder; its struggles became weaker and weaker. It made one last violent attempt to break free, which almost succeeded, but Maude held steadfast. Finally the cougar was still, becoming blessed dead weight in Maude's aching, trembling arms. If she maintained the pressure now, the cougar's fluttering heart would still. It was the right thing to do, the practical and the tactically sound decision. Her strength was faltering and her wounds were demanding attention. She might not be able to do this again. . . .

She let the slumbering cougar slip to the cave floor. If she needed to do this again, she would. She knew it.

She bound the cougar with knots that would tighten the more the cat struggled to free itself. She wrestled with loose rocks and small boulders to choke up the cistern and conceal it. No other animals would be poisoned by whatever unearthly force slumbered beneath the cold water. Maude went out into the chill predawn of the scrubland and scouted a few plants she needed to undertake what she was trying next: some wild licorice and creosote.

She ground up the plants she harvested and added some of the powders in her satchel and then worked the compound into the bloody carcass of a small desert hare Maude hunted down and skinned. She left the medicated meal in easy reach of the unconscious and bound cougar. She ran her hands over the cat's sleek flank, scratched it behind the ears and felt a tremble of a purr rumble in the golden lady's chest.

She mended her wounds as best she could, given her resources, applying poultices to the wounds to ease blood loss and minimize infection.

Maude collapsed, hot, tired and exhausted from battle and blood loss, onto a cool corner of the temple floor. She dreamed of Constance's city of bones and its inhuman inhabitants.

She awoke to a low growl and a foul smell. Maude was sore, tired and cold. The wound on her back was warm and pulsing with pain. She stood silently and banished her own discomforts as well as she could, using her training. The mountain lion was awake. It had eaten the hare. It seemed that Maude's concoction had worked. The cougar had gotten ill and had vomited on the cavern floor. It was thrashing and trying to free itself. Maude approached it slowly.

"It's all right, golden lady," she said, keeping eye contact with the cat. "That feels better, doesn't it?"

Maude's hand flashed out. Her nails sliced through the rope effortlessly. And the action seemed to startle the big cat as it shook off its bonds. Maude stood her ground, her hands at her side. The cougar snarled at her.

"Go," Maude said. "I'm glad this ended with no one dead. If you hunt people again, I'll find you. It won't end this way twice."

The mountain lion ascended the stone stairs out to the open air, to the scrubland. She paused to regard Maude with a roar. Maude met her eyes. The cougar looked away and continued her climb and was gone.

Maude looked around the temple, frowned at the mystery of it and then began her own climb upward, back to the fading night and the trek to Golgotha. She knew she would make it home.

Strength

Mutt shouted to two local men he recognized riding a buckboard wagon down Bick Street, headed out of town. George Minter and Eustace Bloom were new hires, working for Sarah Pratt, the mayor's wife, out on her ranch. They pulled the wagon to a halt.

"We got a mess in the alley, fellas—a murder," Mutt said. "You have horse blankets or cloth we could pitch up to cover up the entrance?"

"Yeah, I think we do," George said. "Happy to oblige, Deputy."

"You gonna take orders from some damned heathen savage, George?" Eustace rumbled. He was drunk, but even when he was sober Eustace was an ass. "Hell, it's a damn miracle the fucking 'deputy' isn't running up and down the street, naked and drunk off his ass on firewater."

"You caught me on a rare clothed, sober day," Mutt said, and turned back to George. "Appreciate the help, George."

George turned and whispered to Eustace, "You are lucky he's too busy right now to pay attention to you, or your stupid ass would be in jail."

Hatred aimed at you was kind of like being caught in the rain, Mutt reasoned. It was uncomfortable as hell at first but once you were good and soaked in it, you really didn't pay it too much mind, even though it was still unpleasant. Mutt had been hated by so many people for so long, he hardly felt the sting of it anymore. At least that was what he told himself.

With George's help, Mutt was able to nail a pair of horse blankets up as a crude curtain at the entrance of the alley. It was less than two hours to sunup and most folks were off the street by now and home in bed, hoping their wives hadn't heard them sneak in. A small crowd of the hangers-on gathered on the narrow mud- and shit-rutted path that was Bick Street. Others lurked on the partly warped wooden planks that were laid out on either side of the street, acting as sidewalks to allow gentlefolk to avoid the filth of the road. Many of the Dove's working girls and some of their clients gathered on the porch to see what the commotion was about. There was almost a festive, party atmosphere to the gawkers, which made Mutt want to shoot each and every last one of them in the face. A few of the "Doves" ducked through the side door of their building to peek in the alleyway. When they saw what remained of their sister, the screaming began. The cry went up on the wind. Sadly, such sounds were all too familiar in the night air of Golgotha.

"Y'all git on back inside now," Mutt shouted to the girls. Most obeyed, but a few and their male company crept out into the alleyway to get a closer look. Mutt desperately wished the sheriff were here. Jon Highfather was a leader; people respected him, liked him and listened to him. Mutt was none of that on his best day. He didn't talk pretty and most of the town hated him and the rest were afraid of him. Jon wouldn't be back till tomorrow, so Mutt had to do it his way and Jon could apologize to everyone for him when he got back.

"Listen up!" Mutt shouted. "This is now an official investigation of the sheriff's office."

"And what does that mean, Deputy Red Nigger," one of the drunken miners on the Dove's porch shouted back. A roar of laughter came up from the crowd. Mutt walked over, grabbed the miner by the collar and pulled him off the porch and over the rail, into the dirt. Mutt drew his pistol as fluidly as breathing and cocked and aimed at the stunned drunk on the ground. Mutt fired a single round. The crowd gasped and a few of the Doves screamed. One swooned and fainted.

The miner blinked and opened his eyes. There was a smoking bullet hole in the dirt next to his head.

"That's Deputy Crazy Red Nigger, sir," Mutt said loud enough for everyone to hear. "The next one of your pasty-faced lick-fingers who says anything other than 'yes sir, Mr. Deputy, sir,' to me, I will put a hole in you and let all the stupid leak out. Y'hear!"

The miner struggled to his feet. Mutt frowned and wrinkled up his nose. "Get your ass home, and for God's sake, clean it up, you done gone and shit yourself."

The miner staggered-ran toward his buddies, who rushed him away into the night, at arm's length. He was rubbing his ears from the blast of the gun.

Jim walked up, still a little pale, with a big gent beside him.

"Doc Tumblety weren't home," Jim said. "I left a message with his boy, Row-ley. Clay said he'd come, but he weren't none too happy about it. And this here is the Dove's manager."

The man was over six foot eight, a good foot taller than Mutt at least. His muscles were barely contained by his clothing. He was dressed in an odd mix-ture of workingman and dandy: a simple linen white work shirt with a short collar, denim dungarees and heavy boots like those the miners wore, but also a proper gentleman's waistcoat, made of brown dyed linen with brass buttons, and a gold watch chain attached to the coat and arching to the pocket. The man had brown hair cut fashionably short with a thick part from forehead almost to his nape. He had a short, neatly groomed beard and hazel eyes that gave away noth-ing of the intent behind them. He had an ugly wooden cudgel that looked small in his hands. He carried it as a walking stick. Mutt nodded at the giant.

"You're the manager now?" Mutt said. "What happened to Ladenhiem?"

"Left town," the man said. "Seems there was some kind of a problem with spi-ders? Things crawling out of people's dreams, webbing them up, drinking them dry, or some such nonsense. Man was obviously a laudanum fiend."

"Oh, yeah," Mutt said, snapping his fingers. "He was one of the ones got caught up in all that. Funny, I thought old Ladenhiem had more sand in him than that. Oh, well. Handle's Mutt, pleased to make your acquaintance."

The manager nodded. "The girls call me the Scholar," he said. "As good a name as any. How do you do, Deputy? Mr. Negrey here says we have an issue in the alleyway."

"If by issue you mean a cut-up whore, then yes, we do," Mutt said. "Can you tell me who she is?"

"I've seen her about," Jim said. "Never got her name, though."

The Scholar nodded in the direction of the body and the two men started back toward the closed-off alleyway. Jim fell in to follow them, but Mutt stopped him.

"Crowd control, Jim," Mutt said.

"Mutt, I ain't gonna fire and fall back no more," Jim said. "Promise."

"I need you out here," Mutt said. "These folks like you a damn sight more than me. I'll fetch you presently. And don't worry about getting sick. A man sees something like that and don't get queasy, something broken in him."

Mutt and the Scholar parted the blankets and entered the alleyway. The stench hit them instantly. Mutt noticed the Scholar seemed unaffected. They moved down past the open alleyway door and around the small crowd of Doves and clients that were gathered. One man, with salt-and-pepper hair and wide muttonchops in an unbuttoned pair of trousers and nothing else, was ducking under one of the slimy lengths of suspended gut, trying to reach the dead girl's torn body.

"Take another step and I'll throw your ass in jail," Mutt said to the man's back.

"Go to hell, Chief," the man said, trying to avoid the blood and bile dripping off the intestines. "I don't gotta listen to you when the real law is out of town. 'Sides, I always wanted to know what it was like to diddle a dead . . ."

The Scholar grabbed the man by the spine. His fingers, the sizes of gun barrels, squeezed the flesh and bone. He yanked the man back and lifted him several feet off the ground, one-handed. The man screamed. The Scholar tightened his grip on the spine.

"Be quiet," the Scholar said softly. "Take the pain." The man tried to stop screaming, and began to sob and whimper. Mutt stood back and pushed his hat up on his head, watching the show.

"If I apply a little more pressure, you will never feel pain again below your neck," the Scholar said to the man, turning him around to view his face. "Mr. Macomber."

"Well I'll be damned," Mutt said, "Max Macomber. Your wives know you out cattin' about, Max? Not very churchgoin' kind of behavior, now is that?"

"I'll have your filthy mongrel hide hung up to tan," Macomber snarled through tears of pain. "I am a personal friend of Mr. Bick and when he . . ."

"Mr. Bick has entrusted me to manage his business here," the Scholar said. "You disgust me with what you proposed to do with the dead woman's body and furthermore, you had not negotiated an acceptable price with the house to undertake such activities, Mr. Macomber."

The Scholar moved the dangling man back to the alley door of the Dove's Roost and set him down. Macomber doubled over in pain, gasping. He looked up at the manager and the deputy.

"I'll see both of you fired for this! That popinjay, Pratt, was a fool to ever let Highfather hire you. Can't trust a savage like you to guard an outhouse, and I will talk to Malachi about you tomorrow, you lummox, I assure you."

"Very good, Mr. Macomber," the Scholar said. "Good evening, sir."

Macomber disappeared inside, aided by a few of the Doves. A few girls and patrons still hovered by the open door.

"Could y'all please stay the hell back!" Mutt said. He and the Scholar moved closer to the girl's body. Someone had set a lamp near the edge of the black lake of blood.

"Old Max means it," Mutt said. "He's part of the Bevalier machine. Rich as he is ornery. He's going to give Harry Pratt a hard time next year in the mayoral election. You may not be at this job very long."

The Scholar said nothing. He leaned closer to look at the dead woman's sliced face, wrapped in blood and shadow.

"Molly James," the Scholar said. "They call her Sweet Molly, or called her, to be more precise. She was an employee here for the past year, I believe."

Mutt looked hard at the Scholar. "This means less to you than a spit, doesn't it?"

"Deputy, I'm paid to look after Mr. Bick's business interests here," the Scholar said. "Miss James was a commodity and, as such, her loss is regrettable. But I sincerely doubt you will go home and shed any tears for a dead whore, as you so elegantly put it."

Mutt didn't reply. There was a commotion from the alley entrance as Jim and Clay Turlough stepped through the blankets. The sky was lightening to a slate blue. Somewhere a nightjar was singing.

"Well, I want to know who the 'commodity' was dating tonight," Mutt said. "I'm sure a meticulous fella like you has all kinds of records and such."

"I'll discuss it with Mr. Bick," the Scholar said.

"You do that," Mutt said. "Then have that information over to the sheriff's office by noon today, y'hear?"

"Well, I'm here," Clay said, walking up on the two men.

Clay Turlough always had a weird smell about him, Mutt thought. Chemicals, and something sour, something spoiled and not right. Mutt was amazed that horses loved Clay as much as they did, given his scent. He owned the only livery in Golgotha and was also the town's resident taxidermist. Clay was skinny, almost cadaverous, dressed in a stained work shirt, suspenders holding up baggy canvas work pants. Tufts of white hair orbited, like sparse clouds, around his liver-spotted pate. His hands and half his vulture-like face were pitted and streaked with scars from a fire he had survived last year. Clay made no attempt to hide his disfigurement; in fact, most times Mutt thought Clay wasn't even aware of it.

"Mind telling me why you needed me out here, Mutt," Clay said. "My experiments are at a very crucial . . ."

Clay trailed off as he regarded the girl's body and what had been done to it.

"You want me to . . . untangle her and take her home," Clay said.

"Yes," Mutt said. "Clay, you think you can help us figure out what sumbitch did this to her?"

Turlough scratched his head and walked closer to the tangle of guts that stretched out of the victim. He no longer heard Mutt; he was deep in his own mind, now. Seeing the scene in multiple dimensions, formulating, equating.

He touched one of the taut tubes of intestine with his forefinger and traced it back, walking to the wall of the alley fence where it was nailed. It vibrated slightly as he did and gore spattered off into the pool of blood. He examined the nail. Jim looked at Mutt and then back to Clay.

"He's no carpenter, doesn't know his way around a hammer," Clay said. "Wrong kind of nails to use for this wood. He used old A cuts, when B cuts would have been better. He also has half-moon divots in the wood where he missed the nail several times and hit the wood."

"You said 'he,'" Jim said.

"Mmhhm," Clay said, only half listening to Jim. "Men's shoes, not boots like you and Mutt tromped all over the scene, but a gentleman's shoe. Size eight and a half, I'd wager. This was a man's work. A man with a great deal of hatred for the female of the species and very little fear of capture or consequence. He has nothing but contempt for the law, fellas."

"Wish we had a photographer to catch all this stuff," Mutt said. "Might be things here that could help us find the sick bastard. I'd like Jon to give it a once-over too."

Clay seemed to snap out of his fog and shuffled off, muttering about getting something out of the wagon.

"Did you get his scent?" Jim asked. Mutt shook his head.

"Nope, whole place smells of death and crazy," he said. "I couldn't pick a man scent out of all that. Can't pick up much of anything."

"I trust you will get this cleaned up as quickly as possible," the Scholar said. "This has been a disruption of the evening's activities and while I am sympathetic to the cause of justice, I have Mr. Bick's business to run."

"Well, ain't Mr. Bick jist the biggest toad in the puddle," Mutt said.

The two men continued bantering. Jim shook his head and looked toward the dead girl they were arguing over. For some reason Jim thought about his little sister, Lottie, grinning, laughing. She'd be nine now and Jim wondered if she was safe, if she was even alive. He wondered who Sweet Molly was to someone somewhere—daughter, sister, friend?

A woman, one of the Doves, was kneeling near Sweet Molly's body. Jim hadn't even noticed her walk over. She was looking at the shoe print Clay had pointed out. The woman was in her thirties and slender, with brown hair falling down her shoulders. She had a rather ordinary face, not plain but not beautiful either. Her dark eyes were bright and intelligent. Jim saw the woman kneel closer to study the shoe print.

"Ma'am, you need to leave that be," Jim said, stepping forward.

The woman looked up and saw Jim staring at her and smiled. Her whole face seemed to change and the intelligent look behind her eyes dimmed. She opened her robe and let Jim get a better look at her thin undergarment and stockings. Jim blushed and looked away.

"Ummm, Mutt," Jim said, patting the deputy on the shoulder.

"Yeah?" Mutt said, pausing from his verbal sparring match with the Scholar. Jim pointed in the woman's direction. "Oh," Mutt said. "You want us to get this finished, then you need to keep your girls out of the damn alley, Scholar."

The giant looked up and gestured to the woman, who was already stepping away from the body and the blood.

"Kitty, inside. Now," the Scholar said, and the woman rushed to the alley door and darted inside. She gave Jim one last look, and for a second the gleam returned to her eye.

"Who is she?" Jim asked.

Mutt grinned. "Trouble for you, short britches."

"Her name is Kitty Warren," the Scholar said. "She's new."

Jim started to say something about the woman's close examination of the print and then decided to bite his tongue in front of Bick's man.

"I'll leave you to your business, Deputies," the Scholar said. "It has been a pleasure to meet you both. I will discuss your request for client information with Mr. Bick today, Deputy Mutt. Good morning."

"I liked Ladenhiem better," Mutt said to Jim as the giant walked away. "Even with the spider-things all over him."

Clay returned a few minutes after the Scholar and the last few onlookers from the Dove had retired inside. It was almost dawn and the alley and the street were blissfully quiet, at least for a little while. He was carrying four large glass jars and several smaller ones balanced on top of them. He also had a large wooden box-like contraption slung over his shoulder on a strap and a large coil of copper wire wrapped over his other shoulder.

"What is all this humbug, Clay?" Mutt asked.

Clay began to set the jars up carefully in different positions around the alley-way. There were strange objects bobbing and floating inside the glass containers. Clay affixed copper wire to a metal post on the lid of each jar. Jim walked over to one as Clay set it up. At first he thought there was a bunch of grapes hanging in the fluid-filled jar. Then he saw what it actually was.

"Are those . . . eyeballs?" Jim asked, squinting in the predawn.

"Yep, they are, Jim," Clay said. "Strands of eyeballs, connected by their optic nerves at the back of the eye to a cable of copper electrical wiring running up through the top of the jar and now connected to an external set of wiring."

Jim looked to Mutt. Mutt shrugged.

"Well, Clay, I have to tell you those are . . . the . . . finest . . . eyeballs all stuck together in a jar like that, that I've . . . ever seen," Mutt said. "Yessir. What are you going to do with your fine jars of eyeballs, Clay?"

"This here," Clay said, connecting the last of the jars to the coil of wire, "is my occustereograph."

"Oh," Mutt said. "That clears things up."

"This device is based off another invention of mine, the occuscope," Clay said, either unaware of or uncaring of the deputy's mocking tone. "The occustereograph imprints images off the eyes from multiple angles and directions. I then can use my occuscope to merge the images into a truly fully immersive photographic view. It's based off the work of Professor Wilhelm Kuhne, head of the Department of Physiology at the University of Amsterdam. Herr Professor holds the theory that the eye can hold its final image for some time after death. We've corresponded quite a bit over the last few years."

"Are these human eyes?" Jim asked.

"Ya know, Clay, I can fetch Bertrand Fisher, over at the *Golgotha Scribe*. He takes pictures," Mutt said. "No need to use up all your fancy eyeballs."

If Clay heard either of them, he didn't reply. He connected the copper wire to posts on top of the wooden box. The box had a large hand crank on the side, and it reminded Jim a little of a dynamite detonator. Clay nodded to answer some question in his own head and began to crank the wooden box. As he turned the crank faster and faster, blue sparks snapped from the posts. The thick gel-like fluid in the jars began to glow with a faint blue light. Jim swore he saw one of the eyeballs move, then focus.

The whole process took about ten minutes. Some of the jars began to bubble and smoke, and several of the eyeballs popped from the heat the process produced. The sun was peeking up over the ridge of Rose Hill when Clay finished his work with the device and began to pack up. A few work wagons were beginning to make their way down Bick Street on their appointed rounds. The town was waking up, and they were finished, just in time. Clay carefully gathered up Sweet Molly's remains with Mutt's help, even taking samples from the swamp of blood and mud on the alley's floor. He measured and sketched the boot print and made meticulous notes of every detail of the alleyway.

Jim noticed the tenderness and care Clay used in the process, and part of his concern for Clay's sanity began to fade. Then Jim recalled when he had first met

Clay in the desert, how the old man had studied and pondered over the carcass of a dead coyote. A strange look of peace and something else, something Jim didn't want to try to understand, had crossed Clay's face as he watched the animal breathe its last breath. Jim realized that the taxidermist was looking at Molly's body the same way he had looked at the coyote.

"Jon and I will meet up with you in the next day or so, Clay, so you can tell us what's what. Square?" Mutt said. Clay grunted in the affirmative. He climbed up on the wagon and drove away without another word. As the wagon bumped and jumped down Bick Street, one of the girls that worked at the Dove came out back with a bucket of water and dumped it on the pool of blood. Jim watched as she repeated the process, until the alley was no longer what it had been a few hours ago, no longer a door to Hell. It was just an alley outside a whorehouse.

"C'mon," Mutt said, slapping him on the back. "Let's git that baby goat and git home. Mrs. Proctor should have breakfast waiting."

In the wagon, Clay Turlough's mind was a crashing torrent of thought and theory, cause and effect. He was eager to get the female's remains back to his workshop at the livery. The girl still had good hands, good feet, and some of the organs had not been completely butchered. In fact, the exact ones he needed were still pristine and he had to race against the enemy of time to secure them. He'd slap some data together for Jon Highfather and Mutt to give them a trail to chase, a killer to find. But now his mind was on the grand project and how this female's death put him maddeningly close to completion of phase one. A few more deaths and everything should be ready.

Whatever this one's name had been he couldn't recall at this moment. Jim had said it, but it was lost to Clay; she would join the company of the others in the heavy, still darkness of the cold room, awaiting immortality, of a sort, as a bride awaits her groom.

The Ace of Cups (Reversed)

The night was near its end when Augustus Shultz returned to his little cottage, nestled in the green cradle of Rose Hill. The house had only been finished a few months ago, and it still took Auggie some effort to think of this place as home. Rose Hill was where the well-off folk of Golgotha settled: the Mormon businessmen, whose families had helped found Golgotha over twenty years ago; the mayor; the bankers and those who had struck it rich with silver and wanted to show off their good fortune—they all built fine homes up on Rose Hill.

Auggie was a shopkeeper, a grocer; he was used to living in a cramped little apartment over his general store on Main Street. Before that he, and his late wife, Gerta, had lived in a tiny dwelling back in Germany. This house was exactly what he and Gerta had dreamed of when they were young, but Auggie still felt like a stranger passing through his own door.

The metallic click of the lock seemed very loud in the darkness and silence of the deep night. The moon was retreating behind the hills and the stars were cloaked in clouds tonight. There was a fire burning in the hearth, or at the least the dying remains of one. A simple meal was set out on the old Hepplewhite dinner table he'd found in a shop over in Virginia City. There were fresh flowers in a vase on the table. He caught a whiff of the rose water she used, as he closed the door quietly, and smiled at the memories the scent brought to him.

Gillian Proctor was dozing in Auggie's comfy high-backed leather Sleepy Hollow armchair, a quilt draped around her. The Widow Proctor, as she had been known until recently, was a striking woman, slender and tall but with a very feminine form. Gillian's black hair had strands of silver that caught the light of the fire. She normally wore her hair up tight, in a simple, utilitarian chignon bun, but now it fell around her face and down to below her shoulders. The small round wire spectacles Gillian wore were perched on her nose. A book lay open on her lap. Half a glass of wine sat on the floor next to her chair.

Her eyes fluttered open and she smiled at Auggie. Her eyes always reminded him of black opals and the way she looked at him always took his breath away.

Auggie was a big man, broad, heavy and tall. He wore a thick handlebar mustache the color of rust, and the fringe of hair that circled his sun-freckled bald head was the same color. He was strong, strong enough to lift and toss massive two-boll sacks of flour off a wagon, strong enough to lift pork barrels weighing twenty-eight stone. But Gillian Proctor, the way she looked at him, the way she made him feel, made him as weak as a child inside. Auggie stood in awe of how a woman like this could love him. If Gillian knew what he had been about again tonight, he knew she would never look at him that way again.

"Mmm, hello," Gillian said. "I must have dozed off."

"*Ja*," Auggie said. "I'm sorry I woke you."

"I made us a spot of supper," Gillian said. "I suppose we could just call it breakfast. You must be starved."

"Uh, no," Auggie said. "I am afraid I am not hungry."

Gillian closed her book, the FitzGerald translation of *The Rubaiyat of Omar Khayyam*, and pulled aside the quilt and stood. "Is everything all right, Augustus? I got worried."

Auggie crossed the distance to her and scooped her up in his arms, lifting her off the floor, no easy feat given Gillian was a good half a foot taller than the grocer. He wished he had time to clean up and change clothes. It felt profane to hold her in the same clothing he had . . . He struggled to push the unpleasant thoughts out of his mind, and focus on Gillian.

"*Ja, ja.* I am fine," he said, holding her tight. "I'm sorry I worried you, *mein Schatz.*"

"Where were you?" Gillian asked.

"I had to deal with some things at the store," Auggie said, stroking her hair as he held her. "It took longer than I expected."

Gillian froze in his arms. She pushed herself away from him gently.

"You weren't at the store," she said. "I checked there, several times."

Auggie looked down at the floor and rubbed his face. "We . . . we must have . . . missed each other."

"Auggie," Gillian said, "please tell me what's going on. You've been so tired, you look like you haven't been sleeping and you are a terrible liar. I want to help you, my love. Please . . ." She paused and touched her cheek where it had been resting against his coat and examined her hand, rubbing the fingers together. "Is . . . is this blood . . . and makeup?"

Auggie stepped toward her. "Gillian, I can't explain to you right now, but please . . ."

"Will used to say the exact same thing to me when he was out all night gambling," Gillian said, summoning the memory of her late husband. Auggie had never cared much for Will Proctor and his irresponsible treatment of Gillian. "Those words are poison to me, Augustus."

Gillian pushed her glasses up on her nose. She walked toward the door and took her simple cotton shawl from one of the pegs beside it.

"Augustus, I think we have both showed each other how much we love and trust one another over the years." She turned to address him as she slipped her shawl over her shoulders.

"We've been through so much together. I lost Will, you lost Gerta. We had to get past those losses and learn to live again on our own before we could try to live together. We went through that awful mess last year, but it brought us together."

The "awful mess" was Auggie's greatest shame. He had slowly confided the tale to Gillian over the past year of how his grief over his wife's passing had been so great, so all-consuming, he had taken part in horror and madness. Auggie had agreed to allow his best friend, Clay Turlough, to reanimate Gerta's head and keep it alive in a jar using a type of scientific alchemy that Auggie still didn't fully comprehend. Auggie had lived a twilight existence alongside his dead wife until Gillian, and her love, had brought him back to the world of the living. Gerta had finally known peace and been freed from her hellish undead existence, perishing in the fire that destroyed his store last year.

Auggie had feared that when Gillian knew the whole, terrible truth, she would shun him. But she had listened and she had understood and the truth had made them stronger. Now, he was falling into an even deeper hole of macabre secrets and he feared that it was too much for even this remarkable woman to forgive or forget. Auggie feared the truth this time would shatter them.

"I think we've paid our dues for a little happiness, don't you?" Gillian said. "We're to be married in a few weeks. That makes me very happy. You are who I want to grow old with, my love."

Auggie wanted to go to her, to hold her and kiss her, explain, ask forgiveness, if there was such a thing for what he was doing. He stood his ground. He knew

what was coming next, could feel it in the tone of her voice. There was steel behind the quavering, the near tears.

"Something has changed, Augustus," she said. "Something has changed in
you in the last few months and you won't talk to me about it, won't let me help you.
Tell me, and please be honest, do you still want to be with me?"

"*Ja*, yes. With all my heart. Yes," Auggie said. "I can't imagine a life without
you, Gillian. You remember how happy I was when you said you would be my
wife?"

Gillian smiled; it hurt Auggie to see the pain in that smile. "You danced a
little jig, as I recall," she said. "Please, Augustus, tell me what's happening?
Whatever it is, darling, we can get through it together."

She was an amazing woman, far better than he deserved. He opened his
mouth to tell her, looked down, shut his eyes. He was still and he said nothing.

"Is it the trouble with the store, with Bick?" she said. "I know how much stress
he's put on you. Horrible man, already richer than Croesus and it's still not
enough for him. Is that it?"

He wanted to say yes and leave it at that. It was true, in part. To rebuild the
store, buy this land on Rose Hill and raise a new house had taken all of Auggie's
savings and more.

With the bank temporarily closed after the troubles last year, Malachi
Bick, the wealthiest man in town, had stepped in to offer loans and financial
stability until the Golgotha Bank and Trust was back on its feet. Bick's First
Bank of Golgotha had given Auggie loans to rebuild his general store after the
fires of last year and to help him secure his dream home for Gillian. While at
first it had seemed like a true act of Christian kindness, as the months wore
on, many, Auggie included, had begun to see Bick's act as a way to gain control of the few things in Golgotha he didn't already own. But by then it was
too late.

"It is . . . it is not that easy, Gillian," Auggie said. "Bick is part of it, *ja*."

"But not all of it," Gillian said. "And you're not going to tell me. Not going to
tell me why you are not sleeping, why you are coming home a hair before the
rooster crows, covered in someone's blood and ladies' paint. No, Augustus, it
doesn't sound easy at all. It sounds like trouble."

Auggie struggled to find a way to even begin to explain the nightmare his life
had become these last few months; how she was the only light, the only hope he
saw now.

Auggie looked at the woman he loved, her hand on the door to leave, the
pain, confusion and distrust like a ghost in the room between them. Auggie's

blue eyes locked with Gillian's. She had never seen him look so grim. It was almost like looking into the eyes of a stranger and it frightened her. The timid shopkeeper departed. This grim man spoke now.

"*Ja*. Yes. Very bad trouble, Gillian. Very bad. Evil. But I will fix it. I will. For you, because of you. Because I love you. Because I want to start my life again with you and I'll do whatever I have to to make this all right."

"Don't start with lies then, Augustus," Gillian said, opening the door. "Nothing really good comes of them; nothing is ever truly fixed with a lie. Good night. I love you. You know where to find me if you want to talk."

"Gillian, please, let me walk you home, it is still very dark."

"I'll be fine," she said. "It's almost dawn. The boarders will be up soon and I need to have breakfast ready for them. I'll see you at the shop later today, if you'd like that."

"*Ja*, very much. Please." He walked to her, she to him. The kiss was gentle, almost timid. He didn't want to hurt her and she didn't want to be hurt.

"Good night," Gillian said, stepping away. "I love you." She closed the door behind her.

Auggie stood and looked at the door for a long time. He felt the air catch in his lungs. He felt something begin to crack inside him. He felt the anger swell.

"*Gott verdammter Narr!*" he said, wanting desperately to break something, to do something, to fix all this. All Auggie could do was clench his fists and try to let the rage pass. Life had taught him long ago that anger was a storm that left far too much wreckage in its wake.

He sat in his chair by the dying fire. Her scent lingered there, taunting him with happiness. He was so weary but he knew sleep would evade him. Once he closed his eyes, they were there. Waiting, staring, accusing, like they were every night when he tried to sleep, like they had been for months when this waking nightmare had begun.

Auggie had anticipated that the boom from the Argent Mine being reopened would grow Golgotha as it had before. The lure of silver would attract new people; new families looking to settle down, miners, prospectors and adventurers would arrive as well and that would mean more customers and more prosperity. It should have worked that way. Malachi Bick, however, opened his own store up on Argent Mountain, near what had been the squatters' camp, but was now becoming a thriving miners' settlement, almost a town within a town. The Argent Company Store sold all the things Shultz's General Store did, and they extended credit to the miners on the Argent Company payroll as well. Add to that that Auggie's business had been pretty much out of commission for months while he rebuilt and restocked. Many of his best customers had headed up the mountain to buy from Bick.

When he reopened, most of his regulars came back, preferring the calm of Main Street to the raucous tumble of the miners' camp. But not all, and few of the new customers came with them. So in less than a year, Auggie Shultz had lost business to the man he owed a large sum of money.

To add insult to injury, when Auggie began to fall behind in his payments, Bick's men would come to Auggie's store and take parts of Auggie's inventory to restock the company store, as "interest" on the late payments for the loans. So when Auggie didn't have the items his customers needed due to the depletion of his wares, it drove more and more people up the mountain to the company store.

The sky was lightening through the leaded glass windows that overlooked the Hepplewhite table. Auggie knew he needed to get up soon, wash up, change and head off to open the store. He sighed and rubbed his sore eyes.

He briefly considered taking down the green glass jug of ale he had brewed a few months ago and draining it, to chase off the awful feelings inside him, to maybe dull his memory enough to let him sleep. What was the point of going to the store today? A handful of customers, a few more creditors coming by to re-mind him he was behind. Standing behind that counter with a false smile and kind words, when all you wanted to do was scream and bash their patronizing, selfish faces in. If he were gone tomorrow, gone today, they would just walk up the hill and not even look back.

He suddenly wished Gerta was still here. Still floating in her jar, so easy to talk to about everything, so much easier . . . better?

No. It was *easier* to talk to his dead wife than his living bride. That didn't make it better. It made him weak. Gerta had been dead for a long time and he and Clay had forced her to remain in this world in a frightening twilight of life in death, in hell, all so Auggie could take her out and cry to her when he felt alone and overwhelmed. He had been selfish and cruel to do that to her. Gerta was free now, dead in the fire, and that was best. He also remembered what drink had done to his papa when he was a boy. His father screaming, raging against his mother, his sister. Papa never struck any of them but often his words were so painful, Auggie would have preferred to be beaten.

No, none of that was the way to go. He stood, already growing sore and stiff from the night's exertions. He needed to get cleaned up and get to the store. It was Tuesday, and Mrs. Dockery would be in for her medicines and the Widow Stapleton would be by to collect her packages that had arrived from back east. People needed the store, people needed him. They were good people too. He was just tired and worried and feeling very guilty about what he was doing, what he was part of.

It had to stop. The sickness, the evil, it had to stop. He had to stop it, no matter how difficult it would be.

Auggie Shultz trudged to his bedroom, weary but determined to begin battle with another day and terrified at what the night would bring to him.

The Queen of Cups

The morning stage groaned to a halt at the Golgotha station a quarter till noon. The Wells Fargo Station, a new edition to the town in the last eight months, was a narrow little building on the corner of Prosperity and Main Street. It housed the coach clerk, a privy with water basin for the passengers and driver, and a table with as much food and drink as the budget allowed. The crowd waiting to board the stage clustered on the station's narrow porch for shade in the unseasonably baking temperatures of November in the desert. Many of them were talking about the murder of one of the public girls from the Dove's Roof that had occurred the night before. Others tried to pull the conversation to less grisly fare, instead discussing the upcoming mayor's race or plans for the approaching Thanksgiving holiday.

The crowd let up a cry when they saw the battered Concord coach rumble down the street and creak to a stop in a cloud of dust.

"Look at that, will ya," a man in a sweat-soaked tweed suit said. "Ol' shake-guts is fifteen minutes early, I tell you what! Modern conveniences! Don't they just beat the Dutch! I can't wait to ride on that there transcontinental rail they just finished. It's in all the papers—quite the do, I hear. A mechanical miracle. New station just a spit away down by Hazen too. Hell, Golgotha could get her own dogleg if the town keeps a-growing!"

"Won't catch me on one of those infernal engines," another man, in shirt-sleeves and suspenders, said. "Too fast, too dangerous! Hear the damn things blow up! Give me a good horse or a carriage any day, yessir!"

Several of the passengers picked up their bags and began to crowd the stairs in front of the station. Their enthusiasm was curtailed by the sight of the first passenger disembarking as soon as the stepping block was set down by the driver. The man, quite green in complexion, stumbled out, fell to his knees and began retching profusely in the manure-covered street.

"Welcome to Golgotha Station," the grim-looking driver said. He had a fringe of graying blond hair and a drooping handlebar mustache. He called out to the heaving man and the other passengers that climbed down after him.

"Listen up! You got an hour for vittles, pissing and to stretch yer legs. It's first come, first serve for seats and just cause yer ass was in one up till this point don't mean you put yer damned brand on it!"

A young woman in her early twenties stepped off the coach and blinked at the bright November daylight. A handsome gentleman offered his hand to help her down. The girl refused with a polite smile and climbed down herself. She was pretty, with long brown hair that held hints of gold when the sun hit it just right. She wore it pulled back from her face with a simple purple ribbon. Her eyes were a striking violet, the color of wild flowers in spring. She wore a plain blouse, dyed with butternut, a skirt and ankle boots, which peeked out from her skirts. She tried to wrestle her large, worn leather humpback steamer trunk free, among the press of other passengers who were trying to do the same.

"Stand aside for a lady, you damned, stinkin' boodle!" the driver boomed as he pushed through the passengers and grabbed the girl's trunk for her, hefting it like it weighed nothing.

"Thank you very much," she said. "I don't think I could have made it through that crowd, without elbowing someone or getting mashed."

The driver set her trunk on the edge of the porch and removed his dust-covered campaign hat. He smiled; his teeth were tobacco-stained. He looked down and mangled his hat in his hands.

"My pleasure, ma'am," the driver said. "Lady as grand as you don't need to be exertin' herself."

The girl smiled. "Well, thank you, sir. You are very kind, Mr. . . . ."

"Haslam," the driver said. "Robert Haslam, knight of the ribbons, at yer service, ma'am. Most folks call me Pony Bob."

"Well, thank you, Bob. I'm Emily. Emily Bright." She extended her hand and he took it, shook it gingerly and then half-bowed.

"You got family here, Miss Bright?" Bob asked.

"I certainly hope so," Emily said with a nervous smile. Pony Bob looked confused and she waved her remark off. "Yes," she said. "I'm meeting my father here."

"Well, good for you," Bob said, and absently scratched his crotch. Emily tried to ignore the act. "Lady like you shouldn't be out in this godforsaken boneyard without a proper escort. Glad you have yer pappy to look out for you. Can't be too careful in these parts. Golgotha's got a bad reputation, there are some salty folk here about . . . and the town's supposedly full'a haints and curses and spirits and such, too, if'n you believe in that sort of thing. I took this route six months back, I've seen things here that I can't . . . rightly explain. Try not to dwell too much. Keep the Good Book handy, shootin' iron too."

Emily pushed a stray hair out of her eyes. The heat was horrid for this late in the year. "What did you do before this, Mr. Haslam?"

"I used to ride for the Pony Express back before Wells Fargo bought 'em," Bob said. "Went to work for them after the war."

"You were a Pony Express rider," Emily said. "How exciting! I've read of your exploits!"

"Well, Miss, those dime novels are one part in apple pie order to six parts camp canard!" Bob said. "Truth out here is a sight more peculiar than what they can cook up in New York City.

"Had a friend named Billy Tate. Young boy, rode the route at fourteen. Tough as they come, a real son of a gun, that little fella. Anyway, he got into a dustup, shot dead up by Ruby Valley. Dang snakes, the fucki—I'm sorry, miss. The Indians, the Paiute got him."

"How awful," Emily said. "I'm so sorry, Bob."

"Thank you kindly," he said. "Thing is, I've seen him, Miss Emily. Recent. I've seen him on the trail. Laughing and smiling, riding his dead horse. Raced the coach for a spell last month. His shirt all torn up from bullet holes, and arrows . . . You be careful hereabouts, pretty missy, y'hear? This place, it ain't like other places."

"Yes," Emily said softly. "Thank you, Bob. Be safe on the road, won't you?"

The old driver gave her his stained smile and laughed. "Thank you kindly, Miss Emily. Pony Express, it didn't git me. The war didn't take me, I'm dam— darn sure the trail isn't goin' to either. Good Lord bless you and keep you."

Pony Bob sidled off, scratching his behind as he went, and headed for the station. Emily stood at the edge of the porch and watched as the town rumbled by. Horses, carts, buggies, wagons full of goods and wagons full of miners. Chinese workers in their black, loose-fitting clothes, cowboys, businessmen puffing huge cigars, fine ladies hiding from the sun under parasols and extravagant fallen women swaggering more than most men. Indians on horseback, stone-faced, proud and aloof, moving along the knife's edge between their world and this one. Somewhere dogs barked and she heard children laughing. A baby was crying.

"You seem kind of lost, child," a man's voice said from the behind her. Emily turned. There was a black man sitting on a bench in front of O'Brian's Meats, the small smoke and butcher shop next to the coach station. He looked old, maybe in his sixties, but it was hard to tell because his head was shaved. He wore a simple linen work shirt, suspenders, and canvas workpants. A walking stick carved of dark cherry wood rested against the bench. Even from where she stood, Emily could see the intricate carving and detail on the stick: tiny rows of figures marching in a line spiraling down the length of the cane, hundreds of them, reminding Emily of Egyptian-like hieroglyphics. The old man's eyes were milky white with cataracts and his head was pointed in Emily's general direction, but his gaze was unfocused. He stared into darkness.

"Me?" Emily said, walking toward the old man. "Are you talking to me?"

The old man smiled. "Yes, I am. How are you today, young lady? Welcome to our fair town. Please come sit with me. I'll scoot over a bit and give you room. Your trunk will be safe right where Mr. Haslam set it."

Emily sat, grateful for a place to rest for a moment. All around her was chaos and bright movement. Here, next to this blind stranger, it was cool and relatively quiet. The smell of smoke-cured beef made her realize how long it had been since she'd eaten.

"I expect they will feed you over at the Falls," the old man said. "I know it's hard to put down food on the trail and harder to keep it down." Emily looked at the old man, tilting her head.

"How did you know I was hungry?" she asked. "And what is the Falls?"

"Educated guess," the old man said with a broad smile. "And I mean the Paradise Falls Saloon. That's where you'll find who you're looking for?"

Emily turned toward the old man, leaning to him. He smelled like warm leather and sweet pipe smoke. "Did Caleb send you to meet me? How could you know all this?"

She noticed he had a small piece of wood in his hands and a narrow jack-knife. The knife danced along the surface of the wood quickly as he carved, shavings drifting down to the ground.

"I am a friend of Caleb's," the old man said, "but I'm sorry to say he didn't send me. I wish he had."

"So he has passed," Emily said. "He's gone?"

"'Bout a year ago. There was some trouble in town, some folks tried to kill his father. Caleb saved him. Cost him though."

"I see," Emily said. She felt sick and tumbling inside. She wanted to cry, to break down and weep like a child, but this land, this town, did not seem forgiving to weakness. She would grieve her loss in private, as soon as she could be alone. The old man stopped whittling long enough to pat her hand, gently.

"I'm sorry, dear. Terrible sorry to be the one to tell you too."

"I suspected when his letters stopped," she said. "I just hoped I was wrong."

They sat quietly for a moment. The old man went back to his sightless whittling. Emily rubbed her face and sighed.

"We all have to leave this world," the old man said. "Got no choice in that, but a person get to choose how and why he's going to go out. If he does it for love, that's about as good a way to go as you can hope for, I'd surmise. He was a fine man and a good . . . friend."

"Yes," Emily said. "He was. I'm sorry, I'm Emily."

"Miles," the old man said. "Miles Press. Pleased to make your acquaintance, Emily."

"Why did you say that about the Paradise Falls?" Emily asked. "Who do you think I'm looking for?"

"Everyone who comes to this town," Miles said, "they are either looking for , or they're hiding from ."

"That's a clever answer," she said, "but it doesn't really address . . ."

"I've lived in this town since before it was called Golgotha," Miles said. "Might say I have a queer relationship with the place. Town took my eyes; bit of bad blood long 'fore you were even born, m'dear. But it gave me insight for my loss. I know you are here to find someone. Find someone Caleb told you about. I know you will find him at the Paradise Falls. And I know you play a part in the game."

"What game?" Emily said. "I'm not playing at any game, Miles."

"Aren't you?" Miles said, smiling. He stopped whittling and held up the small piece of wood. It was now a tiny figurine and it resembled Emily almost perfectly. Down to the smallest detail.

"How did you . . . ," Emily stammered. "Are you really blind? How could you?"

"We each have our talents, Emily, don't we now? Like your paintings?"

Emily stood. "How do you know? Did Caleb tell you? I . . . I don't understand."

"Sit, child," Miles said. She did. "I watch the folks come to this town, day in, day out, year in, year out. I take their measure, see what part they play in the game."

"I swear I don't understand what you mean," Emily said. "Please, what game?"

Miles pointed to the ground in front of the bench. "Tell me, girl, what do you see there?"

"Dirt, sand," she said.

"Why are we sitting here, instead of out there?"

"It's cooler, the shade, the shadow."

"The shadow," Miles said. "Yes, see there the terminator between the light and the shadow. That is this place, that's Golgotha. It drags people here from the light and from the shadow. Each has a part to play. I've known this town for a very long time. My father taught me the truth about this place, rest his good soul. And I have been playing a very long game with this town, a very long game. And now," he said, holding up the small wooden Emily, "you're in the game. Either on the side of light or on the side of shadow."

"Which one am I?" she asked, fascinated by the tiny figure. It seemed so real, as if it would suddenly open tiny violet eyes. "Light or shadow?"

"Can't say," Miles said. "Would be cheating. Must of us zig and zag a bit. The world tends to shake you back and forth as you go."

"And everyone in town is playing your game?" Emily said.

"Yes," Miles said. "I have a model of the town at home. That is the game board. I have my pieces and the town has hers. She's a very good player. Very sneaky."

"And what if I don't wish to play this game?" Emily asked.

"Then you would never have come here," Miles said. He turned his head as if he were tracking something. "Ah, here comes your shining knight now. Oh, Deputy Jim!"

Emily looked up. A handsome young man with hay-colored hair and a silver star on his vest walked by. He stopped and looked at Miles, and then saw Emily. He smiled and brushed his hair out of his eyes.

"Hi, Mr. Press," Jim said, then nodded to Emily. "Ma'am. Can I help you folks?"

"Yes, Jim, Miss Emily here is just arrived in Golgotha and she is looking for accommodations. I believe they will have a place for her over at the new hotel, the Imperial. Could you please carry her trunk over for her and she'll be along presently. She's to meet someone first."

"Oh of course, yes, ma'am. Happy to oblige," Jim said, and hefted the humpback trunk. "It will be waiting for you right there, Miss Emily."

"Thank you, Deputy," Emily said, smiling.

"Just call me Jim," he said. "Everyone does. Welcome to town, Miss Emily. Holler if you have any trouble."

The deputy struggled down the street with the large trunk. Emily stood and straightened her skirt. "I suppose I should be on my way too," she said. "I suppose Jim helping me and me departing now are all part of your game with Golgotha?"

Miles laughed. "No, no. Nothing so fatalistic, my dear. If you know how everything turns out, that's a rigged game. The town may be a ruthless player, but she tends to be a fair one. If she takes something from you, she tends to give you something back. Remember that, it may help you down the road to remember that. It's a pleasure to meet you, Emily."

He pointed across Main Street to an opulent-looking three-story building, painted gray with black trim, that stood at about ten o'clock from where they were. There were balconies on the second floor, overlooking Main Street, and smaller balconies on the third floor, guarded by sinister gargoyles and brooding angels on parapets.

"And that is the Paradise Falls and you'll find what you're looking for there. I sculpted most of those gargoyles and angels a long time ago. I can still see them, see through them. Good luck, child. We'll talk again soon."

"Thank you, Miles," Emily said, patting the old man's shoulder gently. He smiled at her.

Emily stepped down from the shade of the porch to the heat, grit and light of Main Street. She attempted to navigate the mud, straw, dust and manure that constituted the street. She dodged horses and wagons as well as she could. Several riders paused and doffed their hats to her as she crossed.

From his bench, Miles ran his callused thumb over the surface of the carving of Emily Bright. He looked out with sightless eyes toward the bustle of Golgotha's busiest street, the constant ebb and flow of humanity that ran past him.

"Your move," he said to the dry desert air.

Emily stepped through the cherry wood and stained-glass doors of the Paradise Falls. The saloon was beautiful, easily as nice as many of the establishments in San Francisco. There was a wide stage with a lowered red velvet curtain. A piano sat off to the right side of the stage, currently unattended. A man with a long, sad face, who looked for all the world like a Basset hound, tended the polished mahogany bar with brass railings and foot trails that stretched in a massive "L" along the right-hand side of the saloon. Numerous round tables for drinking filled most of the center of the room. The left side of the saloon was taken up with a freestanding carpeted staircase that led up to a landing, partly overlooking the saloon floor, and then another staircase that led to the open second floor. Finally, there were gaming tables scattered around the base of the staircase and into the shadows on the left side of the saloon, including faro tables and an ash and walnut J. E. Came billiards table, lined in red felt with ornate wood carving on the legs and sides. There were about two dozen patrons, all men; most of them looked to be miners and cowboys. A few "ladies of the line" were drinking with the men and attempting to conduct some business. A man in a dirty collarless linen shirt suddenly obstructed her view of everything.

"You lost, miss?" the man's booming voice said. He had a touch of an Irish accent. She looked up from the chest to the face attached it. A pale man with freckles, a mop of red hair and a small bowler hat on his head. He had piercing blue eyes and a practiced scowl. "Don't seem like your kind of place."

"I'm here to see Mr. Bick," Emily said, trying not to sound nervous. "It's very urgent."

The man with the bowler deepened his scowl. His eyes flicked up to an office door on the second floor. Emily could barely make out the milky, frosted glass pane of the door past the man's bulk. "I'm afraid Mr. Bick is indisposed right now, miss. You care to leave him a message I'll make sure he gets it."

"I don't think you understand, this is very important," Emily said. "He'll want to see me. I traveled all the way from . . ."

"Lots of people travel to see Mr. Bick," the redhead said. "Lots of people think whatever they need to see him about is very important. But you're just going to have to wait like the rest of them, darlin'." He placed a large hand on her shoulder, gently, and began to turn her back toward the saloon doors. "Now come along, this is no place for you."

The upstairs office door opened and Emily heard two men talking as they exited the office. She caught a glimpse of them as they approached the staircase.

"You need to address this now, Harry, before Rony turns it into a campaign issue for you," one of them said.

One was very handsome and well dressed; a brocade waistcoat of blue and black caught her eye. He was long of limb with a fine mane of rust-colored hair, a handlebar mustache and muttonchops. The other man was also dressed in finery—a dark maroon shirt with a vest and pants of black. His hair fell in curls to his shoulder in a half-shingle. He sported a black mustache and goatee. Emily's eyes widened as she realized who the man was from Caleb's many accounts. The bouncer's insistent hand tightened on her shoulder and he began to wrestle her to the door.

"Mr. Bick!" Emily shouted. "Mr. Bick!"

"All right, lass," the bouncer said, impatience in his voice. "Enough of that."

He was forcing her through the saloon doors. Emily grabbed his wrist and pulled his hand off her shoulder effortlessly. The larger man was stunned by how easily the girl broke his grip. Emily shoved him, her palm to his chest, and he flew backward toward the bar, his derby flying off his head. Emily sprinted to the stairs and ran up them to meet the two men descending as the bouncer scrambled to catch her, but she was too fast for him.

"Mr. Bick," Emily said as the men paused in their descent. "My name is Emily. Emily Rose Bright. My mother was Clance Bright of San Francisco and you, Mr. Bick, you are my father."

The Emperor

Harry Pratt, mayor of Golgotha, was running in a forest the color of blood. Blood, in fact, dripped from the branches and the wide, thick leaves. It spattered down out of the sky, a thick, hesitant rain. The floor of the forest was slick with it and it splashed his boots as he ran from the thing that pursued him. He could hear its grunting, its panting breath behind him.

He ran past trees where people he knew, people he cared for in the town, were nailed and flayed, still screaming, begging him to save them, to kill them. His wife, Sarah; his friend and mentor, Antrim Slaughter; scores of townsfolk were all looking at him with pleading eyes, accusing eyes. He veered to the right as he ran from the shambling thing. Sheriff Jon Highfather hung suspended from a tree upside down, one leg straight, the other cocked at the knee.

"You can't outrun it, Harry," Jon said, blood burbling from his mouth. "Turn and fight."

Harry couldn't find his sword, the gold and silver mythical Sword of Laban—the first and greatest blade ever forged, the archetypal blade from which all other swords of legend descended.

"Here it is, Harry, my love," his dead wife, Holly, said to him. She was standing there in white, smiling, beautiful, alive and looking the way he remembered her, not how she had been at the end—hollow and filled with darkness, when he had been too late to save her. She wore a translucent white veil and held the sword with both hands, arms extended. The blood began to stain and soak into her white gown in slow, fat drops. She still smiled at him through her darkening veil. "Take it, it's yours."

He grabbed the weightless, flawless blade by the hilt and turned to face the lumbering, howling thing. The pain was exquisite, fire searing his palm as he dropped the blade into the deep puddle of blood at his feet, his hand smoking.

"Unclean!" dour Rony Bevalier said. The town Mormon elder had taken Holly's place: a figure in white, but Bevalier was caked in dust and spider webs. Spiders crawled along his cobweb veil. His pale, water blue eyes boiled with hatred. "Sodomite, man-lover, freak, unworthy!"

It was coming, fast closing. It was gigantic, covered from crown to toe in foul, long dirty hair. It bore a man's face, full of pain and anger, red eyes seeing only murder.

"And now art thou cursed from the earth, which hath opened her mouth to receive thy brother's blood from thy hand."

It was Malachi Bick's voice. Perched on the branch of a great, hemorrhaging tree, the saloonkeeper had large black wings like a bird's, extending from his back, and they, too, were slowly being drenched in blood. "When thou tillest the ground, it shall not henceforth yield unto thee her strength; a fugitive and a vagabond shalt thou be in the earth and whosoever slayeth you, vengeance shall be taken on him sevenfold." Bick held a skull in his hands, blood pouring from it, soaking the soil, soaking everything.

"It's going to be okay, Harry," James Ringo said, taking Harry's burned hand in his own. The pain faded. Ringo was so beautiful; his eyes were calm and dark and serene, full of love and confidence. "It's going to be all right, as long as we are together. . . ."

There was a roar and Harry spun. The Great Hairy Man was upon him, on top of him. Ringo's fingers slipped away from his own and he was alone and the entire world was a bellowing face of endless rage, and Harry could do nothing to stop it.

"Mr. Mayor?"

Harry's eyes snapped open. He was soaked in sweat. He was on the couch of his office again, panting in fear. His assistant, young Colton Higbee, stood over him looking very concerned. The young man was from a good Mormon family and wanted to be a lawyer. He had served Harry very well over the last few years. "Sir, I'm sorry to wake you. . . . Actually, I'm not. You appeared to be in a great deal of distress. You have a meeting in less than an hour, sir."

"I do? What time is it?"

Harry rolled over and sat up on the couch. He slid out his father's pocket watch and popped the lid open, rubbing his wet, disheveled hair. Inside the watch was a browning, faded photograph of Harry's late mother.

"Almost eight, sir," Colton said, pushing his wire spectacles up on his nose and then smoothing his centrally parted hair, which was slicked down tightly with a generous application of macassar oil. He handed Harry a hot cup of Arbuckle coffee with a little bit of cream.

Harry drank deeply and sighed. "Mother's milk," he mumbled.

"Another late night, sir?" Colton said. "Sir, if I may, when was the last time you slept more than a few hours, or at home?"

Harry ignored his young aide and took another sip of coffee as he looked for his boots. "What is on the agenda for today, mother?"

"You have a campaign meeting before noon with Mr. Bick at his office," Colton said. "Sheriff Highfather wanted you to know he's back from his trip to New Orleans and that the business he had there has been resolved. He also wanted to inform you there was a murder last night at the Dove's Roost."

"Client or girl?" Harry asked, yawning.

"Girl, sir," Colton said. "The sheriff says he is investigating. While there is little chance there will be much public cry over the death of a prostitute, public safety is an issue that we have been hearing a lot about from voters. You may also want to discuss with the sheriff the issue of hiring more deputies."

Harry nodded. Colton continued. "Sarah has some papers out at the ranch you are supposed to sign in regards to the sale of the twenty acres to Mr. Wickshire and his family. Max Macomber has expressed the opinion to me this fine morning that Deputy Mutt should be relieved of his duty. His words were somewhat less eloquent. I assured him you would give the matter all the attention it deserves and meet up with him at his shop today. Then a meeting tonight at six at the Presbyterian Church with the Ladies Temperance League."

"God," Harry said, "I'll need a drink after that."

"They tell their husbands who to vote for," Colton reminded him, pouring some heated water into the tin washbasin stand, near the door. "Also, sir, I wanted to bring to your attention the numerous promissory notes that arrived from San Francisco. They are for several thousands of dollars and were presented by your friend, Mr. Ringo. The parties are requesting payment."

Harry frowned. James had said nothing to him about borrowing money, or going to his old home in San Francisco; of course it had been a while since they had talked. A pang of loneliness stabbed Harry.

"Pay them," Harry said. "From my personal accounts, please, Colton." He drained his coffee mug and sighed. "Who do I have this morning?" Harry asked.

Colton smiled. "Your favorite. . . ."

———

Harry hated meeting with Golgotha's Mormon elders. It reminded him of the most dreary memories of his childhood, when his father, the great, stern Josiah Pratt—Priest of the Second Order, the Patriarchal Authority—twenty feet tall, with lightning coming out of his eyes and a face made of scowling stone, would make him come to these meetings when all he wanted was to be out playing in the sun with Holly and the other children. Now, thirty-four, he felt the same way—he wanted out of here, badly.

"This is a serious position we find ourselves in," Brodin Chaffin said. "The Argent Mine reopening has reignited the boom we had before everyone thought it had gone bust, but it is also bringing with it problems that our community simply cannot abide."

Chaffin was a stocky man in his mid-thirties, clean-shaven and well dressed. He looked at the other men around the table in the cool, shadowed meeting hall of the tabernacle off Absalom Road, next to the church and near the temple building.

"Our people, the men of our faith, have held respected and prominent positions in the business community of Golgotha since we founded the town, and now we are in danger of being overcome by outside, foreign business interests; of losing our control."

"Yes," Rony Bevalier said, nodding. The elder was as dry and pale as ever, his face a rutted road of wrinkles and furrowed scowl lines. For an instant Harry saw Bevalier wrapped in webs and spiders as in his dreams. He shuddered and shook it off. "Our community was founded on Mormon values, and with Mormon blood and sweat. Unless something is done and done soon, Golgotha will be another cesspool of filth, mongrels and moral turpitude, like what has already befallen Virginia City and Carson City."

"With all due respect," Harry said, sitting up in his chair. "The boom is creating some challenges for the town, but in the long run, growth from the Argent and from our proximity to the transcontinental railroad is good for everyone's business."

"You need to be concerned about your own people's businesses, not everyone's," Bevalier said. "What are you first, Pratt? A politician or a Mormon?"

"I could ask you the same question, Elder," Harry said, meeting the old man's withering gaze. "You seem to be more interested in protecting business than extending welcome to our new neighbors."

Bevalier reddened and turned to his fellow elder, Antrim Zezrom Slaughter. "Explain to me again why this impudent dandy is here?"

Slaughter, Golgotha's highest-ranking Mormon, a high priest and the sole reason that Golgotha had a fully recognized temple in the middle of the desolate wasteland, smiled and nodded to Bevalier. Slaughter was dressed in black, as usual; with silver hair, gray eyes and standing six foot two, he was an imposing figure.

"I think both of you need to leave that election at the door," Slaughter said. "There isn't enough room in here for it and the church's business. Rony, Harry's family was instrumental in creating this town. He is the guardian of the relics of our faith that are located in the caves below his family home, and then there is the matter of his position as a defender of the faith and protector."

Harry waved Slaughter off. "Sir, I'd prefer not to get into all that."

"If this limsy is the One Mighty and Strong," Bevalier said, "then I'm Daniel Boone! This town needs a real leader, not this sorry mop."

"I never claimed to be that!" Harry said, standing. "I never asked for any of this, and I'm sick and tired of your constant—"

"Enough!" Slaughter said, slapping his palm on the table. "Both of you. Harry has earned a seat on this council, and he has earned all of our respect. And you, Rony, you will keep a civil tongue in your head or I'll have something to say about it."

All four men at the table were silent. Slaughter finally spoke.

"Well, another productive meeting," he said. "Our next order of business . . ."

When the meeting adjourned, Slaughter took Harry aside.

"You need to learn to not let him goad you like that," Slaughter said. "You have more important things to concern yourself with than playing political slap and tickle with Rony."

"If I don't put him and that glad-handing nob of a son of his in their place, I'll be out of a job. What could be more important than that?"

Slaughter reached under his coat and removed a packet of letters. He handed them to Harry.

"This is," Slaughter said. "Your commitment to your people and the faith."

Harry looked at the letters. "What are these?"

"Correspondence," Slaughter said. "Letters, telegrams, requests for help from the One Mighty and Strong. Word has gotten out about what you did last year, Harry, about how the sacred plates revealed themselves to you. Ours is a new faith, and it is not always welcome in this land. The faithful need heroes, they need you, Harry."

Joseph Smith, the prophet and founder of the Mormon faith, had been a friend to Harry's late father. Smith had commissioned Josiah with a great task to seek out and protect the mythical relics of the faith—divine treasure of Heaven.

They found the impossible trove in a cave here in Golgotha, and the Pratt family built a mansion over it.

Last year, the sacred golden plates given to Smith by an angel had revealed themselves to the most unlikely of readers—Harry. Armed with some of the divine items, Harry had been instrumental in saving Golgotha and the world from destruction. Slaughter and others believed that Harry was the fulfillment of the Prophesy of One Mighty and Strong—a great hero and leader who would guide the faith in its hour of greatest need.

Pratt looked at the stack of letters in his hand. They felt much heavier than they should. He leafed through them and shook his head.

"Requests for help with bad crops, range wars, poor business, sick children, religious intolerance and bigotry. Ghouls? *Ghouls?* And what on earth is a 'skin-walker'? What do these people expect me to do? Ride in on a unicorn and smite their troubles with the Sword of Laban? What do they want from me?"

"Hope," Slaughter said. "Hope that the future is bright and good. That tomorrow will be better."

"I can hardly get myself reelected to this one-horse town," Harry said. "How can I give anyone hope?"

Slaughter saw the stress in the younger man's face, and the darkness in his eyes. He rested a hand on Harry's shoulder and patted his back gently.

"I believe in you, Harry," Slaughter said. "Even if you don't."

It was after dark by the time he finished for the day. Harry was exhausted. He rode his horse Knight, a sorrel Morgan stallion, slowly up Rose Hill toward his mansion. He didn't want to but he needed to clean up and change clothes before he headed back to the mayor's office and the couch.

There were lamps lit when he entered the main hall.

"Lamarr!" he called out to his servant, but there was no answer. For second a trickle of fear fluttered in Harry's chest at the thought that Holly, bleeding darkness, would turn the corner and rush toward him eager to wring his neck.

Instead there was the thump of boots and James Ringo stepped into view. The dusky-skinned piano player's hair was brown, shot through with coppery strands and worn long like the Indian men wore theirs. Ringo was clean-shaven, but a shadow of a dark beard remained on his face. He was wearing only trousers and boots. His muscular frame was wiry and lean. His bare chest was scarred with the looping trails of knife wounds and the puckered craters of bullet wounds—a history in flesh of his youth in the Barbary Coast of San Francisco, but he was still beautiful to Harry. Ringo held a glass in each hand. He offered one to Harry.

"Welcome home," Ringo said. "I was beginning to think I was going to be drinking alone. I was thinking a drink, then I drag you upstairs and give you a bath. I'll do your back. Hell, I'll do your front."

"What the hell are you doing here?" Harry said. "Where is Lamarr? What if someone sees you?"

Ringo set Harry's drink on the hall table and took a long draw on his own. "I see," he said. "We're back to this place. Understandable, but still disappointing."

"What are you talking about?" Harry said. "I came home to grab clothes and clean up. I need to get back to work. What do you mean—'back to this place,' exactly?"

"You, back to the old pattern we had when Holly was alive. You love me, you spend time with me, you hate yourself for it, you run away and try to hide in your responsibilities and deny who you are, and I get to hold us together until you get sick of pretending again, start hating your duty again and run back to me. You haven't been to see me in over three months. It gets old, Harry, and all that running must exhaust you."

"Not so old that you can't make your way to San Francisco and spend a hell of a lot of my money there," Harry said. "You find yourself a new 'one true love'?"

Ringo walked past Harry into the parlor. Harry picked up his drink and followed.

"Fuck you, Harry," Ringo said. "I had debts, very old debts, and the people I owed caught up to me and shook me down. Not all of us were born into fucking nobility. I'll pay you back."

Pratt snorted and sipped his drink. "Don't let it concern you. I always told you to use the money if you need it. Look, I'm sorry you are feeling neglected," Harry said, "but I have so much coming at me and I have so much more responsibility now. I don't have the time to . . ."

"To be in love with me," Ringo said. "To let me help you carry the burden?"

"You can't understand this." Harry sat back in one of the French-made upholstered chairs. "I can't afford to make mistakes. Too many people are counting on me."

"Am I a mistake to you now, Harry?" Ringo asked. He sat cross-legged on the oriental carpet on the floor, a few feet from Harry's chair. He fished his makings out of his pocket and began to roll a cigarette, setting his drink next to him. "Harry, not too long ago you said you wanted to run away to San Francisco. You loathed your responsibility, your duties, now they're killing you. When was the last time you slept all night? When did you eat a proper meal?"

"I'm . . . more than I used to be," Harry said. "I had a little boy walk up to me today on the street and thank me for saving his life during the insanity last year. I don't remember him, don't remember saving him. James, people's lives depend on me here—especially here—and I have to be focused on that or people will die."

"Like Holly died," Ringo said.

"Don't," Harry said, and drained his glass. "You weren't even there, so don't you dare."

"You're right, I wasn't, but I would have been if you let me," Ringo said. "Harry, I would stand with you at the gates of Hell. Holly is dead, and I know you blame yourself for her dying. . . ."

"I ran her through with a goddammed magic sword, like out of a fucking fairy tale," Harry said, snarling. He smashed the glass in his hand. Ringo jumped and crawled toward his lover. "I killed her, and maybe if I had knocked her out, or done something different—something some real hero, like Jon Highfather, or the real fucking One Mighty and Strong, would have done, maybe if I had talked sweet to her the last time I saw her instead of being a selfish, evil-hearted bastard, she would have been safe at home and not out where those sick bastards got her. I . . ."

It all came rushing out: all the sadness, all the regret and the anger, the fear and self-doubt. Harry wept and Ringo knelt before him, took his bleeding hand and gently removed the broken glass as best he could, kissing Harry's wrist and the uncut places on the back of his hand.

"Shhh," Ringo said, taking a doily off an end table and wiping away the blood as best he could. "You hush now, love. I got you."

"I've lived here most of my life," Harry said. "I've seen some terrible things, but there was just so much death, so much dying and I was the one doing the killing. And . . ." The sobs rose again in him. "And they all think I'm some kind of hero now, some damned prophecy, me! I have to be good enough for their damned holy books; I can't afford mistakes, or weakness. I can't let anyone die anymore. I can't afford to be . . ."

"Human?" Ringo said, and pulled Harry to him. He kissed the mayor on his wet eyes in an attempt to banish the tears, then kissed Harry's forehead. "Harry, you are one of the most caring men I ever met, and you are a hero. You were afraid and you set that aside and did what needed to be done. Holly understood. She would never have wanted that thing walking around claiming to be her. You freed her. You saved the town, you saved all of us."

Ringo kissed Harry softly, tasting the tears and feeling his ragged sobs with each breath. "And I love you, and you can always be human with me. I love you."

Ringo kissed him again and Harry joined the kiss. Harry ran his good hand through Ringo's hair and Ringo cupped Harry's face. The kiss grew deeper, hungrier. They were on the carpeted floor, knocking over Ringo's drink and scattering his tobacco and papers. Harry kissed the tips of Ringo's fingers, then his palm and then his wrist. Ringo's hand slid along Harry's chest, teasing, then slid lower. Both of them wrestled with their clothes, both too hungry for the other to relent from touching, kissing, long enough to remove them.

"I love you, Harry," Ringo said, panting. "I missed you."

"I love you too," Harry said, trying to catch his breath. The words were true, but it was still an alien feeling to him to hear them come out of his mouth. "I feel very lost right now, like every step could be a mistake that ends me, ends everything."

"It's going to be okay, Harry," Ringo said, kissing him, deeply. "It's going to be all right, as long as we're together."

Harry froze for a second, the words from his dream echoing in the present. Something old and savage and hungry was coming, maybe already here. Its silent, terrible roar bleeding over into his dreams.

Ringo felt him tense and pulled him closer. "Let it go, Harry," he said. "I have you. Let it be till tomorrow."

Their mouths, their bodies, their hearts became one. They devoured each other, worshiped each other, and healed each other. They collapsed exhausted on the parlor floor, holding one another tight. And for the first time in memory, Harry Pratt slept a deep and, mercifully, dreamless sleep.

The Moon (Reversed)

Sheriff Jon Highfather, newly returned from Louisiana, leaned back in his chair and rested his boots on his desk, his hand folded across his chest. He had arrived home to Golgotha this morning and was trying to untangle the events of last night.

"Okay, now this weird goat-eating thing, you were chasing it across the roof and it was . . ."

"Ugly," Jim said, looking at Mutt. The Indian nodded, looking straight at the sheriff.

"Make-yer-eyes-itch ugly," Mutt said.

Jon slid his feet to the floor and leaned forward, elbows on his desk. He was a lanky, handsome man with sandy hair. The only feature that marred his good looks was the trio of rope burns that looped around his neck. Jon usually covered the scars with a kerchief, but their existence was well known and part of the reason many thought Golgotha was protected by a dead man.

"And this critter is the reason I have a baby goat, eating the blankets in the clink," Highfather said, nodding toward the goat kid, who was contentedly munching on the mattress in one of the jail's cells.

"Billy," Jim said. "His name is Billy, Sheriff."

"Can we keep him?" Mutt said.

Highfather sighed. "Can I go back to Creole zombies trying to kill me, please?"

The iron door groaned, opened, and Clay Turlough entered, carrying a large leather bag.

"Good to see you, Clay," Highfather said. "How are you?"

"Jon," Clay nodded. "Jim, Mutt." He paused and watched the goat eating the fabric with gusto. "Whose goat is that destroying your jail cell?"

"Technically, it's Harry's," Mutt said with a wide smile.

"I see," Clay said, blandly. He sat the leather bag on the floor next to Highfather's desk, opened it and removed an odd, lamp-like apparatus. He pushed aside papers and a few books from Highfather's desk to set the device flat and even on the surface. Jon grinned and moved to get out of Clay's way.

"Make yourself at home, Clay," Highfather said. "Thanks for helping us on this."

The device had a wide, rounded column and above it, almost like a lampshade, was a ring of wide barrel-like protrusions of differing lengths, pointing in all directions. The barrels seemed to be made of metal with glass lenses. The whole contraption reminded Highfather of a magic lantern—a device that could produce images off glass slides, projected onto a screen. He had seen one in a playhouse in Philadelphia shortly after the war.

"What is that thing, Clay?" Mutt asked.

"This is my occuscope," Clay said. He opened a door in the column to reveal a glass cylinder full of amber liquid and eyeballs. Highfather blinked and Mutt leaned in to the sheriff, smiling.

"I told you I wasn't joshing," Mutt whispered. Clay continued his explanation, unperturbed.

"I got some very good images from the occustereograph in the alley last night and I harvested the eyeballs that provided the best visual representations of the event. . . ."

"You mean, 'murder,' Mr. Turlough," Jim said.

"Yes, yes, Jim," Clay said, nodding as he raised the inner chamber of the column and struck a match to ignite the projector's lamp-like wick. "Murder, as you say, and quite a clever one at that. As I was saying, the eyeballs that held the best images are combined here and once I adjust the focus . . . Jonathan, Mutt, could you please see to the windows?"

Highfather and Mutt closed the heavy interior wooden shudders and the jail was plunged into deep darkness. Shadows jumped and shivered in the tiny flame of Clay's match. The wide cloth wick ignited and Clay shook the match to snuff it. He slid the column on the device back into place with a metallic click, hiding the flame. The room was pitch black for a moment, then Clay twisted several knobs, like adjusting a microscope, and suddenly the alleyway of the Dove's Roost and the horribly mutilated body of Sweet Molly were all around them. On every wall, every surface. Unlike a regular photograph, the eyeballs seemed to capture details to a depth where it felt as if you were there, as if it were happening right now. It was unnerving and miraculous all at the same time.

"Clay . . . ," Highfather said, shaking his head in wonder.

"White man's magic," Mutt said, and whistled. "Could make a king's ransom on this, Clay. They'd line up down the street to see a picture show like this."

"Would they?" Clay said, clearly having never considered the prospect of making money off his invention. "I've cogitated building a circular room to provide a better immersive experience. The proper chemical hallucinogens would also enhance the verisimilitude considerably, of course. Perhaps dispersed via a nebulizer-like medium."

Highfather tried to bring Clay out of his musings and back to the present. The effort was background noise to Jim. The odd amber-colored light of the device played across Jim's face. Any other time he would have been amazed and delighted at Clay's wondrous achievement, but now all he could see was the dead woman and the things this unknown beast had done to her.

Again, Jim saw Lottie, his little sister. Saw her bleeding from a bullet wound he'd inflicted in his mad race to avenge his father's murder. Molly may have had a brother somewhere, a family. He hated the thought of them ever seeing her like this, as the killer had left her. Jim swallowed hard and turned in his chair, away from Molly's ghastly surgical grin to Clay.

"Mr. Turlough," Jim said, ice in his voice. "Sorry to interrupt, but did you find anything that will help us catch him, sir?"

Clay, Jon and Mutt all grew silent.

"I have made some observations on the subject, yes, Jim," Clay said.

"Molly," Jim said. "She ain't no subject, sir. Her name was Molly James."

Clay looked at Jim, the tufts of his wild hair like smoke in the bright lantern light. He nodded. "Yes, of course, Jim," Clay said. "I think I have."

"Well, let's have it, Clay," Highfather said. Clay walked away from the occuscope. He began to pace the room as if he were teaching a class, the murder scene painting him at every angle as he walked.

"I am certainly no lawman," Clay began. "However, I must confess a certain fanaticism for the romance of the adventures of the late Edgar Allan Poe's fictional investigator, C. Auguste Dupin. I read and reread 'The Murders in the Rue Morgue' many times , and 'The Purloined Letter' is one of my favorite pieces of fiction. I had the privilege of meeting Poe in Richmond, Virginia, before his death and assisting him with a most delicate and macabre matter. The man was brilliant."

The sheriff and his deputies remained silent, even as Mutt gave Highfather a questioning glance. Clay continued, as he paced.

"The basis of Dupin's method of investigating a crime," Clay said, "was a process Poe called 'ratiocination.' In short, it is the use of intellect along with imagination to build the commission of the crime in one's mind, to even attempt to think as the criminal thinks. Dupin was such a master at this as to be considered a mind reader."

"This is 'in short'?" Mutt whispered to Highfather.

"I have not fully had time to assemble all the particulars of the crime in my head," Clay said, as matter-of-fact as if he were discussing chores in the stable. "However, I have made some observations that may be of help in catching the villain."

Clay walked over to the part of the projection that showed the strands of the girl's insides nailed to the rickety fences.

"I took the liberty of examining the scene today in full daylight," Clay said. "These divots on the fence where he missed the nail with the hammer and a closer examination of the nails themselves turned up some interesting bits of data. One: The murderer had planned out what he was going to do to the girl in some detail, including bringing the proper materials and figuring out a way to mask his labors."

"How's that?" Highfather said. "I know this alley and he's not more than fifteen feet from the Roost's side door and not more than twenty-five or thirty feet from the front porch. Even drunk and horny as a bull, someone on that porch should have heard all that banging of the hammer."

"I found fibers embedded in the divots and tangled in the nails," Clay said.

"Fibers?" Jim said.

"Threads," Clay responded, "strands of cloth. I think our killer wrapped the head of the hammer in cloth to muffle its noise."

"What good does thread do in helping us track him, Clay?" Mutt said.

"I examined the threads and they were brownish gray and there were some black threads. The material was poor quality and coarse."

Highfather snapped his fingers. "A blanket," he said. "An army blanket. A Union army blanket. They have a black stripe and they are that color exactly."

"Very good, Jonathan." Clay nodded. "I examined some of the materials we have here in Golgotha and came to a similar conclusion."

"Well, hell, Clay," Mutt said. "That don't exactly narrow it down, army blankets are all over the place, and lots of folks got them."

"True," Clay said. "But few will have one cut up to cover a hammer and fewer still will be originally from back east, so that will help narrow it down."

"How can you know that he's from back east?" Jim asked.

"The military commissioned the Mission and Pacific Mills of San Francisco to create new blankets for the troops stationed out west," Clay said. "This was not a California blanket. It came with its owner from back east."

"You think he's a soldier?" Highfather said.

Clay shook his head. "No," he said. "He has too fine a shoe. He's a gentleman. Plus I'd wager most soldiers know their way around a hammer and nail. I'd make inquiries to Mr. Benham, the cobbler, and see if he recalls making or repairing shoes of that size and with similar wear on the sole as the prints we discovered in the alley. You can compare them to the drawings I took of the print details."

Jim looked at Mutt. The Indian shook his head. "That is a scary noggin, Clay," Mutt said. "Glad you don't have any desire to be murdering anyone. We'd never catch you."

Clay scratched his head. "The man who did this is disgusting, Mutt. To have this kind of imagination and use it for . . . this. Pathetic."

"It's like magic, like a fortune-teller, all this" Jim said.

"Nonsense, m'boy," Clay said. "It's rational thought. Trumps superstition every day of the week."

"Anything else, Clay?" Highfather asked.

"The nails," Clay said. "He bought them at Bick's company store up on Argent. Auggie's store has never carried this fashion of nail. Our local blacksmith, Wayland Smith, didn't make these nails. Bick's store has ones just like it in stock presently.

"The girl had some dust on her," Clay continued. "Most likely from rock. May have been up near the mines or her killer was. The stars, the moon or numerology may play a part in his madness. He despises women, I'd wager he'll strike at Dutch gals—prostitutes—again, but in a pinch, any woman will do for him. No woman in Golgotha is safe until he's caught. Oh, and Jonathan . . . he's not going to stop, not until he's ready to, or has completed whatever ghastly work he is about, or you catch him, or kill him."

"Why?" Highfather asked.

"Because he knows he's smart enough to keep getting away with it and crazy enough to want to keep the game going with you, with the forces of order. Because if it was me, I'd keep going too."

The iron door creaked and blinding light flooded the jail. Everyone who had been in the darkness groaned. A figure swaggered into the dark room, his shadow, cast from the doorway, blotting out much of the washed-out crime scene on the walls.

"Why in damnation are you people sitting about in the dark?" Dr. Francis Tumblety bellowed. "Queerer than a Virginia fence, I declare!"

"Oh!" Highfather said. "Come on in, doc. Shut the door, will you. Clay was just showing us something."

Tumblety slammed the door with a crash and the darkness swallowed the room again. "Ah, yes," Tumblety said, "Mr. Turlough and his mechanical amusements. How droll. Surely, Jonathan, you are not relying on children's toys now to aid you in your endeavors?"

Tumblety was the closest thing Golgotha had to a doctor, though his credentials were questionable at best. He had coal black hair and a large drooping horseshoe-style mustache. His eyes reminded Highfather of coal someone had spit on, in both color and content.

He wore a large, frayed and smelly black military-style bang-up with numerous medals and commendations pinned to it. Highfather had tried a few times to discuss the good doctor's military service and how the odd mishmash of service ribbons from so many different services, nations and, in the case of the War Between the States, sides, all came to be on the doctor's chest. Tumblety blustered and thundered through such conversations with little information and much noise.

The doctor took a chair from the wall and dragged it over to sit beside Jim. He placed a filthy-looking hand on Jim's knee.

"There's a good fella, Jim. When you going to come see old Dr. Tumblety for a checkup? A strapping lad your age, in the flower of his golden youth, needs to make sure everything is in proper order, yes?"

Mutt leaned across Jim and glared at Tumblety. "You take that hand off that boy's knee right now, doc, or all your equipment is gonna be broke."

Tumblety sputtered and began to redden in anger. Highfather tried to head it off as quickly as he could.

"So, Doctor, you had a chance to take a gander at the girl's body yet?"

"I most certainly have not!" Tumblety said. "Why you saw fit to summon a common horse groomer to the scene of the whore's demise instead of a learned man of letters is beyond me, Jonathan. Why you leave your boy, that savagerous, dirt-worshiping half-breed, in charge of making decisions while you are indisposed is also a mystery to me."

"Hey!" Jim said, standing. "Nobody talks that way about Mutt!"

"Jim," Highfather said. "Sit down, and hush." Jim did, but his cheeks and ears were flushed with anger.

"You see," Tumblety said. "The savage is a poor influence on this callow youth."

Highfather walked around to the front of his desk and put his hand on Clay's shoulder while Clay was opening windows, deactivating and packing up his invention.

"Much obliged, Clay. If you think of anything else that might help, I'd like to hear it."

"I'm still trying to figure out how he got her there," Clay said. "I checked on the other side of that fence and there are wagon tracks back there, right up to the fence. I think he came and went by way of a wagon and I don't think he initially grabbed her in the alley. I think he grabbed her, restrained her and then took her by wagon to the alley to finish his work."

"Why the alley?" Jim asked. "It was so close to people."

"Exactly, Jim" Clay said. "To show us his craft. I made sketches of the wear on the wagon wheels, Jon. Hopefully we can locate the owner of the conveyance."

"I concur with Turlough's findings in that respect," Tumblety said. "However, I, too, examined the scene and I surmise that it is much more likely that it was a group of individuals instead of single man."

"But we got only one set of prints in the alley," Jim said.

"Exactly," Tumblety said. "One man aided by his fellows into the alleyway to dispose of the slag's body and then helped back over the fence from the bed of the wagon."

"That is plausible," Clay said. "There's nothing to dismiss it and it clears up a few bits of confusion. I think the doctor may be on to something there."

"So we got a crew of killers, not jist one?" Mutt said. "I don't care for it."

"Me either," Jim said. "Everything Mr. Turlough said about how this crazy sumbitch is, he sounds like he's too stuck on himself to have help. Thinks he's a huckleberry above a persimmon, y'ask me."

"Well, there you go," Tumblety said with a rough guffaw. "The ignorant half-breed and the doe-eyed child think they've solved the crime. I don't envy you your job, Jonathan. I shall be in touch with my results of the examination of the whore's body. Turlough, be a good fellow and deliver it over to me before you get back to shoveling manure."

Tumblety departed without a backward glance.

"I miss him already," Mutt said.

Clay finished packing up his equipment. He headed toward the door with his bag.

"Few more tests I'd like to run on the girl if you don't mind, Jon," Clay said. "After the good doctor there gets ahold of her, she'll look more like a Thanksgiving turkey than a body."

"Take your time, Clay," Highfather said. "And thanks again. You did good. I may have to read this Poe fellow myself."

Clay departed and Highfather sat down again behind his desk and exhaled with a whoosh.

"So, with all that said, where is everything else at right now in our happy little town?" Highfather asked. "You tend the salt circle at the old cemetery?"

"Yep," Mutt said. "Every day. Place makes my hackles jump, but I took care of it. Don't need that kind of trouble crawling back up right now."

"Good," Highfather said. "What else?"

"Widow Stonehouse says the people in the paintings on her walls are moving about again, but no sign of the Marquis of Stain or his knights in any of the pictures yet, so hopefully it's just weird with a little 'w,' and not something we have to tend to for a spell."

"Okay," Highfather said. "Anything normal, ordinary sheriffs have to tend to? Please say yes."

"I hear tell Bick and Ch'eng Huang have a new shipment of dope headed into town in the next few days from back east," Mutt said. "If I can squeeze the delivery point out of one of my people, we can crash the ball, if you want?"

"My invitation must have been lost in the post," Highfather said. "Let's. Anything else?"

"Got a lead on the horse thief that cleaned out Bertrand Knox's stable. I was going to follow it up," Mutt said.

"Sounds square," Highfather said. "Well, I got something I need to chase down tomorrow for Charley Pegg, the sheriff over in Washoe County. Got a lead on that train robbery that happened a few weeks back. Told him I'd follow it up."

"Need any help?" Mutt said.

Highfather sighed.

"I wish," he said. "If what Charley told me is square, Nikos Vellas might be mixed up in this, too, but we're stretched too thin as it is. I'll manage. Harry keeps promising more money to hire deputies."

"Who's Nikos Vellas?" Jim asked.

"Gypsy," Mutt said. "Greek I think. Showed up in town a few months back and has been making himself indispensable to most of the criminal bosses up at the mining camp. He's gotten a very bad reputation, very quick." Mutt turned back to the sheriff. "You be careful, Jonathan," Mutt said. "Even your luck has got to go bust sooner or later."

Jim cleared his throat. "Um, Sheriff, Mutt. What are we doin' about Molly? About what Mr. Turlough said?"

Highfather nodded. "It was pretty ugly last night, wasn't it, Jim?"

"The most horrible thing I've ever seen, sir," Jim said. "Whoever did that needs to be put down, 'fore he hurts someone else."

"Yes," Highfather said, "he does, but we only have so many hands to do the work and I have to prioritize what gets dealt with first. We'll make the inquiries to the merchants like Clay said when we get a second to catch our breath. We'll keep our eyes open."

"So," Jim said. "Catching horse thieves and train robbers is more important than catching a killer that does . . . things . . . like that to a lady?"

Highfather struggled with words. Mutt looked at the boy.

"Jim, those aren't ladies, they're whores," Mutt said. "Things like that are kind of occupational hazards for them and it's a damn shame and we will catch the bastard, but sometimes a gal will pick the wrong customer and things like that happen."

"Clay said any woman in this town was in danger," Jim said. "We intend to wait until a 'real' lady gets cut up? 'Sides, whatever she did to make ends meet, Molly was always real kind to me in the street," Jim said. "Seems poor to make her wait. Listen, y'all got other things to deal with, Sheriff; let me take a crack at it, see what I can run down."

Highfather looked at Mutt. The deputy nodded.

"Boy's got a fire under him to take the case, I say let him," Mutt said. "'Sides, he's sweet on one of the Doves."

"Gol-darn it, Mutt!" Jim said, swatting the Indian's shoulder. "I am not!"

"Well, if you say so, but you're a shade or two redder than me right now," Mutt said.

Highfather and Mutt laughed.

"You got your teeth into this one, don't you?" Highfather said to Jim. "All right, the case is yours, but, Jim, you need to be careful. Women who do that kind of work, they don't always tell the truth."

"And that makes them different from most of the rest of this town, how?" Jim said.

"Don't sass me, boy," Highfather said. "Just watch yourself; I don't want you to get taken advantage of."

Jim reddened a little more. "I can handle myself."

"Just make sure no one over at the Dove's Roost handles you," Mutt said, slapping Jim on the back. "They'll charge you."

The Empress

Morning at the Dove's Roost was a groggy, ponderous thing. Some of the women, who had been granted the night off, were up early to straighten and clean the parlors and public rooms, while others fetched and boiled water, gathered firewood and prepared breakfast for everyone. The Scholar awoke at dawn every day. He did not partake of alcohol, or lie with any of the women, ever, so he was up, bathed, dressed and wandering the Roost, cudgel in hand, like a keen-eyed menacing mastiff.

Several of the Doves, curious about the Scholar's stoic regimen and his impressive body, had peeked in on him in the bath and discovered his strange secret. The Scholar was tattooed. From the base of his neck to his wrists and ankles, he was covered in lines of fine, delicate cursive script. Like a book made out of flesh. In fact, there were lines of more words in between the lines of words. The covert discovery and his penchant for always carrying about a tome to read gave him the nickname. Most girls had no clue that his real name was Montgomery Quire; he was simply the Scholar. No one had ever dared ask him about the tattoos, or even acknowledge they knew of them. He worked very hard to keep them hidden, even chopping wood and tending to house repairs always in full shirtsleeves.

Those who had worked the night before were allowed to sleep in till noon. But most were up earlier to grab breakfast and then retire until they were required to be back on "duty" at midday. All guests had to be out the door by six, unless they had paid extra to make other arrangements. The Scholar and the house madam, a silver-haired Swede in her mid-forties named Agathe Hamsun—or "Ham," as she was called by the regulars—made sure there were no stragglers.

The routine of the late morning and the early afternoon continued. Cleaning, bathing and tending to any bruises, lacerations, bite or strangle marks, burns or other occupational inconveniences that might impact the ability to make money. Some of the women read, a few wrote letters home. Other slept or did needlepoint or mended each other's stockings or clothes. They talked and joked. Sometimes they argued and fought more fiercely than any man could imagine. Some drank, though Ham and the Scholar were quite strict on drunkenness—if you were too full of the bark juice, then you didn't work and you didn't get paid.

Ham was something of an expert on the life of a public girl. She had been one herself for over twenty years and then became one of the most well-known and respected of madames on the East Coast. She had been offered her position by Bick ten years ago.

She had a painted fan an old lover of hers in Boston had brought back from the Orient. It had steel veins that Ham had sharpened to a keen edge and she could use it to great effect. It was her experience that once a man's face was cut, he tended to that and forgot what he was going to lay hands on you for. If it didn't work the first time, then you just kept beautifying him.

After the breakfast dishes were cleared, Ham and the Scholar sat at the dining table by the kitchen and discussed house business. It had been a grim morning for most in the house, with Sweet Molly's murder last night. While the Scholar scribbled in the house ledger, Ham sipped her tea.

"I don't suppose you are willing to give the girls a night off," she said. Her accent was two parts Boston and one part Stockholm. "Seeing someone you know cut up like that . . . They deserve a chance to mourn, or at least recover."

The Scholar didn't even look up from the ledger he was notating. "Can't afford that," he said. "The murder will decrease business anyway. I'm afraid not, Agathe."

"You mean to tell me that Malachi, of all people, can't afford a dip in his profits for one night?"

"Mr. Bick entrusts me with such decisions," the Scholar said. "And I deem it unwise to close tonight."

Ham looked at him and shook her head. "You really do have ice in you, don't you? It's all bottom line for you, isn't it?"

"No," the Scholar said. "It isn't. I feel very sorry for Molly. If I had known she was freelancing away from the house I would have dealt with it and she would still be alive."

"She was trying to make some extra scratch to send home to her kids and mother back east," Ham said. "Can't fault her for that."

"I can," the Scholar said, finally looking up from the ledger. "Because now her family will receive nothing and they have lost her. It was very poorly thought out, on her part."

"Did you tell the deputies she was working away from the Roost?"

"I did not," the Scholar said. "I endeavored to get them out of here as quickly as possible. The law is almost as bad for business as murder. I am not paid to do the sheriff's job for him."

Maude Stapleton cleared her throat as she entered the dining room by the kitchen door. Maude carried a wicker basket of laundry in her arms and a smaller covered basket on her wrist.

"Morning, Mrs. Hamsun, Mr. Quire," she said, setting the laundry on the table.

"Mrs. Stapleton," Quire said, standing. Ham nodded to the laundress. "We . . . It's just normally one of your Chinese girls delivers, ma'am. We don't get many ladies of your position around here. What if someone saw you enter? Your reputation?"

"To the best of my knowledge," Maude said, "this house is full of ladies, Mr. Quire. I've never cared much for being told where it was proper for me to go. And my reputation is mine to defend, if need be. Thank you so much for your concern."

Ham looked impressed, the Scholar stunned. "No, no, of course, ma'am," he said with a slight bow. "Of course."

"I hope you two don't mind the intrusion," Maude said. "I let myself in. Jiao is indisposed today. She's a touch under the weather, so I'm taking care of the deliveries myself today.

"Mrs. Proctor made a few pies and some bread and buns for everyone," Maude continued, setting down the covered basket. "We're all sorry for the loss."

"Very kind, Mrs. Stapleton," the Scholar said, closing the ledger and scooping it off the table. "I'll have one of the girls collect the fresh linen and deliver you the washables. Good day, madam." He nodded to Ham, who was still sitting. "Agathe."

Ham gestured to Maude. "Please have a seat. Tea? You can tell me all about the doings in Virginia City. I understand you only returned this morning?"

"Yes," Maude said. "Thank you, that would be lovely." She grimaced a bit as she sat down.

"Hurt yourself?" Ham asked, pouring Maude a cup from the pot.

"The coach from Virginia City must have been more . . . vigorous than my body could handle," Maude said. "Pulled a muscle."

Ham smiled and offered Maude the cream and sugar. Maude declined. "May I share an observation with you, Mrs. Stapleton?" Ham said. "I notice every once in a while that you do not move the way you should."

Maude paused in mid-sip. "I'm afraid I don't understand."

"I've been in places like this since I was twelve," Ham said. "I've made a living and survived by reading people—the way they walk, move. Things about them they can't hide with words or bluster or pretty manners. It tells you who they really are and you, Mrs. Stapleton, every once in a while, I see you and you move differently."

"Different how?" Maude said.

"You move like a killer," Ham said. "You move like you know you are a wolf in a world of sheep."

Maude smiled, politely, and sipped her tea.

"Cake?" Ham offered her guest.

"Yes," Maude said, "please," and took one off the offered plate.

"Of course I know that isn't the case," Ham said, smiling.

"Yes," Maude said. "Of course."

Two young women in their late teens, a few years older than Maude's fourteen-year-old daughter, Constance, entered the dining room. One girl was black and slender, the other white with red hair and much more curvy, with prominent hips and bust. Both were dressed in stays and frilled pantalets.

"Ah," Ham said. "Ample Alice, Black Pearl, grab the laundry for Mrs. . . ."

"Mannish Maude," Maude said, smiling and standing to greet the two girls. "At least that was what they used to call me as a child, when I beat all the boys up."

The two girls laughed, as did Ham. Maude shook both the girls' hands in turn. "Pleased to meet you, Alice, Pearl . . ."

"Harmony," the black girl said. "My real name is Harmony."

"Pleased to make your acquaintance, Harmony," Maude said. "That is a beautiful name."

Ham stood. "You said your Chinese girl was feeling poorly. I have a remedy that might help her. I'll fetch it."

Harmony and Alice gathered up the laundry and began to sort it. Alice peeked in the covered basket.

"It sure was kind of y'all to make a fuss over poor Molly," Alice said. "I hope she gets a fair shake, bless her soul."

"I'm sure Deputy Mutt and the sheriff will make sure her killer is found," Maude said, finishing her tea. The two girls laughed.

"What?" Maude said. The girls looked at each other and then Harmony looked to Maude.

"They say you're sweet on Deputy Mutt," Alice said.

Maude reddened a bit. It was strange and a little nice to have a reaction to something that she didn't automatically regulate. "And who, pray tell, are 'they'?" Maude said.

"Folks around town," Alice said. "I think he's real sweet, ma'am. He shot a fella that was gonna cut me up once. I think you could do a lot worse."

"Thank you," Maude said. "I think he's nice, too, but the deputy and I, we're just friends."

"Yes, ma'am," Alice said, and went back to folding clothes. There was a silence in the room for a bit longer than there should have been. Alice began to snort a little out her nose and all three women burst out laughing.

"Stop it!" Maude said, wiping a tear of laughter from her eye. "We are!"

"Well, he sure does look at you like he's sweet on you," Harmony said.

"Really?" Maude asked. The girls nodded. "Has the deputy ever been a . . ."

"Customer?" Harmony said. "No ma'am. He's a heartsick fella. He hides it like a whore does, behind jokes and pretending to not care. But he's about the loneliest man I ever did see."

"I wish your deputy had been here last night to save poor Molly," Alice said. "She was a really good girl. Didn't deserve to go that way."

"I'm sure they will catch whoever did it," Maude said.

"Doubtful, ma'am," Harmony said. "Wish they would."

Alice nodded as she picked at a sweet bun she had retrieved from the basket. "Men like that can do whatever they want to us and get away with it. Just the way it is. We're . . . who we are and no one cares what happens to us."

"Do you care?" Maude said. "Do you care what happens to you?" Alice looked at Harmony. The slender girl shrugged. Alice licked the sugar off her fingers. "I guess I don't care much to die and no one should die like Molly did." She crossed herself and made a face as she saw Molly splayed across the alley in her mind. "You're a nice lady, Mrs. Stapleton, but things are different for women like you. No one cares what happens to whores. Have to sneak off to see crazy, mean, old Dr. Tumblety when we get beat or cut or all poisoned up with a baby in us. If we don't make enough, can't pay the house, can't pay our families, we have to go off and sneak about, take our chances alone with no one like the Scholar to protect us. Hell, he finds out we're freelancing, he'll beat us himself."

"You can kill us and gut us like animals," Harmony added, "and there'll be two younger ones to replace us coming off that stagecoach. Lot of girls looking for a way to keep their belly full and the rain off their heads. If I cared, I'd still be crying and you can't make no coin if'n you're busy crying."

Maude sat very still. Her eyes were looking elsewhere. If not for her wealth and her training, she could be one of these girls. Alone on the edge of the world, a world that was over 90 percent men. No jobs, no property, no prospects. If not for a few fortunate accidents of birth, Maude and Constance might be exactly where these women were, where Sweet Molly had been.

Alice looked at Harmony and then lowered her head.

"I'm powerful sorry if I offended you," Alice said. "Just felt I could talk plain to you, ma'am."

Maude nodded. "No, no. You didn't offend me and you can talk to me, Alice. In fact, I want you two to tell me everything you can about Molly. I want to help."

It was a little later in the afternoon when Mutt walked into Maude's laundry, on the corner of Dry Well and Prosperity Road, battered hat in hand. Maude smiled brightly when she saw him, like sunlight sparkling off water. Constance and one of the Chinese girls, Ron, looked up from their work to smile and laugh quietly. Chuan continued to stir the massive brass cauldron of hot, soapy water and dirty clothes and chatted softly in Chinese to Ron as she glanced at the deputy and Maude.

"Mrs. Stapleton," Mutt said. Maude paused in her advance to meet him and gave him a mock frown.

"'Mrs. Stapleton'?" Maude said. "You here on official business, Deputy, or did you just bump your head?"

Mutt grinned and mangled the brim of his hat in his hairy hands. "Nah, Maude, I'm jist trying to do this the right way and I ain't too good at it."

"Trying to do what?" Maude said. Mutt stood up tall and straightened his vest and shirt, then looked at her.

"Mrs. Stapleton, Maude . . . It's been well over a year and a day and I do see you've stopped wearing your black and . . . I was wondering if . . . I was hoping you'd do me the honor of . . . Shit," he muttered the expletive under his breath, and Maude, wide-eyed and blushing, laughed softly with him.

"You're doing fine," she said.

"Would you do me the honor of accompanying me to Mrs. Proctor's tonight for supper? Please."

"Nothing would please me more," Maude said. "Thank you, Deputy."

Mutt smiled and Maude thought, if it was possible, he even blushed a little.

"Good deal," Mutt said. "I mean, thank you, ma'am. I'll pick you up here at six?"

"That would be splendid," Maude said, a little of her South Carolina belle accent slipping out. "I shall count the minutes."

"Six," Mutt said.

"Don't be late," Maude said.

The Three of Swords

Boyle "Liver-Eatin'" Douglass was a trapper, tracker and trader along the Kicking Horse Pass in the Canadian Rockies. Douglass gained his nickname for his reputation of eating the livers of the Nakoda Indians who made their home in the Pass. Douglass, a true physical giant of a man, murdered whole Nakoda tribes in their sleep and literally bathed in their blood during a feeding orgy. He told a reporter from Montreal that he hated the Nakoda for murdering his wife and infant daughter and that he took the natives' own practice of eating the livers to give you your mortal enemies' strength and power.

This was mostly a lie. Douglass had never married or had a child and the Nakoda had never wronged him. However, it was true that he gained strength with each liver he ate—growing taller, physically stronger and hardier. He also craved them the more he ate. In the fall of 1870, having consumed over 120 human livers, Douglass was seven foot two, 450 pounds of muscle, madness and hunger. He was so strong now that he could rip the livers out of his victims with his bare hands. His invitation to head to the United States for a true feast was given to him out of the still, dead mouth of one of his latest victims. Douglass possessed one and it was number thirty-one.

The Queen of Pentacles

A few clients drifted into the Dove's Roost during the lazy, hot hours of the late afternoon. Many had favorites, others were just passing through. Day customers were mostly out-of-towners, drifters or cowboys. The locals came under the cloak of darkness, so their wives and family, church mates, business partners and neighbors wouldn't see them.

Deputy Jim Negrey walked into the entrance hall of the Dove's Roost. He looked around as if something were going to jump out of the walls and bite him. Several of the Doves muttered and giggled at his entrance.

"Well, hello, handsome," one girl said, laughing. "It your first time, darlin'?"

"Oh my, what a sweet young deputy," another woman said. "I hope he's not here to arrest me. I ain't got no weapons on me, see?" She leaned forward and Jim blushed at the view.

Madam Ham greeted Jim at the entrance to the main parlor. She was an imposing woman, a good head taller than Jim, and while she was older, she was still very striking.

"Deputy Jim," Ham said. "Is this business or pleasure?"

"B-business . . . ma'am," Jim said. "I was hoping to get a little more information about the unfortunate events last night. Sheriff asked me to look into it."

"Well, I'm glad to see Sheriff Highfather is giving Molly's death the attention and resources it deserves," Ham said blandly.

Jim looked at her.

"I know I'm not exactly the biggest toad in the puddle, ma'am," he said. "But

I aim to find the devil that done did this and make him pay. Miss Molly was always very kind. I figure I owe her for that kindness to see this man hang."

"Kind?" Ham said. "She was kind. Did you and Sweet Molly . . ."

"Oh, no!" Jim said, shaking his head and growing as red as the belly of a rooster. "I've never . . . I mean, she and I didn't . . ."

Ham patted the young man on the shoulder. "It's all right, Deputy, don't have a fit. How can I help?"

"Well," Jim said. "I had some questions about Miss Molly's, um, work."

"Yes?" Ham said as she led Jim to an empty sitting room slightly down the hall from the entrance. Jim pulled out the chair for Ham and she sat, smiling and shaking her head, as Jim sat across from her.

"Ah, you Southern boys," she said. "Chivalry is very attractive. Shame you graycoats go madder than a pissed-on hornets' nest when you get riled, but at least you don't go mad like that cockchafer that did in poor little Molly."

"I'm real sorry for your loss," Jim said, and Ham was amazed to see the boy meant it.

"How old are you?" she asked.

"Sixteen," Jim said. "Just turned in September."

"Well, late happy birthday, Deputy," Ham said. "You've never seen a girl torn up like that before, have you, sweet boy?" Jim shook his head. "I'm very sorry a boy like you had to. What's Jon Highfather thinking, pinning a star to your chest?"

"I earned it, ma'am," Jim said. "Molly have any kin hereabouts? Regular clients? Soldiers, by any chance? Ex-soldiers? Anything might mean something to help us find who done this."

Ham was about to answer when one of the girls from the front parlor entered. "I'm sorry to interrupt, Ham, but that lady you talked to from San Francisco last month, she's back, asking for you."

Ham stood and Jim rose as she did.

"Excuse me, Deputy. I'll be back shortly." The madam and her charge walked down the hall. Jim sat back down, ran a hand through his hair and looked around the shadowed parlor.

"You here about the girls that done got killed?" a voice said from the darkness of a French-styled couch. "Mean to catch him or you jist trying to make the mayor and the sheriff look like they give a damn?"

Jim stood and turned. A woman was stretched out on the couch, languid. She was dressed in inexpressibles—long striped stockings of red and black, a black stay with red garters clipped to the stockings. She was the same woman from last night, in the alley. The one who had taken such an interest in the footprints.

Jim swallowed, hard. He'd never seen a woman stretched out like that before, moving almost like a cat, sunning herself. He wanted to keep watching but he figured the sheriff wouldn't do something like that, so he looked off to the side of her.

"You're . . . you're Miss Warren, aren't you? Nice to meet you, ma'am. I was going to ask Mrs. Ham if I could talk to you for a spell."

"Well, ain't I jist a lucky girl," she said, her eyes shining and just for him. Her voice had a familiar twang to it; it reminded him of home, of Ma and Lottie, though he felt very uncomfortable thinking about his mom and sister in a cathouse. Miss Warren's accent sounded like home. "Please," she said, "call me Kitty, and may I call you Jim?"

She stretched out on the couch, on her belly. She was a handsome woman, Jim couldn't ignore that. Slender, with curves in all the places he liked best for girls to have, and in the clothes she was half wearing, her curves were very evident. Her eyes were brown and they held you, as if she had reached out and taken your hand. It wasn't so much her physical appearance that was magnetic, as was her bearing. It was comforting and exciting all at once. A very heady mix. Jim sat back down in the chair. Kitty smiled.

"Talk away," she said.

"Are you from West Virginia?" Jim asked. "'Cause you sure sound like it."

Kitty nodded, sat up and clapped her hands. "I jist knew you sounded like you were from over there. Whereabouts you from, sugar?"

Jim started to answer, and then remembered exactly why he wasn't at home anymore and that he had a price on his head.

"Lots of places," he said. Kitty nodded.

"Been through there a few times myself," she said. "Nice view."

Jim laughed, as did Kitty. "You saw me the other night, didn't you?" she said. "Over by poor old Molly, bless her soul."

"Yes, ma'am," Jim said. "You were looking at those shoe prints. I was wondering why exactly?"

"Your momma raised you real good, Jim," Kitty said. "You treat me real fine and that is rare, make a woman feel like a lady."

"Thank you, ma'am," Jim said.

Kitty climbed off the couch and walked slowly toward Jim.

"I had to leave home young too," she said. "Got married way too early. Cart 'fore the horse. Didn't want it, but he was a real gentleman with me and I have no complaints. He passed and I had to leave to find work out here. Couldn't stay home, some bad things happened. Left our only baby with my mama to raise. Had to."

Kitty was in front of him and Jim could smell the sweet aroma of her skin. He looked up into her warm, dark, compassionate eyes.

Kitty nodded. "Little one was sick when I left a few months ago," she said. "Frets me to no end, not knowing if she's well or . . ."

"I understand," Jim said. "I had to leave when my little sister Lottie was . . . hurt, real bad. I haven't been home in about two years. Just thinking about it . . ."

Kitty ran a hand over his cheek. "You poor thing. I knew it was something similar to my miseries. You had that look about you. Jim, may I ask you a question, please? And please be honest."

"Sure, Miss . . . sure, Kitty, anything," Jim said.

"Why didn't Sheriff Highfather come out to investigate himself? I know it's not uncommon for a public girl to get herself killed, but I heard he was a decent man. . . ."

"Oh, he is," Jim said, standing. "He sent me because he had to go deal with some train robbers, up at the mining camp."

"Train robbers?" Kitty said.

Jim nodded. "Yeah. He is a good man, 'bout as good as they come. He just got a lot of irons in the fire, Kitty."

"He's up there facing those robbers all alone? Goodness!" She was very close to Jim. It was hard to think of other things when she was so intently focused on him, and he really liked the attention, he had to admit.

"Naw," Jim said. "I don't think it's a whole gang. He mentioned just one fella named Vellas. Sheriff can handle it. He's a hard case, Sheriff is."

"That's what I heard too," Kitty said, and then she blinked. "Wait, did you just say 'Vellas,' Nikos Vellas?"

"Yeah," Jim said. "How did you . . . Hey, what happened to your voice, your accent? You joshin' me?"

Kitty's whole posture had changed. Gone was the slow, languid, seductive gait in her body and voice. She was more like a coiled spring now, full of purpose and energy.

"Damn it to hell!" she said in a very non–West Virginia sounding way. "He's here? Okay, listen to me, Deputy. Your sheriff is in a world of danger. You need to get him help as quick as you can. I'm headed to him now. Where is the meet happening?"

Jim narrowed his eyes. The way she spoke now, the earnestness was still there. He wanted to believe her, what she was saying.

"Who are you?" Jim asked. "And why should I trust you, if all you been saying to me is put on?"

"I'm here to help." Kitty took Jim by the shoulders. "And yes, some of what I said was lying, but most of it wasn't—those are the best lies, the ones with truth in them. And I swear on my baby and my husband's graves that if you don't help me get to Jon Highfather, he's going to die. He has no idea what Vellas is and what he's capable of. I do. Where are they, Jim?"

Jim looked into her eyes. They had changed, but at the core of them she was still the same woman with whom he had felt such an immediate connection. The distrustful part of his brain, which on occasion he called his "Mutt brain," whispered that she had fooled him once with her seemingly endless sincerity, and she could be doing it again. But Jim decided he couldn't risk the sheriff's life on that.

"West slope of Argent," he said. "Old prospector's shack near Backtrail Road. Sunset."

"Thank you, Jim," she said and started to sprint from the room. Jim grabbed her arm; they were both surprised at how firm his grasp was.

"Hold it," he said. His voice was much deeper and more forceful than he imagined he could be. "Now you answer my question that you fancy-danced all over. Molly James."

A newfound appreciation and respect showed in Kitty's eyes. "Molly was freelancing for the Nail—Niall Devlin—behind Ham and the Scholar's back."

"Devlin? That sidewinder up at the mining camp? He's mixed up in everything dirty."

Yes," Kitty said. "The Nail has been stealing away some of Bick's girls and getting them to work for him up at the camp. She was working away from the house last night, without any backup. Now hurry up, Jim! Time's wasting."

She ran off toward the back of the Roost and up a narrow flight of stairs. Jim watched her ascend and rubbed his hair and then shook his head.

Madam Ham came back, looking troubled. "Deputy, I'm sorry. I have some business I need to address. Might we talk again tomorrow?"

"That will be fine, ma'am. I actually need to run myself. I'll be back in touch."

"She wasn't troubling you, was she?" Ham asked. "Kitty? I've had a bad feeling about that girl since she came to us a few months back."

"No, ma'am, she was fine. Just keeping me company for a spell," Jim said. "Now if you'll excuse me, please. Sheriff needs me."

Jim opened the ornate front door to the Dove's Roost and was halfway off the porch when he was suddenly grabbed and spun about. It was Becky, she of the yellow ribbons, the girl Jim and Mutt had rescued last night from the Elysium's dining room and the goat-sucking creature. She hugged Jim fiercely.

"Oh, Deputy Jim," Becky said. "The girls told me you were here to help us, to find who killed poor Molly. You are a good man, Jim Negrey."

She pulled him closer and Jim's arm just slid around her waist, like it was supposed to, like it had a mind all its own.

"You are my hero," Becky said, and kissed him softly on the cheek. "Come visit me."

Then, as quickly as she had grabbed him, she was gone back into the house and Jim could hear the laughter of the girls that greeted Becky.

Jim stood, looked back at the closed door and then turned toward the street. Constance Stapleton, Maude's daughter, was standing near the edge of Bick Street, about twenty feet away from him, a wicker basket of laundry on her hip.

Jim had first noticed Constance in the days after the horrible events of last year—the plague of the Wurm. Constance had been tending to the ill, helping with the bereaved of the dead. She was beautiful. The devil would dance in her wide, dark brown eyes, a wicked intelligence and humor, but there was a wisdom and a sadness in the darkness as well. Her mouth was small but she had full lips and an almost demi-smirk most of the time, like she knew a joke you didn't. She had thick lashes and expressive arched eyebrows. Her skin was pale and perfect, like fine china, and her thick, straight, long brown hair fell below her shoulders, pulled back into a simple ponytail. Jim had been trying to get up the nerve to talk to her for months. They saw each other often, but neither seemed to find the ability to cross the gulf and say more than just hello. Now, Constance had that slightly amused look on her face and one raised eyebrow.

"It's not . . . ," Jim stammered, jabbing a thumb back toward the door. "I wasn't . . . I . . . Official business."

"Mmmhhhmm," Constance said, her smile widening at the deputy's blush and discomfort. "She sure looks like she could conduct official business." Constance walked up Bick Street toward Prosperity. Jim watched her go, still flustered. Constance stopped and looked back at him. They both looked away quickly.

Jim whistled and rubbed his face. He suddenly snapped his fingers.

"Sheriff!" he exclaimed to no one and ran off in the direction of the jail. The sun was a red-lidded eye, slowly closing in the west. If Kitty Warren were telling the truth, when it closed, it could spell the end of Jon Highfather's life.

Justice

The approaching night's cold crept up the ridge of Argent Mountain, settling into the ground and the stones, as the sun retreated behind the distant mountains. Jon Highfather's legs were cramping from his hours of sitting in wait. He had tied his horse, Bright, to a safe spot in the small stand of cottonwoods about a half-mile from the spot where the criminals were to meet.

A few weeks ago, the Central Pacific Railroad line had got hit by bandits. It was a new kind of crime, robbing a train, but it harkened back to the days of the old highwaymen and their modern descendants, the stagecoach robbers. This, however, was much grander a payoff than any coach. The gunmen had taken over $40,000 in gold off the train.

Charley Pegg, the sheriff over in Washoe County, had contacted Highfather by telegram that the man responsible for masterminding the train robbery was coming out of hiding and headed toward Golgotha looking for a fresh horse and supplies.

Highfather aimed to interfere with that transaction.

The weather had turned, as it often did in Nevada in the late fall. One day would be unseasonably hot, the next day you might find frost on the ground or even snow. The night was turning bitterly cold and Jon wished he had a campfire and a pot of hot coffee. Instead, he had an old army blanket wrapped around him, a loaded 12-gauge short-barrel shotgun, his new Winchester rifle, and his old Colt .44 revolver on his hip. The two rifles rested, propped on his saddlebags to insure that they didn't swell or jam because of the cold. Mrs. Proctor had prepared him a cold lunch of shaved ham, cheese, some hard bread and a bull's-eye canteen of water. The remains of the meal resided in his bag.

He had settled into his hidden roost on the western slope by early afternoon, after tending to his usual daily duties. The site for the criminals' rendezvous was a rotting abandoned miner shack from the days of Argent's first boom. It resided a few hundred yards off the narrow rutted path the locals called Backtrail Road— the only road granting access to the Argent Mountain on its western side. Backtrail was also synonymous with dirty deals because it gave parties access to Golgotha without having to ride down any of the primary well-observed roads. It was the outlaw's preferred entrance and exit point for the town.

Truth be told, despite the reason for his being here and the cold seeping into his bones, Highfather liked sitting here. The view from the western slope was beautiful. The sun was sinking on the horizon, a silent furnace of orange and red, drowning at the end of the world. The shadow lengthened on the mountains and stretched across the arid, cracked north from the base of Argent, through the rough scrublands and the lush belt of pasture and farm country that blessed Golgotha, making it an emerald jewel between the teeth of two deadly wastelands.

It was beautiful country, a beautiful world. And spending the day on the side of a mountain, admiring it, was a pleasant change from his usual days and nights of conflict, terror and stress. Everyone always looked to him for the answers, to save the day, to make the monsters go away. No one in Golgotha understood what it felt like to be just as scared, just as confused and just as desiring of having someone show up and make it all right, and there being no one there. Who saves the savior?

For the hundredth time today he considered resigning. Mutt and Jim were more than capable of handling the strange things that visited Golgotha almost daily. They had shown him that numerous times now.

He'd never come to Golgotha to be the law, to wear a star. If the good townsfolk of Golgotha knew the full story of their beloved sheriff, what he had been and done before he pinned on that silver star, Jon was pretty sure they would run him out of town on a rail.

He walked into town five years ago, after crossing the 40-Mile on foot, more dead than alive. Within forty-eight hours, he'd found himself the only thing that stood between the people of this town, strangers who'd welcomed him like family, and a creature of chaos and evil—a thing made of sawdust, straw and hatred, that called itself Bodach-ròcais. Five years he'd worn this star, experiencing things no one would ever believe. Maybe he was insane and this was all a delusion, a fantasy. Maybe it was still 1865 and he was back in Saint Elizabeth's Hospital, locked away, talking to his dead brother Larson. No. He was sane, as sane as he was capable of being after all he had seen in the war and in Golgotha. Where could he go after all that? Back to the homestead, to his parents and their accusing eyes? Eyes that saw Larson whenever they looked at him.

He had planned a home, a real life, with Eden when they met here in Golgotha, but the town had devoured her, left her dead, worse than dead. Highfather could never go home. This place was all he had now. So, again, for the 101st time today, he talked himself out of resigning.

The sun was a razor cut of brilliant light on the edge of nightfall when he heard the wagon clatter along the northeastern part of Backtrail Road. The northeastern trail ran up Argent to the entrance of the mines and eventually wound around to the miners' camp and hooked up with Prosperity Road. It was dusk and it looked like the deal was about to go down. With Malachi Bick firmly in control of Golgotha, and Ch'eng Huang and his Green Ribbon Tong undisputed lords of Johnny Town, there were several men competing to be crowned the criminal king of Argent Mountain. One of them would be meeting the train robber tonight, and if what Charley's source had told him was true, Nikos Vellas would be with them.

The wagon was a buckboard, with a saddled horse reigned to the back of the wagon. A man Highfather didn't recognize drove the horses from the wagon seat. He carried a pistol on each hip. There was something covered by canvas in the back of the wagon and there were two men crouched next to it; both had rifles. Highfather recognized them from the mining camp, pros named Clement and Dodd. They used to do dirty work for Wynn, the owner of the Mother Lode Saloon and the old lion of the mountain—the original criminal boss of the camp, undisputed until this past year.

At first, Highfather figured with two of his boys here, it was Wynn behind this, but then two more men on horseback, cradling shotguns, rode by flanking the wagon, and following behind them was Bruce "Half-Guts" Mitchell, and Highfather knew Mitchell was calling the dance.

Mitchell, so the story went, had been a quartermaster in the 4th Regiment out of West Virginia, a Confederate unit. He was nearly cut in half by a stray cannonball, losing half his insides in the process, but being too damn mean to die. Folks who had crossed Half-Guts claimed he lost his soul as well as his innards, making a deal with old Scratch himself as he lay dying on the battlefield. Soul or not, Mitchell had come out west after the war and set up shop in Golgotha a few months after the Argent Mine was reopened. He possessed an uncanny knack for getting people together with what they wanted with not a lot of questions or laws getting in the middle of it.

Mitchell was a stocky man, blond, with bright green eyes, hair parted to the side and a full beard. He wore an old Confederate gray bang-up and a saber still hung on his belt. A lever-action Winchester was in a saddle sheath and one of Mitchell's hands rested on the stock.

The party came to a halt just off the intersection of the roads, about fifty yards from the shack. One of the men in the back of the wagon climbed down, lit a lantern and stood near the center of the group. Mitchell climbed down off his mount, a blood bay quarter horse, and proceeded to fire up a pipe.

Highfather slid down to his belly and rested his arms on the saddlebags. He claimed his rifle and took bead on Mitchell, using one of the saddlebags as rest for the rifle barrel. The wind was picking up as the light faded. A few flurries swirled about in the cold night air.

"Where the hell is he?" Mitchell's man with the lantern grumbled, and began to pace. Mitchell, nonplussed, puffed his pipe and admired the last sliver of light on the distant mountains.

"Patience, Clement, is a virtue," Mitchell said. "They will show. We're holding the goods after all."

"That foreign fella gives me the creeps," Clement said, adjusting the lantern. "Don't trust him."

"Mr. Vellas may be a gypsy, but he is a very well-connected gypsy. He located the goods quickly and at a price that was very fortuitous to us to say the least, since I am charging the gentleman who needs them a damn sight more. This is America, Clement. We welcome all kinds to our bountiful shores. The more ante in the pot, the bigger the take for the winners."

Clement spit a brown stream of tobacco juice in the dirt near his boot. "Still don't trust the damn gypsy, sir. He's always too damn happy."

As if he had heard the gunman, a dark shape detached itself from the shadows of the dilapidated homestead and moved through the overgrown field of sacaton grass swaying in the wind. Mitchell's men drew their guns and aimed at the figure, but once the man stepped into the light of the lantern, Mitchell gave them a sign to lower their weapons.

"Mr. Vellas," Mitchell said. "We were just talking about you, sir. No horse?"

Nikos Vellas was stocky and olive-skinned, with black hair and eyes. He lumbered more than walked and each movement implied great bulk and power. He wore a simple collared work shirt, a black frock coat, and black canvas pants. He appeared to be unarmed.

"I do not like the horses and they do not like me," Vellas said. His voice had a booming, hollow quality to its timbre. "I prefer the rail, yes?"

Nikos paused and looked up the hill in Highfather's general direction. A chill ran through the sheriff's spine and his grip on the rifle tightened. Nikos smiled.

"What?" Mitchell asked.

"Nothing," Vellas said. "I see you located the horse and the cache, yes? Do you have my payment?"

"Right here," Mitchell said, reaching into his coat. He withdrew a thick packet of papers bound by a thin leather cord.

"Here you go, sir," Mitchell said.

"It is accurate and to the level of detail I requested?" Vellas asked.

"Yes, very," Mitchell said. "Just as you requested. May I ask why you wanted so much information about the town's geography, the people living here? Mr. Bick?"

"You may inquire," Vellas said, slipping the papers into his pocket, "but I have no intention of explaining myself to you, Mr. Mitchell. Some things it is better not to know."

Vellas smiled. "Clement here doesn't care much for a man who smiles too often," Mitchell said. "He figures it ain't genuine and you're hiding something behind it."

"Oh, I do," Vellas said. "Much to hide, yes? But I smile because I am happy and life is good, Mr. Mitchell. You should learn to cultivate a smile; life is too short to frown."

"Too damn long to smile," Mitchell replied, "in my estimation."

There was the sound of approaching hoofbeats from the west and a lone rider appeared out of the darkness swallowing the road.

"Ah," Mitchell said, "and here is Mr. Chapman now."

The horse's stride was uneven and the poor animal appeared exhausted. The rider looked tired but did not slump in the saddle. He brought the horse to a stop and dismounted. Chapman was gangly, with the look of a vulture about him—a narrow face with a large nose and short graying hair. He was wearing clothes better suited to the city than riding the trail and they were covered with dust. The gunbelt he wore looked out of place.

"You Mitchell?" he said. Half-Guts nodded and the two shook hands. Chapman gave the smiling Vellas an odd glance and then looked back to Mitchell. "You got the supplies, the horse?"

"Yes," Mitchell said. "All that is required is for you to cross my palm with the agreed-upon coin, my good sir."

Chapman walked to the horse and unslung his saddlebags. He opened one and removed a stack of money. He counted some of the stack off and handed it to Mitchell, who inspected it and nodded in approval. Mitchell nodded to one of his men, who led the fresh horse that had been tethered to the back of the wagon over to Chapman, who busied himself with putting the rest of the money away and transferring his bags to the new horse's saddle.

"I want to congratulate you on the job your boys pulled up there in Verdi," Mitchell said. "Real innovative, robbing a train. I think you fellas may be on to something there."

One of the men on the back of the wagon removed the canvas cover and handed Chapman another saddlebag. Chapman busied himself loading it onto the fresh horse.

"There's the food, water, compass and maps and all the rest you were asking for," Mitchell said, watching Chapman struggle with the bags. "I have to ask, Mr. Chapman, sir, have you been in this business long . . . robbing, I mean? I know the fellas that pulled the job have been hitting the Wells Fargo lines for years, but I was just wondering . . ."

Chapman spun, looking nervous and agitated. "I am trying to get the hell out of here! Jesus, you are the most damn chatty criminal I've ever met! The law is everywhere and they are looking for me! No, no, I'm not a hardened criminal, I'm a Sunday school superintendent, for fuck's sake! I planned it and it's going to make me rich and I am done with it, you understand, damn it!"

Mitchel nodded serenely to one of his men on the horses. "Oh I do, sir. I do. Perfectly. Now toss that gun on over here."

The two men on horseback leveled their guns at Chapman.

"What . . . what the fuck is this?" Chapman sputtered.

"Such language from a Sunday school teacher," Mitchell said. "I figured you were new at this when you pulled that wad of shin plasters out of that saddlebag. In my estimation your take of the forty thousand dollars is in there, and I'm afraid I'm just too greedy a son of a bitch to let that money ride off, especially with such a criminal mastermind like yourself.

"It's a shame really. So many genuine villains out west these days, real hard cases, and a shave-tail like you comes along with a fine idea like robbing trains. Irony. Throw down your saddlebags and that iron on your hip and you can ride on out of here on that expensive new horse you just bought."

Chapman opened his mouth but no sound came out. His hand wavered near his pistol and Highfather knew what the fool was thinking. Highfather took a breath, stood and leveled the rifle on Mitchell's chest. The moon was rising behind him and silhouetted him to the party below.

"Mitchell!" Highfather shouted. "It's Jon Highfather. We got a bead on you dead-bang. I want all of you to lay down arms and be still and there will be no trouble."

"He's alone," Vellas said, still smiling to Mitchell. "All alone."

"Shut the fuck up!" Mitchell said to Vellas. Chapman was panicking, looking up at Highfather and then back to Half-Guts, his hands moving near his gun and then up to his chest again and again.

"Wouldn't recommend you do that, Mr. Chapman," Highfather called out. "Good way to end up dead."

Clement looked at Half-Guts.

"He's s'posed to be a dead man, Mr. Mitchell," Clement said.

"So I hear," Mitchell said. "Let's find out. Light 'em up, boys!" he shouted to his men, and then dived for cover behind the wagon.

Highfather remembered his first battle. It was in the war, at First Manassas. Larson, his brother, had nearly pissed himself. Jon saw the plumes of gun smoke vomit out toward them and this great, soul-stealing fear had come over him, began to eat him. He looked at his little brother and heard the hiss, felt the heat of an angry round narrowly miss him. And the fear was gone, and the paralysis with it. He moved to cover Larson and advanced with his fellows, his gun cracking as he fired into the lines.

"Follow me, stay low," he shouted back to his brother, and Lawson nodded and did as he was told. And they lived, and Jon Highfather learned the secret to surviving a fight: have something in you stronger than fear.

The two men on horseback, Clement, and the gunman in the back of the wagon all opened fire on the shadow before the moon. The shadow dropped and tumbled down the hill, covered by the night and the tall grasses, the bullets a swarm of hornets whining all about. The shadow came up in a crouch, rifle in hand, shotgun slung in a back sheath. The rifle bellowed as Highfather fired. The man up in the wagon grunted and staggered backward, but stayed on his feet and returned fire. Highfather cocked the lever on the rifle and fired again. The lantern exploded and darkness swallowed the hillside. There were the flares of fire from the gun barrels and some burning oil splashed on the side of the wagon, but not enough yet to give much light.

Highfather skirted to the right, keeping low and moving through the grasses toward the old shack. He cocked the Winchester, chambering a fresh round. Mitchell's boys were still firing, chopping up the grass where he had been a few seconds ago. Mitchell was a wily old grayback and he'd get them under control in a second, start directing their fire and then Highfather would be in trouble.

He was too far away for the shotgun to be much more than an annoyance right now. He had to get closer, but closer was not an easy thing at the moment.

He heard shouting and wild galloping in the direction of the western road down the mountain. Mitchell was cussing. That would be the great train robber, Chapman, rabbiting. The distraction gave Highfather a few seconds and he took them.

He bolted for the shack, firing with the rifle again as he cleared the cover of the grass onto the open dirt crossroads. He had committed the rough locations of the shooters to his mind's eye and now he aimed from memory and calculated anticipation of movement. A hot branding iron scraped his left arm and it felt like a steam locomotive at full speed clipped him. Highfather staggered, almost fell but stayed on his feet. He flipped the Winchester, cocking the rifle's lever with his one good hand—the one holding it. The gun rocked back into his hand, the lever snapping back into place. It was a tricky maneuver, and Highfather had spent a lot of time practicing it. The practice paid off. The rifle barked again, Highfather using the flash from the shooters' barrels as a target. He dived through the doorless entrance of the old abandoned shack a second ahead of a dozen bullets and fell on the cabin floor, made up of cold dirt, the rotting remains of wooden planks and molded canvas.

There was a whirr near his ear. Highfather looked up slowly into the shovel-headed face of a hissing rattler a few feet away from him. The snake was resting on part of a rotted board, scared, and coiled to strike.

The Six of Cups

"Quite an entrance," Bick said to Emily, as he closed the door to his office. "You certainly display the theatrics of someone who is my daughter. Please, have a seat, my dear."

Emily sat on the tufted red leather love seat that was near the office door. "Thank you," she said. "I came a long way to meet you, to look you in the eyes, and I'm afraid I simply did not care to wait. My apologies."

Bick laughed as he walked to the liquor cart to the left of his desk. He poured himself a tumbler of cognac from an ornate rectangular cut-glass bottle. He proffered the bottle to Emily and she declined with a shake of her head.

"No need for apologies," he said. "I understand completely. And, again, a character trait well in keeping with my child."

"I *am* your child," Emily said to Bick's back. The saloonkeeper didn't turn.

"Yes, Bick said. "You are."

"Mother died giving birth to me," Emily said. "Her family was not terribly kind to a bastard. With all the wealth they had at their disposal, they could have hired someone to care for me and I'd never have been spoke of again. However, they deemed it more efficacious to simply drop me on the steps of 'the old brown house' of the Sisters of Charity. I was less than a year old."

"You speak very well, given your upbringing," Bick said.

"Thank you," Emily said. "I worked very hard to do so. Books were the only family I had, growing up."

"There are worse families, I can assure you," Bick said as he sat on the love seat, beside Emily. "What was it like, the orphanage?"

"I always felt different," Emily said. "Alone. I endured the place. When I was old enough I was released, I worked whatever jobs a girl of my position could find and I discovered I had a talent for painting, like my mother. I struggled but I survived. One day Caleb came to me with money and his story . . . and yours."

"You know what you are? What I am?" Bick said.

Emily nodded.

"I am the daughter of an angel and a human woman. I believe the theological term is Nephilim?"

"I was with your mother for almost a year," Bick said. "I wanted to be with her forever. She was a brilliant artist, Emily. I met your mother when I was in a bit of a crisis about my purpose and the Almighty's intentions with the universe, with people. I was led to ponder that perhaps God was not as benevolent as I had come to believe He was in His plans and experiments. I saw your mother's work in a gallery in San Francisco and it was like the human soul speaking to me, reassuring me, when my God was silent and would not. I determined I had to meet the artist, to know her. My duties forced me to return to Golgotha. I sent word for her that I wanted her to join me. I received word back she had died giving birth to you." He paused at the memory. "Years later, I told Caleb about you, when he first came to me and told me he wanted to search out all his brothers and sisters."

"How many of us are there?" Emily asked.

"I couldn't say," Bick replied.

"That many?" Emily said. "So I'm not the only one that you lost track of. How did Caleb come to find you?"

"That is a very long story for another day," Bick said. "Caleb spoke of you often and with great pride. If you had a guardian angel in your life, it was him, not me."

"Yes, he was," Emily said. "He was very kind to me. I loved him very much. He took good care of me; he spoke of you often too. He tried to explain the way you were, explained that you couldn't be different any more than the ocean could not be wet. He told me you loved him, loved me and loved all of us in your own ways, as best you could."

"If you had written to me earlier, I could have been prepared to meet you at the stage," Bick said, "or arranged more civilized methods of conveyance for you to Golgotha."

"I liked the stage," Emily said. "All those people jostled together, the coughing, the smells—even the stink! The stories they told, the songs. It was so . . . alive."

Bick nodded. "Yes. I feel that way whenever I visit a large city."

"Besides that, I wanted to surprise you," Emily said. "I wanted to see you without preparation. I wanted to ask you why you let me spend over seventeen years in an orphanage in San Francisco."

Bick drained a good third of his glass in a single drink.

"Because," Bick said, "I am a black-hearted villain. You've been in town a few hours, surely you must have heard that by now?"

"I have yet to fully experience your reputation firsthand," Emily said. "It sounds as if I will have something to look forward to. Caleb, of course, told me about you from his experiences being with you."

"And what did he say?" Bick asked.

"That you traffic in prostitutes and deal with criminals and worse," she said.

Bick feigned surprise and insult.

"I am a respectable, upstanding pillar of this fine community. One of the founding fathers of Golgotha, if you will, since my family was here even before the Mormons arrived."

"Your family?" Emily asked.

"I must change my identity every so many decades to avoid being discovered for my true nature. I have taken the name Bick for some time now."

"Oh, yes, of course," Emily said.

"I am a sober-minded sage, town elder and civic leader," he said, raising his glass in salute.

"Who consorts with evil men," Emily added.

"I do," Bick said. "I truck with malefactors most foul, politicians even! I have for a very, very long time, my dear. It has been my sad experience that the 'criminals and worse' of this world are the ones who have the power and the will to get things done. I wish it were otherwise, but that whole 'meek shall inherit the Earth' homily isn't very likely."

"How can you say things like that?" Emily said. "Given what you are, where you come from? You know better, don't you?"

Bick finished his drink and walked over to the cart to make another one. "An excellent question: Who better than an angel of the Lord to know the ethical landscape of the cosmos? If only it were that easy."

"It . . . it isn't that easy?" Emily asked. "You're an agent of God Almighty. You were created directly by God—the one true God—to act in His name across the universe. You . . ." She paused and pointed to the drink in Bick's hand as he sat back on the love seat. "Does that even affect you?"

"It does if I allow it," Bick said, and took another swallow from the glass. "And at the moment, I'm allowing it. So, God Almighty . . ."

"Yes," Emily said. "You . . . you've seen Heaven, lived there, right? You have seen God, spoken to Him."

Bick leaned closer to her, his eyes intent. "Tell me, Emily. Do you recall much about your early life when you were an infant, when you were one, two years old?"

"No, not really," she said.

"It's the same for me," he said. "I have been here for millions of years, Emily, living in flesh more than spirit for most of that time."

Bick emptied the tumbler again. He looked at the empty crystal.

"I remember . . . it is very cold here compared to there," he said. "I remember that when God looked at me, when He spoke to me, it was the most contented feeling I have ever experienced, but I cannot hold His face in this piece of meat you call a brain. I can't remember most of Heaven anymore, but yes, I know it is real."

"You said 'He,' " Emily said. "God is a man? That's what they say in church."

"God simply is." Bick said. "Humanity embraced It. They gave It color and gender, shape and form. They put words in Its mouth. They always have and they still do, perhaps they always will. I experience God as a 'He,' but God is too vast to be held prisoner by language or biology."

" 'They,' " Emily said, "not 'you.' Humanity is 'they' to you and me. I'm not human, am I? I mean, I've known for years, but when I hear you say it, it becomes real. I'm outside the things you are talking about."

"No, just the opposite, you are very much a part of it," Bick said, leaning toward her. "You are in both worlds, Emily—you, Caleb, all of those like you—you are born of flesh *and* the infinite . . . and have the best of both worlds. I'm an exile in this world. You are not. This is your home."

"What do you mean by the infinite? You mean other children of angels?"

"Angels, demons, spirits," Bick said, "and more than that. I'll tell you a little secret, Emily. Consider it a part of your birthright. There are myriad gods, as many as the human experience could summon. I can't see God's face anymore, but so many humans can picture Its every detail. Your mother could, in her art. It's one of the most remarkable things about humanity, their capacity to dream, to see without sight. You still possess that too. You truly have the best of both worlds within you."

"I . . . I don't understand," Emily said. "You're saying that there is not just your God—the one true God in Heaven? That humanity dreamed your God and all these other gods and spirits and devils up? How can that be, since you and all the angels and God existed before men existed? If they are fabrications of man, then how can you have agency—how can you even exist? How can there be more than one all-powerful, all-knowing being when, by definition, two or more such beings would undermine such claims?"

"You're an artist, correct? Like your mother?" Bick asked. Emily nodded. Bick held up the empty glass tumbler. The light from the massive window behind his desk, which provided him with an excellent view of Golgotha's Main Street, caught the cut glass and refracted the light.

"As an artist, let's say you met a man who has been blind since birth," Bick said. "How would you describe the color blue to him?"

"I would tell him to feel ice, to touch water, to let the wind caress him, and I would tell him that it was all like the color blue," she said.

"So you would give him associations to provide an analogy to the color," Bick said. She nodded. "Do you think any two people would give him the same analogies?"

"It's doubtful that they would," Emily said. "It's subjective. Each person would experience blue differently."

"But the color blue exists separate from people, correct? It is an objective part of this reality? Yes?" He turned the glass in the light and the prism of colors shifted.

"Well, yes, but . . . ," Emily said, struggling to articulate her thoughts.

"Is there a perfect blue? An ideal blue, Emily? A 'one true blue'?"

"No," she said, and smiled. "I mix the pigments up each time I paint and it's never exactly the same."

"And do you think blue would exist if there was no one in the whole universe to see it, to name it, to define it as light blue or dark blue, baby or cerulean or navy or midnight? Would those colors exist as potential waiting to be defined or as reality waiting to be experienced?"

"I think I'll have that drink now," she said.

Bick smiled and nodded

"We shall make a philosopher out of you yet," he said.

Bick escorted Emily to the Imperial, located off Prosperity Road, near the northern base of Argent Mountain. The land, past the western border of Johnny Town, was already beginning to fill up with new homes and businesses, all fueled by the silver boom.

He instructed the manager of the hotel, Lionel Kinkaid, to give her the finest suite in the new hotel and a line of credit for any shops or stores in Golgotha.

"That is very generous of you," Emily said as she wandered the expansive suite on the top floor. It was dark outside now and Emily looked down on the town from her balcony window. "I assure you, I won't abuse your hospitality. I came to Golgotha to find what happened to Caleb, but also I wanted to see you, see what you were like in person."

"I'm sorry if I disappointed you," Bick said.

"You didn't," Emily said. "Though you still haven't fully explained why you never came for me. I do not accept that you are merely evil and capricious."

"There are many in this town that would debate that point with you," Bick said. "At any rate, I am sorry for your difficult upbringing and my part in it."

Emily shrugged.

"I'm not sure I believe that either," she said.

"I know you have just met me but you can believe that. I am sorry you had to endure that place."

"I wouldn't give up my years in the orphanage, now," Emily said. "They made me stronger, gave me eyes to see the good in even the worst pits life may drop you into. Life can be horribly painful and dreadfully unfair, but the colors and the hues, the final tapestry, it's worth the suffering, made more beautiful by it, sometime."

"Human experience, human perception never ceases to amaze," Bick said, offering his daughter her shawl. "Humans can sense so little of the universe around them and yet they use the feeble senses they have along with an indomitable spirit to find order in chaos, discover beauty in horror. Amazing. May I have the honor of taking you to supper? I'm sure you are ravenous."

Emily allowed him to drape the shawl over her shoulders. "Yes, very," she said. "Thank you. 'Ravenous.' Do you even need to eat?"

"No," Bick said. "I don't, but I enjoy it very much. Some days I even get hungry."

Emily shook her head. "I know I'm not, but I still feel quite human."

"The best of both worlds," Bick said opening the door for his daughter. "The best."

The High Priestess (Reversed)

Night fell on Golgotha. The evening was in full swing at the Dove's Roost. The piano player, who, by whorehouse tradition, was always called the Professor, was playing an off-key rendition of *Come on in Old Adam, Come in!* in the main parlor. With the Scholar and the Professor in attendance at the Roost, many of the girls had come to call their home and workplace the university.

All three downstairs parlors were crowded with clients and public girls, drinking, laughing and flirting.

The Scholar made his rounds, ever-present cudgel in his hand as he prowled the halls of his domain, ever vigilant for trouble. He nodded to Ham as she greeted a horde of drunken miners in the foyer. She nodded back and gave him a strange smile. He frowned and then walked down the first floor hall to his office.

He knew someone was in the office as soon as he opened the door. The lamps he had lit earlier still burned, but now several others did as well. His office was decorated, as was the rest of the Dove's Roost, in French décor. He didn't care for it—too effeminate for his taste. His one addition since arriving had been to add bookcases to accommodate the personal library he'd had shipped from Baltimore. He always found comfort and peace in being surrounded by walls of words.

He choked up on the cudgel as he stepped inside, expecting a snooping employee or a thieving customer.

The woman sitting at his desk was bewitching. The Scholar had learned long ago to not allow his reason to be swayed by a pretty face or a sharply leg, but this woman gave him pause. She was short, no more than a few inches over five feet; her hair was a mane of ebony tresses that fell down to the middle of her back and covered her breasts. Her complexion was a shade lighter than cinnamon and her eyes were hazel constellations flecked with emerald. Her body was lithe, and she appeared to be dressed in a loose black poet shirt, covered by an unbuttoned vest with a peacock pattern of black and green silk. She stood as he entered and he saw she wore blousing harem pants with a matching peacock pattern of green and black. Intricate spirals, chains and mandalas of henna decorated both her hands and forearms. She smiled and it was like thrill of first kiss. However, the Scholar noted her eyes did not smile. They were clear and even in their stare— ready. She stepped out from behind the desk and there was a faint jingle. She wore no shoes and had toe rings with tiny silver bells on them.

"Who are you?" the Scholar asked.

"The new owner of the Roost," the woman said. Her voice held the accent of many places, but none he could place. "I was going over our books," she said, nodding toward the large leather book open on his desk. "You keep good records."

"Thank you." The Scholar moved closer to the woman. "But I'm afraid you will have to leave Mr. Bick's property."

"Mr. Bick's property—that'd be you, wouldn't it?" she said.

"I have no desire to harm someone as lovely as you," the Scholar said calmly. "But I will if you don't come along."

The woman smiled. "You are quite the flatterer," she said. "Let's see what you have, my stoic friend."

The Scholar knew what was coming a second before it happened. She used the edge of his desk to support her arms as she launched a double-legged kick at his chest. It was an impressive feat of acrobatics and of strength. He prepared to grab her legs as they approached his chest, but then she twisted and arced with her whole body into the inch or so below his knees. He realized the chest kick was a feint just as his legs gave and he crashed onto the floor. The pain was significant but he endeavored to ignore it. He swung the cudgel at her temple as she lighted on his chest. She deflected the heavy wooden club with her forearm, which gave him an opening to grab her hair and yank her hard, off him and across the room. She turned the throw into a tumble and came up crouched low to the ground and with one leg fully extended away from her body. The Scholar had seen African sailors in Baltimore's Inner Harbor perform similar tumbles and feats of muscular liquidity while their shipmates clapped and pounded drums. He had inquired into the odd mixture of boxing, tumbling and dance.

"You know Engolo," he said. "Impressive."

"More impressive that you know what it is," she said. "Your nickname is well suited to you, Scholar."

She tumbled, hands over feet, and ended up before him in a handstand of sorts; both her feet snapped and caught him under the chin. She felt the crunch of his jaw. He responded almost as quickly with a hold, slipping his arm between her legs and around her waist, locking his hands, and then fell forward, smashing her under his weight and hearing the air rush from her lungs at the impact. Reeling from the other's assault, both of them crawled to opposite corners of the office floor. A little blood pooled at the Scholar's lips and he wiped it away on the back of his hand. The woman winced and tested one of her ribs, hissed with pain and then smiled at the Scholar.

"You know Nuba fighting," she said, nodding. "Very good, my friend."

"I dabble. We both obviously grew up in large port towns," the Scholar said. "And spent a great deal of time at the docks. And I know the names of the people I call friend."

"Rowan," she said. "Black Rowan."

"A pleasure to meet you," the Scholar said. "Shall . . . we continue? Shall . . . we . . ." He found it hard to speak. "What, what . . . did you . . . do to me?"

"Drugged you, about an hour ago when you drank that mug of coffee in the kitchen," Rowan said. "I'm surprised it took this long to register with you. You are a remarkable specimen."

"You . . . ," the Scholar muttered as the world blurred and slid away from his view and darkness fell. "You . . . are the most beautiful woman I have ever seen."

The Scholar tried to rise, made it most of the way and then collapsed facefirst on the floor. Rowan groaned and made her way to her feet. The door to the office opened and Ham entered, fan in hand, and closed the door behind her.

"Is he dead?" she asked Rowan.

"No," Rowan said as she sat down behind the desk again with a groan. "A man that can keep books that good, and fight that well, is too much of an asset to kill. I'll need him. When he wakes up, make him a job offer."

Ham nodded. "Do you want me to start bringing the girls in so you can explain how things are changing, boss?"

"Yes," Black Rowan said. "I'll explain it to Malachi Bick, in person."

The Three of Swords

Charles Cook was a lord of iron and steam, one of the four "Robber Barons" to ally under the banner of building the first transcontinental railroad. Cook, the fifth wealthiest man in the United States and the richest in California, was known by all as a man of sterling character and impeccable breeding—one of America's new breed of self-made men. His contributions would lead to binding and changing the nation forever. He said as much in his speech when the final, golden spike was driven to complete the first transcontinental, while he stood beside his contemporaries, like Leland Stanford, T. C. Durant and the honorable Governor of Nevada F. A. Tritle, who presented a solid silver spike, of the finest Nevada silver, to be added to the other ceremonial spikes driven at the august event.

Charles hated Indians. He was convinced at a very early age that they secreted an odor that, once it clung to you, was virtually impossible to scrub off—you'd stink like a savage. He also despised their worship of dirt and pagan-sexual-animal demons, all affronts to the church and God. As such, he hired veritable armies of violent, vile mercenaries, mostly ex-military men for the North and South, to harass, chase away and slaughter any Indian tribes that got in the way of his beautiful dream of a unified nation.

Charles enjoyed killing foreigners and eating them. To this end, he employed a secret private army whom he called his Praetorians. Each Praetorian was sworn to Charles unto death, through rites of sexual torture and ritual cannibalism. His agents snatched his victims off the foggy streets of San Francisco. After torturing them for a few nights, he'd eventually kill them, skin them and eat them. Charles had a trophy case of their skins, scalps and bones that he would often admire in his hidden torture chamber. His favorites were Irish girls. They tasted the best in his stews.

Charles received a telegram from his old friend and confidant, requesting his presence and the use of his Praetorians for an exercise in debauchery and bloody excess. Charles was promised all he could eat. He readied his men for the orgy of slaughter to come. Charles's was lucky number seven.

The commander of his Praetorians, who had slaughtered and raped his way across the Great Plains in service to Charles and to their mutual mentor, could only find sexual gratification by fucking the still-warm guts of dead Indians. He was Col. Bradley Whitmore (Ret.), famed Indian fighter and hero of many tall tales and dime novels. His was number eight.

The Hierophant

"Sheriff's in trouble!" Jim shouted to Mutt as he threw open the door to the jail. It was almost dark and Jim had run to Clay's livery to fetch his horse, Promise, and Mutt's Muha.

"Up on Argent?" Mutt said. Jim nodded.

"Got word that this Vellas bushwhacker may be more trouble than we thought," Jim said. "Golgotha-style trouble."

Mutt stood and unlocked the gun cage behind Jon's desk that held rifles, shotguns, pistols, ammo and other, less conventional items. There were charms—Indian, African and Chinese—wooden stakes, white candles and chalk, silver bullets, a bag of rock salt, a crucifix, a sealed glass jar full of rattlesnake rattles, a bundle of sage held together by twine, a cold iron knife, holy water blessed in Rome, a small dream catcher made out of bones and feathers, a Ba Gua mirror and a collection of tattered tomes.

"Any idea what he is? What can take him out?" Mutt asked as he pulled down a rifle and grabbed a box of shells.

"No," Jim said. "Mrs. Warren just said he was in serious trouble."

"Mrs. who?" Mutt asked, pausing. Jim waved a hand in frantic dismissal.

"Never mind, never mind. I'll tell you later! We got to go help—"

The iron door creaked open. Father Whitley Thorne, the sole priest of Golgotha's small Catholic congregation, entered. The father was in his sixties, raw-boned, with a face deeply lined with wrinkles and scars. There were prominent scars on his knuckles too. The father's nose had clearly been smashed a few times in his life. His short hair was the color of snow and his piercing blue eyes almost seemed to burn out of the darkness. He wore a battered black hat and a long black coat. He always presented an aura of serenity and power to Jim. Now he seemed agitated, maybe even afraid.

"Deputy Mutt," Thorne said. "Deputy Jim, there's been a break-in at the church. Someone is in there. They sound mad as a hatter! I saw them up at the altar. I called out to them and they said something in Latin. I decided I should get you."

"What did they say, padre?" Mutt said.

"He . . . he said he was leaving a tithe for 'the boss,'" Thorne said softly.

Jim and Mutt looked at each other.

"Go look after the sheriff," Jim said to Mutt. "I'll help the father. Muha is tied up outside."

Mutt nodded. "All right. Watch yourself. You shoot whoever this is if they come at you. Don't try to bring him in, just kill 'em. You hear me, boy?"

"Gotcha," Jim said. "Go save the sheriff. I'll be okay."

Saint Cyprian of Antioch's Catholic Church was one of the older buildings in Golgotha, having once been a small stone fortress built by unknown inhabitants of the region, perhaps part of the Bick family. It squatted on the southern rise of Methuselah Hill like a silent gray gargoyle.

Jim rode ahead while the father walked back. He didn't know much about Catholics, except what the folks back home said. They were not thought well of in Southern Baptist country like his home in Albright, West Virginia, he knew that. However, more than rants about papal control, false prophets, graven images and the Whore of Babylon, Jim remembered what Pa had said once while they were fishing and talking about a Catholic family that had just moved into Albright. "Don't make me no never mind, son," Billy Negrey had said. "When we faced the elephant in the war, it didn't matter much how the Jonathan next to you talked to God, or if he did at all. We were in it together, and that was all that mattered. I remember really well an Irish Catholic named Leary saving my backside, more than once. Don't judge someone by anything other than what they do, Jim. It will always guide you straight."

Jim tied Promise to the hitching post outside the stone stairs and double doors that led to the chapel and drew Pa's Colt .44. He moved cautiously up the stairs and reached for the handle to one of the doors. The handle was wet. When Jim pulled his hand back and looked at it, it was black in the moonlight with fresh blood.

He pulled open the massive oak reinforced door, causing it to groan audibly, and wiped his hand dry on his pants. The bitter November wind rushed into the cathedral, swirling desert dust with it, like an angry ghost. The massive candles near the doors fluttered in the wind as Jim walked in, silhouetted in the bright moonlight. The chapel was silent and empty.

There had only been about thirty or forty Catholics in Golgotha when Jim had arrived a year ago, and now with the boom there were probably close to a hundred and fifty. Father Thorne was the only clergy at the church, though Catholic clergy and monks often visited St. Cyprian's to do research in the massive catacomb of a library underneath the old fortress. Jim had heard Highfather say that this tiny little church out on the edge of nowhere had an occult archive only rivaled by the Holy City of Rome, itself. But tonight, there were no visiting scholars, no congregation and no priest. Just Jim, the invading wind and the shadows.

Jim walked slowly down the main aisle toward the huge, heavy, wooden crucifix, which hung by wires at the front of the chapel. Hundreds of white votive candles, held in rows by metal racks on both sides of the main altar, were lit and struggled to endure against the desert's cold breath. Paintings and statues of the Virgin Mother sat among the walls of trembling light.

Jim thought the main altar was alight with prayer candles, too, but as he stepped into the island of illumination at the front of the chapel the terrible realization came upon him. A woman's body, in tattered clothing and wet with fresh blood, was draped across the altar. Her abdomen had been opened and her intestines arranged around her on the altar, spilling out. Some had slid onto the floor, staining the wood. The stench of opened bowels fought for dominance over the perfume of lingering incense

Jim sighed and steeled himself. He tried to replace the nausea and fear with anger and resolve. The woman's eyes had been removed from her skull. Two tall, red tapers had been jammed into her eye sockets and burned strongly. Her ears had been hacked off. Another, thicker red candle, also burning bright, had been jammed into her mouth, blood trickling from the edges of her torn lips, mixing with the red wax. Small red votives had been placed over both of her nipples; the flame from them flickered and danced. The red, hardened wax had solidified around them and left frozen tracks down the sides of her breasts and onto the polished wood of the altar. A gold basin, normally used to hold holy water, sat on the floor before the altar surrounded by, and covered in, blood, excrement, wax and bile. The woman's eyes, ears and tongue had been carefully placed in the bowl.

Something Clay had said suddenly pierced the fog of numb horror that had enveloped Jim's mind. *He likes to show his craft.* Jim spun, and peered into the inky darkness of the chapel.

Suddenly, Jim had an idea. He quickly pulled his father's jade eye from the pouch about his neck and held it up with his bloodstained hand. The moonlight through the open doors caught the milky white orb, with its ring of frosted jade, etched with tiny Chinese symbols.

The eye had resided in the skull of Jim's father, Billy Negrey, after he lost his own eye in the war. The jade eye had been given to Billy and implanted in the dead of night by a group of Chinese monks for still dubious reasons.

The eye seemed to drink in the moonlight, greedily, then began to glow, surrounded by tiny, fiery motes of brilliant emerald light-blazing green fireflies.

"I know you're still here!" Jim shouted out, his voice echoing through the cold dark chapel. "You're not gonna get away this time! Not from me, you sumbitch! Show yourself!"

The flame of every candle burning in the chapel suddenly erupted in green brilliance, illuminating the whole room. In the back of the chapel, near the last few rows of pews, a black-cloaked figure in a floppy brimmed Stetson and long military-style coat suddenly became visible as the shadows were driven back by the unearthly candlelight. A red scarf covered most of the killer's face. The murderer looked about, startled and surprised.

Jim raised his pistol and fired even as the dark-garbed murderer bolted for the open doors, keeping low between the rows of pews. A section of one of the wooden benches exploded as the .44 ball struck it, narrowly missing the cloaked figure racing by. Jim fired again as the killer cleared the pews and was silhouetted against the doors. If the bullet struck him, the killer did not seem to react, disappearing from sight. Already the flames were settling down and resuming their ordinary color and radiance. The room fell back into shadow as Jim raced down the aisle after the murderer. He reached the front doors and stood at the top of the stone stairs, scanning in all directions for any hint of movement, any sign of where the murderer had fled. There was nothing. Then, suddenly, the crack of a whip and response of two horses to their impatient master. A wagon clattered into view, the cloaked killer whipping the horses into a galloping frenzy. Jim fired again as the wagon passed, but once more there was no indication of a hit as the wagon and its unknown driver vanished around the bend of the hill out into the scrubland and then the deep desert.

"The hell you do!" Jim shouted, and leapt half the steps down to where Promise was reined. He grabbed the saddle horn fiercely to pull himself up onto his horse. The whole rig slid off his horse's back, knocking him to the ground. He examined the cinch strap and saw it had been cleanly cut. Jim grabbed his horse blanket and threw it on this loyal, willful, little brown mustang. He holstered his pistol and pulled himself up onto Promise, taking the reins.

"Come on, girl!" He snapped the reins and gave her a gentle prompt by squeezing his legs. Promise snorted and galloped off after the wagon into the desert darkness. Jim felt Promise open up and run for all she was worth, as if she knew whom they pursued, and why he had to be stopped. The boy and his horse raced across the scrubland as thousands of stars burned above them in the indigo night. He saw Molly James in the alley, the woman in the chapel. Jim squeezed his legs, urging Promise on, and leaned forward, willing them to catch up, coaxing a little more speed out of her. A little more . . .

Ahead in the darkness, Jim saw the shape of the wagon clattering along past the southern road onto Main Street, a cloud of dust behind them. Jim had suspected the killer would try to double back and head into town on the southern road. But the wagon had passed it and was off the road, bouncing dangerously, threatening to overturn or break a wheel. The wagon was beginning to slow and Jim and Promise were overtaking it. Jim drew his gun and pulled on Promise's reins to cut off the horses. The wagon horses slowed, then stopped and the wagon with them. Jim stayed on Promise and slowly circled the wagon, pistol at the ready. It was empty. No driver, no one hiding in the bed. The cloaked killer had bailed out in the darkness and used the runaway wagon as a diversion.

Jim slumped. He holstered his gun and wiped the trail dust off his face. He looked out into the fathomless darkness.

"Damn," he said. "I'm sorry, Molly."

The Star

Highfather, staring into the cold eyes of the rattler, heard shouting outside, Mitchell calling for his men to hold their fire.

"I think I hit him!" someone shouted.

"I'm bleeding like a stuck pig over here, goddammit!" another voice cried out, tinged with panic.

"Clement's dead!" a third voice yelled.

"Can't kill him, sumbitch is a haint . . . ain't really alive! Been hung three times already. . . ."

"All of you shut the hell up!" It was Mitchell. "Hush."

The rattler was ready to strike. Mitchell's men were forming up. Jon's eyes locked on the rattler.

"Go on," he said to the snake's merciless eyes. "Do it."

"Hey, the bastard's right here in the dirt," a voice extremely close to Highfather said. It was one of the men who had been on horseback. He was a shadow in the doorway, rifle in his hands. Highfather grabbed the edge of the plank the snake was on with both hands. Ignoring the pain in his left arm, he rolled and flipped the snake in the direction of the gunman in the open doorway. The man screamed and dropped his rifle as he fell back, the rattler hitting his chest, dropping to the dust in front of him, striking again and again in terror all the way down.

Highfather scrambled and grabbed the rifle; he slid it aside and drew the shotgun from his back. He emptied both barrels of 12-gauge buckshot into the gunman's chest. He flew backward and laid still in the moonlight. The snake slithered toward the high grass and disappeared. Mitchell and his two remaining men opened fire on the shack. Highfather dived back for cover out of the door-way. Holes exploded in the crumbling walls of the shack, bullets whined and ricocheted all around him

Highfather snapped open the breach of the shotgun and pulled the hot empty shells out. He fumbled in the pocket of his barn jacket, fishing out two fresh cartridges. He loaded them and returned the shotgun to his back sheath. His left arm was wet with blood and throbbing with pain, but he could still use it—a good sign. Another rain of bullets ripped through the shed. Jon ducked and felt the air scorch inches from his face. He popped up a second after the barrage and returned fire with his rifle. One round and he was out. He ducked and dropped the empty gun, grabbing the dead gunman's rifle as more bullets ripped apart the shack and bounced around inside. For a second he was back in the war, pinned down with Larson ten feet away, screaming and bleeding, his brother's arms and legs reduced to bloody mist. The cannons exploding. . . .

No. No, he was here, now, and he would be dead if he let his mind slip. He popped back up off the dirt floor and aimed the dead man's gun into the dark-ness. The shattered lantern had done its job: the wagon was burning now in the crossroads of Backtrail Road. Mitchell was smart enough to get his boys away from it, out of the light. They were in the high grass, where he had been, and they would move up on him, quiet. He grabbed a handful of bullets from his pocket and quickly loaded both rifles. He was a little dizzy from losing blood and shivering from what he hoped was cold, not shock. He ignored it as best he could by focusing on the task of pushing the cartridges into the gun.

The night had settled and the wind howled across Argent Mountain. Snow flurries swirled and danced in the moonlight.

"Sheriff, why don't you come on out and we talk about this?" Mitchell's voice echoed above the crackle of the burning wagon.

"'Cause I'm of a mind not to get shot, Half-Guts," Highfather shouted out of the doorway. "You and your boys care to head on home, I'm sure we can just call this square. What do you say?"

There was a scream and a gurgle from the grass to the right of the shack and Mitchell's last man staggered out, a bloody ragged hole in his chest where his heart should be. He staggered into the crossroads, tried to talk, fell facefirst and was still.

"What in damnation was that?" Mitchell shouted. He came out of the grass to the left of the shack, a Colt Navy revolver in his hands, swinging it between the doorway of the shack and the tall grass his dead soldier had staggered out of. "That your fucking half-breed deputy, Sheriff?"

"No, I'm afraid it was me, yes?" Vellas said, stepping from the grass into the fire light of the wagon. The gypsy was smiling and covered in fresh blood; steam from the heat of it rose off him like smoke. The dead gunman's heart was clenched in one of his large, hairy fists.

Vellas turned to regard Highfather, who was now leaning against the shack's doorway, looking at the blood-splattered man.

"You, Sheriff, live up to your indestructible reputation. Very impressive; you took out three seasoned killers who were on guard, by yourself, and you are still standing. Very good, yes? I shall enjoy eating your heart."

Highfather leveled the rifle at Vellas. Mitchell was pointing his revolver at him as well.

"You crazy, sick son of a bitch," Mitchell said to Vellas.

Vellas laughed and took the heart and tore a bite from the sturdy muscle as if he were biting into an apple. He chewed it with gusto and walked toward Mitchell. Mitchell fired into Vellas's chest, again, again and again. Highfather saw the .44 bullets rip through the bloody man and blast out his back, taking chunks of flesh and sprays of blood with them.

Vellas remained standing and raised the heart above his head. He leaned his head back and opened his mouth, squeezing the torn heart like a sponge and pouring the lifeblood from it into his mouth and across his face. Mitchell fired again and again, until the pistol was empty. Vellas staggered but did not fall from the lethal wounds.

"Your blood is thin," Vellas said, the heart blood gurgling out of his mouth as he spoke, spilling down his chin. He spit the blood at Mitchell, who, to his credit, Highfather noted, stood his ground and did not look as terrified as he surely was. Vellas tossed the savaged heart away. "My father's blood sustains me and he is strong."

He closed toward Mitchell. The old soldier narrowed his eyes.

"I'll see you in hell, boy," he muttered to Vellas.

Gunfire tore the air like a knife. Bullet after bullet ripped into Vellas and spun him as if he were being hit by a rain of sledgehammers. Jon Highfather advanced with a rifle in each hand, even his injured left arm steady as stone. He moved and fired both of the Winchesters, flipped them both back by the levers, one-handed, and then forward until they snapped the levers back into position, chambering a new round, spitting out the smoking empty cartridge. He fired again, repeating the action as he moved closer and closer to the staggering Vellas with each blast.

"You get on home, Half-Guts," Highfather said, slurring his words slightly. "We'll settle up another day. This kind of thing is my jurisdiction. Run."

"Don't cotton to leaving a man alone with a hell-spawn like this, even a god-damned lawman," Mitchell said, stepping back and trying to reload his gun.

Highfather continued herding Vellas back toward the burning wagon, bullet by bullet. The bloody man was no longer smiling; each round made him wince and stagger back more and more. "Just go, damn you, or I'll shoot you next!" Highfather shouted. "Tell Mutt what went down if I fall. Now go on!"

Mitchell ran toward one of the horses that had shied away when the shooting and the fire started. It was standing nervously in the field by the crossroads. Mitchell climbed in the saddle and rode off toward the mining camp without a glance back.

Highfather kept shooting even as the world seemed to dip and falter at the edges of his vision. Vellas was almost into the roaring fire of the wagon, a few steps more . . .

One rifle, then the other, clicked. Empty.

Vellas grinned through a mask of blood and wounds. "Thank you, father," he said as he reached down and grabbed a red-hot wagon wheel with both of his hands. He hissed in pain at the heat and his hands smoked as the flesh charred. He looked at Highfather as he grunted and ripped the massive iron wheel off the wagon. The wagon slumped with a crash. Vellas hurled the steaming, massive wheel at Highfather, who scrambled and staggered to avoid it, dropping both empty guns in the process. The wheel clipped Highfather's shoulders and upper back as he ran, knocking him off his feet and carrying him with it as it careened into the shack. The decrepit, bullet-riddled cabin groaned and collapsed on top of Highfather with a crash.

The sheriff lay in the ruins of the shack. His back throbbed and for a second he feared the wheel had broken it and paralyzed him. He groaned and forced himself to move, pushing the broken boards, rusted nails and tar paper off him. He heard the bloody man's laughter as he rose from the wreckage.

"Good, you don't break easy," Vellas said. "'The sheriff who cannot die' . . . It's been a long time since I had one that wasn't easy to kill."

Highfather staggered out of the debris; his clothes were torn and he had cuts, bruises and scratches all over his body. His upper back was red and raw from the burns he suffered from the burning wheel.

"Wish I could say the same," Highfather said, and stepped forward, trying to stay awake and pushing away the blissful, painless darkness. "What are you exactly? Most fellas like you come around here, they got some evil scheme or master plan or such. A few like to rave about it, makes things a mite easier. You got any raving in you, Vellas?"

"I am my father's son," Vellas said, the fires of the wagon roaring behind him. "A scout, a harbinger of what is to come."

Highfather took another step. "I hate it when they get all cryptic," he said. "You're under arrest, Vellas. Stand down, or I'm going to have to get rough with you."

There was the whinny of a horse and the thud of hooves at full gallop. For a second, Highfather thought Mitchell may have come back, but it wasn't him. The rider appeared on a gray Appaloosa, thundering down the high road from the miners' camp. She had brown hair falling to her shoulders, fluttering in the biting wind. She wore a black bolero hat and coat that looked a bit too big for her slender frame and snapped in the wind like wings. A black corset—worn under the coat—revealed smooth, pale skin. She wore men's trousers and a gun belt with twin holsters, one strapped to each thigh. The guns were in her hands and she drove the charging horse with her legs only, moving between Vellas and Highfather. Without a word, the woman opened fire on Vellas, both revolvers barking as she emptied them into the bloody man. Vellas staggered back, again toward the blaze. More holes exploded through his tattered flesh. Vellas roared and drove his fist into the horse's flank as it rushed by at full speed. There was a horrible, hollow crunching sound. The horse screamed and flew through the air, bloody foam spewing from its nose and mouth. It fell and was still, ten feet from where it had stood. The woman was pinned under the dying animal's shuddering bulk.

"Nikos Vellas!" the woman shouted as she struggled to free herself. "By the authority of the federal government of the United States of America, I order you to surrender and be bound for your crimes."

"I already did that," Highfather mumbled. "I'm arresting him." The sheriff fell face forward and didn't move.

Vellas dropped to his knees, the bullet holes in him smoking. A piece of the dark sky tore itself loose and lighted before the bloody man. The crow croaked at him and cocked its head. Vellas removed the packet of papers that Mitchell had given him from his jacket. It was pierced with bullet holes and stained with blood. The crow took it in its black beak.

"For my father," he said. The crow flew away, toward the moon.

Vellas climbed to his feet and staggered toward the trapped woman. He loomed over her on the opposite side of the dead horse. "You're that bitch that hunted me in Saint Louis and Raleigh, aren't you? This is revenge for what I did to your friend, yes?" He laughed and coughed up some blood. The woman struggled to reach one of the guns that had fallen from her hand. Fumbled for bullets in her coat pocket. Vellas leaned forward, his hand resting on the horse. He swatted the pistol out of her hand and it thudded a few feet away. His wet, torn face looked down on her as she struggled. The woman spat in his face.

"I will kill you with my bare hands, you bastard," she said, still fighting to get free. "With my last breath in me, I will find a way to kill you."

"Unlikely, yes?" Vellas said. "I think I shall spend some time on you and then drink the sweet terror out of your heart. It will heal me. Your heart, and then the good sheriff's." He glanced around. "Now where did he get to? Did you pass out somewhere, Sheriff?"

Highfather charged the bloody man from the darkness behind the woman. It wasn't pretty, but it was the very last ounce of energy left in him. He used the dead horse's body as a vault and launched himself toward the still grinning Vellas. As he flew through the air, Highfather unloaded both barrels of the shotgun into Vellas at point-blank range. The bloody man gasped in pain and staggered backward. Highfather latched onto Vellas like a stubborn dog biting. He tossed the shotgun and drew his .44. Vellas, his titanic strength beginning to fade, pounded on Highfather's back and sides as the sheriff coughed blood and groaned. Jon jammed the Colt into Vellas's face and emptied it. Both men, locked in a death dance, fell into the roaring fire of the burning wagon. The crossroads grew silent.

The woman the locals called Kitty Warren struggled to free her legs from the dead weight of her horse. With a final growl of effort she did. Pain ran up her leg and she nearly passed out from it, but she didn't dare. She recovered one of her pistols, frantically loaded it and limped toward the fire.

Jon Highfather, his face black with soot and smoke streaming off his burnt clothing, crawled out of the blaze. He struggled to his feet and Kitty helped him as best she could. They took a few torturous steps away from the fire and Jon whistled as best he could. In the distance there was a whinny. Jon looked at the woman holding him up and whom he was helping to hold up in turn.

"Are you hurt? Are you okay?" Jon mumbled. It was hard to keep his eyes open. The woman broke into a smile. She had small, even teeth and her smile was charming because Jon was pretty sure she didn't do it often.

"I'm fine," she said. "Hurt my leg when my horse fell, but . . . I'm good. How did you . . . with the wagon and the fire?"

They staggered back toward the ruins of the cabin. There was the sound of a horse approaching.

"Knocked him onto the back of the wagon, I went low, under it. Less fire down there, less smoke, more air. Got a little singed crawling out, but I've had worse."

"I'll just bet you have," Kitty said.

"Not my time," Highfather said.

"What?" she asked.

" 'Not my time.' It's . . . it's something I say a lot, kind of like my saying, if you will," Highfather said. "It's nothing. Thank you for riding in and saving me. You look familiar, who are you?"

"I've been going by Kitty Warren," she said. "Been here a few months, but my name is Kate, Kate Warne. I work for the Pinkerton Agency and the United States government."

Highfather laughed. It cost him. He winced in pain and Kate steadied him. "Well, you are the prettiest Pinkerton man I ever did see."

"We need to get you to a sawbones," she said. "You're obviously delirious. And then we need to talk. Your town is in danger, Sheriff."

"If you save my life, you get to call me Jon," he said. Behind them the cart shifted with a crash as it burned itself out. Both Warne and Highfather spun, ignoring their injuries and leveled pistols at the blaze, guns cocked. Nothing emerged from the fire. Vellas's corpse vomited black smoke into the night as the fire consumed it.

"Town in danger, huh?" Highfather said. "We're just about due for one of those."

The Three of Swords

Professor Elias Zenith was used to dealing with the ignorant and the shortsighted. His work in expanding on the research of Luigi Galvani into fluidic transmission of electricity via the nerves throughout the body of an animal—so-called animal electricity—was seen with scorn and ridicule by the simpletons at the Missouri School of Mines and Metallurgy, where he had acquired a teaching position after his troubles in Boston. "Just teach the classes on metallurgic analysis that we hired you to, Professor Zenith," the rock-headed dean had rumbled. "You can work at your hobbies and scattershot theories outside the classroom, thank you very much." The fool! The ant-brained imbecile! The "subtle fluid" was the key to mankind's future, to making one as mighty Zeus of old.

Zenith had to leave Boston when they discovered his Alessandro Volta–inspired battery experiments on the street urchins. It was unfair! He was so close to the realization of his dream. In his electrical utopia, Professor Zenith saw a world where those versed in the ways of science were immune to the dreary and dogmatic rules needed to govern the filthy mongrel mobs of chattel that would make up the brute servitor and experimental subject classes.

After months of covert work in his filthy laboratory in the catacombs of the Boston sewers, Zenith had learned exactly the proper methods of application and the correct dosages of electrical energy to apply to the human body to break bones, disrupt the brain, stop hearts, make skin burn and cook internal organs. This addendum to the sum of human knowledge was purchased cheaply, by Zenith's reasoning, with the lives of eighteen children, orphans living on the streets of Boston.

An additional twenty-eight "subjects" died as he developed and refined his method to pump and maintain saline water in the subjects' bodies and then add the proper chemical mixtures, along with copper wire implants to the brain, spine and heart, via catheters. The end result was an organic voltic pile—a living battery capable of storing and releasing electrical current. Granted the batteries tended to scream endlessly in agony until they caught fire and exploded from within, but in later models he would simply remove their vocal cords to eliminate that distracting byproduct. It was all a manner of fine-tuning the process to keep the batteries alive indefinitely. He was so close to achieving his life's work, and it was so infuriating to have to pretend to hide his genius because the world was run by moral cowards without a shred of will to do what science demanded.

So, when the letter arrived from California, written on sturdy, cured human skin, and told him that his longtime patron had taken an interest in seeing his work come to fruition and wanted to know if he would enjoy working with a bigger laboratory with many more test subjects, the professor agreed eagerly. He set out with a wagon full of his finest inventions, a human nervous system floating in a jar that he was tinkering with, and, of course, the token of his patron's devotion and, dare he say it, love. Professor Zenith possessed the ninth one.

The Nine of Cups

Gillian Proctor felt very self-conscious as she waited in the darkness in the small stand of bushes behind Shultz's General Store. A year ago she, Auggie and Clay had hidden here as they'd tried to avoid the hideous stained creatures their fellow townsfolk had been transformed into. Now she waited here to find out the truth about her future husband and the reason for his own transformation into a sullen stranger.

Maude Stapleton had given her the idea the other day when the two were having coffee and discussing Gillian's obvious upset.

"I can't spy on him. I love him, Maude," Gillian had said. Maude Stapleton had a sadness and a wisdom in her eyes, and in the year since Maude's husband, Arthur, had died, the two had become good friends. Gillian remembered how terrifying it had been to lose her own husband, Will, years ago and how difficult it could be to be a woman alone at the ragged edges of the world. Gillian knew Maude held secrets and didn't press about them, but she also knew Maude was a good person and a good friend, and that was really all Gillian needed to know.

"You love him, right?" Maude had asked as they sat on the porch of Gillian's home, which she had turned into a boardinghouse to make ends meet after Will had died. The two had developed a ritual of having coffee and talking before they began their busy days.

"With all my heart," Gillian said. "He's a decent, loving, caring man, the best man I ever met."

Maude nodded and sipped her coffee. "Auggie has been nothing but decent and as open as a book as long as I've known him," she said. "So if he's behaving this way, shutting you out, he's in some kind of trouble and you and I both know very well that men think they can handle any trouble that comes their way and that they love to protect us 'shrinking violets' from it."

Gillian sighed and nodded.

"You are probably right, but I can't just meddle in his private business."

"When people you love are in trouble, you do what you have to do," Maude said. "Often you discover what you are capable of when push comes to shove. It can surprise you."

"I wouldn't even know how to," Gillian said.

Maude smiled. "Well, I might be able to give you a few suggestions. . . ."

It was dark, except for the few sparse streetlights that had been lit about an hour ago, and Gillian was dressed in a very unfamiliar way for her. A dark shirt and dark trousers that had belonged to Will. She had a belt tied tight about her waist to hold the loose clothes on. Her hair was tied in a tight bun to stay out of her face. She felt like a skulking thief, but there was a thrill to this, she had to admit.

There was a clatter of wagon wheels down Dry Well Road, behind her, then the sound of the wagon leaving the road to turn just past the Salvation Square flophouse that a former preacher, Christopher Marlowe, ran. There were worn ruts where so many delivery wagons and horses had taken the shortcut to gain access to the back doors. Folks joked that in a few more years, it would be its own unofficial little road running between Main and Dry Well.

A wagon came into view and stopped behind Auggie's store. The lone occupant was Clay Turlough. Clay climbed down from the seat and knocked on the back door to Auggie's. After a moment Auggie appeared, grim faced and looking exhausted.

"Clayton," he said. "I . . . we need to talk. I am done with this madness. It is wrong, what you are doing is sick. Those girls . . ."

Clay regarded Auggie, then shrugged. Gillian couldn't see Clay's face, but from Auggie's pained expression, the odd inventor to whom emotion was a greater mystery than any science had let a tiny drop of hurt and disappointment slip from his visage for a second.

"Suit yourself, Auggie." Clay turned and headed back to the wagon. "I started this on my own and I can finish it on my own."

Auggie stepped out of the doorway. "Clay! You can't do this, your health is poor, man, and since the fire . . . you can't handle them alone. You need to . . ."

Struggling, Clay managed to climb back into the wagon with great effort. "Tonight is the last one I need, by the dawn my work will be complete. I'll manage, Auggie, don't you fret. I know it's a lot to ask of someone. I appreciate the help."

"I appreciate the help you've given me with the store, the loans," Auggie said. "Can't you just stop this?"

Clay looked at him but said nothing. Auggie muttered a curse in German and then locked the door to the store and climbed in the wagon. "*Verrückte*," he mumbled as he climbed into the seat. "Let's get this over with, *ja*?"

Clay slapped the reins and the wagon clattered down the narrow alley between the two streets, headed toward Prosperity Street.

Gillian waited until the wagon was swallowed by the darkness between the streetlights, and then she ran quickly down the alley. Her feet felt odd in oversized boots, and she almost stumbled a few times. She was out of breath by the time she reached Prosperity. Then she could see the wagon turning onto Pratt Road. Clay's livery, his home and barns were all off Pratt. Gillian began to walk up the road as the wagon disappeared from sight.

It took her about fifteen minutes to reach Clay's. She stood on the road and tried to make out any details in the pitch darkness. The only light came from the moon and stars, which were playing hide-and-seek with banks of swift-moving dark clouds. The bunkhouse for Clay's workmen had been built inside his fences in the last six months. It was dark, too, as the hands had to be up and at work with the horses well before sunup and were already asleep.

Gillian walked up the road. The wind was cold, a reminder that winter would be upon them all soon even here in the desert and that the Earth was tilting far from the sun and deeper toward the void. The high grasses that bordered the road and Clay's fences swayed in the November night. Gillian felt a little fear trickle into her chest. It was a dark, lonely road and this was Golgotha. People disappeared or worse here all the time. She looked back and saw the feeble flickers of the streetlights, the dark silhouettes of slumbering homes and the warm but distant glow of the mining camp up on Argent, which was pretty much alive and awake around the clock. It suddenly dawned on her just how narrow a ledge of civilization separated her, separated all of the good folk of Golgotha, from the ravenous beast of the wilderness. Gillian quickened her pace up the road to Clay's livery. The wagon wasn't here. Gillian cursed silently. Pratt Road dead-ended at Clay's place. If Clay's wagon wasn't here, he and Auggie had turned onto Old Stone Road. That meant they could be headed along that seldom-used eastern road out of Golgotha, or south to Rose Road that ran along the backside of Rose Hill, or north up Pauper's Rest Road, headed to either the old graveyard that had been there as long as anyone can remember, or past that to Boot Hill where the poor and the nameless were all buried. Gillian moved across the exercise yard to the entrance of Clay's smaller barn that was opposite the stables. Clay had made substantial improvements and expansions to both the stable and the barn in the last year and Gillian was sure that the barn's expansion was more for Clay's experiments than to accommodate more client horses. She struggled with the heavy wooden door and was afraid for a moment it was locked. She dug in her heels and pulled with all her might. The door creaked open and Gillian fell backward on her rump. Getting to her feet, she noticed the interior of the door was reinforced with heavy lead plates.

There was a strange sound from inside the dark building. It was a shrill squeaking, like metal scraping against metal rhythmically. The barn had an odd smell, combining something burnt, the smell in the air after a thunderstorm, sour chemical odors, and the faint whiff of feces and rotting meat. It dawned on Gillian that Clay usually smelled this way as well.

There was a row of oil lanterns hanging on a hook next to the door. Gillian took one and examined it. It was a strange design. It had a handle on the bottom of the metal oil reservoir, and there was a trigger-like device alongside the handle. The globe of the lantern was an orb instead of the typical slender chimney and there was no hole in the top of the globe for smoke to escape from, or for air to feed the flame. Gillian squeezed the trigger. There was a sharp click and the cloth wick in the center of the orb ignited with a bright flame. Gillian looked at the wondrous device, smiled and then entered the dark barn with the light guiding the way.

There was a workbench to the left and a large flat table near the center of the room. An odd contraption that looked like a wagon wheel with glass globes was suspended by a chain over the central table. She noticed a new addition: a large metal door on the back wall of the barn. There was an odd-looking switch beside the door. The peculiar squeaking, scraping sounds seemed to be coming from behind the metal door.

Gillian drifted to the workbench. It was covered in wooden crates overflowing with all manner of wire, gears, cogs and scraps of metal. There were also clear glass jars with mummified animal parts floating in a yellowish fluid. One held a dead toad with two heads growing out of its squat, gray body. There were piles of rolled paper and more papers stretched out on the table and held down with animal skulls and a rusty hacksaw. The papers were covered with scrawled diagrams and plans for all manner of machines and devices. The most prominent was some kind of engine or device Clay visualized mounted on the back of a wagon, complete with a large flagpole extension. Its purpose was a complete mystery to Gillian. She noticed a picture frame in one of the boxes next to a pair of rusted buggy seat springs. She picked up the frame; the glass cover was cracked. It was a medical diploma, with honors, from the Medical College of Hampden-Sydney, with Clay's name on it. It was dated 1845.

"You wily old coot," Gillian muttered. "Clayton, you are a doctor."

She replaced the diploma and moved with the lantern to the right side of the room. There was a military-style cot there with crumpled, stained blankets and a pile of books at least two feet high next to the bed. A smokeless lantern-globe like hers hung on the wall by the cot. There was also a closed door on the right wall near the foot of the cot.

The majority of the rest of the wall was covered in butcher-paper sheets, filled with drawings, scribbled notes and esoteric formula. There were weather pattern predictions and calculations for the whole world formulated from bird migrations, anatomical diagrams of wasps and worms, a calculus to determine political victories and losses into the 1900s based upon the population density of states and predicted states and the lunar cycle, star charts and extrapolations of the locations of stars unseen from Earth due to a "shroud of dark material," detailed drawings of the canals and possible cities upon Mars, diagrams for devices that used eyeballs to capture images like a camera, something called a "spirit lantern" to make ghosts visible to the human eye (its primary component was a cat's brain), an odd mathematical formula based on the overall casualties from the Civil War that seemed related to Jon Highfather's famous ability to cheat death and plans for a balloon vehicle designed to reach the stars.

Gillian was in awe. It was Clay Turlough's mind spread out on paper. It was beautiful and complex and bewildering. It was wonderful. Then she noticed another island of drawings and formulas pinned farther down the wall, away from all the rest, and her smile faded. Anatomy sketches of a human, female body occupied several large pages of butcher paper tacked to the wall. The figure in the drawings was headless and there were disturbing segmented lines at various places along the form that reminded Gillian of the placard at the butcher shop showing the customer the various locations of the different cuts of meat one could obtain from different animals. Meat.

The measurements of the headless form were on one of the diagrams as well. They were Gillian's measurements, exactly.

The fear came back, rushing in, taking her breath. Reason almost left her, but she struggled to maintain it and won. Fear and panic did her and Auggie no good now. She had started this to discover what trouble her love was in and now she knew. Auggie had told her how Clay had helped him keep Auggie's dead wife

Gerta's head alive, in a sense; how fiercely Clay had fought to do it. Auggie said it was the most emotional he had ever seen the odd genius. Gerta had perished in the fire, and Gillian agreed with Auggie that was for the best. Clay's obsession with death, and with preserving, playing with life, had reached some horrible new height. And Augustus, sweet, loyal to a fault Augustus, was up to his bushy eyebrows in it.

Gillian steeled herself and attempted to open the door near the cot. It opened easily and she stepped inside the dark room, holding the lantern before her like a shield. The first thing that struck her was the scent, like burnt molasses, acrid and sweet. There were large barrels and crates in the room, scattered everywhere. She stepped deeper into the room, sweeping the lamp before her. There were glass-walled tanks on tables running along the walls of the room. One cylindrical tank in the corner held a bizarre creature floating in a clear, but slightly cloudy, solution. It was three or four feet tall, barrel chested, hairy all over with a large head, massive closed eyes and razor-sharp teeth like a reptile. Membranes drooped under the dead thing's arms, like wings, and its hands had sharp, wicked-looking claws. Fresh bullet holes covered its chest. A simple placard mounted on the front of the tank said *Goat-vampire, xeno-specimen G174.* Gillian shuddered and turned the light away from the creature's tube.

Most of the tanks were empty but a large one contained something that devoured the light of her lamp, some viscous darkness. Gillian stepped closer to it. There was a chain attached to a ceiling hook, hanging down and partly submerged in the oily black fluid.

The sweet-burnt scent was very strong coming from the tank. It had taken on a musky quality as well and Gillian suddenly shuddered as she felt her body responding to the peculiar and slightly offensive smell. It was as though every square inch of her skin was alive but her mind began to feel as if it were stuffed with cotton. She was flushed and her clothing seemed too tight and the tightness was arousing her. Lascivious thoughts better left to the bedroom swarmed in her head, and Gillian fought to push them away. Only moments ago, she had been terrified and upset. This was not natural; this was something being done to her, done by the stench of the oily substance. She dipped her fingers into the tank, and suddenly pulled them back as reason reasserted itself. Gillian looked, horrified, at the thick black slime that coated her index and middle finger. The urge to stuff her wet, glistening fingers under her nose and deeply inhale the obscene scent was almost more than she could stand, but she knew instinctively that if she did so she would be lost to these alien thoughts and feelings. She knew what real desire was, knew true longing and the pleasure and awareness of her own body and this . . . this was a cheap narcotic shadow of it. She pushed it away, out of her head as much as she could, and wiped the ooze off on Will's old pants. There was movement in the tank, something swimming through the midnight darkness, attracted by Gillian's fingers. She leaned down close to the glass and tried to peer into the oily morass. It smashed against the glass with great force and Gillian jumped back with a shriek. She thought it was a snake. The burst of fear helped clear her head and she stared at whatever it was in the tank. There were several of them gliding through the oily slime like eels.

A terrible memory assaulted Gillian. The Stained. Last year, after the troubles in which so many had died, they'd called it a plague of the Black Vomit, but Gillian knew better. Everyone did, but no one wanted to admit it. Some horrible, pneumonic sickness had gripped Golgotha and transformed friends, neighbors and family into soulless monsters who oozed a black oily substance from every orifice. The same black oily substance in the tank before her.

"Oh Clayton," she said. "Why couldn't you just leave it alone, let it die?"

She moved cautiously toward the tank again, reached carefully over the churning surface of the obsidian fluid and grabbed the chain that was submerged in it. She lifted the chain, which had some weight to it; something was hanging from it. Slowly, the decapitated, mostly rotted skull of a woman rose from the oozing blackness, her tattered scalp still clinging to dank hair, resembling black seaweed. Parts of her skull, picked clean, were evident and scraps of her flesh hung loosely to other parts of her head, drooping and clumping like wet paper. Her eyes were empty, raw sockets and her lipless mouth gaped stupidly. Black things, like segmented worms, about six inches long, slithered out of the head's eye sockets, mouth and even the tattered ears. They made fat, plopping noises as they dropped back into the inky fluid of the tank.

Gillian nearly retched and dropped the chain, causing the head to sink back into the tank with a slow suctioning sound. She staggered back, hand over her mouth, and tried desperately to push the thoughts and images out of her mind. She had no clue who this woman was or how Clay had come into possession of her severed head. The thoughts that had troubled her back on the road to the livery returned, but with a much more visceral, sinister taint to them. *People disappeared all the time in Golgotha:* strangers, wanderers, vagrants, prostitutes. What if Clay needed them, needed meat for his experiments?

And Auggie, her Auggie. Sweet, kind, loyal . . . Auggie, with blood and women's makeup on his clothes. Oh, no, no, no, no, no . . .

She turned, the panic rising in her, struggling for a foothold of reason and calm. The light from her lantern caught another tank near the end of the row.

The liquid in it was smoky, slightly amber-colored, as though it contained a diluted version of the worm oil substance. Another head floated in it, bobbing, submerged and apparently perfectly preserved. It was a young woman, perhaps in her twenties; she had been beautiful, her hair was black and floated behind her like drifting wings. There was something familiar about her. Gillian knew her but she couldn't place . . .

No!

Gerta. It was Gerta, her best friend. Gerta with the gray hair and the wrinkles. Her dear old friend who had died at the age of forty-eight. Gerta, Gertie . . . Auggie's Gertie . . . Oh Clay, how could you do this?

The eyes of the head snapped open. They focused on Gillian, pupils narrowed in the bright lantern light. The mouth opened, tried to speak . . .

Gillian ran, dropping the lantern. As she released the trigger, the flame vanished with a snap just before the lantern crashed to the floor and shattered, without igniting a fire. She snorted the stench of the tank room out of her nostrils as she bolted back into the main barn.

There was the sound of a wagon arriving in the exercise yard just outside. Gillian spun about, looking for a place to hide. She ran to the large metal door at the back of the barn and struggled to open it, praying it led to an exit. The door hissed open and a blast of frigid air passed over her, colder than the winter wind outside. The strange squeaking metal-scraping noise was louder, having been muffled by the door. The light from the open door revealed nothing of the interior. There were no windows, no light, only a cold and sightless void. Gillian heard Auggie's booming voice at the open door to the barn. She stepped quickly into the cold room and shut the metal door behind her. It was absolute darkness, like you experience underground. The squeaking noise, which Gillian was pretty certain was some type of contraption Clay had developed to keep the room so cold, was the only sound. The thick, metal door blocked out the sound from the rest of the barn.

Gillian tried to calm herself. She knew both of these men. She thought highly of Clay, and was in wonder of his intellect. She understood how awkward he was trying to puzzle out people, who simply made no logical sense to his mind. And she loved Auggie, loved him with every ounce of her being.

She backed away from the door; the thick insulating India rubber that sealed the jamb cut off even the tiny sliver of light from the cracks around it.

Will had been the man she fell into love with, been charmed by, as a girl, but with his passing, with the mercy of experience that time grants, she knew Augustus Shultz was the love of her life. Surely these men would do her no harm.

The image of the head in the tank, fat black worms sliding out of it, vomited into her brain. She struggled to push the idea of the man she was to marry being anything other than noble and good out of her racing mind.

She bumped against something in the darkness. She turned, haltingly, toward it and gingerly felt the invisible form, trying to fathom what she was feeling. There was a table . . . and something cold and smooth atop it. She moved along it its length until she felt fingers. It was an arm, icy, still, lifeless. It was a corpse on a table. She felt the rough cloth of a simple sheet partly covering the body, and suddenly Clay's diagram with the cut lines was before her mind's eye. She recoiled and moved away only to bump into something else in the darkness. The speed knocked her partly over it. Cold skin, breasts, and a ragged, damp cavity above the breast, which her fingers slipped into. Another table, another corpse.

Gillian was reaching the end of her self-control; she envisioned a great frozen hall of tables in this unnaturally cold room, filled with dead women, raw material for Clay Turlough's imagination. She staggered, hitting another table, another body. She had no idea where the door was, how to get out. She wanted to scream, but she swallowed it and steeled herself as best she could, being in the dark with the dead.

There was whoosh of air escaping over the constant whine of the mysterious machinery and a bright square of light appeared to her left. She heard Auggie's voice over the squeaking of the machine.

"Where do you want me to put her?" Auggie said.

Clay had one of the globe lanterns in his hands and its light stabbed into the darkness of the room. Gillian could see there were over a dozen tables with bodies in the cold room. They all seemed to be women. "Over here," Clay said, stepping into the cold room, gesturing with the lantern to an empty bench off to the left of the door. Gillian slid down behind one of the occupied tables; the floor was smooth stone and cement, with clean straw scattered everywhere. She peeked over and saw Auggie carrying a woman's corpse; she was dressed in tattered nightclothes and stockings. She looked like a prostitute. Her face was smudged with thick pancake makeup, dried blood and dirt, and her chest and belly bulged, as if the insides had been disturbed and then returned to the cavity. Her face was young and it was familiar to Gillian, but no name came to mind. She felt very sad for the anonymous girl cradled in Auggie's strong arms. The look on her fiancé's face in the lantern was not that of a savage leering killer; it was sadness. He felt for this girl, too, and he carried her gently, like she was fragile, and with respect. He lowered her gingerly on to the wooden table, covered her with a sheet and crossed himself.

"Does that make you feel better?" Clay asked. It was not a malicious question. He sounded more like a child, trying to understand something that bewildered him.

"*Ja,*" Auggie said. "It does. It's asking the Lord to watch over her poor soul to protect it from evil and give her peace."

"Hmm." Clay nodded. "Doesn't seem to be terribly effective. Soul wouldn't need protecting if the transportation for it was designed a bit more sturdily. I don't think this God fella is a very good engineer."

Auggie shook his head. "Clay, how can you say such things about your own creator. . . . *Ach!* I can hardly hear myself over that infernal squeaking! Always squeaking in here! What is that?"

"The pulley and fan system," Clay said. "I designed the cold room on essentially the same principles as Mr. Andrew Chase of Chicago's refrigerated rail car."

"*Ach, du meine Fresse!*" Auggie said, his voice tired, stressed. "I just asked a simple question. Why can't you ever just give a simple answer?"

Clay continued, unabated. "However, I employed solidified carbon dioxide as the cooling agent, and since I didn't need it to move, like a rail car, I employed this steam-powered pulley and fan system to force the cold air around the insulated room."

"This is the last one, Clay," Auggie said, interrupting. "No more. This is not right, what we are doing."

"Yes, yes, it is the last one," Clay said, oblivious to Auggie's intent. He lifted the girl's hand and examined it carefully, then her wrist. "This is exactly what I needed. It's very fortuitous . . ."

Auggie sputtered. "Fortuitous? Clay, this girl is dead and was buried. Her life, her future, has been stolen from her. How can you be so inhuman?"

Clay continued to examine the dead girl's fingers carefully. "It's just death, Auggie. It's a natural process. I have never understood why folks get so emotional about it. We don't make much fuss about other bodily functions . . . well, most of them anyway. My first memories as a child were of death. It's a problem to be solved, not some cosmic decree, not fate or the will of some fickle god. We live, we die. What we are doing here, the research I'm involved in, could change the human race, and make death no more of an inconvenience than a case of the sniffles."

He put the girl's hand down and rested it on the table. Auggie covered her again.

"As for the manner of her death," Clay said, looking at his friend and tightening his jaw. "I assure you it was gentle compared to that poor child over there.

Your god seemed not up to the job of protecting her last evening. Maybe she didn't pray hard enough for her life."

Clay gestured to one of the tables near where Gillian hid. The light cut the darkness and Gillian tried to push herself closer to the floor.

"Is that the girl murdered in the alley last night?" Auggie whispered.

"Yes," Clay said. "More like butchered. Monstrous. We have a fiend among us, a lunatic with a penchant for cutting up innocent women in a most gruesome manner. He knows his way about a knife, I'd wager. A skinner, a butcher, someone with medical training . . ."

"Like you," Auggie said quietly. "Like you, Clay."

"Yes." Clay nodded in agreement. "Exactly like me."

The two men paused and were silent. Gillian had a horrible image of Clay drawing a blade and driving it into Auggie's chest.

Clay blinked a few times, seemingly confused by the stern look on Auggie's face. "Oh," he finally said, "you suspect it's me that's killing these girls. Preposterous."

Gillian bumped against the table she was hiding behind. The cold, stiff hand of the girl on the table slid out from under the sheet and caressed Gillian's cheek. It was too much. She couldn't contain herself any longer. Gillian let out an audible gasp of revulsion, jumped up and rushed into the lantern light. Both Clay and Auggie froze in mid-speech.

"I want to know everything, you two," Gillian said. "I want to know why you are keeping those vile, murderous worms alive. I want to know what you are doing with poor Gerta's head and where these women's bodies are coming from and what you're doing to them, Clayton."

Auggie looked at Clay, horror blooming in his weary eyes. "Gerta? Clay, what is she talking about? You told me Gerta was gone . . . destroyed in the fire."

Clay sighed. He opened the door to the cold room and walked out, Gillian and Auggie following.

"I know this may seem strange to you, Gillian," Clay said, "but if you will listen and keep an open mind . . ."

Gillian rushed to the workbench and grabbed a scalpel stained with old blood and rust. She brandished it and Clay stepped back, away from her.

"I will listen, Clayton, and you are going to tell me everything, and then we'll see if I go to the sheriff and tell him exactly what you've been up."

"Gillian, please put that down, before someone gets hurt, yes?" Auggie said. "You know I'd never let anyone hurt you, darling."

Gillian hung onto the blade and backed into the workbench.

"I love you, Auggie, but no more secrets. I want the truth and I want it now, or else I go to Jon Highfather."

Clay and Auggie looked at each other. Auggie nodded to Clay. "I want the whole truth, too, Clay," Auggie said. "I think we both deserve that."

Clay looked at the ground and then nodded. "I reckon you both do," he said. "Well, to start off with, I've discovered the secret to eternal life."

The Emperor (Reversed)

Twenty-one years earlier . . .
April 10, 1849
San Francisco

San Francisco hummed with a song of life, surging, mad, vibrant. The streets were teeming streams of faces, noise and commotion: different languages, shouting, street vendors hawking, whistles, music from voices and instruments, shouts of anger and bursts of laughter, the barking of dogs, the shrill calls of exotic birds, the mouthwatering scents of cooking from dozens of different cultures around the country and the globe, the stench of gutters overflowing, the honeyed voices of women from windows above the crowds urging clients to come up to call.

One word had turned San Francisco from another sleepy port town to a boomtown with hundreds of newcomers arriving daily—gold. Whole crews were jumping ship as soon as they docked at Clark's Point. Overnight, hotels, general stores, saloons and whorehouses all sprung up due to demand.

Malachi Bick walked through the teeming throngs, smiling in wonder. The crowd seemed to naturally part for him. Despite the grim reason for his visit to this blooming Bay City, he couldn't help but marvel at the life, the energy, teeming here. He loved cities, loved being among people. After his long isolation in the desert, he had to admit he was happy to be away from Golgotha, if only for a little while.

He turned left off Broadway onto Kearney Street. The neighborhood got a bit rougher here and much more bawdy. He paused outside a saloon called Dennison's Exchange, which faced toward Portsmouth Square's sprawl of open-air markets, peddlers and street performers.

Bick turned back toward the saloon. A small girl, maybe seven years old, stood looking up at him with intense green eyes.

"Hello," Bick said.

"My mum is sick and playing the sleeping game with a man and my da is gone off to sea," she said. "I'm hungry." The child was dressed in a thin, filthy dress; her bare feet were black. Her skin was golden and dark, her ebony hair a wild mane that fell below her shoulders. She resembled a tiny, disheveled, dark lion.

"What's your name, child?" Bick said.

"Rowan," she said.

"You are a very good liar, Rowan," Bick said, and handed the girl one of the newly minted gold dollar coins. "You almost fooled me and that is very hard to do."

"Is this real?" The child snatched the coin and clutched it to her chest. Bick nodded.

"As real as anything is, girl. Off with you now, before I take it back."

Rowan laughed and ran away.

Bick entered the cool, smoky darkness of the saloon. The place was tightly packed and the rumble of the patrons' conversations and the warm, mahogany of the black piano player's voice as he sung "Old Rosin the Beau" made Bick wish he could sit and enjoy a drink and soak it all in. A young boy of perhaps six with dusky skin and long curly black hair, shot through with coppery strands, accompanied the piano player, obviously his father. The boy was quite good.

Bick approached the stairs leading up to the private rooms on the second floor. Several Mexican and Indian women were leaning over the rail of the stairs, negotiating with saloon patrons. Two men lounged near the foot of the stairs, guns on their hips. They looked up as Bick approached.

"I'm here to see him," Bick said.

"He's busy," the one wearing the bowler said. The other, an Indian with a necklace of mummified human ears, crossed his arms.

"I know what you've done, Jeremiah," Bick said to the man in the bowler, his voice oiled steel. "You, too, Simon," he said to the Indian. "All the terrible things. All the lives you've ended. That family that came in on the Hastings Route. What you did to their children after you killed them. . . . The preacher in Nacogdoches you crucified. . . . I can see them, see their eyes staring into you as you snuffed out their light."

Both men's eyes widened as Bick stared them down. Jeremiah began to weep. Simon clutched at his chest.

"Look at them, look at all of them," Bick said. "Can you feel their gaze clawing at your eyeballs, your soul? Can you feel them crawling inside you? They have something to share with you."

Both men fell to the floor shuddering, convulsing, sobbing. Simon rolled over and began to heave. The whole bar was silent, except for the weeping of the two men.

"We did it for him," Simon mewled. "We did all of it for his glory."

"Yes," Bick said. "I need to have a word with him about that."

Bick walked over them and began to climb the stairs. He tipped his hat to the shocked prostitutes as he passed them.

He kicked in the bedroom door, third on the left. There were four women, all nude, slumbering even after the crash of Bick's entrance. Ray Zeal was sitting up in the bed, naked and smiling at Bick.

"Malachi, my old friend," Zeal said. "You look as miserable as ever. I take it you dealt with my men on the stairs and at the door? Pity, they'll be no good to anyone after that. Now if my boy had been here, then you would have had a fight on your hands."

"We need to talk, Ray," Bick said. "Now."

Zeal was just over six feet, with a slender, muscular build. His hair was spun gold, curly and falling in loose locks down to his neck. He sported muttonchops but was otherwise clean-shaven. His face was perfect, like a Greek statue, and his smile was both infectious and sincere, as if Zeal were smiling with every fiber of his existence. And of course his teeth were perfect too. Zeal climbed over the pile of slowly stirring women and stood beside the bed, completely unconcerned with his lack of clothes.

"Alone," Bick said, nodding to the women. Zeal laughed and clapped his hands.

"Ladies, wakey-wakey! I know I promised you a good long rest after our horizontal refreshment, but I'm afraid I must entertain an old friend."

A few of the women began to climb out of the bed, groaning, and slipped on robes. One didn't stir. Zeal leaned over her.

"Out!" he bellowed. "Now!" The woman jumped to her feet, terrified, and fled the room, still in a state of undress. Laughing, her peers followed her and Bick closed the door behind them. By the time the door closed, Zeal's smile was back at full brightness.

"And what occasion drags you away from your dingy little hellhole in the desert, Malachi?" Zeal asked as he leaned against the bed and pulled on a pair of denim work pants.

"Guess," Bick said, grabbing a chair by the door and sitting down. He began to roll himself a cigarette. Zeal pointed to Bick and held up two fingers. Bick sighed, nodded and began to roll a second cigarette. "It's about the skull. Do you have any idea what it's done? How many people are dead or half mad because of it?"

Zeal shrugged. He slid on a gray shirt and began to button it. It appeared to be made of silk or some other smooth, shiny material. It rippled like water as he buttoned it. "You mean it's not locked up tight and safe in that cave of yours?"

"Of mine!" Bick said, tossing the cigarette at Zeal. The blond man caught it easily, the smile never leaving his face. "It is your responsibility, your duty! You left it in Golgotha because you were tired of guarding it and wanted to go play in the world." Bick gestured to the room.

"And played I have," Zeal said, sliding on a pair of heavy black boots. "You should really try it. It's an amazing world, if you enjoy slumming, Biqa. Can we just drop the whole 'Ray-Malachi' thing? It gets tiresome and the children are all out of the room. Grown-up time."

"As you wish, Raziel," Malachi Bick, the angel Biqa, said. "I'm not the one who chose 'Ray Zeal' as a traveling name anyway. It's a bit cheeky."

"Cheeky!" Raziel said. "Not at all, it has the flair of the dramatic and it denotes a positive outlook on life. I like it. It's just nice to drop pretenses and let your wings down, so to speak, with someone from the old hometown."

Biqa lit his own cigarette, then the golden angel's as well. Both angels were silent for a moment as they enjoyed the tobacco.

"Any word from home?" Raziel asked.

"No," Biqa said. "There's never word from home."

"Do you ever consider that perhaps we are just two lunatics sharing a delusion? That we are no more angels than the moon is made of cheese?" Raziel said.

"No," Biqa said. "This reality is not our home. We are not from here. This is just the crossroads. Our home is the Radiance. We are here to perform our duties for the Almighty. Your duty is to guard that skull, and you have shirked that responsibility for far too long and people have died for it."

"And what would you have me do, Biqa?" Raziel asked. "Sit in a dark cave staring at a moldering old hunk of bone until the stars burn away?"

"Yes," Biqa said. "If that is what is needed to secure it and keep that thing from being loosed on this world, the other worlds, then yes."

Raziel exhaled smoke through his nose and shook his head. "Back home, you would never have dared speak to me in this manner. I was the Keeper of Secrets, the vessel of divine knowledge, one of the Princes of the Second Heaven. When the Almighty whispered mysteries, he whispered them to me.

"Don't presume to lecture me on my duties, Biqa. How many times have you snuck away from that pit you guard? How many divine bastards have you sired, even knowing what such a birth always does to the mortal mother? Tell me, Biqa, how far have you fallen?"

"Not so far that I have forgotten who I am and what I am," the dark angel said. "Not so far that I disobey my orders. I do my job as well as yours. It escaped using a child, Raziel, a child! If either of the things we guard escape, everything ends—mine quickly like a bomb, yours slowly, like rabies. You cannot simply desert your post."

"My post." Raziel laughed and fell back on the bed, his long legs over the side, still touching the floor. "My post, our orders. Do you fancy yourself a soldier, Biqa? Did you slay many Voidlings in the War of Darkness, the First War?" He sat back up, quickly; the smile was now a sneer.

"Did you hear the sound of the war against the rebels, against Lucifer's traitorous army, while you were down here standing watch over the mother of the Voidlings and playing patty-cake with the monkeys? Did you see the Pearlescent Gates burn and fall? Did you spill your brother's blood on your blade, listen to it hiss as it boiled? Hear the howls, the begging, the screams of rage and terror as they were cast out?

"You are no solider, Biqa. You are the same thing I am, an exile. You, for questioning His motives and actions in the War of Darkness; me, for daring to give divine knowledge to the monkeys that my fellow Archangels of the Sephirot said they were unprepared to receive, the hypocrites! Exiles, Biqa. Not quite fallen, not quite whole, in-between, given meaningless tasks, cosmic busywork and kept away from the balm of the Radiance for our transgressions."

Biqa exhaled smoke. "I've seen my share of war," he said. "All of them. Despite what you think, Raziel, our tasks are far from meaningless. I used to think I was an outcast, but I've come to believe that I was sent here to learn. This Earth, this world, is a classroom. I'm here to learn lessons and I do fail, oh, do I fail, but I remember why I am here."

Biqa regarded the cigarette and dropped it at his feet, crushing it out with his boot.

"I think I'm very sure of why I'm here too," Raziel said. "And I think I have gleaned any lessons I need to out of this construct of decay, illusion and death."

Raziel stood holding the cigarette by his lips as he slipped on a brocaded vest of blue and left it unbuttoned. He picked up a gun belt off the table by the bed and a cavalry saber, sheathed. He buckled on the belt and then affixed the sheath to it.

"Do those lessons include setting yourself up as a false god to these people?" Biqa said, his eyes on the guns and the blade at the golden angel's belt.

"Oh, that," Raziel said. "You mean my little congregation."

"Yes," Biqa said. "That. You have followers, more than that, worshipers, a cult. Across the globe, small bands of cutthroats, murderers. Sick, evil predators, like those two downstairs. They commit atrocities for you, in your name—Raziel. Explain yourself."

Raziel laughed again. He walked to Biqa and knelt on one knee before the sitting angel, leaning in close to his face.

"Explain myself? To you? Very well . . . old friend.

"You see, Biqa, what I discovered in the wars was that I liked killing, maiming. I loved it. I loved that my creator gave me a purpose, and that purpose is to slaughter. It thrilled me, it made me feel like the Almighty understood me, loved me so much he gave me wars and rebellions to slake my thirst for blood, for murder; that he created this whole charnel house, this joke of a world, just for me."

"You've lost your way, Raziel," Biqa said. "Perhaps it was the skull; it may have influenced you. . . ."

"Influenced me," Raziel laughed, looking into Biqa's dark, calm eyes with his own brilliant, shining blue ones. "Biqa, I was made to be the skull's guardian, its master. I felt this way before the Earth was even forged. I felt this way from the instant of my creation. What things do you think the Almighty was whispering into my ear all those countless eons? Words of endearment? Of joy and peace and love? No. He dipped his tongue in the blackest blood and he whispered to me of slaughter, of death, of torture and atrocity. That is your creator, Biqa. He built this entire lovely, lovely playground so that he could tear it apart, abuse and neglect his toys and listen to the terrified screams of the monkeys as they tried to understand. And only I was capable of comprehending that desire, that uncontrollable urge to control, to destroy and to feed on terror."

"I don't believe that," Biqa said.

"Really?" Raziel said. Only a few inches separated the two angels' faces now. They bore into each other's eyes, their inhuman wills clashing like sabers. "Well, if what I am doing is so abhorrent, so against the Almighty's plan, then why am I being allowed to do it, Biqa? Why isn't He stopping me? For that matter how can I even exist as I am, unless I was created this way by Him? And why would God make a bloodthirsty angel unless He intended him to be. I am part of His grand design, as much as gravity, or the flowers, or disease. Or you, sweet, dark Biqa."

Biqa said nothing and Raziel smiled his perfect smile.

"Can't answer that one, can you? My 'cult,' as you call it, is made up of humans who are created in my image—they have hungers, fantasies, which must be fed. They are artists in pain, fear and slaughter. In short, they are like me and I am their god. And the skull is my Holy Grail, can't you see that? That is why I was tasked to stand watch over the mortal who crafted the power in the skull, and in time, his remains. I've even figured out why the Almighty wanted me to stand over the mortal, and, trust me, it had nothing to do with moral outrage. It was fear. God fears the skull. It all makes sense to me now, Biqa. I wish you could see but I'm afraid you're just too stunted in your vision. Your morality limits your comprehension. Beings such as us should strive to be less myopic."

"All I see is a petty, egotistical tyrant," Biqa said, standing. "A servant who thinks himself a master and has set up his own pathetic excuse for a religion to justify his madness, and his own treason. I'm taking guardianship of the skull. You are no longer fit to protect it . . . Ray."

Raziel's smile dimmed. He stood, resting his hand on the hilt of his saber. He slapped Biqa on the shoulder, good-naturedly.

"Of course, old friend. Keep the skull. Keep it safe in your little empire in the dust," the golden angel said. Bick stood and opened the door. Zeal's smile faded and his blue eyes burned.

"Keep it for me like a good servant, until I come for what is mine."

Bick shut the door. The thought of Ray Zeal, what he represented and why he was allowed to exist was a shard of troubling doubt buried deep in the angel's mind. He also felt a trickle of something he tried to push away seep into the core of him.

Bick was afraid.

The World (Reversed)

Twenty-one years later . . .
November 20, 1870
Nevada

"I hope you'll forgive the intrusion," the woman said as she strode into Malachi Bick's office on the second floor of the Paradise Falls as if it belonged to her. She was a beauty, to be sure: short, lithe, exotic with long black hair, falling in ringlets far below her shoulders. She was dressed in a loose tunic, pants and vest of green and black. The Scholar was with her, Bick noted, dressed in his usual workingman attire and vest, cudgel in hand. The fact that his men downstairs were not all over the two indicated that they had already been dealt with. Bick rose and turned to his guest, who was sitting in one of the high back chairs before his desk.

"I am sorry our chat has been interrupted, Emily," he said. "I believe I'm taking an unexpected business meeting. Perhaps I could call upon you later at the Imperial?"

Emily Bright stood and regarded the dark woman and the giant bearded man who accompanied her. Emily had been afforded a chance to rest and settle in at Bick's new hotel. She was in a clean, comfortable blouse of cream and a black skirt that fell to her booted ankles. Her hair was loose and draped her shoulders.

"I'd like to stay, if I might," she said. "I'm keen to see the inner workings of the man who owns Golgotha." She looked at the woman who now leaned on the edge of Bick's desk, smiling. "I know you."

The woman looked Emily up and down, dismissively. "I doubt, that, dear," she said. Emily was unperturbed.

"You're from San Francisco," Emily said. "I've heard rumors of some esoteric society you're mixed up in, the *coven la nan deyès a siren*? And something about purchasing spy balloons from the war? I saw you in the city once. They call you the Queen of the Barbary Pirates. They call you a few other less flattering names, too, not to your face, of course . . . dear."

Bick smiled at the exchange. He sat down again behind the desk and gestured for the two women to sit in the chairs. They did. The Scholar stood beside and behind the dark woman's chair.

"You reputation precedes you, Black Rowan," Bick said. "This is Miss Bright," he said, nodding toward Emily. "Only recently arrived in town. We were catching up. How may I be of service to you?"

Rowan held out her hand and the Scholar dropped a small cloth bag into it. Rowan tossed it across the desk to Bick, who caught it easily. He opened it and dumped a thick pile of currency and heavy gold and silver coins onto the desktop. Bick looked at it and then back to Rowan.

"And this is what, exactly?" Bick asked.

"Your cut," Rowan said. "You're the house, so it's a straight fifty percent of the cream straight off the top."

"My . . . cut," Bick said, looking at Rowan and then to the stone face of the Scholar. "Of the profits from the Dove's Roost. My business, my property. I see."

"There has been a change in management," Rowan said. "I'm in charge of the Dove's Roost now. I'm in charge of what happens to any public girls anywhere in Golgotha now: freelancers, saloon girls, camp followers, crib ladies, all of it. I'm having talks with Mr. Wynn, Half-Guts Mitchell, the Nail and Ch'eng Huang to explain to them as I'm explaining to you.

"I'd enjoy watching your talk with Huang," Bick said. "And what exactly are you going to explain to all of us, Lady Rowan?"

Rowan leaned forward in her chair, her eyes narrowed and focused on Bick's, and even he was drawn into her gaze.

"These women, they are under my auspice and my protection," she said. "The Scholar and Ham will continue to do their jobs and you, as the owner of the property, are entitled to a handsome cut of the profits, but I own this trade in Golgotha now, not you. Those women are now like craftsmen, protected by a guild of sorts—mine."

"You working for her now?" Bick asked the Scholar. "So much for your much lauded loyalty, it seems, Mr. Quire."

"No, sir. I still am currently in your employ," the Scholar said. "Miss Rowan's machinations were unknown until she sprung them upon me. I defended your business interests to the best of my ability, Mr. Bick, and I was soundly defeated by the lady, a most humbling experience, I can assure you. When I awoke, the situation was explained to me much as it was just explained to you. I am here today to give you this."

The Scholar removed an envelope from his jacket and handed it to Bick. Bick took it, but didn't open it.

"My resignation from your employ," the Scholar said. "If you refuse to accept it, I will continue to act as your advocate to the fullest extent of my resources, Mr. Bick, and will even move against Miss Rowan to kill her, if you wish it. Words are all we have in this life to mark our passage through eternity. My word is my bond and I break it for no one. Currently, as your advocate, I would urge you to accept the generous terms being offered to you."

Bick looked at the Scholar and smiled. "I apologize for impugning your honor, Mr. Quire. You have been a loyal and exemplary employee. You are relieved, sir." Bick slipped the envelope into his jacket pocket.

"Thank you, sir," the Scholar said. He turned to Black Rowan. "I am currently without employment and would be honored to accept the position you have offered me."

Rowan nodded. "Thank you, Scholar." She turned back to Bick, who was unreadable, his fingers steepled and resting against his pursed lips. "And you, Mr. Bick, do you also accept my offer?"

"I always like to know the motives of those I am getting into business with," Bick said. "You are well connected and have many profitable endeavors on the coast and elsewhere in the world, so why come to my little corner of nowhere? Why inject yourself into my business?"

Rowan sat back in the chair and crossed her legs. "It's a pity you are not as invested in the details of your businesses as you are in your business partners, Mr. Bick. Were you aware that in the last two days, two of your loyal employees have been savagely murdered? One last night, found on the altar of St. Cyprian's. They were murdered while freelancing for a poacher in your territory? The man's name is Niall Devlin, but I'm sure you are more familiar with his nom de guerre, the Nail. He puts them out there with no protection and they are terrified to cross him or tell you for fear of your retaliation. They did it because they needed more money, and for that, they have been tortured to death and mutilated. You knew that, didn't you, Mr. Bick? Perhaps that's what you and the pretty Mrs. Bright were discussing when we so rudely interrupted."

Bick's eyes darkened. Rowan felt as if a shadow had just fallen across her heart, but she refused to show this man weakness.

"Did you know?" Rowan asked. "Did you give even a drop of golden piss about any of them?"

"I didn't know." Bick said. "Did they have family?"

"They goddamned do now," Rowan said, her voice like a knife wrapped in silk. "I'll look after them. I'll deal with the Nail. I'll deal with the man that's hunting them and I'll keep them safe and make as many of them as rich as I can."

"Why?" Bick said. "How do I know you aren't someone like this 'Nail,' someone looking to move in and exploit these women, looking for profit?"

"I talked to every girl at the Dove," Rowan said. "Every girl in the street or the camps or the saloons, every girl I could find; and I gave it to them straight. They don't want to work for me, I get them a ticket on the stage out of town and a week's pay. They stay here and work around me, cut me out: I give them a first-class beating and the same ticket out of town.

"You, Mr. Bick, have your eyes on the horizon. You haven't spent enough time in the dirt. You don't know how it feels to fall, to live in the shadows. Me, I have one business concern here and one business only, and I will tend my garden and take good care of my lilies and pull any weeds out by the roots."

"Very poetic," Bick said, "but not really an answer. And you'd be surprised the falls I've experienced in my time, Lady Rowan. So I ask again. Why here, why now?"

"I have my reasons for being in Golgotha," Rowan said. "And they are mine. I hope you can understand, being a man who also enjoys the cloak of anonymity. So, do we have an arrangement, Mr. Bick? You don't really want us to discuss such ugly unpleasantness as what happens if you say no in front of the lovely Miss Bright, do you?"

Bick looked to Emily. "What do you think?"

Emily stared straight at Rowan as she spoke.

"I think that Black Rowan lives up to her reputation," she said. "She is a pirate and an agency of lawlessness and chaos. I think that if I spoke something I knew was true and she repeated my words, I would doubt their veracity."

Rowan's gaze remained fixed on Emily's violet eyes. Bick was impressed by his daughter's fearlessness. Emily returned her gaze to Bick.

"However, what she says about the women, about looking after them, protecting them . . . I believe her in that. And it sounds as if they need protecting."

"Then we have an arrangement," Bick said, rising. Rowan stood and extended her hand. Bick took it and kissed it. "Consider this a welcome gift to our fair town, for such a resplendent and capable woman." He looked at the beautiful pirate and the darkness once again fell upon her heart, like a hand of ice had clutched it.

"And if you decide to expand your business interests in Golgotha further, Lady Rowan, then we shall have that ugly, unpleasant conversation, I assure you. Please rouse my men downstairs on your way out, if you will be so kind."

Rowan, somewhat shaken, withdrew her hand. She and the Scholar departed without another word. Bick closed the door behind them.

"Well, this is shaping up to be an eventful month," Bick said to Emily.

"So why did you just let Black Rowan take over the Dove's Roost?" she asked him. "You lost control of that part of your world now?"

"The worst thing to do is let your enemies decide the battlefield," Bick said. "I know where she is now and I know her plans in the short term, at least. If Rowan decides to stay here, then I will either control her or eliminate her. A shame, too, if I must. Lovely woman, a breath of fresh air, really."

"Eliminate? I don't understand you," Emily said, shaking her head. "You act like a villain but with your resources, your . . . abilities, these people should love you. You could make this desert into a garden for them," Emily said.

"No," Bick said. "My powers have diminished considerably over my time here."

"But half of near infinite is still . . . godlike."

"I, those like me, we're not gods," Bick said. "We're servants, agents, nothing more. This is your world, mankind's world. We can't, we shouldn't interfere too much here; it's not what all this is here for. I'm here to do a job, fulfill a duty. Did Caleb explain that to you?"

Emily nodded. "Yes, he said you were tasked to guard a . . . thing, older than God, than time or even death . . . sealed away under the Earth. Caleb said its presence is why so many strange things happen in Golgotha, why the town attracts so many odd souls. He said that if this creature got loose it would destroy everything, everywhere."

"Last year, it almost did," Bick said, "because I was careless, because I was too busy being human to do my job properly and because I trusted someone else to safeguard what I was entrusted to guard. My mistake was paid in blood, rivers of it, not the least of which was Caleb's.

"I've spent the last year making sure that everything in a hundred miles of here is nailed down tight, under my control, making sure I have something over everyone so that if I need to I can control or destroy any man, woman or child in this town, because I just might have to do that to make sure I never fail in my mission again."

"That's horrible," Emily said. "What of trust? You just said this world is ours . . . theirs? How can you say you don't want to interfere in man's destiny when you are clearly doing that here? If you clutch at something too tightly it slips through the crack in your fingers or you crush it. You don't want either one to happen. You have to trust."

Bick shook his head. "I trusted in my Creator, have obeyed His words to me loyally and for it. I'm an exile. I trusted men here to protect my secrets and defend this world. They fell to greed and weakness. They almost let the most terrible thing in all creation loose. I have met an angel that tells me God whispered horrors and nightmares into his ear since before time began. Is that my God? Is that the God who showed me mercy and love? How can that be? No, I can't afford to trust, Emily. I have to control and, if necessary, crush."

"That is very sad," Emily said. There was a brief silence before she spoke again. "Do you trust me?"

"I don't know yet," Bick said. "I'd like to. It's hard to believe in anything or anyone when you have heard God's voice but can't recall it, when you have heard the choirs of the Radiance, but Heaven is silent now."

"Well," Emily said, patting his hand, "welcome to the human race. We trust every day and we have far less awareness than you do. Faith is dangerous, but hopelessness is death. We stumble about in the universe with a blindfold on and hope the powers that be don't trip us."

Bick took his daughter's hand, squeezed it.

"I think I believe in you," Emily said.

"Well," Bick said, "that makes one of us."

The Three of Swords

The smoke from the fine home on Joseph Street in New Orleans led the intrepid volunteers of the Fireman's Charitable Association to smash down the kitchen door on a Saturday in late October, 1870. Inside they found two black servants, former slaves, chained to the stove in an advanced state of starvation and showing signs of long-term torture. They set the fires in hopes of dying in them, to end their suffering.

Upstairs the men of the FCA, and the local constabulary they had summoned, discovered an antechamber to Hell in the mansion's attic. Dozens of servants, all former slaves, shackled to the walls and floor of the narrow, cramped, hot room. Some had been experimented upon. One woman was in a small cage, her bones broken and reset to resemble a crab. Another man had been the subject of a crude attempt to alter his sex—breasts and sexual organs taken from one of the women had been stitched to the man after his own genitals had been hacked off. Several of the victims had their hands sewn to parts of their body. Some died of starvation after having their mouths sewed shut. One woman had her arms and legs cut off and her skin mutilated to resemble the patterns found on a caterpillar. The ones that hadn't died begged their rescuers to kill them.

The author of this macabre and inhuman tableau, one Mme. Delilah LaTour, was the mistress of the house and widow of a well-respected Spanish ship captain. She was skinny to the point of looking unwell, with coal-black locks that fell well to her waist. The surviving servants told stories of the Madame pleasuring herself while either torturing the servants or simply watching the maimed and the mutilated struggle to survive. A collection of amputated and taxidermied phalluses in *her bedroom had been well used. All told, with the bodies found in her "garden," she had ended forty-two lives and tortured and ruined another fifty that they knew of.*

LaTour had fled the property when she was given a warning only moments before the firemen arrived. The warning came from the mouth of a crow, which lighted upon her gatepost and told her what was to come. It was the same crow that gave it to her as a gift long ago. The crow told her to flee west and to meet her god, the Lord of Torture, Pain and Suffering. It told her that her good works were not yet at an end. She grabbed a small bag with a few precious possessions, trophies of her victims and, of course, it. Mme. LaTour's was the eighteenth.

The Devil

It was early morning the day after Highfather and Kate had survived their violent showdown on Argent with the late Nikos Vellas. They had made it back to Highfather's house just off Absalom Road, in the dark of night.

To call it a "house" was being very generous. It was a one-room shack that the sheriff had built a few months after coming to Golgotha, figuring he'd build something better later on. He never seemed to find the time for that, though. There were still stakes in his yard, marking the places for a large addition—a master bedroom, a nursery—a home for more than one. The stakes were old and rotted now.

Highfather had helped Kate, with her injured leg, off his horse, Bright, and the two had stumbled to the door in the freezing cold and the stygian darkness. He found his key while Kate helped keep him from falling over. She had bound his bullet wound on the mountain as well as she could, but it was hard for Jon to stay conscious. Once the door was opened he had managed to light the lantern hanging on a nail next to the door. The room was filled with warm yellow light. Jon sat the lantern on the kitchen table.

There was a wrought-iron bed with a small side table, the kitchen table with a few chairs, some sparsely filled shelves and bookcases, cupboards, a wood stove, a wash basin and mirror and an old, frayed George III wingback chair by the window. Sitting above the hearth that had no fireplace yet was a bouquet of dried flowers in a crystal vase. They were the only real decoration. They had been a bridal bouquet. Highfather began to make a fire in the stove.

"You take the bed," he muttered. "There's fresh water in the pitcher here if you'd care for any. Privy is out back, if you need it."

"We need to get you to a doctor," Kate said with a groan as she sat on the edge of the bed.

"If you knew the doctor we had hereabouts, you wouldn't be so eager to get to him," Highfather said. "I'll keep."

"This looks like every policeman's house I've ever seen," Kate said as she wrestled off her boots, hissing as she began to work the boot off her tender leg. "How often are you here a week? Two, three nights?"

The fire caught in the stove and Highfather shut the stove's small door. "Bunks at the jail are just fine most nights," he said. He slowly limped to the corner chair and eased into it. Every part of him ached. Kate got both boots off. The red and black stockings she was wearing were in tatters.

"I usually don't wear my inexpressibles out to a shoot-out," Highfather said, "but that's just me."

"I could either change clothes or run save your hide," Kate said, pouring sand from her shoes. "Please don't make me regret my choice."

Highfather leaned his head back and closed his eyes. "No, ma'am," he said. "Just thankful for the assist, Kate . . . Kate?"

He opened his eyes with great effort. Kate was asleep, her stocking feet dangling over the side of the bed. Highfather grunted as he stood. He lifted the Pinkerton agent's strong, well-shaped legs and shifted them over on his bed. Then he pulled a quilt up over her. He dimmed the lantern on the table, locked the door and sat back down in his chair. He was asleep before he even got his boots off.

There was a persistent banging at his door shortly after dawn. Highfather blinked and tried to stand. His whole body felt as if it were made of fused bones and broken glass. He snapped open the door and saw Mutt and Jim looking at him. They started to open their mouths to speak, but he cut them off.

"Yes, I'm alive," Jon said. "Yes, I am hurt. Yes, Agent Warne saved me. Yes, I want the doc over here after you fellas collect whatever bodies are up on the ridge. Pay special attention to Vellas. He's liable to jump back up. Anything else?"

Mutt looked past him and saw Kate stretch lithely in the sheriff's bed, like a cat sunning herself. The Indian's eyebrows raised like a drawbridge.

"Whoa," Jim said as he saw Kate sit up and blink, still wearing the skimpy attire he saw her in at the Dove's Roost.

The evil smile spread across Mutt's face and he opened his mouth to speak.

"No, we didn't," Highfather said to his deputies and shut the door in Mutt's grinning face.

———————

When the deputies returned from asking Tumblety to come check on the sheriff, Jim told Highfather about the dead public girl at the church and his pursuit of the killer. The victim had been identified by the Scholar as a young German immigrant known only as Rica. She had been at the Roost for a little less than a year. She had no family here but sent money home to her sisters and mother in Chicago.

"I would have made it to the scrap to help," Mutt said to Highfather and Kate. "But I decided it would be quicker to cut through the mining camp than circle all around the mountain to hit Backtrail Road. I ran smack into the middle of a little disagreement between Wynn's boys and the Nail's crew. By the time I gentled them all down, you and Agent Warne here had headed on down the mountain and left a lot of dead bodies behind you."

"Well, you didn't miss much," Highfather said. "He threw a wagon wheel at me. That was new."

"Flaming wagon wheel," Kate corrected.

"The mining camp is getting too crowded for all them desperados, Jonathan," Mutt said. "Sooner, later, it's gonna blow and we're gonna have us a war."

"A bunch of normal criminals trying to kill each other, for good old-fashioned greed," Highfather said to Mutt. "Let's hope we live long enough to see that in this town."

"Clay's looking over the wagon the killer was driving out into the desert," Jim said. "I'm sorry I let him get away,"

The sheriff shrugged. "Hell, Jim, you got a damn sight closer to bagging him than anyone else has. You did real good, Deputy. I'm proud of you."

Jim beamed like the sun.

"Thanks, sir," he said. "I'm gonna get before Doc Tumblety shows up. He's always trying to touch me as he asks me a lot of questions about, um, stuff I rather not discuss in front of Miss. Warne."

"Come on," Mutt said to Jim. "Let's scare up some grub. Tumblety makes me want to punch him till he stops jawin'."

"Go on, "Highfather said. "Truth be told, Jim, I don't care much for the doc laying hands on me either."

"Well done, Jonathan," Dr. Francis Tumblety said upon arriving at the sheriff's home. He spoke in his usual gruff bellow. "You not only managed to undo that swarthy, degenerate Greek goat-banger, Vellas, you also received mere minor injuries in the exchange. A true testament to your superior bloodline and moral and national character."

Highfather winced as Tumblety poked and prodded the raw gunshot wound in his left arm with stained, dirty fingers thick as sausages.

"Here," Highfather said through gritted teeth. "That's . . . great . . . Doc."

Kate, dressed now in a narrow skirt that fell to her ankle boots, a simple white blouse and a dark bolero jacket and hat she had fetched from her bags at the Roost, leaned against the wall in the corner by the window with her arms crossed, watching the exchange with slight amusement. "See," Tumblety said, taking his hands away. "Hornet claimed a hunk of meat, but nothing else. The blood loss made you weak, but you stanched that well enough."

Highfather's bare chest was covered front and back in scars, bullet and knife wounds, claw and fang marks and, of course, the three sets of rope scars about his neck.

"Miss Warne was gracious enough to help me keep from bleeding out," Highfather said to the doctor, "till I could get ahold of you, Doc, and get you over to give the hit a look-see."

"Hmm." Tumblety looked to Kate with narrowed eyes, then back to Highfather. "Well, you are dashed lucky then, to trust your ephemeral soul to the Asclepian ministering of some water-kneed quean."

"Pardon me?" Kate said. Tumblety turned back to her.

"Hush now," he said. "Men are talking."

Kate started to say something, but Highfather gestured for her to wait.

"The burns are also minor," the doctor continued. "Some singed hair, a bit of redness and swelling on that Olympian body of yours, Jonathan. Dashed lucky, like you danced between the flames. Certainly adds to the legend of the sheriff who cannot die, eh? Good bit of balderdash for the superstitious, what? We know better, don't we, eh? You bleed as well as the next man. I'd hazard to say your preternatural reputation is due, in large part, to my care."

"Yeah, Doc," Highfather said. "Don't know what we'd do without you."

Tumblety handed Highfather an envelope out of his physician's bag. "This is all that remains of the possessions of that ram-headed gobbler, Vellas, as you requested. I had to set Turlough in his place. The man was insistent on examining the remains, but I set him straight to his station. Not much on Vellas, I'm sorry to say, but these items seemed to endure the fire with great fortitude."

"Well, thanks for coming by, Doc," Highfather said, hopping off the wooden dinner table he had been sitting on while Tumblety took a look at his arm. He winced a bit when he did.

"Of course," Tumblety said. "When that cherubic lad, Jim, came to me like a vision of beauty and mercy, I knew I must make haste to your domicile." He glanced again at Kate. "A pity a strapping male specimen such as yourself feels the need to keep such company. I'd preferred to examine you away from unscholared eyes." He extended his hand while Highfather retied the cloth bandage around his bicep. "Always happy to be of service to an agency of lex loci."

"Oh," Highfather said. He fished in his trousers and handed the doctor a silver dollar. "Much obliged, Doc."

Tumblety pocketed the coin and gathered up his bag and medal-festooned coat. "A word to the wise, Jonathan," he said as he went about his task. "A man in your position must show great care in trucking with adventuresses. Their horrid female sex is replete with disease that can lay a man low faster than any bullet. Beware, I caution you as a physician, beware!"

"I've seen better sawbones in a Chinese brothel," Kate said. Tumblety's face grew ruddy with rage and he strode toward Kate with hatred glazing his eyes. "Shut your mouth, you haughty bitch! I'm going to beat the sass out of your whore gob!"

Highfather moved to stop Tumblety, but by the time he rested a restraining hand on the blustering doctor's shoulder, Tumblety was staring into the short barrels of two .36 Colt revolvers Kate had cross-drawn from under her short jacket. Tumblety stopped abruptly and gasped.

"Are you just?" she said coolly, cocking both guns. "Tell me, you pompous gasbag, who's going to reattach your ugly face when I blow it all over the walls?"

"Jon . . . Jonathan! You are the law here! You're not going to allow this . . . this . . . to . . ."

Highfather dropped the doctor's coat and bag in his hands as he led Tumblety to the door. "Naw, Doc. I'm not going to let the mean lady shoot you in the face this time, but you may want to consider trying to talk nicer to folks in the future. Thanks again."

Tumblety stood outside the door, his face purple.

"Filthy slut," he snarled.

"I'm a damn fine shot," Kate said. "I can shoot that little amusement you call a pecker off you from over here quicker than you can kill a patient from incompetence."

"Thanks again, Doc," Jon said, and slammed the door in Tumblety's face before the angry doctor could summon a retort. He turned to Kate. "And that's our first-rate medical care here in sunny Golgotha. He may seem pretty horrible at first, but after a while, you come to realize that deep down inside, he's much worse than that."

"Why don't you people get a real doctor out here?" Kate asked. She decocked her guns, carefully, and holstered them in the curious shoulder rigs she wore under her jacket.

"Well, he's what we were able to attract in the bust years," Highfather said. "That and our last doctor turned out to be some kind of . . . thing . . . that turned people into stone . . . and drank their memories, or something like that. One 'fore that, I had to stake him through the liver and bury his head on an eastern-bound railroad track . . . or was it westbound? Anyway, he was all monstery too. At least Tumblety is human, a creepy jackass, but human."

"Monsters . . . ," Kate murmured. "How long have you been sheriff here, Jon?"

"I'd cypher it seems like . . . about a thousand years, give or take," Highfather said. He slid on his shirt and began to button it. "Have a seat, coffee should be ready."

He pulled Kate's chair out for her and she sat. "Thank you," she said. Highfather took down two porcelain mugs from a cabinet and then fetched the coffeepot from the top of the small wood stove he used to heat his house and for cooking. He poured her a cup, then himself, returned the pot, and sat down across from her.

"Can you tell me why the U.S. government sent you to my town and why you didn't tell me?"

Kate sipped her coffee. "Like I said before, your town in in terrible danger, Jon. However, from the reports I've read, what you've told me and what I've seen since I've been here, that really isn't anything new, is it?"

"Reports?" Highfather said. "What do you mean reports? About Golgotha? Kate, tell me what's going on here?"

"Well," she said, "you saved me up there, too, and I've seen and heard enough to trust you, Jon, but here's the thing. My presence here and my work and even who I am have to stay as quiet as possible."

"My deputies know about you, and you can trust both of them with your life," Highfather said. "And no one listens to anything Doc Tumblety says anyway. We'll hold our peace. That's kind of how we do things around here anyway."

Kate nodded. "Your younger deputy, Jim, is a sucker for a pretty leg, but he seemed trustworthy enough. If you vouch for your men, that is good enough for me. Golgotha is part of why I'm here, Jon. Let me give you this from the start. Fourteen years ago, I walked into Allan Pinkerton's office in New York City and applied for a job."

"*The* Allan Pinkerton," Highfather said. "Scottish fella, hobnobs with presidents, has the detective agency with that big eye symbol, 'we never sleep,' and all that? That Pinkerton?"

"Yes," Kate said with a strange smile. "The legend himself. Apparently he was hiring for office help and for detectives that day, and he asked me what I was there to apply for. I told him I was a month late on my rent and would take any job he might have. We began to talk. He's a fascinating man, remarkable mind. He hired me as a detective on the spot."

"Never heard of a female Pinkerton man before," Highfather said. "Did you enjoy the work?"

She smiled. "I'm impressed. I usually get a lecture about how that's no work for a lady and all that claptrap. It's refreshing to not hear it."

"I've seen you in action," Highfather said. "You can handle yourself just fine."

"You actually live up to your reputation, Jon Highfather," she said, then continued. "Yes, I loved my work. It was exciting, challenging and I discovered why Allan had hired a woman. Men will tell things to a woman in confidence they would never spill to a man. I had adventures, Jon. I got to help keep President Lincoln safe from an assassination attempt on him before the war, during the inauguration. I met Lincoln, Jon," she said, her eyes brightening. "A little dirt-poor Five Points girl from Cross Street got to meet the President of the United States and help keep him alive. How could I do anything but love a job like that?"

"What was he like? Lincoln?" Highfather asked, as he sipped his coffee.

"Sad," Kate said. "He hid it behind humor but if you spent any real time with him, you could feel it leaking out of him. He seemed a good man.

"Allan worked for the president during the war as head of the Union Intelligence Service. That was when the odd reports and accounts began to filter in to him. Tales of cultists trying to summon some nameless ancient god in the swamps outside New Orleans; some giant winged creature with eyes like glowing dinner plates terrorizing the people of West Virginia; a man claiming to be the devil's son performing miracles and inciting riots in Chicago; murderous frog men in Loveland, Ohio; headless Confederate soldiers with flaming sabers overrunning Union positions and slaughtering every man before falling over dead. The list goes on and on.

"Allan Pinkerton has a very precise and detail-oriented mind, but it's fluid as well. He took to investigating these claims, as much to debunk them as to verify them. When he began to see more and more of these fantastic stories that could not be rationally explained, he brought the matter to the president's attention.

President Lincoln was receptive to these fantastic tales since he had nearly died in an assassination attempt by an assailant that could only be described as a Confederate sorcerer, earlier in the year.

"The last document the president signed the night he was assassinated by that sorry secesh, Booth, was an executive order to create the Office of Special Intelligence Resources, Investigation, and Security."

"Sounds fancy enough to beat the Dutch," Highfather said, rising and refreshing both his and Kate's mugs. "And what is all that, exactly?"

Kate took a sip and resumed. "It's an esoteric branch of the Secret Service, which the president also signed into being the night of his death."

"Secret Service works like the Marshals as I understand," Highfather said. "Work any cases they care to: murders, bank robbery, try to hunt down folks passing bum script, too, I gather."

Kate nodded. "Yes, and we carry normal Secret Service credentials. Our department is under the independent authority of Allan Pinkerton and the Pinkerton Detective Agency. We're tasked with investigating activities and individuals of a preternatural nature that may prove to be a threat to the Republic. Allan reports directly to the president and his cabinet. We investigate the things that go bump in the night, Jon. I've been at it for five years."

"I expect if it's anything like around here, you all don't make the papers too often," Highfather said.

Kate laughed. "No, no we don't. In fact, I was declared officially dead two years ago; most of the senior operatives are."

"Dead? Don't you have any family?" Highfather asked.

"No," she said. "I guess Allan is the closest thing I have to that. I'm officially 'buried' in his plot, next to where he will eventually lie. Considering the kind of work I do, it's best I don't have anyone to fret over."

"Sounds like Pinkerton looks after you pretty well," Highfather said, looking straight at Kate as he took another drink. Kate waved her hand dismissively and laughed.

"Oh, no, no. Nothing like that. Mr. Pinkerton is a married man."

"'Mr. Pinkerton,' not 'Allan,'" Highfather said. Kate blushed and nodded.

"Very astute, Sheriff. You are quite a detective yourself."

"None of my business, Kate," Highfather said. "Pretty woman like yourself, man would have to be dead, buried and married not to notice you about."

"Is that so?" she said, smiling and tracing her finger along the rim of the mug. "Well, aren't you quite the charmer, Jon Highfather?"

"So what led you here?" he said.

"Changing the subject?" she said, laughing.

"Getting shot's a damn sight less dangerous than dancing around pretty words with a woman, Kate," he said. "So why are you in Golgotha and why have you been spying on us without at least checking in?"

"A wise man, you are. It's called 'assuming a role,'" she explained. "Allan developed it during the war. You go into enemy territory under a false pretense and with a false identity and cover story. It's very effective, especially for me, as a woman. I walked past you quite a few times as a fancy girl and you never gave me a second glance. That hurt my feelings a little bit, to be honest."

"My heart is as pure as Galahad," Highfather said, grinning. "And my head is as thick as Gibraltar. So you were pretending to be one of the Doves for better part of two months. . . ."He let the implication hang in the air.

"It wasn't the first time I've had to do something like that, Jon," she said. "Doubt it will be the last."

"How can Pinkerton do that to you?" Highfather said. "If he cares about you, loves you, how could he send you into . . ."

"Allan Pinkerton cares about duty first, country second, and everything else third," she said. "He expects the same from his employees. He didn't make me do anything, Jon. This is dirty work, and I knew that going in."

Highfather shook his head. "I'm sorry, Kate. So you were tracking Vellas?"

Warne shook her head. "No, your boy Jim just dropped his name and I knew what he was capable of, so I took off to help you. I lost a good friend and a good partner to that evil bastard a few years back in Saint Louis. Vellas had been killing folks for a long time. We think he slaughtered a settlement near Fort Chambly in the northeast—forty-three men, women and children—all by himself. It felt damn good to see him finally go down."

"Well, if it wasn't Vellas, then who?"

Kate sighed. "This past summer, in the District of Columbia, someone started murdering women. His targets were all public girls, but very high-class ones— the secret mistresses of some of the congressmen and other government officials who reside in the District. The killer sewed his victims' eyes shut as part of the mutilation of the bodies. He claimed five victims. I want him and I think he's here."

"Why here, Kate?" Highfather said. "Not that he wouldn't fit in. But our Dove killer hasn't sewn any eyes shut as far as I know. The only thing in common is they both prey on public girls, and even then it's a long stretch from a senator's girl to working the Dove's Roost."

"All very true," Kate said. "And again, excellent detective work. However, I have one piece of information you are lacking that explains why I've been hiding out and looking for my killer here, Jon. Our District killer's fifth and final victim was murdered in a suite at a very posh hotel in the District. She was slaughtered without a sound. He painted the walls in her blood. . . ."

Kate's face became ashen and Highfather knew. He knew she was in that hotel room, right now, trying to snort the thick coppery stench out of her nostrils as she visited with the ripped and savaged dead. Instinctively, his hands went across the table and took hers. She looked at him as if she didn't quite recognize him. He nodded, his lips moved, but he said nothing, just held her hands, anchoring her, like he had wished someone could have anchored him through all those horrible, frozen tumors of memory. Eden had, Larson had, until they became part of the atrocity gallery's exhibits. Now he had no one to hold his hand as he walked between the screaming, looping paintings. But Kate did, at least this one time. He squeezed her hand and she squeezed his back.

"Does it ever get easier?" she said softly, finally.

He shook his head. "No," he said. "If Pinkerton is your armor, Kate, then use him. You walk this alone, it will eat you alive."

"How do you manage?" she asked.

"I'm a dead man," he said.

She pulled her hands away from his, crossed her chest with them, hugging herself.

"Our District killer, he wrote on the walls in her blood. One word over and over and over."

"Let me guess," Highfather said.

"Golgotha," she said.

The Three of Swords

Chi Mo Duan was cast out of the venerable Green Ribbon Tong of Chinese mystics, assassins and trained killers. Duan had been a member of the tong in Hangzhou and was considered one of the finest killers the secret society had ever produced. His downfall came due to his mental instability and bloodlust against the city's community of Chinese, Muslims and Jews, whom he viewed as "infected." His wanton, bloody killing sprees drew too much attention to an order whose greatest weapons were silence and anonymity.

Duan had the arrogance and presumption to voice his disgust with the direction of the tong to its leader, Ah Kung Ch'eng Huang, within the tong boss's underground sanctum far beneath the squalid Chinese city's streets. For his presumption and lack of respect, he was told to leave China or die, and was warned by Huang himself to stay out of Chinese communities across the globe. He was an outcast and unwelcome.

Duan sailed to America in 1865 and began to wander the railroad camps that dotted the American West, driving rail spikes into the eyes of his thirty-one Chinese and American victims. The Union-Pacific Railroad dicks who unsuccessfully tried to hunt him and stop him came to call him what the Chinamen who feared him called him: Yeng-Wang-Yeh. The Lord and Judge of the Dead.

Duan's was number thirteen. He headed west, inspired by the voice in the dying sun to seek out one who could give him his fill of blood, and of revenge.

The Knight of Wands

"You must do everything through being, nothing through acting," Ch'eng Huang said. "The first and last step of being comes from the breath. Breathe."

Jim sat in the venerable Chinese tong boss and mystic's inner sanctum, cross-legged on the carpeted floor. He was struggling to place his hands in the first mudra position while regulating his breathing. The shadowy room's walls were covered in astrology charts, horoscopes and ancient tapestries. The shelves of the room held all manner and shape of bottles holding numerous questionable liquids, crumbling scrolls, worm-eaten books, and trinkets of brass, glass and jade. A heavy brazier of hot coals and dozens of candles about the room provided the only light. The pouch Jim normally wore about his neck by a leather cord lay in front of him.

"You taught me this the first day," Jim said. "I've been practicing, just like you told me. I breathe real good now."

"No," Huang said. "You practice breathing well. You must make it part of you, part of being, Jim, if you want to open your energy, want to access it."

Jim had been coming to Huang, with his long white beard that fell to his knees, his dark, almost infinite eyes and his robes of green silk, for almost eight months now, to try to understand the artifact that was his birthright—his father's jade eye.

The eye's original owner, Huang said, was Pangu, the god that created the universe. One of Pangu's eyes became the sun and the other, the left eye, Jim's eye, the moon. Apparently the Eye of the Moon had been stolen by another Chinese god and returned to men, and from there had made its way to Billy Negrey.

Huang sat on cushions behind a low table of teak in the center of the opulent room on the second floor of Huang's sprawling saloon, brothel and opium den, the Celestial Palace.

The Palace was the heart of Huang's empire in Golgotha, as the Paradise Falls was Malachi Bick's stronghold. Huang controlled the four or five blocks of narrow maze-like streets that the white locals called Johnny Town, which housed the growing population of Chinese who called Golgotha home.

Jim closed his eyes and tried to relax. He exhaled deeply, feeling it all the way to his abdomen, and then slowly, deeply, filled his lungs again, breathing all the way to his lower stomach. He kept doing this, emptying his mind as Huang had taught him to do. His breathing deepened and thoughts diminished. He was breathing and feeling very good.

He was uncertain how long he was like this before he heard Huang's voice.

"Good," Huang said. "Now bring forth the eye."

He imagined the eye was between and above his eyes. He felt his body fill with light with each deep, cleansing breath. Jim slowly directed the light to the pouch he could see in his mind and slowly the eye rolled out of its own volition. The light lifted it off the floor and the eye arose, held aloft seemingly by nothing. It hovered before the boy's head.

"Very good," Huang said quietly. "You are doing very well, Jim. Now, today," Huang continued, "we will work toward using the eye to open doorways. It is a gateway to many different worlds and powers, if you can unlock the proper doors."

"Is that why you're always talking about keys?" Jim said.

"Chi," Huang corrected, "and in a manner of speaking, Chi can be used to open many doors, within and without."

"The eye ain't never done nothing, 'cept at night in the moonlight," Jim said. As he spoke, the eye faltered in the air before him. He gasped and tried to right it. It dropped a few inches, then remained hovering.

"The eye is tied to the moon, true," Huang said. "But it is also tied to the sun, its brother eye. The moon reflects the sun. It will work in the day, but it requires more effort on your part to make it do so, Jim. Now stop diverting your attention, stop jabbering. Breathe, be."

When Jim had first arrived in Golgotha, he'd worried that Ch'eng Huang had wanted to steal the eye. The eye; his father's pistol from the war; and Jim's horse, Promise, were all he had left of his family and his life before he began his run. Talking with the old man, at the urging of the mysterious Malachi Bick, had proven to be the right thing to do and Jim had been able to use the eye to save Golgotha and possibly even the world. That part seemed very unreal even now, a year later. Folks in Golgotha tended to make their way through a disaster and then try as hard as they could to forget all about it, cover it up, hide it. Jim didn't agree with doing that, but he could understand it.

Huang said the eye had nearly infinite power but that it could only be unlocked by a Wu, a trained sorcerer, whatever that meant exactly, so Jim had asked Huang for instruction. He had come a long way, mostly learning how to calm himself and to focus his mind. He had begun the long and treacherous path of joining his mind to the mudras, the finger meditations that Huang said were a critical component of unlocking the jade eye's secrets. Now, almost a year in, Jim saw he had so much further to go, but he was determined to master the eye, and to make his pa proud.

"I want you to imagine the eye in the center of your forehead, as we discussed," Huang said. "I want you to feel the coolness of the glass against your skin, feel it connected to you."

"Okay," Jim said after a few moments.

"Now, imagine standing on a plain. Feel the wind move around you, through you. Feel the wind caress your face, your hair. Hold that image, that feeling, don't let it fall away."

Jim's eyes were closed. He felt the dry desert wind kiss him. He was riding Promise across the scrubland at the edge of the desolate 40-Mile. It was warm, but not hot. He could feel the grit on his pursed lips and smell the leather of the reins. He was there; the rhythm of Promise's gallop was hypnotic.

"Good," a distant voice said. "Now I want you to open the eye. Imagine opening your other eyes wide, but you are only opening the jade eye. Wide . . . wider. Feel the wind pass through you, through the eye. Wide open now. . . ."

Jim saw through the jade eye. The world was painted in lines of force, cause, effect and color, brilliant, prismatic strands of thread tied to everything. Swirling winds of gold, crimson, azure and emerald roared, vibrating the humming, resonant cords. The eye saw the music of the world.

Jim felt arms about his waist. Soft, slender, strong arms warmer than the desert wind that was against his face. He felt a head resting on his shoulder. He turned and saw long brown hair fluttering , shining, in the sun. Constance Stapleton, her wide, brown eyes looking at him as she raised her head from his shoulder. She looked beautiful, but a little sad. She was saying something but he couldn't hear. Constance leaned closer to his ear.

"Wider . . . ," Huang's faraway voice said. "Open."

Jim's eyes opened. He was back in Huang's chamber. Huang had placed a large cylinder of a green candle on the low table between them. Its wick was trailing black smoke. A few of the papers behind the old man fluttered as did the wisps of his beard. The jade eye began to drop and Jim held out his hand. It fell into his palm with a soft thud. Jim closed his hand around the eye and looked at Huang.

"Adequate," Huang said, his face quickly recovering from some surprise. "A good start."

One of Huang's men, a member of the notorious Green Ribbon Tong, brought tea and cakes. Tattoos festooned his arms. Guns and axes hung from his belt as he entered and exited like a servile ghost. Huang prepared the tea for himself and his young guest.

"So last night, at the church, I got an idea to use the eye to try to find the murderer of these women," Jim said as he accepted a cup from Huang. "And it worked! I made all the lights in the church flare up and found him. He got away, but the eye did what I wanted it to do . . . sort of."

"The eye's power comes from the moon," Huang said. "Moonlight is a redirection of the sun's true light. The eye's powers are tied to misdirection, distortion, mystery and reflection. It is good you are growing more confident in its use, Jim."

"Well, I wanted to ask you," Jim said. "The first thing I learned the eye could do was let me speak to haints—y'know, the dead. Last year I was able to talk to Mr. Stapleton and he helped identify his killer for us."

"Yes?" Huang said.

"I tried the same trick with the two dead girls," Jim said, "last night, when her body and Molly's were both over at Clay Turlough's place, but I got nothing. I was wondering if I was doing something wrong?"

"First of all, what the eye does is no trick," Huang said, somewhat indignant. "It is a power of the highest order, tied to the creation of the universe. Second, these women, they were of a low station, yes? Few ties to their homes and families? Such lonely and isolated people, ones at the fringes of society, they have few anchors to hold their spirit here and few to miss them, to mourn them. Also they were torn from this world in a most savage and horrible way, correct?"

"Yes," Jim said coldly, his jaw set. Ch'eng Huang nodded.

"You have a great capacity for compassion, boy," Huang said. "Have a care. Emotion is the fuel that drives a sorcerer, gives him power when all other resources have failed him. Too much fuel ignited devours everything."

"What happens to people like that, fringe people, when they die?" Jim asked.

"The same thing that happens to everyone else," Huang replied, "exactly what they have trained their souls to expect. Now tell me of your vision from today."

"It was like I was there, in the desert," Jim said. "At first it was me imagining what you were talking about—the wind."

"Yes," Huang said, nodding. "I wanted to see if you could open the door to the House of the Tiger, the land of the wind. I have undertaken your horoscope and you are born under the tiger. Though your element is wood, not wind, you were successful. You did very well, Jim. However, there was something else that happened?"

"There was a girl with me," Jim said. "She wasn't, then she was."

"I see," Huang said, smiling thinly. "And how old are you now, Master Negrey?" he asked, already knowing the answer to the minute and the second.

"Sixteen," Jim said, sipping his tea. "Last month."

"Ah," Huang said. "Well, that explains the girl, doesn't it?"

Jim reddened. "No, no. I knew her. It was Constance, Widow Stapleton's daughter. It felt like a memory more than anything."

Huang set down his tea and stroked his beard. "The eye sees into all the worlds. It is possible you opened a door to some other world as well, perhaps the Realm of Dreams, where the God of the Dreams, the Duke of Zhou, holds court. He is lord over the dream-eaters and the nightmare carrion—the Baku."

"So I shared a dream with Constance?" Jim said. Huang nodded. "How do you know all these things and how can they all be real? The God my ma and pa taught me about? The gods you talk about as if they live down the street. Mutt's 'family'—the spirits the Indians talk to all the time. How can all that be?"

Huang opened his palms and gestured about the room. "This world is the stage. Mortals are the performers in the show, and it was written for them. Your world is a house full of doors, Jim. This is part of the reason the eye has such great power, it opens doors."

"'Your world,'" Jim said, leaning forward. "Not *our* world. Who are you, Mr. Huang? What are you? How come you never go out of Johnny Town, ever?"

Huang smiled. "Part of the true power of sorcery is opening to understanding and the thrill of discovery. Tell me, Jim, what do you think I am? Tell me."

Jim regarded him without fear, with calm discernment. "You lead your people," he said. "No, you protect them. Not just here, all over. But you never leave Golgotha. . . . You are some kind of guardian for Chinese folks."

"You are very astute, Jim," Huang said. "My people have a myth, a legend of a god who shares my name—Ch'eng Huang—the God of Cities, Moats and Walls, Divine Magistrate of Heaven and Earth, God of Ramparts. It is said he is everywhere my people gather in numbers, here in Golgotha and in the railroad camps where my people toil to build the bloodlines of this rowdy, raw, wondrous land. He is in the streets of every Chinatown, and every city, every village in China. He is said to have been born a mortal whose service to his home, his community, elevated him to godhood upon death. Ch'eng Huang protects the homes and businesses of the Chinese people in this new world as he does in their ancient homeland."

"Are you? You mean to say . . . ," Jim said.

Huang gestured with open palms.

"I simply tell you a story of my homeland, and the interesting coincidence that I share the name of this divine and magnificent being."

"So why do you stay in Johnny Town—uh, I mean in your neighborhoods all the time?"

Huang laughed for the first time since Jim had met him. It was a warm and terrible sound all at once.

"Ah, my dear boy, words like 'Johnny' mean nothing to me. They only have power to harm or diminish if that is allowed in the mind and heart. People fear the alien, the different. Whites fear my people as my people fear and distrust yours. It is human nature, mortal nature. Never let words wound you, Jim. The core of humanity is too bright, too resolute to bend to fear.

"I remain in the communities of my people because that is where my . . . authority is absolute. Past those borders other powers hold sway, just as their power diminishes within my realm."

Jim was quiet. He picked up the eye off the table. "This is really the eye of a god. A god. It's too much to figure out. Makes my head hurt."

Huang nodded. "As wise a response to the infinite as any I have encountered. This is a bright new age of mortals. Look at all that has been accomplished . . . the marvels! You've created and changed gods, bent them to your imaginations: electricity, the telegraph, the locomotive, steam power. It's your time, Jim. The direct interference of other powers in this world, it would only hold you all back."

"If that's the case, then why did those monks curse my dad with this damn eye?" Jim asked. "It drove him half crazy, gave him near constant pain and never did a single trick for him, as far as I know. Why do it to him? Why interfere and give him a god's eye when he was just a simple man, a decent man."

"As I said before, your father must have been a remarkable man to endure the stress of having something so vast and powerful joined to him physically," Huang said. "The obvious reason that the monks brought it to America and entrusted it to your father was that it was in danger of falling into the hands of someone who would use the eye's power for evil. They sought out a good human being, one devoted to life and humanity. They found your father. It was an honor, and a terrible duty."

"When I talked to Pa through the eye after he passed, he told me I needed to keep it safe," Jim said.

"Yes," Huang said. "In the wrong hands, the eye could lay waste to the Middle Kingdom, to this world. The Monkey King, Sun Wukong, stole it from Chang'e, the Goddess of the Moon, to give to humanity as a gift. However, as with most things involving the Monkey King, he didn't think it through very well and soon lost interest in what became of the eye. It fell to mortals to keep it safe. It fell to your father and now it falls to you, Jim."

Jim slid the eye back into the pouch and replaced the cord about his neck. "Keep it safe from who?"

Huang grew silent. He examined the tea leaves in his cup. "That is a question for another day. You are making acceptable progress. . . ."

"You said I did good," Jim interrupted, smiling a little.

"Adequate," Huang said. "You have your feet on the path of sorcery. We will see if you can stay on it. If not, then I still foresee you could make a half-decent Fu Yao Da Chia. "

"Come again?" Jim said.

"A hunter of demons—a hero, or sorts," Huang said. "Don't let it go to your head, boy. Demon hunters tend to flunk out of every respectable enterprise before they fall into the profession. They all possess one singular trait, though."

"What's that?" Jim asked.

"They are insufferably persistent."

"Demon hunter it is," Jim said.

Huang stood as Jim did.

"I have not yet given up that you may claim the title of Wu, one day," Huang said.

"Are you really a god, Mr. Huang, sir?"

"No," Huang said. "I am a crazy old man who has learned a few conjuring tricks. Does that make you feel any better?"

"It would if I believed you," Jim said.

"Belief is a wonderful and terrible thing," Huang said.

Walking through Johnny Town, the sun flashing off his badge, Jim observed the bustling crowds of Chinese populating the maze-like streets.

More Chinese were coming every day to Golgotha, looking for work in the mines, anywhere really, as the grand race of the transcontinental railroad came to an end. There was still railroad work to be done—Jim had once considered that life himself—but the massive numbers that had been needed to connect east and west were being let go.

Laundry lines connected many of the buildings in Johnny Town, with clothing drying and fluttering in the dry desert wind. Old men sat outside Tieshan Tehuai's market and café, talking softly and watching the river of faces drift by. Children ran, laughed and played. One little boy stopped in front of Jim.

"*Huìzhì niúzǎi!*" the little boy said and, lighting-fast, drew a finger. "*Pēng!*" the boy said, unloading his finger on the hapless grinning deputy.

Jim winced and doubled over, clutching his chest with a gasp.

"Awww, you got me!" he exclaimed. The little boy laughed.

"*Nǐ shì yīgè qiángdà de hǎo qiú, xiǎo niúzǎi,*" Jim said, with many awkward pauses. He ruffled the boy's hair. Huang had been teaching him Chinese and Jim tried to pick it up anytime he could. Highfather and Mutt knew a smattering, too, but Jim had taken to the language very quickly. Huang said it might have something to do with possessing the eye. The boy laughed at Jim's clumsy attempt to speak Chinese, and stuck out his tongue. Jim laughed again.

The boy's mother ran over and grabbed him by the arm "*Yufi! Fù zhèyàng de shíjiān, bùyào làngfèi!*" she said, then to Jim, "So sorry, Deputy Jim. Yufi like you very much. Hear stories about you!"

"Stories?" Jim said. "About me? Huh? Well, I like Yufi too. *Xièxiè. Yǒu yīgè hěn hǎo de yītiān.*"

The mother was a little politer, but it was still obvious to Jim his lingo stunk.

He walked on. The first time he had come to Johnny Town it was in the dead of night and it had terrified and confused him. Jim had learned since he had come to Golgotha that the few streets that made up Johnny Town on the maps didn't even begin to adequately describe the narrow labyrinth-like streets that sometimes seemed to go on for miles when they simply couldn't, as though they shifted and changed of their own accord; how doors and alleyways seemed to disappear from one moment to the next. It was even more byzantine at night. He had slowly discovered if you focused on a destination, you would eventually reach it, but that the route might be different each time. A story he'd heard from several folks in town, including Mutt, was that a drunken cowboy had shot a woman and child in the heat of an argument gone wrong. He fled into Johnny Town to hide from the law. They found his emaciated body three weeks later in a Johnny Town alley. He had died of starvation and dehydration. Jim was pretty much the only person with a star on his chest that regularly patrolled Johnny Town. Word had gotten out to the Johnny Town residents that Ch'eng Huang was mentoring the boy. The locals liked the idea of having one of Golgotha's lawmen patrolling their streets alongside Huang's private army of enforcers, the Green Ribbon Tong.

Today he could feel a little tension on the streets due to the murders even here in Ch'eng Huang's kingdom. Jim hoped his presence was helping to keep the peace.

Jim walked down Bick Street—Johnny Town's equivalent to Main Street— and crossed over Prosperity Street and out of Huang's domain, walking past town hall and the office of the *Golgotha Scribe* newspaper. As he walked, he overheard bits of conversations in the air, like flies. Some were talk about the "whore killings," others were gossiping about the upcoming mayoral election next year. A few were still puzzling over the mystery of the house on chicken legs that had appeared overnight a few months back and then up and walked out into the desert, not to be seen again. A lot of talk involved Malachi Bick and the shady deals he had done over the years and all the dirty dealing he had undertaken since the big trouble last year. Folks knew he had put a hurting to Auggie Shultz's business and many others.

Jim knew it was Bick who had gathered him, the sheriff, Mutt and Harry Pratt together to save the town last year from the thing down in the mines. Bick's family had resided here for centuries to protect these lands and make sure the thing in the mines never escaped to wreck the world. It was Bick who had given the evil they were fighting a face and helped come up with a plan to defeat it.

Jim wondered, if the townsfolk knew they all owed their lives and their families' lives to Malachi Bick, would they still lick their chops to see him fall? Most likely. People loved to see the high and mighty hit the dirt. And Bick had taken advantage of a lot of people when they were down and out. Maybe he did deserve a little ass-whooping.

Where did payback end exactly? Charlie Upton had murdered Jim's Pa. Jim killed Charlie. One day Jim might get shot or hanged for what he did to Charlie and someone like Mutt or Jon Highfather might seek revenge in his name. How far back did the blood flow? When was it enough? Could anything ever get square?

Jim paused at the corner of Main and Prosperity. Constance Stapleton, looking even prettier than in his vision, was talking to two of her friends, Harriet Rees and Jacoba Thorborg. The three girls were laughing. Constance had a basket of clean laundry on her hip. She looked over and saw Jim and said something to her girlfriends. They looked over at Jim, too, and then laughed, waved and departed, headed down Main. Constance crossed the street toward him, smiling.

"Deputy," she said. "Just come from visiting your girl over at the Dove's Roost, or headed over there now?"

Jim got redder. "She ain't my girl," he said, "and no, just making my rounds over by Johnny Town."

"Just teasing you," Constance said. "People getting ready for Thanksgiving. You got plans?"

"Just eating at Mrs. Proctor's and then I guess do my rounds. Not much for church," Jim said.

"My mother and I will be eating there too," Constance said. "So guess I can view this legendary appetite of yours firsthand."

"Shoot," Jim said. "It ain't all that!"

"Well, that is not what Mutt or Mrs. Proctor say," Constance said. "They say you unhinge your jaw like a rattlesnake and shovel it in!"

They both laughed. It felt good. He looked at her. She had a faint line of freckles across her slender nose and her brown eyes were huge and bright. A few stray hairs fell from under her bonnet.

"What?" Constance said, looking away. "Why you staring at me?"

"Nothin'," Jim said. "Sorry. You still Jess Muller's girl?"

It was Constance's turn to blush. "I most certainly am not anyone's girl, Deputy." She handed him her basket and Jim took it. Constance crossed the street again, headed down Main. Jim followed beside her.

"Heard you were sweet on him," Jim said.

Constance looked away. "Jess is a fine fella, but he's . . . No, I gave him the mitten," she said. "Why you so interested?"

"I had a kind of . . . a dream," Jim said, "about you. We were . . ."

"Riding in the desert," Constance said. "Together, on your horse."

"How did you know that?" Jim asked.

"I have . . . dreams, since all that mess last year. I have very . . . strange . . . dreams. I dreamt that one last night, you and me."

"Well, I was wondering if you'd like to go ride tomorrow. My dream was . . . it was real nice, and I'd be honored if you'd consider accompanying me."

"I'll need to get my mother's blessing," Constance said. "She'll want to talk to you. What time?"

"Tomorrow morning," Jim said. "I'll come by the laundry, if that's all right? I figured we could ride up Argent in the morning, while it was still cool, if that is okay with you and your ma. You can be back in time for chores and lunch."

They arrived in front of Shultz's General Store and paused.

"It was cool in the dream," Constance said. "But it wasn't Argent Mountain. Windy but not hot. It was a nice dream, at first anyway."

"What do you mean?" Jim said. Constance took the basket out of his arms.

"My dreams don't usually end well," she said. "It's probably nothing. I'd love to go, if I can, Deputy."

"Jim," he said. "Please call me Jim."

"I'd love to go, Jim," she said, smiling. "See you tomorrow. Don't get shot tonight and stay clear of that Dove's Roost."

Jim laughed. "Yes, ma'am." He opened the door to Auggie's store for her.

"See you tomorrow," she said, and disappeared inside the cool darkness of the store.

Jim headed farther down Main, toward the cut-over for the jail. He was so happy he forgot to wonder how Constance's dream ended.

The Three of Swords

If you're riding through Kansas and the sun is setting and you're thirsty, hungry or you need a place to lay down your weary bones to rest, then the quaint little tavern run by a family of German emigrants, just off the road in a secluded stretch of countryside, will seem like providence.

The Brecht Family Lodge offers the lonely traveler all manner of amenities—a roaring hearth, good hearty stout brewed in the traditional German manner, good food and a beautiful barmaid. Guests enjoy the hospitality of the lodge so much, in fact, that many of them decide to stay forever. At last count twelve, including a circuit judge and a little girl, are resting comfortably in the garden behind the lodge. An indeterminate number of patrons ended up as garments or as meals for the masters and mistresses of the Lodge—the Brechts.

The innkeeper, Herr Brecht, or Pa, as he insists guests call him, is six foot four, and fat, with thinning blond hair. He usually has a bloody meat cleaver in his brown-stained hands and can use it like a conductor wields a baton. He enjoys making sausage; don't ask him where the meat comes from.

His wife, known only as Ma Brecht, is even larger in size, especially girth, and speaks no known human language. She occasionally whispers in Pa's ears. She is very good with a shotgun, wielding it one-handed and making it look like a child's toy. Her dry, grayish skin has a scaly, almost reptilian, cast to it.

The couple's son, Ernst, is an imbecile, with a pointed malformation of the tips of both his ears, known as elf ear, and eyes that look red in the proper light. However, the young man is strong and lean of body and is a prodigy with a sledgehammer, the family's method of choice for disposing of guests.

And then there is the siren, the oracle, the Brechts' baby daughter, Hilde. Blond, beautiful and with a pleasing figure, the young woman claims supernatural powers of prophecy and fortune-telling. To some degree, these claims are accurate, as the family's longtime business partner and patron whispers obscenities and portents into Hilde's ear, while she giggles, seeming to listen to empty air. Hilde carries a butcher knife that she is very capable with, once using it to gut a mountain man who resisted Ernst's hammer and was trying to escape while brandishing his impressive blade, called a Kansas City Toothpick. She buried his own knife in his anus while he bled out from a slit carotid on the tavern floor.

The lodge is the third such establishment the Brechts' silent business partner has set them up in. Each has been a huge success, at least by the standards of the management and their patron.

So when Hilde saw signs and messages in the tarot cards she cast one late October night, she told the family they were being summoned by their business partner out west. The family eagerly departed, burning the lodge with four slumbering guests in their very comfy beds, as they had done with their other taverns. Each of the Brechts possessed one. They numbered twenty-two through twenty-five.

The Five of Swords

Augustus Shultz entered Malachi Bick's office, escorted by one of Bick's men. The shopkeeper was still wearing his stained work apron under his coat, having decided to see Bick on the spur of the moment. The emotions churning in Auggie couldn't be held in check any longer and he knew what he had to do.

It was the day after Gillian's discovery, of his and Clay's nocturnal activities, of Clay's revelations. Auggie was exhausted. And today, today had been the final straw.

"Mr. Shultz," Bick said, standing from behind his desk. "An unexpected pleasure. Please, may I offer you a libation?"

Auggie stood awkwardly before Bick's desk, his dirty hands clenching and unclenching.

"Mr. Bick, the men . . . The men from your bank, your men . . . They took over half of my shipment of merchandise that arrived today, right off the wagon."

"Yes," Bick said. "My people calculated that those items sold at the Argent Mining Company Store would be sufficient to cover the arrears on your loans to me, Mr. Shultz."

"Yes," Auggie said, "but if I can't sell those goods in my store, how will I ever catch up and pay you off, Mr. Bick?"

"The current arrangement seems to be working out fine," Bick said. "You seemed quite confident that the boom would increase your sales when you spoke to my people at the bank about taking that loan, Mr. Shultz."

Auggie's fists clenched again. "Why . . . why are you doing this?" Auggie looked at the floor, the blood rushing to his face making him flush. "You know as well as I that you've taken away half my customers with your establishment up at the camp. You know that, yes?"

"What I know is that you have an obligation to me, Mr. Shultz," Bick said, sitting back behind his desk. "You need to honor that."

"A man like you, a great man," Auggie said. "With so many fine things, so much money and power, why would you hurt so many people, Mr. Bick? You have no need to. You could live well, better than most, the rest of your life and still forget every penny you have bled out of the people in Golgotha. I don't understand. You, people like you, will never know what it feels like to . . ."

"To feel helpless?" Bick interrupted, a jagged edge of anger in the black-garbed businessman's voice. "To think that those who have power over your very existence have abandoned you? Don't care or worse, are amused by your plight? Was that what you were going to tell me I don't understand, Mr. Shultz? I assure you that I do, and far deeper than you can ever comprehend."

Auggie was silent, but his eyes burned with anger. Finally he spoke. "Then if you understand it, why do you do it yourself, Mr. Bick? Why hurt so many people? Why hurt me?"

"Because, Mr. Shultz," Bick said. "When one is a predator, beset on all sides by those who would destroy him, you cannot afford to show weakness."

"What you call weakness is mercy," Auggie said.

"What you call mercy I call operating under a vulnerability," Bick said. "I tried it once. It did not end well. I can never afford to do that again, Mr. Shultz. Once nearly ruined everything. Good day."

Auggie remained. Looking down. His hands ached from the pressure of his squeezing them in anger. "Predators can be pulled down, *ja*, Mr. Bick?" Auggie said. His hand slipped into his coat. He felt the cool, smooth steel of the gun against his hot, rough palm. *"Genug hungrige Wölfe können sich einen Bären, ja?"*

"You can leave of your own volition," Bick said. "Or I can have my men beat you and throw you onto Main Street. The choice is yours."

Auggie began to pull the pistol out of his pocket, to shoot this smug bastard in his smug face. He paused, the gun remaining hidden. He felt Gillian's soothing presence, felt her arms around him, heard her voice. He felt her horror at what he was about to do, saw her waste away, dying with him as he danced at the end of a rope. No. He could never do that to her, never. He let go of the gun and turned to walk out Bick's door. He paused as he was leaving.

"I was like you once," Auggie said. "So afraid, so lonely and bitter. So terrified of losing something, someone, that I held them so tight that I almost crushed them, yes? I forgot how to live. I was lucky enough to have someone to remind me, to drag me back into the light. Be careful you don't chase your salvation away, Mr. Bick. Good day, sir." Auggie walked out of the Paradise Falls and headed for Gillian's house. There was something he needed to do. It was time he began taking his own advice.

The Dove killer's abandoned wagon was parked in front of the jail. Clay had driven it over from his workshop, where he had spent the evening examining it. Now as curious passersby wandered past them, Highfather, Mutt, Kate and Jim stood on the porch and listened to Clay's findings.

"There was dust in the bed," Clay said. "Consistent with the rock dust we found on the victim in the alleyway and on the girl killed in the church. It is different in composition from the dust found in the desert. I'd hazard both victims were in this wagon at one point," Clay said. "I also used a presumptive test developed by the brilliant German chemist, Herr Schonbein, to ascertain that there was blood in the back of this wagon—even though it had been cleaned several times. This, I believe, is the conveyance used to move the murdered women about from the sites of their deaths to the sites of their exhibition."

"So we find the owner of this wagon and these horses and we got our fella," Jim said. Highfather shook his head.

"Doubt it will be that easy," the sheriff said. "If he's fine with ditching the wagon, I doubt it's his."

Clay nodded. "I concur, Jonathan. He's too clever for that by half."

"Maybe we can trace it to him, by finding the owner," Kate said. "If it's been stolen or missing, I imagine someone will report it sooner or later."

Mutt walked off the porch of the jail and sidled over to the wagon. He leaned on the backboard and seemed to be concentrating on something. Clay went on.

"I also researched astrology and astronomy and discovered some interesting phenomena that might explain his rush to claim a new victim each night."

"Really?" Kate said. "What?"

"There is a conjunction of Venus, Saturn and the sun at the winter solstice that is approaching," Clay said. "It signifies a need for love, paradoxically difficult to fulfill because of an imbalanced self-image. In such a tangle, hatred and desire can be knotted up. It also tends to be a time of growing strength for those who possess an insensitivity to disagreeable things, kind of a moral blank slate."

"Sounds like our man," Highfather said. Clay nodded.

"Add to that the discovery of the asteroid 111 Ate in August," he said.

"Named for the Greek goddess of mischief and destruction, and the appearance of asteroid 112 Iphigenia in September. Iphigenia is named for the Greek princess sacrificed by her father. This madman thinks the heavens themselves are preordaining his acts. The stars are tumblers unlocking some horrible mystery for him and now is his time to act. I wouldn't be surprised if the number of victims and their profession has something to do with his occult obsessions as well. There are numerous prostitute goddesses in mythologies all about the world."

"Amazing," Kate said. "I'm impressed, Mr. Turlough."

"Observation, data collection and deduction," Clay said with a dismissive wave. "Simple reasoning, ma'am."

"Blood," Mutt said, sniffing and stepping away from the truck. "Fresh and human. Also some chemical smells—I think the victims might have been drugged—and blasting powder. I picked up all those on the bed."

"Stone dust and blasting powder," Highfather said. "Sounds like the mines."

"Molly was working for the Nail," Jim said. "And he's one of the crooks running things up at the mining camps." "So was Rica," Kate said. "They were both moonlighting behind Bick's back for the Nail to make extra scratch. I think we may have found our pattern, gentlemen."

"Thank you, Clay," Highfather said. "Can you give us a little bit more help? I want you to help us lay a trap for this lunatic tonight."

"I don't believe that the moon is a factor," Clay said.

"What?" Highfather said.

"You called him a lunatic," Clay said. "I don't see any indications that the moon is a contributing factor to his crimes. And yes, I will help as best I can, Jonathan. I have a previous engagement this afternoon I must attend to, but I will meet up with you back here by, say, four o'clock?"

"Sounds good," Highfather said. "Oh, and Clay?"

"Yes?" Clay said.

"Your face? Your hand and arms? The scars, they're all better, gone?"

"Yes," Clay said. There was an awkward silence.

"Um . . . How?" Jim offered.

"I just stopped picking at it, and it healed right up," Clay said. The old inventor climbed up onto the wagon and drove it down Dry Well Road without another word.

"Well, that cleared things up," Mutt said as he watched Clay ride away. "At least he's happier than I've seen him in a long spell. If you're going to be crazy, it's better to be happy and crazy."

"True," Highfather said. "All right, we'll meet up at four and figure the best way to catch our man tonight. Agreed?"

"Jonathan," Mutt said. "Can I have a word, private like?"

The two men stepped away from the porch while Kate and Jim talked. They walked down the street toward the old well.

"I . . . I kind of made some other plans for tonight," Mutt said. The confident, almost cocky deputy seemed suddenly very awkward to Highfather. "I . . . I can cancel them if you need me tonight. It's just . . ."

"Oh my God," Highfather said, a smile coming to his face. "You did it. You asked her, you finally asked her."

"What the hell you mean 'finally,'" Mutt said. "Look, I can just tell her that—"

"Go," Highfather said. "We can handle this without you for one night, Mutt. Go."

"Jonathan, I'm serious, I can just—" Mutt said.

"You ain't squirming out of this," Highfather said. "We got Agent Warne here to help us. It will be okay."

"You sure?" Mutt said.

"I'm happy for you," Highfather said. "She's good for you. I've seen it. Between her and the boy," Highfather nodded back toward Jim, "you've changed a hell of a lot from the drunken hell-raiser I had to drag out of the Paradise Falls, what was it, four years ago?"

Both men chuckled.

"I kicked your ass that night," Mutt said, grinning.

"The hell you did," Highfather said. "I seem to recall you ending up in my jail cell."

"I was tired," Mutt said. "I needed a place to sleep off the exertion of kicking your ass."

They laughed again. Both men paused in their walk.

"I hope it goes real good for you tonight," Highfather said. "You both deserve that."

"Thank you, Jonathan," Mutt said. "I was wondering if I could ask your help with one more thing. . . ."

The Three of Swords

The war never ended for Victory Ferrell. Nosirree. He relived it nightly. The slightest sound, the faintest motion, and he was awake, ready for some bluecoat doodle to sneak up and try to slit his throat. He stayed awake for two weeks once because he knew the blue-bellies were out there waiting for him to close his eyes, ease his mind, so they could strike at him.

That was fine with him, though. He liked the war just fine, thank you. He loved it, in fact. He liked the killing, the occasional fire and pillaging, the chaos. He took trophies, a collection of Yankee eyeballs and tongues. Kept them in wax-sealed jars. He liked to rape their women, even after he shot them in the head. Sometimes he had sex with the wounds on the dead bodies of the soldiers when there wasn't a Union whore to be had. It didn't make him no kinda sissy, no sir, even if he did cornhole a few of the bodies.

They said it was because of the things he did, of what he did without orders, without regret, "violated the rules of war and human decency"; that's what his nancy of a commanding officer said. They wanted to hang him, but they needed men too badly and they said some bad things about Victory not being smart enough to understand what he was doing was wrong. So they sent him to the rear of the lines to shovel horseshit and do laundry, like a damn woman.

When the war ended and the cowards and quitters lost, Victory refused to accept the surrender. He began to wander the roads, starting out in Tennessee and going wherever it told him to go. Anyone unlucky enough to cross his path with a kind word to say about the fucking Union, or fucking blowhard U. S. Grant, or even those Southerners who had just up and rolled over like a licked dog and were "trying to get on with their lives," they all met up with Victory's guns and knives. He liked to break into lonely farmhouses and tie the families up, hold war crime trials, spend a few extra days with the wife and kids, before he moved on down the road. In the chill of late October on the roads of Pennsylvania, he was visited in dreams and portents by a pillar of golden, divine fire that told him where he needed to go and what he needed to do. He began to walk west. Victory's was the eleventh.

Death

Everyone dining in Delmonico Hauk's small restaurant grew quieter when Clay Turlough entered. Hauk, a newcomer to Golgotha, had built and opened a small restaurant across the street from the old dried–up well at the end of the road bearing its name. He'd bought the late Odd Tom's old house and built his very popular restaurant on the land adjacent to it.

Clay was dressed in a dirty, collarless white shirt, suspenders and filthy canvas work pants. His boots, while scraped with a knife, still carried the pungent odor of horse manure. Clay wore a black sack coat of decent quality. His hair was its usual eruption of gray tufts from his spotted pate. The surprise was partially Clay's appearance in a public eating establishment and partly in what was missing from Clay's disheveled appearance. The deeply pitted, scarlet-colored scars from Clay's burns on his hands, arms and face all seemed to be completely gone.

Clay navigated through the pattern of tables, seemingly oblivious to the stares and the gawking faces. He sat down across from Gillian Proctor, who looked at him with a pinched, almost sad expression.

"Grub any good here?" Clay asked as he sat and poured himself a glass of water from a pitcher on the table next to a small vase of violet wildflowers. Gillian set her menu down.

"Very," she said. "Thank you for coming, Clayton. You and I have to discuss a few things. Are you sure this is the best place for such a delicate and morbid discussion?"

"I had to come down here to tell Jon Highfather what I gleaned from looking over that wagon the Dove killer used last night," Clay said. "And then we have that thing to do this afternoon, so I figured, I hear this place has decent chow, so why not kill two birds with one stone. I can be discreet." He picked up Gillian's menu. "So are you telling Jon Highfather what I've been about? Grave robbing and such?"

Gillian gestured with her hands for Clay to lower his voice. Clay nodded and went on a bit lower, but it was plain to Gillian that Clay had no idea how to comport himself around people in public.

"If you do they will run me out of town as sure as I'm sitting here," he said. "Not to worry, I won't say a peep about Auggie being involved. I promise."

"Clay, what you told us last night, what you showed us, what you did with Gerta," Gillian said. "You are certain that there is no danger in using it, in doing what you've done?"

Clay waved dismissively. "Pishposh! What possible problem could there be, Gillian? This is the greatest scientific breakthrough of the nineteenth century. What problems could I have possibly overlooked?"

"The kind of problems you wouldn't even think about," she said. "The kind that blindside you because you don't understand as much about life as you think you do, Clayton. Everything isn't a problem to be figured out and solved, especially people, especially when you are talking about something like immortality."

Last night, when Gillian had confronted Augustus and Clay about their nocturnal activity, things had gotten very heated, very quickly. Especially once Auggie discovered that Clay had not allowed Gerta to perish in the fire last year.

"What do you mean, 'eternal life'?" Gillian asked, shaking her head. "You are talking nonsense, Clayton. All you are doing is tinkering with things that got a lot of people killed last year. Those worm things . . ."

Auggie grabbed Clay with a roar and lifted the smaller man off the ground by his collar. "*Gottverdammt!* What the hell did you do, Clay?" Auggie shouted, and smashed Clay against the wall of the barn. "You couldn't let her rest in peace, could you? You couldn't let me have the peace of mind that she was finally happy? No! You had to tinker, you had to meddle! Damn you, Clay!"

Clay was red-faced and obviously in great pain from the jostling Auggie was subjecting him to. Gillian had never seen Auggie so angry, so out of control.

"No!" Clay screamed back at Auggie. "No, damn you! Damn you for just giving up on her! I couldn't just let her fade into memory! I couldn't! Even if you could! You never loved her! Never!"

Auggie smashed Clay against the wall again. Clay drove his bony fist into the side of Auggie's head. Gillian saw all reason leave both men's eyes as Auggie growled and threw Clay across the barn, hurling him into his workbench. The frail old inventor and his tools crashed and tumbled to the floor.

"She was my wife, Clay!" Auggie bellowed, tears of rage and pain streaming down his crimson face. "When she died I wanted to die with her, for her. She was an experiment for you, a test subject, *ja*? How dare you tell me I didn't care for her! She meant no more to you than these poor girls whose bodies you desecrate now! Her soul was at peace and you, you took that away from her, you arrogant bastard!"

"Shut the hell up!" Clay snarled and charged Auggie low, driving his shoulder into the portly shopkeep's stomach and legs, knocking Auggie off his feet and onto the straw-covered floor of the barn. Clay smashed Auggie again and again with his fists and the bigger man blocked them as best he could with his forearms while lying on his back. Occasionally Clay got through and landed a solid blow to Auggie's face.

"You shut your mouth, you stupid, blundering fool!" Clay barked as he punched his friend, over and over. Hot tears burned and blurred Clay's eyes as well. "She's the best human being I ever met on this cesspool of a planet! You were supposed to love her always, not just till her meat failed her, you sanctimonious hypocrite—all prayers and hymns to some imaginary God that does nothing for any of us! Nothing! You left her in darkness and patted yourself on the back that she was having tea in some Bible-school heaven! You idiot! Damn you, Auggie Shultz! Damn you to your childish Hell!"

Auggie bellowed and drove a massive right to Clay's chin; the smaller man flew off Auggie's chest and crumpled to the floor. Both men clambered off the floor and began to circle each other, fists raised. Gillian started to interpose herself between the two old friends, but something in her made her stop. This was old blood being let, poison drawn. They both needed this. The wound was too old and too neglected to remain.

"Who makes you God? What gives you the right?" Auggie said, his wet eyes hooded in anger and pain.

Clay stopped circling and dropped his guard. He looked at Auggie and for the first time the shopkeeper or Gillian could ever recall there was pain on Clay's face, a grimace of soul-deep pain.

"I . . . I love her," Clay said softly. His slight frame began to heave with sobs. "All my reason, all my skill, all of it falls away when I think of her. She . . . she's the only reason I want to be in this world, Auggie. I knew it the moment I first saw her."

Clay sobbed, wrestling with the pain buried in him. Auggie blinked and lowered his fists.

"You have someone else who loves you." Clay pointed at Gillian. "You get to have another life, Auggie. Gertie, she was the only one ever for me. No offense, I know how much you loved her. I respected that and I stayed away. It's just, she was the only one ever for me. It's just how I'm put together.

"I'm sorry, I didn't mean to say all that. You're the best friend I ever had. I just love her and I know I can save her, give her another life, another chance. Even if she doesn't want to be with me, even if she goes away or wants you back, wants another, I don't care. I just want to know she's in this life, sun on her beautiful face and happy and smiling and singing, like she used to. That will be enough to keep me going."

Clay fell in a little on himself, crying, shaking from the tears. Auggie shuffled forward, all the anger gone from him. He wrapped his massive arms around his friend and held him tight.

"You . . . you are a good friend, too, Clay," was all Auggie could think to say. The storekeeper held him tight and let the scientist sob.

It was the witch's hour: three in the morning. Gillian had led them to Clay's house on the compound and she made them coffee in the kitchen and got fresh water and clean towels for the men to clean up from the brawl in the barn. The three of them sat down at the kitchen table.

"Everything, Clay," Gillian said. "Now."

Clay sipped the coffee and winced in pain at the effort. "After last year—the fire at the store and all the townsfolk's changing from exposure to the *lumbricina*-like creatures the infected possessed in their mouths . . ."

"*Lumbricina?*" Auggie said as he dabbed a wet cloth at his swollen ear.

"Earthworm," Clay said. "A very loose analogy to toss around, I assure you. But I was attempting to put you and Gillian at ease by using referential terms that you could understand."

Auggie looked at Gillian. She smiled and shrugged, then patted Clay's swollen, bleeding hands.

"Thank you, Clay. That's very kind of you. Please continue."

"The infected who suffered mortal injuries continued to function," Clay said, "but once the epidemic was over those infected individuals were dead, while those who were infected and avoided life-taking injury were very ill, but recovered.

"It occurred to me that the process by which the so-called worms converted the host's blood into a different substance also provided a method of regeneration and reanimation for the infected that had been effectively killed, keeping the body going past death."

"So you took it on yourself to collect those things," Gillian said, shaking her head. "They're evil, Clay."

" 'Evil' is a word the superstitious use when they can't discern a motivation that fits their view of the world," he replied. "The physical world has no good or evil, Gillian. It has effective and ineffective and these worms and what they do is very, very effective. So, yes, I gathered as many as I could find alive and as much of the fluid as I could acquire as well. In the chaos of the first few days after the plague ended, it was easy enough, while the dead were delivered to me."

Gillian sipped her coffee and said nothing.

"Go on, Clay," Auggie said.

"There was also the matter of the late Arthur Stapleton," Clay said, oblivious to Gillian's silence. "He was poisoned, very effectively I might add, by the so-called worm-blood, which I analyzed and deemed to be highly toxic. So I concluded that the factor that allowed the substance to animate the dead or near dead and poison the living was the worm creature itself. Once I began to examine them and vivisect them, I began to understand what needed to be done and how to create a biorestorative formula from the creature's secretions."

"A bio what?" Auggie said, shaking his head.

"Biorestorative formula, Auggie," Clay said. "It's the secret to eternal life. Processed from the black worm venom and diluted and adulterated with certain other compounds—sodium bicarbonate, alum, garlic, to name a few, some other concoctions of my own manufacture. The end result is nothing short of astounding."

"You sound like a cheap huckster, Clayton," Gillian said, adding more sugar to her coffee. "Hawking your potions off the back of a wagon. I thought better of you."

"And you will again," Clay said, standing. "Not that I care. A moment." He exited the room and Auggie turned to Gillian.

"How angry are you at me?" he asked. Gillian took his torn and bloodied hand carefully, and kissed it.

"Furious," she said. "That you didn't tell me what was happening. You do that to me again and we will have a most tempestuous falling-out, Mr. Shultz, I assure you."

Auggie smiled and winced from his split lip. "I am a very lucky man, Gillian. Thank you."

"Augustus." Gillian held his hands tightly in hers and looked down at the table. "If what Clay is saying is true and he can bring Gerta back to life, then . . . I'd understand if you wanted . . ."

Auggie pulled her close to him. "No, you listen to me, Gillian. Gerta was my wife and I loved her—you know all that. You loved her, too, and it made me very sad when she passed and I . . . got . . . scared and did a foolish thing to try to keep her, a selfish thing. People are meant to grieve, remember, and continue living. I was in that half-life I damned her to as well. You saved me, Gillian—your love saved me, and it saved Gerta too."

"I just know how much she means to you," Gillian said. "And I want you to be happy and I love her, too, and . . ."

The tears were hot on her cheeks and Auggie pulled her closer to him, cradling her in his huge arms.

"Hush, *nun, meine Süße,* still," Auggie said. "No tears, my love. Gerta is my past and it was a wonderful past. You are my future. Whatever happens with this . . . creature Clay calls Gerta, she is an echo of my Gerta, and I can't go back anymore, can't live in death anymore."

"But Auggie," Gillian said, wiping her eyes, "what if Gerta wants to be back with you?"

Clay returned to the room, a large, wide glass Erlenmeyer flask in his hand. He sat down and placed the glass on the kitchen table with a thunk. Inside the conical flask was a solution that looked like equal parts water and swirling ink, the two not entirely mixing. At the terminator of the ink cloud, the clear liquid had an almost purplish cast to it. On the bottom of the flask, curled and unmoving, was one of the black worms. The motion of placing the flask on the table made the thing twitch and drift a little. A small squirt of black ink-like substance excreted from its body.

"Is that thing *alive*?" Gillian said, scooting back from the table. Auggie pulled her close to him.

"Of course," Clay said. "You need it to keep producing the substance, but at a less toxic level. Part of the formula I devised keeps it dormant. This is it, the biorestorative formula. It is capable of healing wounds, regenerating tissue and revitalizing and maintaining dead tissue. With this, death holds no more sting for mankind, and Gertie can live once again. It's my life's work."

"Clayton," Gillian said. "If you created this process and it is such a miraculous product of science, why do you need those . . . creatures for it to work, couldn't you just produce the substance you need from them artificially?"

"Sadly, no," Clay said. "But an excellent question, Gillian." Clay sat down and placed his palm over the wide mouth of the flask. "The worms' biology simply defies all I understand about biology and the process of life and death. They possess numerous traits that would indicate they are dead; however, they also possess characteristics that show they are very much not dead. It's strange—the closest thing I can compare it to is that carnival of murderous hemovores that rolled through town some time back."

Both Gillian and Auggie cringed a bit at the memory.

"Their bodies upon examination," Clay continued, "showed similar signs to the worms . . . to what the superstitious might call 'undeath.' As with the worms, I was able to observe effects caused by their bewildering biology and produce effects I can replicate. As a matter of fact, I used some fluids I collected from their bone marrow in this formula."

"So this gunk is made up of worm blood and vampire juice?" Gillian said. "Sounds terribly scientific, Clayton."

"Science doesn't promise us to unravel every mystery right away, Gillian," Clay said. "It merely promises us there is an answer. One day, we will have the answer of how these creatures function. I think my formula is a large step toward that day. It shows that death is not immutable. It can be defied—cured, if you prefer."

"It sounds like you're playing at being God," Auggie said.

"Well, he's not doing a very good job of it himself," Clay said. "I figured I'd take the initiative. Auggie, if man waited around for God to drop things out of the fool sky for him, we'd still be in skins and living in caves."

Clay reached for Auggie's hand. "Now give me your paw, here. I'm going to show you what my formula can do."

Auggie pulled his hand back and Gillian helped him.

"No," Auggie said.

"Indeed," Gillian said.

"What are you?" Clay said. "Yellow?"

Auggie sputtered, "I . . . I am not . . . not yellow, *ja*? But this is, how did Gillian say, gunk . . . and I will not . . ."

"I've tested it," Clay said, looking at the two and shaking his head. "You think I'd use it on anyone if I didn't know it was safe?"

"If that's the case, Clayton," Gillian said, "then why on Earth haven't you used it on your face and hands? Your burns?"

Clay blinked a few times and then slowly touched his own scarred face. "Gillian! It hadn't occurred to me to do that. It would be an excellent demonstration of the restorative fluid's properties."

Gillian had to smile. "Yes, Clayton, it would. Are you sure this is safe to use on yourself?"

"You saw how it restored poor Gertie's head after the decay and the fire. Observe."

Clay took a long glass pipette with a rubber bulb at the end and drew it full of the fluid. He then carefully dripped the formula over his free hand, turning the hand, to moisten both sides. Auggie and Gillian leaned forward to observe more closely. In less than a minute, the flesh began to return to its normal color and smooth texture. The damage from the fistfight—the bloody torn knuckles—also began to fade, to mend.

"*Süße Mutter im Himmel*," Auggie said. "How can this be?" In less than five minutes, Clay's bony, slender hands and even parts of his wiry arms were completely healed of the horrific burns, of any damage at all. Clay held them up, still damp from the formula that had not soaked into the skin.

"Quackery indeed, Gillian," Clay said. "Science. Pushing back the frontiers of ignorance and superstition. My formula will change the world."

The waiter at Delmonico's brought Gillian and Clay's entrées.

"'Bout time," Clay uttered. "Starved. Smells good."

Clay tore into his roast beef without a care for how his lack of table manners may have troubled the other patrons. Gillian sipped her water and watched him attack the food on his plate, occasionally taking a small bite from her own and chewing it carefully before swallowing. There were smacking sounds from Clay's full mouth and the clink of metal against china. Gillian half expected to see sparks.

"Something still troubles me, Clayton," she said, dabbing her lips with a napkin. "You had a diagram up of a . . ." Gillian looked about and lowered her voice as she leaned forward. ". . . headless woman. . . ."

"Yes," Clay said, as particles of the partly chewed food erupted from his mouth like a volcano. "Template. I needed to calculate the dimensions of the body for Gertie to make sure I could harvest the appropriate-sized parts. That's what took so damn long and why I needed Auggie's help. I had to find the right sizes for everything, or else Gertie would be all mismatched, and I wasn't going to do that to her. It was a damn sight easier with the dog, that's for sure."

Gillian refrained from asking what dog and instead said, "Those were my measurements, Clayton. To the inch. Why?"

Clay paused and grabbed the sleeve of the passing waiter. "Hey, Slick, send another gravy boat over this way, will you?" The waiter nodded and walked away, shaking his head and muttering something in Spanish that Gillian was sure wasn't "the customer is always right." Clay picked at his teeth as he answered her.

"Yes, I used you as the model for the template. I didn't realize it at first but after I saw you and the drawing, I realized it was you. You have a perfect body by the Western standards of beauty, Gillian. Congratulations."

The waiter returned with the gravy in time to hear Clay's scandalous admission. He blushed a bit and looked from Clay to Gillian, then departed as quickly as he could back to the kitchen.

"Pass that bread, will you?" Clay said, unaware of the waiter and Gillian's discomfort.

Gillian blushed and became acutely aware of the other patrons who were now intently trying to eavesdrop on their possibly torrid conversation. Again, she wished that Clay had asked to meet somewhere more private, but that would beg the assumption that Clay Turlough had any idea of how humans worked past a purely biological level.

"I . . . Clayton! Well . . . thank you, Clayton. No one has ever said that to me before . . . in such a manner."

Clay shrugged. "Just stating a fact's all."

"Did you ever consider . . . harvesting my body?" she asked. "Seems much easier than hunting up already dead parts."

Clay stopped picking and eating. He looked squarely at Gillian. "Did I consider murdering you, cutting off your head and attaching Gertie's head to your body? Yes, I considered it as an intellectual exercise, of course. For about ten seconds. Gillian, I know you think I'm some kind of monster—"

"No, Clay, I think very fondly of you—"

"Sometimes," Clay interrupted. "Other times you think I'd do anything to prove my theories. I'm very dedicated to my work, but I'm a straight shooter, Gillian. Auggie is my best friend in the world. Not many folks in this world have the patience to be my friend. You make Auggie happy—happier than I've seen him since Gertie got sick. And . . . I must confess a certain . . . fondness for you as well. You are a brave lady, and you have a reasonably well-stocked brainpan; and you love him, as much as Gertie did. Auggie has lost so much in the last few years. I would never take you away from him . . . and I would never want to do you harm myself. I hope that clears things up for you."

He tore back into the meat and Gillian watched him again, smiling, some wonder and confusion in her eyes, battling it out.

"I must confess a fondness for you, too, Clayton," she said. "I must indeed."

After the demonstration at his kitchen table, Clay walked them back over to the barn and showed them the body: It was on one of the tables in the cold room. It was spallid, dead flesh, stitchwork and, of course, a headless, ragged neck. The hands were missing but Clay explained that the girl who had been murdered in the Dove's Roost alleyway had perfect hands to complete the patchwork body. Gerta's head and brain were fully healed and revitalized in the biorestorative formula.

"I should be able to complete the preparations and undertake the revivication process in the next few hours," Clay said. "You are both welcome to stay."

"I . . . no," Auggie said. His knuckles and face were now healed, as were Clay's injuries; even Clay's burned face was unmarred. "I do not think I should, Clay. I am still unsure that this is what is best for Gerta. She was so unhappy. She wanted to be free from the pain of that existence."

"This isn't like the jar," Clay said. "This is a brand new life for her, a brand new physicality, and I swear to you, Auggie, if she is in pain, if she changes her mind, if she decides she doesn't want this, I will never let her suffer."

"Changes her mind?" Gillian asked.

"Yes," Clay said. "I've spoken to her about this extensively. Well, to her head anyway."

"I . . . I want to speak with her, Clayton," Gillian said. "Alone, please."

Clay took them back to the tank room. As they walked through the barn, Gillian nodded to the elaborate mechanical contraption on the back of a wagon.

"What on earth is this, Clay?" she asked.

"Something I came up with after that bad spate of lightning storms we had at the end of summer," he said. "Still haven't got the kinks out of it yet."

Clay opened the door to the tank room. Auggie stopped by the door, his massive arms crossed.

"Clay says he has to set up the apparatus to talk to her," Gillian said. "You don't want to come in for a moment?"

Auggie shook his head.

"I understand," she said. "Any messages for her?"

"Nothing I didn't already tell her," Auggie said quietly.

"Gillian?" Clay said, and gestured to the door. Gillian kissed Auggie and then joined Clay. The door thudded as Clay closed it and Auggie stood alone.

The tank room was illuminated by numerous lamps. Clay set about his work quickly and efficiently. He poured a powder that resembled salt from a bag into the tank with Gerta's head. The solution rained down as white, slow-motion columns that hit the bottom of the tank and then spread and diffused as swirling clouds of sediment.

"This will stimulate the solution itself to act as an electrical producing medium to power the craniovox," Clay said. "I've been corresponding with a youth in Sweden, name of Svante Arrhenius. Boy's a genius, a prodigy. Helped me with some ideas I had about the conductivity of ion-rich solutions. Solved some of my neurological restoration and construction problems I'd been wrestling with."

Clay took a circular device woven with numerous thick rubber-coated cables and wires, and gently placed it on Gerta's head, making sure it was secured tightly. He ran his healed fingers through Gerta's long floating hair gently. He ran a cable from the device to a wooden box with a crude, circular metal screen on its face and a few thick black toggle switches. Clay attached the cable to the back of the box. He dried his hands and flipped one of the switches. There was a loud snap, a puff of smoke from the box and a strange, barely audible hum in the air.

"This works on a larger scale, but is essentially the same equipment I used on the vox screen I had in her jar," Clay said. He gestured for Gillian to join him by the tank and pointed to odd devices the size and shape of large coat buttons mounted along the front face of the tank's edge.

"Talk toward these and she will be able to hear you through the head harness," he said. "I'll flip the connection to finish the circuit. If you have any trouble at all, I'll be outside with Auggie."

"Thank you, Clayton." Gillian pulled a wooden chair in front of the tank and sat. Clay had set lanterns on either side of the tank and one behind it to provide illumination for the conversation. He snapped the other switch on the wooden box and there was a momentary screech, which rapidly faded. He nodded to Gillian and Gerta and then exited the room, closing the door behind him.

"Hello," Gillian said.

The drifting head opened and closed its mouth, bubbles spilling away.

"Hello, dear friend," a woman's voice, faint but audible, said from the screen on the wooden box. Gillian smiled when she heard the voice.

"I know it must seem a dreadful question but, how do you feel?" Gillian asked.

"I think it must be a little like our memories when we are very young," Gerta said. "I remember . . . things. Other things seems to be dreams or nightmares, I can recall flashes, impressions but not full memories."

"Do you remember dying?" Gillian said.

"The end, yes," Gerta said. "Pain, choking, drowning in my own body. Fear . . . horrible fear. The fear was worse than the dying, I recall. Like tripping in a dark room, the fear of the fall into nothing. I remember talking to you, to Augustus. Clay came once when you were both exhausted and slept. He told me how he felt about me, said he would never have done anything to hurt me or Augustus. Dying feels very . . . cramped, like you are in a tent that's tight with too many people; you just want to step outside and breathe fresh air, feel space around you. Have a moment alone."

Gillian's eyes had grown wet as she listened. "I missed you," Gillian said, her voice cracking. "You were my sister, my mother, my best friend. I missed you so much."

"I missed you too," Gerta said. "I knew you would look after Augustus. I knew you would not let him fall away from the light. Thank you, Gillian."

Gillian choked a little and sniffed, wiping away the tears. "I hope you know how much he loves you," she said. "If I knew . . . If I knew what Clay was do-ing . . . I'd never have . . ."

"Loved him?" Gerta said. "You loved him the first time he told Will to have a care how he talked to you in public."

Gillian laughed and sobbed.

"He's a good man, it's easy to love him," Gerta continued. "I remember the fire. It was awful—sleepwalking in the burning house, screaming, and oil-faced shadows. But I wasn't scared anymore, Gillian. I learned to control the fear in the jar. So many things in life, in death, are so much less terrible than we imag-ine if we can just control the fear. We can survive the jar, we can escape it, if we let go of the fear.

"I remember talking to Augustus, saying our good-byes. He loves me, yes. He loves the memory of me, of us. His Gerta has gone. He loves his Gillian now, and

I want him to have a new, beautiful life with you, my dearest friend. I hoped for that when I was dying—I saw you cling to one another. Your happiness, his happiness, is my joy. I wanted it even more when I escaped the jar, when Augustus finally let me go."

"And now?" Gillian said. "Gerta, I love you. You were always better to me than my own family ever was, and I can, and will, stop Clayton from doing this to you, if you wish. This is about what *you* want, what *you* need, not Clay, not Auggie, not even me. It's your life, your soul, Gerta. Tell me, what do you want?"

Gerta's head tumbled, the raven hair a curtain that drifted between her eyes and Gillian's. The shadows of the lantern made Gerta's old eyes and young face seem almost ghostly and translucent.

"It has been so long since I could move as I choose to move, to have volition. Before that I was ill, so ill, and before that I had grown so old, so quickly, the stresses of life crippling me while my insides still wanted to sing. I have been a prisoner for so long, Gillian. To that damned jar, to my sickness, to my own bed, and in the cage my body became. Death was the only freedom I ever felt and even it was taken away from me."

"The methods Clay is using are . . . questionable," Gillian said. "To say the least. There may be side effects we know nothing about; you may be trading an end to your suffering for more suffering, Gerta. I just want you to go into this with your eyes wide open, not just hearing Clay's pompous claptrap about—"

"Science," Gerta interrupted. "Yes, one of the reasons I long for hands is to be able to cover my ears occasionally. Clay is a fine man, and he loves me very deeply. I know that love blinds him. His religion is science and that blinds him too.

"I'll be honest, Gillian, the prospect sounds too good to be true, but I so want it to be true. I want to live, who wouldn't? I want to have more time, more life. I want to be free. If Clay's formula doesn't give me that freedom, if there are strings attached to it, then I will end this false life, myself, on my own terms. If for some reason I can't, if I . . . change, I want you to promise me now you will kill me. Please, my darling friend. I know it's a lot to ask, but I am asking it of you. Don't let Clay or anyone else stop you, especially me. If you think I have been corrupted in some way, please end that and give me peace. I don't want to live a slave or a monster. Please promise me now."

"Of course," Gillian said. "I promise."

"*Danke*," Gerta said.

"I've missed you," Gillian said. "I have to be honest, I'm glad to be getting my friend back."

"Me too," Gerta said. "Now, tell me all about the wedding. . . ."

The door to the tank room opened and Gillian emerged. Both Clay and Auggie stopped pacing and turned to her. The barn doors were opened and the sky was gray, edging toward dark blue. Dawn was close.

Gillian walked out of the barn toward Clay's wagon.

"Do not botch this, Clayton" was all she said on the way home.

"Everything went fine, Gillian," Clay said, wiping the gravy off his mouth with his sleeve. "She's perfectly lucid and even the scars from the stiches will be completely gone soon. She wanted to come today, but her skin is still a little too sensitive to daylight. It should toughen up pretty soon though, a few more treatments with the formula. She told me to give you her love and her best wishes for the day. She said it meant a lot to her you wanted her there."

"I always did," Gillian said. "I suppose we should get over there, shouldn't we, Clay?"

"Yeah," Clay said as he pulled the wild flowers out of the vase on the table and handed the bouquet to Gillian. "The big old side of German schnitzel has had enough time to get sweaty and nervous now. Let's skedaddle."

Clay dropped a small bag of coins onto the table. The waiter picked up the bag as if it were full of venomous bugs. He opened it and gold coins spilled into his hands. He called out to Clay as he was opening the door for Gillian.

"Mr. Turlough! Sir! This is way too much for your meal! It's a small fortune!"

"Oh, is it?" Clay said, and looked to Gillian. She nodded and mouthed the word yes. "Oh, okay, well you can just call it a tip. Sound square?"

"Yes . . . yes, sir!" The waiter smiled. "Come back any time."

"I get hungry about three in the morning," Clay said. "I just might."

Walking down Dry Well Road, toward Prosperity, Gillian slid her arm into Clay's. The inventor seemed puzzled by the contact but accepted it.

"Promise me please, Clayton," Gillian said. "No more skulking around graveyards, no more body snatching, no more worms, please."

Clay nodded. "Fair enough. Bored with all that anyway. I'm thinking about building a balloon ship to fly across the Atlantic."

"Of course you are," she said, patting his arm. "Of course you are. To think I actually suspected you were murdering those girls, Clayton. I'm sorry."

"No need for apology," Clay said. "An obvious enough deductive fallacy to make. It's taking even me a spell to figure out who's doing it." They continued walking, turning onto Prosperity, headed for Main. "But I intend to. Just been a little busy bringing the dead back to life and all and helping my best friends get their ducks in a row."

"Best friends?" Gillian said, and hugged Clay's arm a little tighter.

Clay straightened his wild hair. "I'm real honored you and Auggie wanted me to be there today, Gillian. Why are you not waiting and doing it when you planned?"

"We don't want to wait," Gillian said as they neared the white tower of town hall. "Something Gerta said. We get trapped so many ways in life, so easy to let things slip away. Auggie just walked up to me this morning and said he wanted to do it today, if I did. I love him and I don't want to spend another night without him beside me."

Clay smiled. It was genuine and Gillian realized it was childlike and sweet. His eyes actually twinkled for a moment and it made Gillian smile inside and out.

"C'mon then, "Clay said. "Let's get you hitched."

In the mayor's office, Harry Pratt stood, looking very happy. Before him was Auggie Shultz, in his finest suit, kneading his derby in his huge, sweaty hands. Off to the bride's side stood Maude and Constance Stapleton.

Clay walked Gillian in front of Harry.

"Who gives this woman into matrimony?" Harry asked.

"I do," Clay said, "proudly."

Clay stepped back to Auggie's side and checked to make sure the ring was still in his coat. Auggie stepped up beside Gillian, who was holding her purloined bouquet. The two looked into each other's eyes. Their hands found each other's and clung tightly together.

"Miss the dress, and the crowd? The priest?" she whispered to him.

"*Nein,*" he said. "All that is important is here."

A tall figure slid into the room. She wore a dark green dress, bonnet and a gray veil that hid her face. She moved to the groom's side and touched Clay's arm gently with her glove. The gesture made her sleeve ride up for a second and caught the shadow of a scar running all the way around her wrist. The veiled lady stood silently next to Clay, the best man, as Harry started to read.

"Dearly beloved . . . ," Harry began.

The Three of Swords

The third one was in the possession of Thug Batra, who sat hidden in a murder garden of mummified victims among sacred assassins in the bowels of Bombay. Thug Batra was not his real name, it was the name the British colonial soldiers muttered under their breaths as they tried to find him, kill him and end his reign of slaughter. "Thug" was not even correct. It was a bastardization of Thuggee, the name of his religion, his holy cause. His given name was Jangir Batra and he was born in a village outside of Bhopal. Some nights he had holy dreams of returning to the city of his birth as a cloud of evil smoke and strangling the life out of all the city's inhabitants for the glory of the Black Mother.

He was secreted away from his birth parents by the Thuggee to thwart the British attempt to crush the religion, to become part of a new generation of assassins dedicated to the worship of Kali through the practice of ritual murder. After his decades of study and training, after he was empowered to use his mind and body to kill as easily as breathing, to move as silently as a poisonous thought, after his hundredth murder before even reaching adulthood, it had fallen into his possession, a final gift from his master—proof that he was ready to fulfill his destiny as the greatest murderer of his age, to dedicate each strangulation to the cause of forestalling the Kali Yuga, the iron age of crushing, the end of the world. In effect, each killing he and his brethren committed helped keep the world going.

He murdered his master and took it. In the years to follow he was personally responsible for 241 murders. The truth he knew in his own heart—he killed for the joy of hearing the life hiss from his victim's lips, for the thrill of feeling them shake and convulse against him and then grow still. He did not kill to hold back the end of the world; he killed for the dark light joy of ending another's personal world. In the fall of 1870 he dreamed of a small town in the wasteland of the American frontier. A golden god of death from the West called to him, called to it. So Thug Batra came, traveling on a ship across the seas, to America, thirsty to slay.

The Lovers (Reversed)

Mutt arrived at the laundry, where the *Closed* placard hung on the door. He rapped on the glass. The door opened and Mutt felt the air spill from his lungs. Maude was in a bustle dress of blue-green taffeta with brown frocked velvet patterns, her underskirt was brown taffeta, as was the bodice's front, and the bodice was adorned with gold buttons. Her hair was up in a chignon and she wore a small capote hat that matched the dress's colors.

For once Mutt had no words. He opened his mouth and then closed it, trying to not look like a fish out of water.

Maude had an equal surprise. Mutt was in a sack coat, white collared shirt, trousers and vest of brown tweed. He was wearing a pair of brown polished oxford shoes with laces. He wore no tie and his top shirt button was undone. Mutt's hair was washed, combed and pulled back into a ponytail with a cord of rawhide. The claw marks on his face from a few days ago were completely healed. He had a bouquet of purple and yellow wildflowers in his big, scarred hand.

"You," Mutt said. "You look like a queen. I've never seen anyone so pretty in all my days."

Maude tilted her head. "You look very handsome and dapper," she said. "You did this for me?"

"Yeah." He offered her the flowers. "Jonathan helped me out some. I just wanted you to not feel bad walking next to me."

"Oh, Mutt," she said, taking the wild blooms and smelling them. "Never felt bad with you by me, just the opposite. Never have, never will."

"No one ever dressed up for me before," he said. "You look like a piece of art. You should be in some museum, not out in all this mess."

"Never figured you for a poet, Deputy" she said. "You, sir, are too kind, and I am starved. Let's go eat!"

He took her hand, escorted her across the threshold. Maude locked the door. Mutt hooked his arm and offered it to her and Maude slid her arm through. They walked across the street to Gillian Proctor's boardinghouse, where Mutt had his room.

"I'm trying to figure out where you hid the weapons," Maude said.

Mutt grinned. "Ain't packing any."

"Not even your knife?" she asked.

Mutt shook his head and she whistled. "You are taking this seriously, aren't you?"

"Not even my star," he said. "No monsters, no ghosts, no spirits, no madmen out to destroy the world, no goat-vampires, no desperados. No nothin', not tonight. I'm officially off duty. How about you?"

"Well, almost nothing," Maude said, looking down. "A few envenomed hat pins, my derringer, of course, and a few knives, oh and my fancy strangle cord. Virtually naked."

Mutt cleared his throat and pulled at his loose collar. Maude laughed and squeezed his arm tighter. He pulled out a pocket watch attached to his vest by a chain, flipped it open and looked at the time. "We still have a spell before vittles are on, care to take a stroll?"

"Of course," Maude said. "You heard about Gillian and Auggie getting married today, didn't you?" Mutt nodded. "Was glad to hear it. They are good people and both of them have had a hell of a year. Bick's done his damnedest to put Auggie out of business."

"If Gillian is on her honeymoon, then who is making dinner at the boardinghouse?" Maude said, stopping.

Mutt's only reply was to glance at the pocket watch again.

Maude looked at the watch. "When did you ever carry a timepiece?" she asked.

"Jonathan loaned it to me," Mutt said. "Came with the vest. I don't use the damned things. Crazy white people thinking some numbers on a dial gives them control over time; more the other way around."

They walked down Dry Well Road, past the jail. They both noticed the looks they were getting and they both worked very hard to ignore them.

"So Jon Highfather is the author of your change in wardrobe?" she asked.

"Partially," Mutt said. "I asked him for help. I've never been out with a lady before and I wanted to do this all right. Jonathan's my friend. He helped me, not that he's exactly a Fancy Dan himself."

Maude laughed. "No, I'd hazard in your work, clothes are pretty low on the list of concerns. How is the sheriff? Else Thaler led me to believe that he had been in some kind of altercation up on Argent?"

Mutt nodded. "He's okay. Got tagged, but not too bad. That quack Doc Tumblety patched him up, which is more dangerous than the shoot-out, if you ask me. Jon pushes that luck of his too damn far."

"Do you think that's all it is, luck?" Maude asked. "I mean, you're his best friend, and you and I have seen our share of . . . trouble in our time. It just seems that all these . . . miraculous escapes of his simply defy luck."

"Is Jon a walking dead man? No," Mutt said. "How does he stay alive? Beats the hell out of me. But something happened to Jon in the war, something that haunts him and changed him. Doing the job here helps him with whatever it was, but I swear it's going to get him killed eventually."

Maude squeezed his arm again. "You really do care about him."

"Yeah," Mutt said. "We talk about our feelings and such in between fightin' off critters like those living cactus things from a few months back and we swap fashion tips. I'm plum sweet on him."

Maude smacked his arm. He winced, then laughed. They walked closer to the end of the road as the falling sun painted the sky in crimsons and oranges.

"What exactly happened with those cactus things anyway?" Maude asked.

"Well," Mutt began, "you remember how I was walking kinda funny there for a spell . . . ?"

They ended up by the old well that gave the road its name. There were a few worn stone benches around the old, crumbling stone well, and a stand of hardy desert willow trees covered in purple blooms grew here, offering the comfort of shade in the day.

The supper crowd from Delmonico's drifted in and out of the restaurant. Most of the patrons were scions of Rose Hill. Several pointed or glanced at Maude and Mutt on the bench together. Maude didn't need to increase her hearing's power and Mutt didn't need his razor-sharp senses to know what they were whispering about.

"Well, at least we've given them some stimulatin' conversation to break bread over," Mutt said.

Maude nodded. Mutt checked his watch again.

"You," Maude said, "are stalling me. What are you up to?"

Mutt shrugged. "Just enjoying the lovely view and trying to make as many white folks uncomfortable as I can," he said. "I have no idea what you are on about."

"I'm talking about killing something and eating it raw, pretty soon here, Deputy," Maude said.

"Long as it ain't me," Mutt said. "I'm good. Just a few more minutes and we can head on over to the spread."

Maude pointed at the well. "Something I've been wondering all the years I've lived in this town, are the stories about this old well true? I've heard it's haunted. That there's some kind of secret tunnel down in it, that the Bick family threw one of their mad relatives down in there and that you can still hear his screams on some nights."

"My favorite is that back before there were any white folks here, the locals used it as a sacrificial well to appease the evil spirits that wander these lands," Mutt said. "Been tempted to start that old tradition back up from time to time. And you, Maude, you are dancing around something with me, now. Something you don't want to tell me."

"You always can see through me," she said. "You are the only one who can."

"I pay the most attention," Mutt said. "I'm kinda fascinated by you, if you haven't cyphered that out yet. Talk to me, straight."

Maude looked out past the buildings to the cool darkness settling over Rose Hill and the desert beyond that. This was harder than fighting the mountain lion could ever be.

"I received a letter from my father in Charleston," she said. "He's coming to fetch me and Constance, like we're errant children. He's already on his way. He feels that this 'unwashed frontier' is no place for his daughter or granddaughter without a man to look over us."

"And how do you feel 'bout it?" Mutt said, without missing a beat.

Maude felt something flutter in her chest and she realized again why this man, this battered and coarse man, was the most miraculous person she had ever met and why he made her feel the things she felt inside whenever he was about.

"You are the only person in this world, except my daughter, who would even think to ask me what I wanted, as if that was an option," Maude said. "Thank you."

"I mean, after all you went through with Arthur being murdered and then almost losing Constance and what you had to go through to save her, I'd understand if you jist wanted to move away from all this badness. A lot of folks do," Mutt said. Something else hung in his throat, more words that he wanted to say. Maude could sense them, but he held his peace.

"It's been my experience that the badness here is balanced pretty well by the goodness," she said. "It's harder to find and it doesn't always come looking for you, but it's here. This is my home now and Constance's. We have roots and I don't intend to have them pulled out."

Mutt nodded, again. Words held. Maude decided not to push that.

"Good deal," he said. "You know whatever happens, I got you covered, right?"

"I know that in my bones," she said. "And I can't tell you how much it means to me."

"C'mon." Mutt stood and offered his hand. "Let's git you fed."

They walked into the dining room of Gillian Proctor's home, which she ran as a boardinghouse, and Maude paused in surprise. No boarders were crowded around the dinner table. The room was empty, except for a slender man in his forties, with aquiline features and short, dark hair, turning gray at the temples. He was dressed in a traditional white double-breasted chef's jacket and checkered pants and standing proudly by the kitchen door. The table had fine linen on it and there was a virtual feast laid out. At the center of the table was a lit candelabrum, bathing the dark room in warm light.

"Welcome," the man said. "Perfect timing. I just chased Jim Negrey out of here. He did help clear the table, good lad, though how he did it with a biscuit in either hand and one in his mouth is beyond me."

"Much obliged, Del," Mutt said. "You really went all out for us. Maude Stapleton, this is Delmonico Hauk, to us by way of New York City."

"Hauk? The owner of the new restaurant?" Maude said.

"Owner, chef, bookkeeper and dishwasher," Hauk said with a laugh. "Pleased to meet you, Maude."

Hauk took Maude's hand and shook it politely and with a slight bow. "When Gillian and Mutt told me about the surprise wedding today and how she was supposed to fix you two dinner, I offered to step up and take over so her and

Auggie could enjoy their honeymoon. I offered Mutt the best table in my place, but he wanted you all to himself."

"Did he?" Maude narrowed her eyes at Mutt in mock accusation. "How long have you and Gillian been keeping all this scheming from me, Deputy?"

"Mutt worked it out with Gillian," Hauk said. "He wanted to make sure I could arrange the meal and get the boarders out of here in time. For Mutt and Gillian, I'd feed them in the back alley. A few of the boarders are in the parlor. If they make too much noise, you tell me and I'll shoo them."

"Thanks, Del," Mutt said. "I owe you."

"Nonsense," Hauk said. "I'd be dead in New York if not for you and I'd never have got the restaurant up and running here without Gillian's help. Tonight is for you two. I'll put these lovely flowers in water for you, Maude, and I'll be right in the kitchen if you need anything. Mind your manners, Mutt."

"Yes, mother," Mutt said. As Hauk departed, Mutt pulled Maude's chair away from the table for her. She sat and he pushed it in before taking his own seat across from her.

"They, uh, they usually say grace before we chow down," Mutt said. "I don't usually cotton to that myself, but I'll do it if you'd like." Maude smiled. Her eyes shimmered in the candlelight.

"No," she said. "But thank you for offering."

"Well," Mutt said. "Let's eat." He gestured for her to begin, but Maude paused.

"Mutt," Maude said. "This is the sweetest thing anyone has ever done for me, ever. Thank you."

"You deserve to be treated fine all the time," Mutt said. "Thank you for lettin' me."

Dinner was the best either of them could recall eating. Hauk had prepared so much food: roasted chicken with fixin's, corn dodgers, greens with bacon and biscuits. Hauk had made a large pandowdy full of apples, sugar and spices for dessert. There were large pitchers of cold water and tea and pots of hot tea and coffee, with an assortment of cakes for both.

"That," Maude said, dabbing her lips with a napkin while Mutt poured her a cup of coffee, "was magnificent. Mr. Hauk's a great chef. What was that about you saving his life back in New York?"

"Long story," Mutt said. "Back when I was a short britches, not much older than Jim. Hated New York. Wouldn't have gone if I didn't have to. Some bad business with my father's family. Like I said, a long story."

"I have trouble seeing you in New York," Maude said.

"Me too," Mutt said. "Almost wrecked the damn place, but I met Del and he's real good people. A very generous fella, Hauk is."

Maude sipped her coffee. "You are a very generous man for doing all this for me."

"Well, if I'm good to you, maybe you'll stay," he said, smiling. "How you going to handle your father?"

"I honestly don't know," Maude said. "But I will. I love him and I don't want to hurt him. Father has business to attend to all over the world, so I spent more time, as a child, with this relative or that relation than with him. Truth be told, he loved me but I knew he always wanted a son to carry on the Anderton name. I was another . . . obligation, like a business debt, and father always saw to his obligations. He was a good provider and he's good man.

"My mother was active in causes that embarrassed him often. Abolition, women's suffrage. He could have forbid Mother from doing those things, relegated her to the role of wife, but he never even tried to because it made Mother happy, never because he thought those causes were right."

"Your mother sounds like a fine woman," Mutt said. "Sorry you lost her. I still miss mine too. She did right by me, when she didn't have to."

"I've told you before about my great-great-great-grandmother on my mother's side, Gran Bonny? She was always more of a parent to me than my mother or father ever were," Maude said. "She was there when I needed her and she actually listened to me."

"You loved her a lot, it shows," Mutt said. "You told me she's the one that taught you how to do the things you do, right? The fighting, the disguise, all that hard case stuff?"

"Yes," Maude said. "She did."

"One tough old lady," Mutt said. "Would have liked to meet her."

"Tough? You have no idea," Maude said, laughing. "She was the most alive person I've ever known. She took life by the throat and refused to let it go until she had wrung every last drop out of it. She could be stubborn and coarse at times, but she was honest and true and she spoke her mind and didn't give a damn what the world thought. You remind me of her quite a bit, actually."

Mutt raised a glass of water in salute.

"I'll take that as high praise indeed. To Gran Bonny."

"She'd hate being toasted with water," Maude said. "Hated the stuff, said fish fornicated in it. I do believe she had wine in her veins. I think she'd like you."

"'Course she would," Mutt said. "I'm charmin' as hell."

"That," Maude said, touching his hand on the table, "you are."

———————

They departed Proctor's boardinghouse well after ten at night. Both profusely thanked Hauk for the wonderful meal and offered to help clean up, but he would have none of it.

"You get her home before she turns into a turnip, Deputy," Hauk said to Mutt. "Pleasure to meet you, Maude."

They turned right onto Prosperity Road. The shadow of Rose Hill stood before them and they began to climb the hill on the narrow, smooth stone path lined with desert willows. The walking path ran adjacent to the simple, but well-attended dirt road that gently ascended Rose Hill, running past the finest homes in Golgotha. Maude's house was near the base of the hill. The two walked, arm in arm, as the moon was beginning to wane. The desert's chill had fallen and it genuinely felt like winter was a wolf at the door. Mutt paused and draped his coat over Maude's shoulders.

"You know the cold doesn't affect me unless I let it," she said softly.

"Humor me," he said. And she did.

The faint perfume of the desert willows kissed the wind as they walked along silently. Maude knew the willows would lose their purple blooms soon, but tonight it felt like they remained here just for her.

"You have given me a perfect evening," she says. "You always give me what I need. How do you do that?"

Again Mutt held back words. Then he said, "I treat you the way you deserve to be treated, Maude."

They turned off the pavestone path onto a dirt one. There was a water pump that acted as a crossroads, with smaller paths leading to each of the circle of homes clustered around it.

"I'm going hunting again," Maude said, pausing at the pump. "I felt I should let you know."

"Mountain lions?" Mutt said.

"No, I'm tracking down the man who has been murdering the women at the Dove's Roost."

"Well, Jonathan and Jim and some Secret Service agent are trying to bag him tonight. Hopefully they do," Mutt said.

"Secret Service?" Maude said

"Yeah, all the way from Washington, D.C.—the hometown of white-man crazy. I'm not 'posed to say anything about 'em being here. Real hush-hush," he said with a grin. "Oops."

"Well, you know you can trust me," Maude said.

"Yes," Mutt said. "I know."

"Well, if they don't get him, I will," Maude said.

Mutt stopped walking. He rubbed his chin as he frowned. "Did you hear what he did to them?" he said. "This man is crazy to wake the snakes, Maude. Whores are real good at reading crazy, too, so that means he's witchy at hiding what he really is."

"Women," Maude said. "People, not whores. And, yes, the women at the Dove's Nest told me exactly what he did to them. That's why I'm going to hunt him down and stop him if you can't."

"Maude," Mutt said. "They are whores. Women, or people, or whatever you care to call them, who sell themselves. When you do that as a trade, you run into men like this one. I'm not sayin' it's right. Hell, I'd like to have a little private time with the no-account who done it, but it is kind of part and parcel of the business they chose."

"Most of these women have no choice in this 'business,'" Maude said. "It's this work or they starve and their families starve. And I've been called 'whore' plenty of times in my life, mostly by men who claimed to love me. You, of all people, should be able to see past a label and see the person, Mutt. Are you just a 'half-breed'? A 'redskin,' any of those horrible labels you've had spit at you?"

"Just names," Mutt said. "Don't mean nothin' except to the damn fools that use them. Don't make you who you are unless you let 'em."

"You know I can handle myself," Maude said. "Why are you being this way?"

"Because I caught a whiff of . . . just a hint of it today sniffing over that wagon," Mutt said. "Something evil, and old, but hard to tag, like smoke from a far-off wildfire. Crazy. Hate and lust all mixed up together. It was like part of his scent but not . . . like a separate thing he's tied into. I . . . I just don't want anything to happen to you and I sure as hell don't want you anywhere near this . . . whatever it is."

Maude put her hand on his shoulder. "If it's some kind of creature, then I need to stop it even more."

"No," Mutt said. "He's human. As human as it gets. That's part of what troubles me. Unnatural things—monsters, spirit things—they make sense in a weird kinda way, but this . . ."

Catching that scent today, Mutt had felt, more than sensed, an animal savagery that spoke to a part of him. This was the human animal at its most debased, its most horrible. No other animal, even mad and frothing, could do something like this. The thought of Maude torn and violated like that filled him with more fear than he could ever recall. This man was to be avoided like the prairie fire or the shuddering diamondback. He was death.

They walked again in silence for a time.

"Do you trust me?" Maude finally asked.

"You know I do," Mutt said. "With my life."

"Trust me now," she said. "He must be stopped and I was trained to do this."

"Fair deal," Mutt said. "Like I said, it's probably moot. Jon and them will nail his hide tonight, I'd wager. But if not, just remember what I said and be careful as hell."

"I will," Maude said. "I promise."

They walked past the Kimball homestead and to her door in silence, holding hands.

"Well," Mutt said. "Thank you for the pleasure of your company. This was . . . this was the best night of my life, Maude."

"Come here." She held his callused hand tighter and pulled him gently forward. Their lips touched. The first contact was soft, tentative, the desire fighting with the fear—the fear of opening to another, of beginnings. They slid together, their bodies fitting with ease, their scents teasing each other, and the hunger began to take ascendance. Their mouths struggled to make them whole, make them one. Then, like calm water moving, they moved their lips apart, moved their bodies apart, as one. Patient in the certainty of the feeling they had shared.

"Now it's the best night of my life," Mutt said with more than a little growl in his voice. Maude smiled at him.

"Good night," she said, her voice soft like velvet. "Be safe as you can be."

"You too," he said.

Maude removed his coat and started to hand it back to him. Mutt stopped her.

"Keep it," he said. "Means I get to come fetch it."

"Yes," Maude said. "Please do. I'd like that."

"Good night," he said.

"Good night," she replied. Maude unlocked the door and stepped inside. A single oil lamp rested on the dinner table, guttering: Constance looking out for her before retiring. Maude closed the door with a click. She rested against it, smiling. She held Mutt's coat tight in her arms.

Mutt stood looking at the door for a moment and then began his walk back down Rose Hill, whistling. This had to be some kind of dream. People like him didn't get that lucky in this life. He'd wake up in some flop with an empty whiskey bottle in his hands, alone.

There was a thunder of hooves as he reached the descending stone path. A half-dozen men with hoods circled him, shotguns, torches and rope in hand.

"There's the no-account red nigger thinks he can walk around and put his filthy hands on a white woman," the leader said over the hiss and crackle of his torch.

"Thanks," Mutt said.

"What the hell you talkin' about, chief?" the hooded man said.

"You just convinced me this wasn't a dream," Mutt said.

The Ten of Pentacles (Reversed)

Kate Warne moved thorough the miners' camp up on Argent Mountain, a huntress pretending to be prey. She was dressed as she had been during her months at the Dove's Roost and was acutely aware of the hungry eyes that devoured her as she moved through crowds made up mostly of men, with a few female camp followers plying their trade among them.

The second shift was done in the Argent Mine and third shift was well underway. The night was cold, the diminishing moon smothered by black clouds. The camp was a labyrinth of shifting canvas walls and filth-filled canals that took the place of streets. You could get lost here very easily and with a wrong turn find yourself in the domain of some petty tyrant eager to relieve you of your coin, your virtue or your life.

Kate knew that the dirty miner staggering along about thirty yards behind her, covered in soot from head to toe and with a half-empty rye bottle clutched in his fist, was in fact Sheriff Jon Highfather. He bumped into folks in the crowd and mumbled apologies as he shadowed her, occasionally faking a swallow from his bottle. Jim Negrey, looking equally disheveled and unkempt, was walking along farther back behind Jon, with an empty water pail in his hands and a few sticks of kindling firewood over his shoulder.

Kate had taught the sheriff and the deputy what Allan Pinkerton had taught her about staggered surveillance, or at least as much as she could in a few hours. Jon would be Kate's primary spotter, then he'd drop back into the crowd and Jim would advance to keep an eye on her, while still trailing behind and attracting as little notice as possible.

Her job was to be the bait. With Clay's insights they had decided to take a run through the mining camp. So far no one had made a report of a missing wagon and two horses, so they were wandering the whole camp, hoping a "new girl" would attract the Dove killer's attention. Kate turned off of the main thoroughfare and headed to the eastern side of the camp that intersected with Backtrail Road. She paused at a ramshackle church, part wooden skeleton and part canvas walls. An old man in black shirtsleeves held aloft a beautiful wooden cross and recited a prayer to the handful of faithful on the rickety pews, bowing their heads.

"Deliver me, O Lord, from evil men," the preacher said. "Preserve me from violent men, who plan evil things in their hearts; they continually gather together for war. They sharpen their tongues like a serpent; the poison of asps *is* under their lips. . . ."

The congregation parroted the holy man's words as he continued. Kate looked around and suddenly she felt like she was a girl again running through the streets and alleys of the Five Points in New York. That was a million lives ago. That girl and her life were dead and buried. She had the job now, she *was* the job now. She had no illusions about her future with Allan Pinkerton. Her empty grave was at the foot of his own future grave. His good lady wife would reside beside him and she would be at his feet. She pushed it away. She was no foolish schoolgirl. She knew the arrangement with Pinkerton when they began the dance. No sense moaning about it now. Eyes were on her, and it felt very good to know Jon Highfather knew that, too, and was in wait. The sheriff had developed a powerful reputation as part of the growing mythology of the West. If he were a self-promoting whore like Bill Cody and had attracted the notice of Ned Buntline, he'd be rich and famous now. But Highfather honestly didn't want to be famous, he didn't want to be a legend. It troubled Kate that now, in the middle of the job, when her mind should be on keeping her ass alive and catching this killer, she was wondering exactly what Jon Highfather did want.

Two men came toward her out of the crowd. Kate moved away from the church tent and turned to face them. Both were too clean to be miners and too rangy-looking to be honest.

"What the hell you doin' here?" the bigger of the two men said. He wore a cheap, slightly crumpled top hat and had two pistols holstered in his gun belt and a third stuffed in the front by the buckle. "You got permission to be dragging your scrawny ass all over the Nail's camp?"

Kate looked confused. "Do . . . Do I need that, darlin'?" she said, with a Texas accent now. She began to tear up. "Oh my. I . . . I didn't know, sir."

Derby looked at his silent companion, a smaller man who looked like he might be partly Chinese. The dark-haired silent man wore his long hair in a ponytail. He had a shotgun sheathed on his back, attached to a bandolier of shells, and a six-gun at his belt.

"You making coin on Mr. Devlin's streets, you pay the freight, bitch," Derby said. Kate was pretty sure these were not the Dove killers, but now she had a new mess to untangle.

Derby grabbed her by the arm and began to drag her toward one of the dark spaces between the tents. "I'm sure we can work something out, here," he said. "Take it out in trade."

A strong hand rested on Derby's shoulder and pulled him around. He released Kate in surprise.

"I don't think so, slick," Highfather said.

"Who the fuck are you?" Derby said. The sheriff's response was to strike Derby on the side of the head with the barrel of the .44 he had already drawn. The man's hat flew off in one direction, his head in the other, and he went down hard.

"I'm the man throwing your sorry ass in jail," Highfather said, flipping over the collar of his coat to reveal his silver star.

Ponytail went for his shotgun, but stopped cold when he saw that Jim had aimed the double-barreled shotgun pistol at his chest. Jim cocked both hammers at once. The deputy had been carrying the short, ugly, gun in his pail.

"You just keep that scatter gun slung," Jim said. "Or a big patch of daylight will be poking through you."

"I could have handled them in the alley," Kate said to Highfather as he pulled Derby to his feet and wrestled irons onto the stuporous man's wrists. Jim was cuffing Ponytail as well. "Our surveillance is shot now. Whole camp will be on us, Jon."

"You're welcome," Highfather said. "My call. You'd probably end up having to shoot them in there. This way everyone stays alive."

Kate shrugged. "I just could have gotten some more information out of them about this 'Nail Devlin' character is all. Well, at least we made a pretty decent sweep of the camp before this mess. No bodies, so signs of our Dove killer. Maybe Mr. Turlough was off about the stars and all that."

"I hope so," Highfather said. "Come on, let's get these upstanding citizens into the clink."

———

The word came shortly after Highfather, Kate and Jim had deposited the Nail's two men into a jail cell. Jon and Jim were busy washing off their disguises and Kate had adjourned to a curtained-off cell to change back into her normal clothes. Brady Bowles, one of the local tradesmen, rushed in, white as a sheet.

"Sheriff!" Bowles shouted. "Come quick! They found a dead girl over in Johnny Town!"

Bowles and a few volunteers kept the crowds back until Ch'eng Huang's Green Ribbon Tong hatchet men showed up in force and established a perimeter. The girl was hanging from one of the clotheslines that were everywhere in Johnny Town. She was roughly twenty feet in the air. Like the other two, she had been disemboweled, her entrails hanging from the bloody cavern of her stomach and abdomen, dripping down on the street below. Some of her guts had been wrapped about her wrists, arms and neck and tied to the clothesline. The blood had drained from her slashed and torn face and she was pale, almost white. Her eyes had been cut out, leaving bloody, empty cavities. She looked like a grisly marionette, left abandoned by some towering puppet master.

Jim stood silent and still as he looked at her. He was far past illness now. A cold rage settled in, the kind he had felt the night he had shot Charlie Upton down for murdering his pa.

"Her name is Abigail Holden," the Scholar said to Highfather, looking up at the dead woman. "She is an employee of the Roost. She hadn't been seen since this afternoon."

"Freelancing?" Kate asked. The Scholar did not take his eyes from the body. He swallowed hard.

"Apparently so," the Scholar said. "Unfortunate. I rather liked her. She was well read for a . . . woman in her position. I thought she was smarter than this."

Highfather excused himself from the Scholar as Kate continued to question him. As he approached Jim, one of Huang's lieutenants, a shovel-faced China-man named Shunli, intercepted him.

"I speak for Ch'eng Huang," Shunli said. "He is most displeased by this atrocity being perpetrated in his community. He says resolve it quickly, Sheriff, or rest assured the Green Ribbon will."

Highfather locked eyes with Shunli. "You tell Huang I'll handle this and he needs to keep his dogs on their leashes and off my streets, or I'll shut all of you down, y'hear me?"

Shunli turned away and departed without a word. Highfather walked over to stand beside Jim.

"You good?" Highfather said. "Stupid damn question to ask. How the hell could anybody be good after seeing that?"

"Sumbitch cut back on us," Jim said, his eyes not leaving the hanging girl. "Maybe even let us . . . let me have the wagon to send us right where he wanted us to be."

"I think you're giving him too much credit," Highfather said. "He's trying to throw us off his scent to be sure, but we're gonna get him, Jim. It's just a matter of time."

"And bodies," Jim said.

The Six of Pentacles

They had shotguns. Mutt had nothing but the sweet memory of Maude's kiss on his lips. He wouldn't have traded it for a hundred guns.

"Walk," the masked leader said, "or we'll cut you in half right here and go visit your whore and her daughter."

"You touch her and I'll eat your fucking heart," Mutt snarled, staring into the barrels of the gun. His eyes seemed to flash with unnatural color in the moonlight and the masked men's horse became uneasy, whinnying and shuffling nervously.

"Move," the leader repeated, and gestured with the gun. Mutt walked down the dark path, surrounded by the horsemen. They came off the road near the base of Rose Hill and led him out to a tall, wide mesquite tree standing alone in the waning moonlight.

"This will do jist fine," one of the men said behind his mask. Mutt arched his head at the sound of the voice.

"Healy?" Mutt said, grinning. "Conn Healy? Is that your special brand of stupid leaking out from under that potato sack?"

"Don't answer him, Conn," another of the masked men said.

Mutt laughed.

"All of you shut the fuck up!" the leader said.

"And that would be Max Macomber," Mutt said. Macomber—powerful, wealthy man. Mutt had crossed him outside the Dove's Roost the night Molly James had died. Seems he took it personal.

"Well, hell, fellas, I didn't know I was dealing with such a rowdy band of masterminds." Mutt laughed again. "Shit, your wives cut those eyeholes for you, and make sure you didn't put the masks on backward?"

"Shut up, you stinking half-breed!"

"Put the rope up over that branch," Macomber said. "That will shut his fool mouth up for good."

While the rest continued to train guns on Mutt, two of the men got off their horses and tossed a rope with a knotted noose already tied over a high branch and lowered it carefully.

"I know it's a foreign concept to you all," Mutt said. "But think for a minute. You do this and you will have more hurt come down on you than any of you want or can even imagine. If I can figure out who you are, you think Jon High-father can't? You can still walk away from this."

"Leesen to him," one of the men with the rope said. "He's skeered." All the men laughed.

Macomber and two other men climbed off their horses as well. They all had shotguns trained on Mutt. "Jon Highfather ain't always gonna be sheriff in this town," Macomber said. "He was a damn fool to put his trust in a stinkin' red-skinned desert ape like you anyway."

"Max!" one of the mounted men shouted. "Got company."

A lone figure on horseback made its way up Prosperity Street, headed for the path up Rose Hill. The rider paused when he saw the silhouettes of men and horses at the tree and rode across the field to join them. It was Harry Pratt.

"What's going on here?" Harry said, seeing the noose and Mutt standing at gunpoint.

"Little rope party for me, Harry," Mutt said. "Didn't you git your invite?"

"None of your nevermind, Mr. Mayor," one of the masked gunmen said. "Keep on riding."

"This man is a deputy," Harry said. "You can't just string him up like a common criminal."

"You hold your peace, Pratt," Macomber said. "This fucking Lamanite had his hands and lips all over a white woman and there is no way in hell we're going to stand for that. Figure our little citizens' vigilance committee would have something nice hanging in the trees to welcome folks tomorrow morning. Now ride on up the hill to your fancy house your daddy built and let real men get to their work."

"You want to kill this man because he was with a white woman?" Harry asked. He looked at Mutt.

Mutt shrugged.

"Go on now, Harry," he said. "I got this."

Harry looked at the circle of armed hooded men, a few with blazing torches.

"Clearly," Pratt said. "Let him go, Max."

Macomber turned suddenly to face Harry, who was climbing down from his horse. "How the hell did you . . . ?"

"A mask can't hide as much as you think it can," Harry said, walking up to face Macomber. "Let him go, Max."

The men chuckled nervously. Macomber pulled the sack off his head. His mean, tiny eyes burned. "Or what, Pratt? You got no gun, and even if you did you wouldn't know what to do with it, unless you could get a vote out of it. Run on home."

"Not without him," Pratt said, nodding to Mutt.

"Fine by me," Macomber said. "Just means it's that much easier to get Rony Bevalier's boy elected next year. Kill this dandy son of a bitch!"

Harry reached under his duster. The man beside Macomber emptied both barrels of the shotgun into Pratt at point-blank range. The horses pinned their ears back and their eyes grew wide at the blast of gunfire. Several of them rose up and pawed the air. Harry flew backward and landed with a thud and was still.

Mutt moved the instant the shotgun was fired. He grabbed a gun away from one of the men next to him, spun to put the unarmed man between himself and the circle of gunmen. Mutt stuck his face in front of one of the spooked horses and snarled. The terrified horse snorted and turned and ran, tossing its rider to the ground with a sick crunching sound. The equally spooked circle of men opened fire and the blasts cut the unarmed man Mutt was ducking behind almost in half. As the dead man fell, Mutt returned fire on one of the shooters and watched him stumble backward, missing most of his face, and fall to the ground.

Mutt turned straight into the twin barrels of Max Macomber's shotgun. Macomber smiled and pulled the trigger. Just as the hammers clicked, there was a blur of brilliance—silver reflecting moonlight, and sparks—as Macomber's shotgun was sliced cleanly in half. Macomber held a stock and part of a trigger, as well as part of his finger. The rest, including the first two joints of his trigger finger, tumbled to the grass. Harry Pratt spun in one fluid motion and disemboweled another of the gunmen with the Sword of Laban, before the pieces of Macomber's gun and finger had finished falling. The last man on horseback spurred his horse and began to ride toward town. Harry brought his blade to rest under Macomber's chin. Macomber had fallen to his knees and was looking at the severed stub of his finger and the blood gushing from it.

"You," Harry said, "are under arrest. You know, I always wanted to say that!"

"You did that real fine, Mr. Mayor," Mutt said as he loaded the shotgun in his hands. He walked over and tapped the ornate breastplate that Harry had strapped on over his shirt and vest and under his coat. The jewel-encrusted armor didn't show the slightest sign of wear from the two solid 12-gauge slugs it had stopped. "Interesting evening apparel for a ride," Mutt said. "I'm sure you got a story for why you got all your getup on."

Harry didn't answer. Instead he looked out across the field in the direction the lone escaping rider.

"And don't worry none about old Conn getting away, there." Mutt smiled as he pulled Macomber to his feet. "Even a genius like him is bound to slip up sooner or later."

By the time Mutt and Harry returned their prisoners to the jail, word was out about the girl murdered in Johnny Town tonight. Mutt decided he'd head over to the crime scene once he wrapped things up at the jail.

Macomber's hand was patched up by Doc Tumblety, who seemed damned put out to be having to make a late call to the clink, especially for Mutt.

"I just came from performing surgery, damn your half-breed hide!" Tumblety growled.

"Francis," Pratt said to the doctor with a sigh. "Just do it, please."

Tumblety mended the stub of an index finger the best he could and staunched the blood. The gunman whose horse had thrown him and broken his collarbone was in another cell, feeling little pain thanks to Tumblety's laudanum. The doctor said he'd be by tomorrow to see about a cast for the man's arm and shoulder. The dead in the field had been collected by one of Clay Turlough's men and were on their way to Clay and then to Boot Hill. Their kin would be notified in the morning, if they had any.

Mutt and Harry walked out onto the porch of the jail. The deputy closed the iron door behind them.

"So you were coming back from practicing your sword work with Professor Mephisto over at the theatre?" Mutt said. "I thought you were already pretty good with that big, shiny pig-sticker?"

"I am," Harry said. "Very. I need to be better."

"And the Prof is better?" Mutt said. "On top of all the other stuff he knows and all the things he's studied? Damn."

"The man has studied with Domenico Angelo in London and Thomas Hoyer Monstery as well," Harry said. "He's as quick with a blade as he is with his wit."

"Why the armor?" Mutt asked, leaning against the rail.

"I need to be used to the weight of it while fighting," Harry said. "Not that it has much weight, thing is as light as a feather, but I still need to know how I can move in it and can't move. It's lucky for both of us I was headed back from practice tonight and was too tired to take it off."

The two men sat in the still of the dark, their faces hidden by deep shadow. A distant gas streetlight puffed, then its flame brightened.

"Why?" Mutt said finally. "You hate me. You always have. And to acknowledge the corn, I hate you too. Why risk your own skin for me?"

Harry was quiet for a time, then finally spoke. "You were out with Maude Stapleton, right?"

"Yes," Mutt said.

"You love her?" Harry asked.

"That's none of your damn business."

"I thought so," Harry said. "I've seen how you two look at each other, how sometimes you want to touch each other so bad and you just . . . can't because then the sky would fall and a whole world of stupid narrow-minded little men like Max Macomber and his idiots would rain down on you and her, and you'd rather cut your own skin off than have her be hurt by you."

Mutt said nothing; his shadow looked out past the porch. "The reason I hate you is because you're free, Mutt. You say what you damn well want, to whoever you damn well please, and you don't care what people think of you, don't care what names they call you. I hate you because I wish to God I could do that, be that. But I can't."

"Why not?" Mutt asked. "It's your damn life, Harry. Don't belong to anyone else."

"Actually it does," Pratt said. "I have so many eyes on me, all the time, expecting me to act a certain way, do a certain thing. More eyes now, a lot more. Even my father's dead eyes looking at me, all the time, judging me. If I fail, if I don't live up to those expectations, I let a lot of people down, and it's just not in me to say, 'To hell with all of you, I'm doing what I want.' I tried that, I ran away from here, but I had to come back. Some days I still want to run—hell, most days. But I wasn't raised that way. I wish I had been.

"I stopped tonight because it burns like hell to know we live in a world where you can't just love who you love, be who you are, where someone who is free, like you, can be hung up in a tree for loving, for being free. To know you have to hide your love, like it's a dirty secret. It's unfair and it made me angry. For all his faults, my father taught me that, too, that something wrong's got to be made right."

Harry stepped off the porch, falling into the moonlight and out of shadow. He climbed onto his horse. "'Night, Deputy. See you tomorrow."

"Night, Mr. Mayor," Mutt said.

Mutt watched Harry ride off and finally disappear in the darkness beyond the few working streetlights on Dry Well Road.

Mutt rubbed his face and let the tension of the last few hours slide out of him with a sigh. He walked off the porch and began the walk over to Johnny Town.

Two shadows detached from the darkness and blocked his path. Mutt cursed himself for thinking too much like a man and ignoring his senses—this was twice in one night. He now picked up that there were four of them, all around him, and they moved quiet, easy, fluid, not huffing and puffing like most white men did.

One of the shadows stepped forward and his face fell into light. He was an Indian, dressed in white man's clothing: work pants, boots, a collarless shirt and an unbuttoned vest. He also had on a gun belt and wore it like he knew how to use it. His long hair was pulled back and he wore a headband with a single black feather in it.

"We need you to come with us," the Indian said in Paiute. "He needs to talk with you."

"Fellas, my plate's been kinda overflowing today, so let's skip the mysterious bit, okay? Who? Who wants to see me?"

"Wodziwob," The Indian said.

"Let me git my horse," Mutt said.

The Three of Swords

The Galveston, Texas, newspaper called him the Annihilator. A clever and ambitious reporter there coined the term after his third victim and the killer rather liked it, finding it appropriately menacing and powerful. He wandered the streets of this booming, industrious, modern city and chose his victims with leisure and discretion. No one suspected him, no one was clever enough, or thought as he did enough, to begin to winnow out his process.

He wore a wooden African Dogon tribal mask when he killed. It had been a trophy from his first victim, a ship's captain. The empty face of the mask spoke to him, it was more his true face than this capricious mockery of emotive skin he was cursed with at birth.

He dragged his victims—male, female, black and white—out of their beds. He slid an ice pick into their tear ducts while they slept, damaging their brains and making them docile, but still aware, as he dragged them out under the merciless stars and unleashed his fury upon them. He had claimed sixteen victims in Galveston when he felt it give him an inescapable pull west, toward his god, toward the face on the mask—toward even greater power and glory. Toward annihilation. His was number six.

The Page of Wands

Dawn brought with it the news that another horrific murder had occurred in Johnny Town last night. There were rumors that the mayor and the sheriff were considering a curfew until the killer was brought to ground. Many citizens disliked the idea of a curfew with Thanksgiving only a few days away. Already, Harry Pratt's political opponents were making hay about the fact that women were no longer safe on the streets of Golgotha under the Pratt administration.

But politics were far from Jim's mind.

The morning was still cool and quiet when he rode up to Mrs. Stapleton's laundry. He tethered Promise to the hitching post beside the sidewalk, knocked and stepped inside, hat in hand. Constance was waiting for him, dressed in a very practical, and slightly oversized, man's collarless shirt, tucked into denim work pants and boots. Her hat hung on her back, held by a stampede cord. Her long brown hair was pulled back into a ponytail and she smiled as Jim entered.

"You look beautiful," Jim said.

Constance laughed.

"I look like a cow-puncher," she said. "But thank you."

Jim turned and waved to Maude. "Mrs. Stapleton."

Maude looked up from the laundry pile in front of her.

"I understand it is your intention to ride off with my fourteen-year-old daughter, unchaperoned?" Maude said, locking eyes with the young deputy.

Constance looked away, trying to not laugh out loud, as Jim's eyes grew wide with a mixture of fear and confusion. "Uh, well, yes, ma'am, but I wouldn't exactly put it like that. . . ."

"Oh, I'm sure you wouldn't," Maude said. "Now, I understand from Deputy Mutt that you fancy yourself quite the dandy, Master Negrey? Is that so? Quite the thief of hearts, are you?"

"I . . . I ain't no dude, ma'am, no sir!" Jim stammered. "I ain't stole no hearts or nothing else, ma'am! Mutt . . . he . . . My ma raised me right, I swear it."

Maude smiled at Jim and nodded to Constance, who was now outright laughing at the boy's discomfort. "Yes, I think she did, Jim," Maude said. "Just a little ways up Argent? Correct? Nowhere near the mining camp?"

"That's right, yes, ma'am," Jim said.

"You two be back by noon, and be careful," Maude said.

"I'll keep her safe, Mrs. Stapleton," Jim said. "I promise."

"Yes," Maude said. "I'm sure you will, Jim." She looked at Constance. "And you keep him safe as well."

"I will, Mother," Constance said. The girl slapped the still off-kilter Jim on the shoulder. "C'mon, you desperado, you. I packed us some food. Let's ride!"

"Oh, Deputy," Maude said to Jim's back as he followed Constance outside.

Jim turned. "Ma'am?"

"Anything untoward happens to my little girl, my treasure, and you will learn whole new definitions of pain and suffering for the rest of your infinitesimally short life," Maude said sternly, and then she smiled. "Enjoy your ride."

Jim helped Constance up onto Promise and she slipped her arms around his waist. It felt good, Jim had to admit, and it also felt comfortable, like this was where he was supposed to be.

"She's a beautiful horse," Constance said.

"The best you could ever ask for," Jim said. "I've had her since she was a foal. Me and Promise have been through pretty much everything together."

"I like her," Constance said, stroking the horse's flank.

"You ready?" he asked her.

Constance nodded. "Let's go."

Jim snapped the reins and Promise took off at a gentle, easy trot, headed up Argent Mountain by way of Prosperity Road.

The road began to ascend toward the peak of Argent Mountain. Jim urged Promise on and the brown mustang began a smooth gallop up the winding road, rising higher and higher, Golgotha behind them. Constance's arms encircled him. Jim couldn't help but smile. Promise took the two young people higher into the savage beauty of the wilderness, their hearts thudding in time to the horse's hooves. She tapped his shoulder and he turned his head slightly to hear her over the powerful drumming of Promise's hooves.

"I know a place we can ride to," she said. "It's got shade and some food for Promise. We can eat breakfast out there, if you want?"

"Sounds good," Jim said.

"Okay," Constance said. "Bear right here at Backtrail Road."

Constance took them to one of the places where she and her mother trained. The site was marked by a huge boulder that both Constance and Maude called "the giant's fist" since it bore a certain resemblance to that. Off about fifty yards from the boulder was a wide rock shelf jutting out from the side of Argent. There was shade and low, flat rocks, big as tables, to sit or lay on, under the cool shadow.

They let Promise wander in the tall grasses off to the west of the stone tables, and the mare contentedly munched her breakfast. Jim stretched out a blanket on one of the wide flat rocks, while Constance gave Promise water from a canteens they had brought.

"She's so good!" Constance said as she walked back under the cool shade. "And smart too!"

"Yeah, I'm pretty sure she's a sight brighter than me," Jim said. "She's kept me alive a lot of times. I owe her."

"I'm pretty sure you've done the same for her," Constance said, handing Jim an apple from her sack. "She loves you."

"You have a horse?" Jim asked.

"My father promised me a pony, just mine, when I was twelve, but he got busy with work at the bank," Constance said. "We have two horses my father bought. They're carriage horses, but I've been riding one of them quite a bit lately," Constance said. "She's beautiful. Her name is Sheba. She's a grulla."

"A smoke," Jim said, nodding and taking a bite of his apple. "Pretty horses, stout, gotta good heart. My pa always said they don't give up."

"Whereabout is your family?" Constance said. "If you don't mind me asking. Harriet Rees says your father was some kind of hero, passed in the war, and the rest of your family was taken from you by Indian raiders on the western trail?"

"You believe all that?" Jim asked, smiling.

"No, it sounded very dime novel to me," Constance said. "So, tell me the real story."

Jim started to wind up the lie, the one he'd practiced till he was perfect at telling it: Dad passed away, mother and little sister back in Kansas; he came out west looking for a job to make some money to send home. Hoped they would come out here one day, to be with him once he made it big. It was a good lie, with plenty of truth and little stories sprinkled in. A fine lie. A safe lie.

He looked at Constance's wide brown eyes and fell into them.

"I have this lie I usually tell most folks," Jim said. "I don't want to lie to you. Ever. It's a bum way to start anything. Especially anything important."

"I'm important?" Constance said. There was no teasing in her voice. A dry wind off the 40-Mile fluttered the edges of the blanket and her hair.

"You feel . . . very important," Jim said, lost in her eyes. "The truth is I killed some men in West Virginia a few years back. They were . . . bad men. One of them killed my pa, hurt my ma and sister. The other . . . he didn't do anything worth dying for . . . he just caught me when I was mad, out of control.

"I ran. My mother told me to run and never come back. My little sister, she . . . got hurt at the end of it. No, that's a lie too—the hardest lie. When me and this other fella were shootin', Lottie got hit . . . most likely by me. The last time I saw her she was bleedin', dying. I honestly don't know if she is alive or dead, if I killed my baby sister."

Jim felt Constance's hand slide into his, clutch it tight and squeeze.

"So that's my family," Jim said, his voice croaking a little. "And that's the truth. I like Harriet Rees' version better, I must say."

Constance smiled. "I'm so sorry, Jim. You can't go home, ever?"

Jim shook his head. "I guess I could if I'm looking to dance on a rope, and that's fair, Constance. I did kill that man in cold blood and he didn't have it coming. He just got between me and my pa's eye."

"Eye?" Constance said.

"Yeah, that's another story," Jim said.

"You're full of stories, aren't you, Jim Negrey?"

"I got a question for you," Jim said, smiling. "How'd you come to know about this place up here?"

Constance sighed. "The lie is, this is a spot my mother and I found to come picnic. The truth is . . . the truth is it's my favorite spot to hide away from the world. I've been coming here for years. When my father was angry, or mother was sad. Only my mother knows about it, and now you."

"Thank you. I'm honored you trust me," Jim said. "I understand. I got a place like that, too, over by Clay's. It's my secret spot to go to when I'm kind of fed up with everyone. It's real beautiful, 'specially when the sun is coming up or sinking. Only Promise, and now you, know about it."

"Well," Constance said. "I am honored to be in such sterling company."

They both laughed and ate and talked about books and songs they enjoyed, people their age in town and places they longed to visit. Constance was both proud and very ashamed. She had lied to Jim, lied expertly, using all the tools and tricks her mother was teaching her: the use of eye contact, the posture and body language, even her tone and inflection had masterfully concealed her lie. She told herself it was only a lie of omission. What she had told Jim was true; it just wasn't all of the truth. Only a fool would be completely honest with someone they just met, she could hear her mother's voice saying in her head. But Jim Negrey had trusted her with a secret that could get him killed and he certainly didn't seem like a fool, far from it.

They ate all the food and drank a good deal of water. The sun was higher in the sky now and the heat of the day was settling in. "I hate to say it," Jim said, hopping off the stone table and petting his full stomach, "but I reckon we need to get you home 'fore your ma puts a few extra holes in me."

"This wasn't my dream," Constance said. "We were racing in the deep desert, full gallop."

"Yep," Jim said. "You're right. I mean, don't get me wrong, this was . . . well, this was great, Constance. But it wasn't what I saw either."

"I'm kind of glad," Constance said. "This is ending much better than my dream did."

"May I ask how it ends?" Jim said.

Constance sighed and decided that maybe sometimes lies were better.

"You try to kiss me and I have to punch you in the breadbasket," she said, smiling.

An odd look came over Jim's face.

"What?" Constance said.

"Nothing," Jim said. "That's two . . ."

"Two what?" she asked.

"Nothing," Jim said. "All right, let's pack up and get you home. I really enjoyed this, Constance."

"Me too," she said, folding up the blanket. "Can we do this again?"

Jim's face lit up.

"Sure!" he said, "you say the word. I really like that."

"Did you mean what you said about me seeming important?" Constance said, not meeting Jim's gaze.

"Yeah," Jim said, "very."

They rode down Argent. Both were quiet and Constance rested her head against his back. It felt good. She hated lying to Jim, it felt wrong, a mistake, but how could she tell him, how could she tell him that her strange dreams always came true, that they had never been wrong. How could she tell Jim that her dream of them galloping across the desert ended with his death?

The World (Reversed)

Bick escorted Emily out of the Paradise Falls and down Main Street toward the Imperial for lunch. It was warm and bright out, but not overly hot today. Bick with his flat-brimmed Stetson, smoked glasses to avoid the desert glare, and silver-headed walking stick took the young girl's arm and led her along the street, interposing himself between the filth, dust and bustle of the main thoroughfare and his charge.

"I'd like to spend Thanksgiving with you," Emily said. "I've never really had a family to spend it with before."

Bick smiled and nodded. He squeezed her arm gently.

"I'd enjoy that very much," Bick said.

The faces that passed them endeavored to be polite enough, but Emily noted almost at once that it was a thinly veiled attempt.

"Mr. Bick, good day, sir," Egypt Whitehurst, one of the stage hands at Professor Mephisto's Playhouse, said and doffed his hat as he passed. Others walked by without a spoken word, but their eyes shouted murder. A few whispered and hissed behind their backs as they passed.

"These people hate you," Emily said when they had a moment between the streams of humanity passing by. "I can feel it coming off of them like heat. Why?"

"They always have, to one degree or another," Bick said. "Either fear or hate, or a charming combination of the two. Fear is useful; hate tends to be counterproductive unless you can aim it just so. They hate me because I own this place, own the land, the water, the houses, the mine, their businesses. I own them. And you always hate someone who controls your destiny without your say-so."

"That . . . that must be lonely," she said.

Bick shook his head.

"No, millions of years of solitude, far from home, is lonely. Crowded hatred is quite cozy after all that.

"They have every right to hate me, Emily. I've used and manipulated them, played on their weaknesses and misfortunes, and I own them lock, stock and barrel because of that. They all know it, too, and they all wouldn't shed a tear if I died tomorrow, most likely they would have a party. But the world will endure and they will all be alive to hate me, and that will suffice."

"A charming sentiment, Biqa." The man's voice was warmer than the sun in the sky. "Ever the noble, stoic sentinel, aren't we? How amazingly boring."

Bick stopped; he moved to interpose himself between Emily and the man blocking their way. The afternoon sun was behind him, so all Emily could see of the stranger was a vague silhouette wreathed in brilliant light.

"Hello, Ray," Bick said. "Why are you here?"

"You know exactly why I'm here," Ray Zeal said, stepping forward and blocking the sun so Emily could see him. He was slender, golden and handsome. Emily stepped back instinctively, though, because of the emotions she received from this man: pure, undiluted anger, cruelty and malice, wrapped in beauty and geniality—like a needle buried in a perfect apple.

"I'm here for the skull," Zeal said. "Where is it?"

"Safe from you," Bick said.

"Oh, Malachi," Zeal said, laughing. "If there is one thing I have learned about this big, wide, wonderful world, it's that there is no place that is safe." He looked past Bick to Emily. "Well, hello there, you sweet little thing. What's your name, darling?"

"She's no one," Bick said. "She's lost and I'm escorting her back to her hotel."

Zeal sniffed the air. He stepped into Bick, crowding him, and reached to Emily's hair. He lifted a few locks with his fingers, pulled them close to his nose and inhaled deeply. His smile broadened. He leaned to Bick's ear and whispered as he looked into Emily's widening eyes.

"A family reunion. How sweet."

"Stay away from her," Bick said. He pushed, hard, and Zeal flew backward, away from him and from Emily. Zeal crashed into a few of the folks moving around them on the street, knocking some of them over. There was shouting, cursing, and a crowd began to form.

"Watch where the hell you're going!" a burly miner shouted to Zeal as he climbed back to his feet. "You damned brick-footed . . ."

Zeal, smiling, lifted the man off the ground with one hand by the throat. He began to crush the man's windpipe. Bick put his hand on Zeal's forearm. The two angels locked gazes.

"Put . . . him . . . down," Bick said. Zeal's smiled slid away and he squeezed harder. There was a snapping, crunching sound like twigs breaking, and the miner's body stopped struggling and hung limp. Zeal tossed the body. It flew across the wide, busy street, with people shouting, ducking and diving for cover. It crashed into the window of Geoff Aggerby's barbershop and dentist practice. Bick tightened his grip and spun Zeal around. He led him farther onto Main Street and away from the crowds on both sides watching the altercation. He raised his walking stick to strike the golden angel.

"Yeah, Malachi," Zeal said, the smirk back on his face. His hand dropped to his saber at his belt. "Let's do it, Biqa! Let's open the ball, right now. Do it, come on! Think how good it will feel to not have to walk on eggshells in this fragile little china shop of a world, to not hold so much of ourselves in any longer, for fear of breaking the props. We can flatten this shithole of a town in a single flutter of a fly's wing. . . . Come on, it will be fun. You might even win."

Bick lowered his stick and let Zeal go. "Get out of my town, Ray, now, or by the Radiant Arch, I will put you down."

"Give me the skull and I'll consider it."

"No," Bick said. "Why do you want it so badly now, after all this time?"

"Because I cyphered it all out and it's a beautiful, horrible jest," Zeal said. "But the joke is just for me and God. You wouldn't get it, Biqa. Guess it's the hard way then, suit yourself. Got a little matter to take up with that pet sheriff of yours too. That fucker went and killed my boy, Nikos. I think I'm going to eat that bastard while he's still living."

"No," Bick said again. "I won't allow that."

"You keep saying that," Ray said. "But 'no' don't mean shit, unless you got the sand to back it up. I'm going to tear your little kingdom apart until I find that skull and I'm going to carve up your sheriff and you can't do a thing about it, Malachi."

Emily ran up to stand beside Bick.

"Get back!" Bick said.

"Oh, the love of a daughter for her daddy," Zeal said. "Tell me, my dear, did your stalwart father tell you what he did to you and to your mother?"

"Stop it," Bick said.

Zeal laughed. "Poor Malachi, so used to being able to order the sheep about, it's hard to deal with a bigger wolf than yourself, isn't it? I feel a certain obligation to the girl; after all, I'm practically her uncle."

Zeal stepped back, blocking more of Main Street. Traffic was stopped in both directions. While people couldn't hear what was being said, everyone seemed very interested in the conflict. More than a few were hoping the stranger would pull out his pistol and shoot Bick. "You see, my dear, your father here fucked your mother, and here's the funny part—bearing one of our children? Well, it always kills the mother. Always, without fail."

"Ray, swear to . . ."

"To whom, exactly?" Zeal said. "Swear to whom, Biqa? If the Almighty gave a shit, how would I even be here, doing all this? Surely He'd stop his own creation and come to his loyal servant's aid? Unless I'm His loyal servant and you're the freak." Zeal laughed. Bick looked at Emily. Her eyes were wet.

"Emily . . . ," he said.

"Is it true?" Emily said. "Is it? If I mean anything to you at all, please, please, tell me the truth now. Don't lie. Is it true?"

"Yes," Bick said, lowering his eyes from hers. "It's true."

"You knew," she said. "You knew it would kill her, and you just did it anyway. I grew up an orphan, in a nightmare, because of you . . . your selfish need."

"Yes," Bick said. "I was selfish . . . and I knew."

Emily ran, disappearing into the crowd. Zeal laughed and clapped. Bick grabbed him again and pulled him off his feet, their faces inches apart. There was a rumble of distant heat thunder and the sky darkened.

"Oh, good, you're finally angry," Zeal said. "All I did was be a good little angel and tell your sweet innocent girl the truth. That sets you free, right, the truth?"

Bick tightened his grip on the golden angel's collar.

"You know, Biqa, I'm tired of you putting your hands on me and not doing anything except hurting my feelings. That stops now," Zeal said quietly, so only Bick could hear. "I didn't come into town alone. I have snipers up on the roofs, enough to turn this street into a slaughterhouse. Now, you will not resist what I'm going to do next in any way, or all these precious townsfolk will die."

Zeal drove a fist into Bick's stomach. The dark angel flew back and fell into the mud and shit in the middle of the road. Zeal walked over and kicked Bick viciously in the face with his boot. Bick rolled over, driven by the force of it. When he looked up, he saw the glint of a rifle barrel reflected by the sun. The shooter was on top of town hall. Zeal grabbed him and picked him up with one hand and began pounding him in the face again and again and again. At first there were only a few shouts from the crowd, a murmur of approval, but when blood flew from Bick's smashed nose and mouth, there was a cheer all down Main Street.

"Kill that son of a bitch!" one voice shouted.

"Rich bastard done bled us all dry, fuck 'im up!" another screamed.

"How you like that, Miiiiisssssttttteeeerrrr Bick!" a mocking voice called out to derisive laughter and more hooting and cheering.

"Bully! Bully!" a voice called out. "Give that codfish aristocracy a sound thrashing! Thought himself above the law for far too many years, you ask me!"

"Make him bleed more!" another voice, shrill with rage, shouted.

Bick was aware, and the pain was real; he wished he could pass out, but he couldn't. A few fat drops of rain began to fall. Zeal stopped punching him and pulled him close.

"These are the pieces of cosmic garbage you are protecting, Biqa. These are the worthless motes of finite shit that you just took a beating to save. And where is our boss? Where is the being you are continuing to serve when it can't get any more evident He doesn't give a fuck about you or your loyal service or any of these meat puppets? Cogitate on that and wait for me to come back here and kill every single one of them."

Zeal tossed him on his back into the muck of the street again and the sky roared almost as loudly as the crowd did. Zeal turned slowly, rotating to address the entire crowd, his voice seeming to grow louder as to be heard over the thunder and the rowdy assembly.

"Good people of Golgotha," Zeal bellowed, smiling. "My name is Ray Zeal and I am a very bad man to cross. This villain, this Malachi Bick, has cabbaged something from me and I intend to get it back. Now, I'm going to ride in here in two days with my crew, and we are going to take this walking shit-stain Bick apart until he gives me back my property. I got no grudge with any of you upstanding folks and your kin, so you just go about your business and maybe enjoy the show."

Laughter arose from the crowd. Bick, his face swollen and bloody, crouched in the mud, still and silent. The rain was falling harder now, running down his hair and his torn cheeks. He had tracked at least three snipers on rooftops and knew there were surely more gunmen in the crowds. Zeal pointed to him and smiled.

"Now, if anyone cares to line up, to stand with this man, and take up arms to defend him, well, then me and mine will have a problem with you. And I swear, anyone who helps this man will get the same treatment he gets tenfold. I hope I've made myself real clear. Go about your business and good day to you all now."

A cheer went up from the crowd and some whoops of joy and excitement. Zeal walked past Bick, looking down at him as he passed by.

"Two days, Biqa. Then my worshipers and I will be back. You had best crawl out to meet me on your belly with the skull in hand. If you do that, I will give these rubes a quick, painless death. If you resist me, then I will turn this place into Hell on Earth. Remember to say your prayers tonight."

Zeal stepped away, disappearing into the rain.

Biqa, Malachi Bick, remained kneeling and tried to find the face of God in the ruin of the road.

The Three of Swords

In the summer of 1870, Elijah Barrows began hunting the pampered and secreted mistresses of the congressmen of the District of Columbia. A tailor by trade, Barrows was guided by faceless forces that drove him to savagely murder and mutilate five women in the deepest precincts of power in the young nation.

His fifth victim died in a suite of the Willard Hotel at the corner Pennsylvania and Sixteenth. He sewed her eyes shut, as he did with all of his victims. The fifth woman was also his muse, for in her blood he was compelled to write his destination far to the west, a place that called to him, screamed to him with promises of blood and fantasy fulfilled and sweet, sweet release. His was number ten.

Barrows wrote the destination of all those chosen to possess one of the thirty-two. The place they were being driven to, like a pack of hungry wolves. Driven by silent, waking dreams, bright, vivid fantasies that long ago failed to supplant the visceral reality found in the warm splash of blood and the rich, coppery taste of human flesh. Murderers, poisoners, rapists, torturers, wanderers, trap-door spiders, hunters, predators, sadists, the mad. All bound together by their secret, bloody god and by their possession of one of the thirty-two.

And all bound for the same destination.

And in distant Golgotha, Nevada, the killer and mutilator of prostitutes, who had claimed three victims, smiled in anticipation. Three down, two to go.

The Magician

They rode north the rest of the night and into early morning before they came to the camp. Mutt had changed clothes before leaving and grabbed his guns and knife. He left a note under Jim's door at the boardinghouse explaining where he was going and to tell Jonathan that he would be back as soon as he could.

Mutt recognized the garb of the men who rode out to meet them—two of them were Goshute, the other Shoshone. All carried rifles and all wore a single black feather in their headbands, just as his escorts from Golgotha did.

"*Behne,*" the lead rider said in greeting. "So this is the famous spirit man, the one that stood alone against the Nimerigar—the man-eater monsters with their poisoned arrows? Who drove them back to their cave cities over forty seasons ago? The two-world walker? The one that owns no name. I thought you'd be less pretty."

"I take it your name," Mutt said in his best Shoshone, "is Talks-Through-Asshole."

The men all laughed, even the one Mutt had insulted. "This way," the Shoshone said. "He's been expecting you."

The inside of the tent was still cool, compared to the rising heat of the late morning on the badlands. Mutt entered, along with the leader of the party that had found him in Golgotha, a man named Mahkah. The tent reminded Mutt of his youth and his late mother. There were blankets and skins arranged on the floor for sitting and sleeping. A simple cook pot hung from a metal spit and a few saddlebags and a small, ornate wooden box were propped in one corner with a rifle and a belt of shells resting on it. The tent smelled of worn leather and rich tobacco. The sole occupant of the tent was sitting cross-legged, drinking from a tin cup of water. He was an Indian. It was difficult to determine his exact age, but his hair fell to his shoulders and was silver. His eyes were as old and dark as the void between the stars. He smiled at his guests with every part of him, not just his face, and Mutt felt his power and presence shine out of him.

"Hawthorne Wodziwob," Mutt said, removing his hat. *"Maiku."*

"Maiku, my friend," Wodziwob replied in Numa, the ancient Paiute language—Mutt's native tongue. "Thank you for coming. I hoped you would."

"I've heard a lot about you over the last few years," Mutt said. "I wanted to see if you were the real deal, like everyone said."

Wodziwob laughed. "I'm curious, what is 'the real deal' exactly?"

"They say you can heal the sick and they say you have walked in the land of the dead," Mutt said. "They say you claim to carry a message back from the dead to the living."

"Is that so?" Wodziwob said. "Please, sit. You must be weary."

"That is a hell of a story," Mutt said as he and Mahkah sat on the furs. Wodziwob offered the men water and they both drank from tin cups like their host. "Supposedly, you claim the dead will rise if enough of the Numu will do these circle dance ceremonies you've been hawking, and some great power from beyond will wipe the white men from the lands and return them to the People."

"Hawking, eh?" Wodziwob said with a chuckle. "For a man whose reputation claims he's got spirit blood in his veins, who has battled the Nimerigar in their cave cities under the earth and helped bind the Uktena, just a year ago, you seem very skeptical."

"The other worlds are real," Mutt said. "I've seen them, been to them and sure as hell sent enough things back to 'em. Jist 'cause they are real don't mean you are. Some folks say you're a fraud. I'm jist trying to figure out where you stand."

"You fought with Chief Paulina against the whites, Mutt? Yes?" Wodziwob said.

"Yes, for a time," Mutt said. "We had a falling-out after he had Chief Queapama assassinated. I chose not to ride with him no more."

"Why?" Wodziwob asked.

"Paulina was a lying, bloodthirsty son of a bitch and whatever happened to him, he had coming," Mutt said.

"Some say you helped the army, a Captain John Drake, to fight Paulina," Mahkah said.

"Is that so?" Mutt said, never taking his eyes off Wodziwob.

"Every man's story is open to interpretation," Wodziwob said. "Good and bad. I assure you that I have nothing but the best interests of our people at my heart."

"Your people," Mutt said. "Not mine."

"Why do you say that?" Mahkah asked.

"'Cause 'our people' called my mother a dirty whore and drove her out of the only home she ever had. Because they took her away from her father and mother, brothers and sisters, turned them against her, against their own blood. Because a bunch of old men who claimed to have the ear of the spirits, like ole Wodziwob here, told her she had disgraced her people, when the only spirits any of those dried-up old hypocrites knew a damn thing about was the coffin varnish they were guzzling up in the elder's lodge. I got to watch her spirit die, day after day, then her flesh. I was the only thing that kept her alive, kept her going."

"So you consider yourself a white man now that you've lived with them, fought with them?" Mahkah said.

Mutt laughed.

"Shit," he said. "I'd rather wipe my ass with a cactus than dream of bein' a white man. Just 'cause I live with stupid don't mean it's catchin'."

"You must be very lonely," Wodziwob said. "No home, no people . . ."

"Oh, I got home and I got people," Mutt said. "My tribe is small and they are pretty funny-lookin' by white or Numa standards, but they've never screwed me over and they never will. I picked my home and my family, thank you all the same. Keep your damn pity."

Wodziwob nodded. "My apologies, I see you are a man who knows himself and his life. You have passed through two of the three crises of life and come out with wisdom. You have fought your inner battles and won them."

"Not all, and not without help," Mutt said. "I sure as hell ain't wise, but I know who I am, and that's good enough."

"Very good," Wodziwob said. "You are exactly who we need."

"Usually when I hear that kind of talk, it means trouble is hitchin' up his horse outside," Mutt said. "Who's 'we'?"

"As you know, the land hereabout is powerful—like you, it straddles many worlds," Wodziwob said. "It is a crossroads of many ancient powers and spirits—a place of mystery and *pua* that has existed since the dawn of the world. And as long as there has been life, since the time when only the animals talked here, since the Dine came to live in these lands, and even now, as the whites swarm over it like locusts, it has fallen to a small, secret council to protect all who live here from the bad medicine of this place and to protect the wellsprings of good medicine that flow here from abuse or destruction."

Mutt grew calm, even solemn, as the old man spoke.

"We were founded by the powerful Puakantï, Be'kiwa-ah, he who was a servant of Esa, Wolf—the creator force, the Great Medicine."

Wodziwob held up a single perfect feather. It tapered from a dark gray at its edges to a deep black. "Be'kiwa-ah gave the first of us this totem of power, that we might call upon him and make his medicine our own."

Mutt felt the power coming off the feather in waves, like the ocean crashing against the land. "We move in shadow and silence," Wodziwob continued, "seeking no glory in our duty. Our reward is how we protect so many with so few seeing the tracks of our passing. As the time of the end grows closer, so, too, does the danger in these lands. . . ."

"Whoa," Mutt said. "'Time of the end'? We went through that last year, the Uktena was bound. The boy, my friend Jim, he used the Ulun'suti—the crystal eye that came from the skull of the Uktena—to wake the dead spirits in the desert. The spirits held the Uktena down in his well. World saved, right? Right?"

Wodziwob said nothing.

"Well, ain't that a little kick of sunshine up your backside," Mutt said. He rubbed his face, and then drank more water.

"Prophet, are you sure this is the one the spirits told you to give the mission to?" Mahkah asked, giving Mutt a sidelong glance of disapproval. "The Snake-Man is powerful and cunning. He has god-venom in his veins, but this man, he is disrespectful and acts a fool. His mind is neither serious nor disciplined. If he fails, then Snake-Man gets the skull and many will die."

"Thanks for the vote of confidence," Mutt said, wiping his mouth. "Hey, what mission? I never said anything about a mission here."

"He is what he is," Wodziwob said. "Born of dust and flame. His blood is as strong as Snake-Man's. Yes, I am sure."

"Who's Snake-Man?" Mutt asked.

"He was one of us," Mahkah said. "Initiated into our council. One of our greatest . . ."

"He was a warrior and Puakantï of the Northern Paiute. He lost his family when the white soldiers came to punish us for trying to stop the white settlers from taking our land. They killed us, we killed them. It grew, like a prairie fire. They called it the Snake War."

"I know of it," Mutt said. "Died down a few years back, I understand."

"Not for Snake-Man," Wodziwob said. "It will never end for him."

"His name is Awan," Mahkah said. "But after his family was destroyed he took the name Snake-Man. He said if the whites were going to call us all snakes, he would be the face and name they would fear in the deepest night."

"He has murdered over a hundred and twenty-five white men, women and children in his search for revenge," Wodziwob said, shaking his head. "And over fifty of his own people, including women and children. He has . . . lost his way."

"You want me to bring him in," Mutt said. "Why the hell me? More importantly, why the hell should I?"

"You are said to be like him," Mahkah explained. "He claims to be the son of Snake—the spirit of wisdom, initiation and healing. A powerful spirit, to be sure."

"And you, they say," Wodziwob said, "are the son of Coyote—the trickster, the bringer of fire and forbidden knowledge. Another powerful spirit."

Mutt shook his head. "Me and my kin, we don't talk much, lest we gotta. Why you after him? What's all this about a skull?"

"It is the skull of the brother-killer, the one known as Pauguk. The skull is home to a powerful Manitou," Wodziwob said. "Old as man. The soul of a thing, the idea given energy. The Algonquian call it Gitche Manitou—the Great Spirit, a god."

"So the skull's holding a god," Mutt said. "Or an idea, or both. Of what?"

"Murder," Wodziwob said. "The skull holds the Manitou of unmaking all things living. It was born out of men, and so terrible that the Great Spirit locked it away in the skull of Pauguk, who dreamed it up."

"Great," Mutt said. "Couldn't just sweep it the hell away. Nope, that'd be too damn easy. Good ole Great Spirit."

Wodziwob lashed out so quickly Mutt didn't even comprehend what he had done until he had done it. The old man slapped both sides of Mutt's face, hard. Wodziwob's face remained as placid as an endless blue sky.

"At some point in your life, maybe at many, the words you uttered could be applied to you. All things exist for a reason—not just the ones we want to exist."

"That include those white men you advertisin' to wipe from the face of the earth?" Mutt asked, rubbing his stinging cheek.

Wodziwob shrugged.

"The spirits talk to me; I listen and tell what they say. I don't always understand it. Perhaps, the driving of the whites from our lands is now the right thing at the right time. I do not question the seasons, or the sun and moon. I will not question the wisdom of the spirits."

"Well, I sure as hell do," Mutt said. "So this skull is out there and your renegade is hunting for it?"

"Yes," Wodziwob said. "He now serves a very bad, very powerful being who is hunting for it. This being is a messenger of the Great Spirit. He believes he does the Great Spirit's work."

"Does he?" Mutt asked.

"The Great Spirit speaks with many voices," Wodziwob said. "He has a different voice for each of us."

"That doesn't really answer my question," Mutt said.

"You get that a lot with the Great Spirit," Wodziwob said. "This spirit messenger calls himself Ray Zeal."

"A white man?" Mutt said.

"He walks as one," Wodziwob said. "But he is older than this world and dangerous."

"Of course he is," Mutt said. "Never met one that was sweet as pie."

"I can tell you where the skull is hidden," Wodziwob said. "The medicine man who helped hide it and worked the medicine to protect it was one of our number. If you can find it and secure it before Snake-Man does, please bring it to me. I can ensure it is kept safe and the Manitou within it will sleep. If Zeal and Snake-Man get it, death and madness will stride the world of mortal man."

"You assume I trust you with this thing," Mutt said, standing. "You never did tell me who this secret council is, exactly."

"We are the Black Feathers," Wodziwob said. "I understand trust is earned. It comes in time, Mutt. We would be honored to have you join us."

Justice (Reversed)

Martin Anderton thought that crossing the Atlantic on a ship was perhaps the greatest discomfort he had ever known until he had undertaken the stagecoach to reach his daughter, Maude, in the little shithole she lived in—Golgotha, Nevada. Anderton experienced the indignity and the crassness of close quarters travel with a number of the unwashed riffraff who were now headed out west in droves to stake a claim to gold or silver, or to get lost in some seedy little cattle camp like this Golgotha—hiding from creditors, the law, abandoned families and past deeds. The proximity he had to endure to some of these people made his skin crawl and each time he thought of his silent, shy, beautiful daughter and his baby granddaughter alone out here in this godforsaken desert now that Maude's husband, Arthur, had passed, he knew he had made the correct choice in coming out to fetch them. However, he had determined by the time the stagecoach reached the Colorado Territories that his return with the girls would be by train.

Besides the constant, kidney-smashing jostling that made one feel as if they had been in a bare-knuckle altercation, the stench from the bodies of his fellow passengers made Anderton seriously consider walking several times. When he could no longer mask his discomfort, one of the other travelers, a whiskey-soaked puke by the name of Dorsey, informed him the stink was far worse if he had come in the summer.

The Missourian had offered Anderton some of his libation as a remedy to the discomforts of the road. He explained it was good stagecoach etiquette to share one's "hooch." Anderton politely declined, since the only thing he could imagine worse than traveling by stagecoach sober was traveling by stagecoach hung-over.

They were close to Golgotha, Anderton was informed at one of the coach stations, in an arid wasteland charmingly called Sand Springs but more suited to an infernal appellation.

"We should be getting on to Golgotha pretty soon, sir," said the Wells Fargo coach driver, a rustic but stalwart chap who went by the folksy sobriquet of Pony Bob. "Odd place to be sure—damned odd, but they got fine vittles, soft beds and clean water. Can't ask for much else this far out."

"No," Anderton said, finding himself in full agreement with Pony Bob. "I don't suppose you can."

So when the coach clattered to a stop hours before they should be arriving in Golgotha, Anderton was already on edge. He slipped the small derringer out of his vest pocket and into his palm as the other passengers began to rouse from the torpor of the trail.

"Everyone out!" Pony Bob shouted. "Unexpected stop, folks. Everyone out of the coach!"

The doors were unlocked and Anderton and the five other passengers clambered out into the blindingly bright Nevada daylight. The coach was surrounded by soldiers on horseback, dressed in tan fatigue blouses, trousers, suspenders, leggings and slouch hats. None of the men wore insignia denoting rank or unit. They were armed with pistols at their belts and sabers. They covered the passengers and the coach driver and his second, riding shotgun, with Springfield "trapdoor" .50 caliber rifles.

Anderton counted about a dozen men surrounding the coach and blocking the road. Off about a hundred yards from the roadside was a large military camp, bristling with activity. Anderton guessed there were about fifty troops in total based here, as well as a sizable civilian presence. Calculating the odds in his mind, he casually slipped his small pistol back into his pocket.

"What gives?" Pony Bob said to the man who seemed to be commanding the troops. The leader had a prodigious, drooping mustache and several days' growth of beard on his grim face. His hand rested on the hilt of his cavalry saber. "All these bodies in government suits? Mind explaining why you're blocking the coach way there, mister?"

"You're headed for Golgotha," the commander said. "You're damn lucky we caught you. Place is sealed up by order of Governor Blasdel of Nevada. Got an outbreak of scarlet fever all over the town. Mayor Pratt asked the governor for assistance and to quarantine the town until further notice. No one in or out."

The passengers began to grumble. One woman seemed faint. "My husband is in Golgotha!" she said to the commander. "Is he all right?" The commander shrugged.

"Couldn't tell you. Last report was there were bodies piling up all over."

The woman swooned and Dorsey managed to catch her and lead her back toward the shade of the coach. Many of the circle of mounted soldiers chuckled at the woman's obvious dismay. Anderton and Pony Bob were both shocked at such a cruel reaction.

"See here now!" Anderton said loudly. "My name is Martin Anderton, founder, president and owner of the Anderton Mercantile Venture Companies of Charleston, South Carolina. I am on a mission of grave importance. My daughter and granddaughter are in Golgotha, and I am willing to take the risk of venturing into the town with any expeditionary or reinforcement force you may be sending in there. I have to get my family out."

The commander shrugged again. He seemed good at it. "Most likely they are already dead," he said blandly. "Even if they are not, no one goes in or out. We've got every route into Golgotha blocked. We'll ship their bodies back to you in South Carolin-ah."

The soldiers laughed at the commander's faux Southern accent. Anderton's face grew red.

"Look here, you blasé myrmidon! I am personal friends with Governor Scott of South Carolina and you will fetch me your commanding officer immediately, or else I can assure you your next command will be digging latrine holes in a worse place than this!"

The Commander's face didn't change at all and Anderton noticed his grip on his saber tightened. Several of the men under his command readied their rifles. The commander looked toward the camp.

Anderton noted a tall, extremely corpulent bald man dressed in a very expensive tailored suit, who was watching the confrontation with the commander while reclining in a high-backed French-style chair that seemed more appropriate for a parlor than the wasteland. The fat man was gnawing on something he held in one hand. A slender black man dressed in the fastidious attire of a butler stood beside the fat man, shading him from the brutal desert sun with a large parasol. The fat man pulled his lips away from his repast and shook his head very slightly to the commander, who in turn nodded and saluted the fat man.

"You have ten minutes to get your horses water and any for yourselves you can scare up," the commander said. He leaned forward and pointed toward the make-shift coral. As he did so, Anderton observed an odd talisman about his neck that fell forward as he shifted and hung free of his tunic—a single yellowed human tooth, with a hole drilled through it to accommodate a thin silver chain. Anderton wondered if it had belonged to an Indian warrior this odd, cold man had slain on the field of battle. "Then you turn this coach around and head back where you came from. You tell anyone you see headed this way to head back. Golgotha is a graveyard until this sickness runs its course and anyone trying to get in or out past us will be shot. That clear enough for you, Mr. Big Bug from South Carolina?"

The soldiers laughed again. Anderton started to protest, but Pony Bob put a calming hand on his shoulder.

"Will do, sir," Bob said to the commander. "I'll telegraph the Wells Fargo offices when we get to the next station with a wire and have them pass the word along as well."

"You do that," the commander said.

Anderton turned to Pony Bob. "If these men are federal soldiers then I'm John Brown's body," Anderton said. Pony Bob nodded in agreement. "What the devil is going on here?"

"Beats me, but once we get back, I'll make sure to contact the home office and give them the real deal," Bob said. "Something is queer here, but we ain't got the firepower to make a fist about it, Mr. Anderton. I'm sorry, sir."

Anderton nodded to Pony Bob. "It's all right. You're right, of course. I just . . . That's my little girl in there, alone, most likely terrified. I just . . ."

"I understand, sir. Let's get the horses watered and get while the getting is good. I'll pray for your girls, Mr. Anderton."

Bob headed off, shouting to the other passengers to make haste to get fresh water and see to their toilet. Anderton swore under his breath and turned back toward the coach. He hated the barbarism of this land. He was eager to get the girls home to civilization, if they survived the plague of Golgotha.

In short order the stage rumbled away back from where it came. Col. Bradley Whitmore, the commander of industrialist Charles Cook's private, fanatical, mercenary cadre, the Praetorians, watched the coach ride off and longed to ride after it and slaughter every person on board. However, Mr. Cook had ordered them to hold, and hold he did.

He rode up to his employer and regarded Mr. Cook as the huge bald captain of industry continued to suck the flesh off the boiled hand of the thirteen-year-old Irish girl who had been in the wagon leaving Golgotha yesterday evening. Cook's lips glistened with the child's fat. He looked up at his loyal commander and smiled.

"I know, I know, Whitmore. You wanted them. I understand. When we take the town, you and the men can wander the streets as bloody gods, slaying as you wish. But for now, a missing Wells Fargo stage would attract too much attention, too quickly. That's why we let the last one pass unmolested out of the town, unlike everyone else."

Since Ray Zeal's declaration to return, Whitmore and his men had been posted on all the roads into or out of Golgotha, posing as U.S. soldiers. Anyone leaving the town, save the stagecoaches, had been detained, tortured for any and all information about Golgotha and her inhabitants, and then murdered. A few men and women had been raped before or after death and a few, like Cook's Irish delicacy, had been eaten.

"That South Carolinian jackass will be trouble," Whitmore said. "He will get the real military involved."

"Snake-Man's renegades are already striking at a few settlements far enough away to keep the real army busy while we secure the town," Cook said. "I also have planted the scarlet fever story in enough of my newspapers around California, Utah and Nevada and sent the appropriate telegrams to ensure no one will be in great hurry to come to poor, isolated Golgotha's aid."

Cook struggled out of his custom chair. His manservant, sweating in full butler regalia in the noonday sun, helped him up. The black man, named Lazare, was not allowed to touch Mr. Cook except with gloved hands. Lazare hated Cook and wished him dead, but Cook had taken the servant's entire family hostage years ago to ensure his loyalty. So Lazare performed his odious tasks to keep his wife and sons alive.

"I'll report to Mr. Zeal," Cook said to Whitmore, as he handed the half-eaten child's hand to him. Whitmore eagerly began to lick the grease and strip the tatters of skin from the bones. "You see if you can get any more information from tonight's main course before we close the books on him."

Inside the main tent, Cook found Ray Zeal studying a large map of the town of Golgotha spread out on a campaign table, weighted down by books, a pistol and a decanter of rum. The map, while burned at the edges and stained with blood and marred with bullet holes, had notes scribbled on different buildings, details of who resided where, the number of people in each home, the names and locations of businesses, the schoolhouse, the churches.

Assembled around the table were some of Zeal's worshipers, like Cook himself. Professor Zenith tinkered absently with some type of coil, only half-listening and dreaming. Thug Batra, the Hindi, with his shaved head, necklace of human knuckle joints and wicked curved knives, stood silently watching everything, but seldom speaking.

Delilah LaTour, beautiful and cruel, was here to make sure she was fully prepared for her and Elijah Barrows's role to play in taking the town. Barrows, handsome, with a boyish child-like quality to him, stood beside the still-as-death LaTour and absently fondled himself, rocking back and forth on his heels. When she glared at him, he stopped touching himself and looked at the floor. It was the only time LaTour smiled.

The giant mountain man named Douglass, and his partner, the equally violent and unstable Victory Ferrell, nodded like children as their god, Ray Zeal—Raziel, the God of Murder and Divine Secrets—explained exactly what he needed them to do.

"So it's important that you two are in place, Victory, at the same time that Madame LaTour and Mr. Barrows are," Zeal said. "You need to be fully secured by the appointed time. All of our infiltrators inside Golgotha already will undertake their appointed tasks precisely at the times we discussed, so no variation is allowable, do you understand?"

"Yes, Lord," Farrell said. "Thy will be done."

"Well, I like the sound of that," Zeal said with a chuckle. He turned to address Cook. "Hi ya, Charlie, how goes the roadblock?"

"Just turned back the stagecoach," Cook said. "Still no word from Snake-Man though, sir."

Zeal frowned and looked on the map at the location of Argent Mountain. A large black X marked the spot the renegade Paiute medicine man had told Zeal was the hiding place of the skull.

"Snake-Man is essentially a Nephilim, more or less, like my poor boy, my Nicky," Zeal said. "If he isn't back by midnight, he most likely suffered the same fate as my son at the hands of this annoying piss-trough of a town's guardians. They shall all suffer our divine wrath."

The air around Zeal darkened and the tent grew very cold. Batra's eyes rolled back in his head as if he were in the throes of ecstasy. Barrows hummed and stroked himself faster, and was surprised to discover LaTour's icy hand joining his own. The tent thrummed with foul energy, churned like blood-filled water crowded with sharks.

"नफरत की मेरी सुंदर भगवान के लिए खून!" Batra shouted.

"Hallelujah!" Ferrell shouted. "Praise be to the Lord of the Slaughterhouse!"

Je suis la servante du dieu de la douleur et de plaisir!" LaTour whispered as she clutched Barrow's manhood tighter.

The blond death god shook off the darkness and slapped his palm on the table, breaking the spell. A broad smile returned to his face and his disciples composed themselves.

"No worry, Bick will give up the skull," Zeal said. "Sooner or later, especially after we close the trap. If he won't do it willingly, the sheep he values so much will make him.

"Then, once we have the skull and have dealt with Bick and the sheriff and the other guardians of Golgotha, we will reopen the town for business, like a trap-door spider, welcoming new followers and feeding on the sweet meat the desert sends us. There is power in that town, primordial, endless, hungry, and it will get along with me a damn sight better than it ever did with poor old Malachi."

"As you have pointed out, sir, they are very resourceful," Cook said. "Surely they will be making contingencies as well."

"Yes," Zeal said. "I'm sure they will, the mercurial Malachi Bick and the legendary Jon Highfather. Oh, I'm sure they have quite a few surprises in store for us, Charlie, but in the end, we will triumph. Do you know why?"

"No, sir," Cook said.

"Because they think like honorable men. They think of containment and just punishment, minimal casualties and valiant combat." Zeal leaned forward and whispered in the industrialist's ear. "And we, Charlie, we think like monsters."

"Now then," Raziel said, clapping his hands. "The plan, from the beginning, everyone's part in detail. Once more from the top, children!"

The Knight of Pentacles

Mutt rode back to Golgotha alone. His horse, a dark, dabbled paint named Muha, galloped across the bright desert, and Mutt urged him on. Mutt's hand dropped to his large sheathed knife at his hip as he crouched low in the saddle and neared the hidden cave on the western face of Argent Mountain, the secret resting place of the Manitou skull.

The skull sounded like a shotgun to Mutt, loaded with uncontrollable rage and hatred, ready to rip the world apart. Shotguns were effective at killing, but the blast caught everyone in its path. Shotguns didn't give a damn who they killed.

Wodziwob had warned him about the Snake-Man as he prepared to depart.

"He is very hard to harm, just as you are, Mutt," Wodziwob said, handing him a canteen of water. "He can be hurt, but killing him is difficult without overwhelming force or something of the spirit world."

"I think I have that covered," Mutt had said.

After the beating he had taken last year at the hands of an exceedingly resilient acolyte of the Uktena, Mutt had gone to Golgotha's resident master blacksmith and farrier, Wayland Smith, to undertake a special project for him. Old Wayland had had his hamstring cut sometime before he ever made it to Golgotha, and he had constructed a special steel brace to allow him to get about and to stand at the forge and the anvil for the hours he needed to do his job. Despite his affliction, Wayland was considered the finest blacksmith in three states. Mutt commissioned a knife from the nearly lame blacksmith, made from the finest steel. It was to be like Mutt's favored blade, a thirteen-inch Bowie knife, with only one significant difference—Mutt added his own blood into the molten steel as the blade was forged and hammered, and the steel was quenched and cooled in Mutt's blood. "Finest blade I've made in a long spell," Wayland said, handing the blood knife to Mutt. "Odd request, but not the oddest I've had since arriving here. May it cut true and deep for you, Deputy." Mutt rested his hand again on the hilt of the blood knife as Muha galloped faster and faster toward home. He was as ready for this as he'd ever be.

The cave was just where Wodziwob had said it would be, on the northwestern slope of Argent Mountain. It was late afternoon, only a few hours of daylight left. The entrance was little more than a small hole obscured by a thick stand of sagebrush. Mutt noted that someone had already disturbed the brush but had moved through it with great subtlety. There were chalk markings, petroglyphs, circling the cave's mouth. Mutt felt a strange ache in the pit of his stomach when his hand crossed the circle of symbols and broke the seal of the cave as he cleared the brush to make his way through. He tried to ignore the nausea as best he could and drew his blade.

The mouth of the cave was so low that Mutt had to squat down to pass through it. After duck-walking about ten feet he had enough clearance to stand, but the cave was narrow and the walls ran at sharp, tight angle. Mutt's face was only inches from the cave wall as he sidestepped farther under the earth. The walls were covered in more symbols and glyphs, which he could see thanks to the feeble sunlight falling through from the distant cave mouth. The feeling, the sick stomachache, like getting kicked hard in the balls, became stronger. The place smelled of warm stones and mummified snakeskin.

Another twenty feet and another sharp twist and he was in absolute darkness. His arms were forced down to his side by the narrow passage. He felt the invisible strands of a spider web cross his face as he tore through it, moving downward. It felt as if small scuttling things were crawling across his face, his scalp and his neck, but his arms were trapped low, so he had to ignore the desire to frantically rub his face, hair and neck. The dusty, oppressive, oven-like feeling of the upper part of the cave gave way to dry coolness and he carefully slid his boots along the floor, seeking each step with slow, steady caution. His instincts screamed at him—this was the worst possible terrain for him to be in, no room to maneuver, to jump and take advantage of his speed and agility. He was pinned by the mountain and at the mercy of any faceless enemy ahead of him. His instincts screamed to him: *Run, head back to the entrance and jump him when he exits with the skull. At least shake off this clumsy two-legged skin and have more room to maneuver in here! This is death!* The man told his instincts to shut the hell up and he kept sliding forward, one dragging, searching boot at a time. Mutt paused. There was something directly ahead of him in the infinite darkness. He could feel it, but he could see nothing. He crouched as best he could, his back against one of the narrow sloping walls. He felt heat and pain where he pressed against the symbols on the walls, smelled smoke, like meat burning, and realized it was his flesh. He gritted himself against the pain and low-walked ahead. Another five feet, he estimated, and he saw light, defused and flickering, swimming in shadow—a torch, off to his right. A few more steps and the entrance to the chamber allowed him to raise his arms. He wiped the cobwebs away as he stared across the chamber. The torch was on the floor of the dry vault. It was a low room, Mutt still couldn't stand. The chamber was about four and a half feet high and roughly twenty feet wide. There was a ledge about a foot in front of Mutt. You dropped down a few feet from the narrow passage to actually enter the circular chamber. The walls were again covered in powerful medicine symbols and glyphs. Mutt's stomach ached and his back still throbbed from proximity and contact with the marks. The skull sat unceremoniously in a narrow, crumbling rock alcove on the far wall. There was nothing particularly unusual about it. It was an old, yellowed human skull, with a fine network of thin cracks radiating out above the left brow. The pattern reminded Mutt of fractured glass. There was a deep, jagged gash in the back of the skull and the teeth were all gone, but the bare jawbone rested at the base of the skull.

Between Mutt and the skull was a man, an Indian. Northern Paiute by the look of his clothing, jewelry and the cast of his features. He was taller than Mutt, and thinner, but he seemed more comfortable crouched in the tiny rock chamber. He wore only a square of long black hair along the back of the crown of his head; the rest of his head was smooth. It gave him an almost bird-like plumage effect. Mutt had never seen the style on a Paiute, but knew it was the way several tribes wore their hair—the Mohawk, the Seneca and the Pawnee, to name a few. It involved a ritual of tearing out the rest of the hair in ragged tufts, enduring the pain of it to protest the mass scalping of Indians by the white man. It was a banner of defiance, an open declaration of war and a warning that the bearer could endure great discomfort, great self-inflicted pain.

He wore a simple leather vest and pants. His feet were bare and his chest, arms and face were covered in war paint, brilliant colors and patterns of red, black, yellow and blue. A gun belt was strapped to his waist and a six-gun holstered and strapped to his side. A pair of tomahawks was also sheathed in his belt. He regarded Mutt with handsome, noble features and cold black eyes.

"And my shadow arrives," he said in a cool, measured tone. "Just in the nick of time. Now the show can begin."

"Show's over, pretty face," Mutt said from the ledge above and drew his pistol with his now free hand. He still clutched the blood knife in the other. "You are coming with me, Snake-Man. Or I can jist shoot you. Don't make me no never-mind."

"Exactly the behavior I'd expect from the son of a coward and a fool," Snake-Man said. He reached back without taking his eyes off Mutt and wrapped his long, bony fingers around the skull.

"I can smash it before you can kill me," Snake-Man said. "Anger the Manitou, let it rage across the world. Even the cave's medicine can't contain such power. You and I can watch everyone go insane, murder and eventually be murdered. Won't that be fun? It's very brittle old bone and you know how strong we can be."

Mutt slid the gun back into his holster. The Snake-Man moved his hand away from the skull.

"Exactly the behavior I'd expect from the son of a shifty, gutless belly-crawler," Mutt said, grinning. "You this Ray Zeal's pet now? He send you out here to fetch him a bone? Seems pretty lowly for such a mighty warrior, after killin' all those women and children and such."

Snake-Man smiled; it was a long, slow thing that crawled across his narrow face. His face was not well suited to expressions of joy. "Zeal needs me. He is a being of spirit. He cannot enter this cave. The medicine placed on the walls here is designed to hold the influence of the skull within and it keeps beings like Zeal out. It is painful even for you and I due to the divine blood burning in our veins. I'm surprised you made it this far without running off with your tail between your legs."

"I like digging things out of their holes," Mutt said. "Dragging them into the light. You can come peaceable, or we can scrap. Choice is yours."

"Yes," Snake-Man said. "It is. You're at a complete disadvantage here, dog-son. This is my father's home, his domain, and his power is strong here. Tell me, did you ever hear the story of the day Coyote and Snake fought?"

Mutt dropped down from the ledge into the circular pit of the room. He was still crouched and he held his knife before him.

"Trust me, if it's a Coyote story, I've heard it."

"'Come, step over me. Do it in spite of me,'" the Snake-Man said, quoting the old story. He made a flourish with his hands and two curved, hook-like gutting blades appeared, attached to rings on both his index fingers. They were about four inches long. "These are my fangs."

There was a dry rattle as he presented them and Mutt realized that Snake-Man had armbands with numerous rattlesnake rattles hanging from them. As the slender man stretched his legs and bent his knees in the cramped space between them, Mutt heard the rattle again and saw he had dried rattles on bands about his ankles too. His eyes were flat and empty as a starless night in the torchlight.

"Coyote was foolish and he tasted my father's venom. He fell from it."

Mutt showed his unusually long and straight incisors.

"Yep," he said. "I seem to recall another version of that story where Coyote tore Snake apart, then he died from the bite."

"He still died," Snake-Man said.

"Yeah," Mutt said, twirling and spinning the blood knife in his hand, faster and faster. "But he got to follow an arrogant asshole into Hell. I ain't afraid of dying, pretty face, and trust me I will take you with me."

Snake-Man crossed his arms across his chest, his finger blades flashing in the guttering torchlight. "Let us dance as our fathers did, Coyote-son," he said.

And sprung out to strike.

Mutt twisted to the left, avoiding one hook blade, as his knife caught the other and blue sparks erupted from the force and speed of the blow. Mutt shuffled, still squatting, and drove a hard right hook toward Snake-Man's exposed jaw. The gaunt man seemed to fold in half, bending his knees backward to avoid the punch and then snapped back, lashing out with a sharp kick that connected with Mutt's face and drove the deputy backward into the wall and the searing pain of the glyphs.

Pressing his advantage, Snake-Man righted himself and lunged again at the off-balance Mutt, both finger blades arcing in and down to tear Mutt's throat. Mutt braced his charring hands against the wall, ignoring the pain and the nausea, bent a knee and snap-kicked Snake-Man full in the face with his boot. The force of the kick knocked the renegade Black Feather back into the walls as well and he gasped at the pain of the burning glyphs through a bloody and pulped nose and lips.

Both men gasped and righted themselves as best they could in the cramped, low cave, moving away from the walls and slowly circling each other.

"Stings a bit," Mutt said, grinning though crimson teeth. He spit blood. "Don't it?"

Snake-Man's hand dropped like the hammer of a gun to his belt and a toma-hawk flashed across the narrow space, sinking into Mutt's left shoulder—his knife arm—with a hollow *thunk*. Snake-Man was already moving before the hatchet even struck home. He scrambled forward, using one hand to balance and support his weight, the other hand flashed out, the gutting hook aimed at Mutt's left eye.

"You tell me," Snake-Man said coolly as he struck.

Mutt lowered his face and turned it, so the hook missed his eye, but tore the skin above it and ripped an ugly crescent of crimson down his face from his forehead almost to his mouth. Mutt drove his knife with all the force his injured arm could muster into the hand that Snake-Man was using to balance himself on. The blood knife sunk through the flesh and bones of Snake-Man's bracing left hand and flashed sparks against the stone of the cave floor, chipping the rock. Snake-Man roared in pain and fell face forward onto the floor. Mutt kicked him savagely again in the side of the head, but Snake–Man was ready for this and drove his right-hand gutting knife deep into the deputy's right calf. Mutt howled in pain and both men staggered back to opposite corners again. The cave was beginning to fill with the coppery scent of blood.

Neither man spoke. They both stared, unblinking, into the other's eyes, wait-ing for the next pass, the next response. Mutt wanted to pull the tomahawk out of his shoulder, but he knew Snake-Man would take advantage of the distrac-tion. An idea flashed in Mutt's mind and he performed the calculations as best he could as his lifeblood seeped out of him. If the deception didn't work, he would be a dead man. For a moment, Maude was in his mind: her dress from the other night; her soft, beautiful face; her strong eyes. Her lips. He pushed Maude out, pushed her away. She couldn't help him in this, only get him killed. He kissed her memory quickly and then chased it away, replacing it with madness and bravado and blood: the crazy urgency of the now. No future, no tomorrow. All that slowed you down.

No more thinking. He chuckled dryly and just did it. This should be fun.

It happened fast: Mutt reached up with his right arm and pulled the hatchet out of his shoulder. As he began to do it, Snake-Man launched himself again, leading with his uninjured right hand, as Mutt had expected, going for Mutt's right hand. Mutt slid straight down to the floor, putting himself in a completely vulnerable position, on his back, his belly exposed. As he slid down he used the extra distance the maneuver gave him to stomp out the light of the torch on the cave floor, so that the whole chamber fell into complete darkness.

Snake-Man missed his target but fell on top of the prone Mutt. He began to respond with a series of terrible blows to the helpless deputy when he felt the cold, hard barrel of Mutt's revolver jammed against his heart and heard the pistol's hammer cock. His own hatchet rested against the thudding artery in his throat. Instinctively, Snake-Man froze.

"You move, you twitch, I blow a hole through your chest," Mutt said through swelling lips. "I want to hear the hooks hit the floor. I'll know if it's a trick and I'll kill you."

There was a faint tinkling sound of metal hitting stone. It was repeated.

"The trickster," Snake-Man muttered. "Very good. You are worthy. We will have many glorious, bloody battles across eternity, Mutt, before I kill you. I will initiate you in true pain, true hatred."

"Yeah, right," Mutt said as he dropped the tomahawk and found Snake-Man's gun belt. He removed the revolver and the remaining tomahawk and tossed them into the darkness. "Now you are going to slowly get up and I am going to keep this gun on you. Any sudden movement, any movement I am unsure of, and I will initiate you into a .44 bullet, and trust me—that is true enough pain. Now, move."

Mutt fumbled about until he found the skull in the alcove. He gathered it up and dropped it in his battered hat and held it close to his chest. Using the alcove as a landmark he and Snake-Man made it across the chamber and struggled and groaned back up onto the ledge. They began the staggering shuffling trek back to the daylight, Mutt's gun resting at the base of Snake-Man's skull.

The sun was a ribbon of burning ochre light at the edge of the world when the two injured men climbed out of the cave. Mutt prodded Snake-Man up the ridge to where Muha waited for him.

"He's coming," Snake-Man said. "Can't you feel it? Like a fever burning hotter across the world. He is sickness and delirium-dream madness. He's coming for it and he will set it free."

"Zeal," Mutt said. As much as he hated to admit it, he could feel it. His instincts screamed to run, to hide, get away from Golgotha. But he couldn't do that.

"Soon," Snake-Man said, turning to smile at the deputy through torn and bloodied lips. "He arrives soon and you were kind enough to carry the skull out of the cave for him and for me. Thank you, Deputy."

Mutt struck Snake-Man hard with the barrel of the gun at the temple. The bleeding, injured renegade tumbled to the ground and lay still, unconscious.

The skull, cradled in his arm, was singing. Singing, but not in a voice any but the monsters of the night could hear. Mutt heard it clearly. It yearned to be free and to drag this world, all the worlds, into blood-soaked chaos.

Mutt saw the last dying threads of the sun slip away. The darkness waiting to claim the sky, to claim the world.

"Soon," Mutt said.

The Devil (Reversed)

Maude drifted through the raucous mining camp, on the eastern side of Argent Mountain, like a half-remembered dream. Her training granted her the ability to walk past others and leave only the faintest memory in their mind, and she did not want to be noticed.

It was pitch black beyond the warm glow of torches whipping in the mountain wind, beyond lanterns and campfires. The darkest soul of the night.

Word of Malachi Bick's thrashing today on Main Street at the hands of Ray Zeal had made its way up to the camp. Many here were celebrating, drinking and singing songs as if Zeal's promised return in a few days to finish Bick off was a greater holiday than the rapidly approaching Thanksgiving. It was clear there was no love lost for Bick anywhere in Golgotha.

Maude had to admit, she loved the miners' camp—it was a little universe of its own, looking down on Golgotha, full of laughter and shouting and music composed of voices, squeezeboxes, jaw harps, spoons, harmonicas and guitars; the soft murmurs and boisterous calls of love making, gossip and arguments. Random gunfire in anger or joy, the smells of cooking meats, stews and fresh-baked ashcakes, unwashed miners, and whores wearing too much scent. The laughter and cries of children, the coughs of the sick and the dying. The camp was life, in all its beauty and horror—alive, vital and uncontained.

The camp had grown nearly fourfold since the new boom began, going from about fifty miners and prospectors to over two hundred. It was now a small city all its own, with less order but fewer rules than Golgotha. It was cheaper to build a home out of canvas and a few planks of wood up here, than down below or across the gulf to the ivory homes on the green slopes of Rose Hill. Some who came to the camp came west to seek out a dream, a new life, a fortune. Others were here to take advantage of the dreamers and tenderfoots. And some were hiding from the law or working hard to make a dishonest living at the edges of civilization. There was danger here as well as joy. Life dancing side by side with death. This was the human soul laid out, living under the bright stars, in the mud.

Numerous new businesses had sprung up here. New saloons challenged the filthy dirt-floored tent that was the Mother Lode. Quacks and old army saw-bones with shaky hands and rheumy eyes offered to remove bullets and babies for a little coin. A few ramshackle churches had sprung up to minister to the weary souls here.

Malachi Bick had opened the Argent Company Store in the camp, offering credit and advances on miners' wages. Part of the hatred for Bick here among the miners was the fact that once you began to buy from the store on credit, it was virtually impossible to ever get out from under your obligation. Bick owned you. News that a man was coming to shoot Bick dead for thievery, to make him suffer first, seemed poetic justice to most.

And of course there were the crime lords of the camp, including the man Maude was seeking out now.

Maude had used the skills she had been taught to alter her appearance—not just makeup and clothing, but posture, voice, even facial expression. It was doubtful Mutt or even Constance would recognize her if they passed her now. She was dressed for work—dark collarless man's shirt, pants and boots. Her hair was tied back and up to conceal its length. A bandana was about her neck, ready to be pulled up to cover her face. At a casual glance, Maude would appear to be a man and given her training, a casual glance is all anyone would give her.

All three of the dead girls had been moonlighting up here in the camp; all three were working away from the Dove's Roost for the man known as the Nail. Maude found herself outside a semicircle of large canvas- and wood-framed buildings that were the base of Niall Devlin's dirty little kingdom. One such tent was the Halla Damhsa, Devlin's dance hall, saloon and brothel. A crowd of men, mostly miners and prospectors, were jostling to get in. A pair of armed toughs stood at the entrance, rifles in hand. Maude had melted into a deep shadow off to the far side of the compound, waiting for some sign of the Nail. After about twenty minutes the crowd parted at the barking insistence of the two toughs on the door, and Devlin exited the tent, accompanied by a woman. He was a tall man with reddish-brown hair, sharp features and hazel eyes, armed with at least three pistols, a knife and a hand axe on his belt. His companion was a small, lithe woman with a mane of raven black hair, dressed in a vest of black and green. The pair passed through the crowd and walked toward the smaller tent on the opposite side of the semicircle from where Maude was hiding. She moved quickly behind the tents, using the deep shadows to cross the gulf in a few seconds. She used her sharpened nail and precise technique to silently tear a small hole in the thick canvas, and peered within.

The tent was Devlin's office. A crude wooden table served as a desk and there were numerous crates and barrels, most likely of stolen goods, in small islands about the room. A large lamp rested on the edge of Devlin's desk and one of Devlin's men, a lanky boy in simple clothes and a vest, sat on a crate, sharpening a knife, his rifle leaning next to him.

"So this is the beauty that has all the big bad men in Golgotha atremble," Devlin said. "Black Rowan, Hellcat of the Barbary Coast. It's a pleasure, darlin'. Care for a touch of the creature to chase away the night's chill?"

Devlin poured a drink from a bottle on his desk. He offered it to Rowan and she accepted it. Devlin poured himself one and raised the glass.

"To the future of Golgotha," he said. They both drank. Devlin offered Rowan a chair and he sat after she did. Rowan paused and looked toward where Maude was watching.

"Problem?" Devlin said.

Rowan shook her head.

"No," she said. "Mr. Devlin, you know why I'm here. You seem an intelligent man, so I'll do you the courtesy of not wasting either of our time. Your days of poaching from the Dove's Roost are over. Malachi Bick may not have been giving the matter its appropriate attention, but I assure you I am. You want to contract public girls in this town, you talk to me now."

"Is that so?" Devlin said, smiling and leaning back in his chair.

"It is," Rowan said. "I have already had conversations with the other gentlemen in Golgotha who make money off public girls, and so far they are all in agreement—that is my business now and you will subcontract through me. You will get a handsome percentage, I assure you, Mr. Devlin."

"And what, love, do you consider handsome?" Devlin asked.

"Forty-five percent," Rowan said.

"I get one hundred percent now," Devlin said.

"Those days are past," she said. "Welcome to the future. Mr. Devlin, no offense, but you are a parasite. You were making a living in this line by existing in the margin and hoping Bick thought you were too small a flea to scratch off.

While he may be well-off enough to afford the occasional flea,I can't and will not. You lured girls away from the Dove's Roost and then sent them out into this tent jungle of yours with no protection, no escort, nothing. They were butchered."

"The cost of doing business, love," Devlin said. "I didn't force those girls to work for me, I gave them plenty of extra work, just like they asked for."

"Then you have the sand to get one of them killed right outside the Dove's Roost," Rowan said. "You honestly thought that you would get away with that? You are a brave one, Nail, I'll give you that."

"Do you know how I got that name?" Devlin said. Rowan shook her head. "My da was a carpenter in Galway. Taught me and my younger brother the craft. 'Measure twice, cut once,' he always said. He died on the boat ride to New York. I got his tools, his chest. Well, some lads on the boat, they figured they had a better claim to my da's tools, so they took them from me.

"When I healed up and could walk again, see again, I went looking for them in Kingsbridge, and I found them. I asked them nice as you please for my da's tools and they laughed and told me they had sold most of them already and they were going to sell the rest and for me to piss the hell off. So I did some dirty work, did some favors for some culchies I knew and when it came time for payment for what I done for them, they held those gobshites down while I nailed their kneecaps and their hands to the floor with my dear old da's hammer and the last few of his nails."

Devlin reached under the table and placed a battered old hammer down on the table with a thump. "This hammer," he said. "I keep a single nail that belonged to my da with me all the time—a good luck charm and a reminder. I'm a patient man, Lady Rowan, and I assure you I always measure twice before I cut. So now, you were telling me about how I should run my business here?"

Rowan nodded. "You were spoiling for a fight with Bick, were you?"

"Testing the waters," he said. "You want the whore trade up here on the mountain and you'll give me forty-five percent of it. Make it fifty-fifty and I'll purr like a kitten for you."

"Forty-eight," she said. "But I'll tell everyone it's fifty-fifty . . . and perhaps I'll do the purring."

Devlin laughed and stood. "Fair shake, love. From one parasite to another, eh? We're both living off Malachi Bick's table scraps and good graces, right?"

"For now," Rowan said. "Like I said, welcome to the future. Bick's slipping. This Zeal character may be the death of him."

"And if that happens," Devlin said, leaning against his desk, "then the race is on, beauty."

Rowan nodded and smiled. She glanced over again to the spot where Maude's rip was, then back to Devlin. "Until then, I intend to call my girls in. No need to give this maniac any more grist for his mill, yes? How many girls are running tonight and where are they?"

Devlin sighed with a whoosh. "Umm . . . three, I think. Little Gold Dollar, Lady Jane Gray and Gold Tooth Betty. All three were working the Tanner Row."

"And where did the dead girls work?" Rowan asked, standing now.

"Tanner Row . . . ," Devlin said.

Maude didn't wait to hear any more. She launched herself skyward, her fingers lightly gripping the wooden frame and the tarp as she cleared the six-foot roof of Devlin's tent with less sound than the wind. She kept heading up, a shadow that tore itself loose from the silhouette of the camp's darkness, sailing another ten feet into the air. She spun as gravity once again tugged at her and dove, feetfirst, curling toward another tent. She landed on the flat edge of a central tent pole for less than a second, on the balls of her feet, and then snapped upward and launched again. Hopping like a ballet dancer, jetéing between the tent poles, swaying as they did, alighting for balance and a solid point only for an instant before hurling herself again and again across the canvas city: invisible, silent, hunting.

Her heart was calm and her breath even. Her soul sang. This was life; this was the gift of freedom Gran had helped her to unlock so long ago. The power to defy gravity, to kiss the night like a lover; the power to right a wrong. Maude paused for a heartbeat on a pole, pivoted as it swayed as if in a gentle breeze, got her bearings and then launched herself again toward the wide, winding thoroughfare that was Tanner Row.

She dropped into a deep cold shadow and with a few quick changes to her attire, hair and posture, assumed the face and gait of a public girl. Stepping out into the light, she swaggered slowly down the row.

"Here's a right handsome adventuress," an old prospector reeking of cheap phlegm-cutter said as he grabbed Maude with strong, dirty hands. "Come 'ere, my randy Dutch Girl. What do you say to a little fuck, eh?"

"Hello, little fuck," Maude muttered in his ear as she pressed gently on the vagus nerve on the side of his neck. It looked like a caress to the untrained eye but the old coot's eyes rolled back in his head and he collapsed, unconscious. His drinking buddies came to his aid and Maude made a few squeaks of feigned distress and quickly slipped away.

She took a cleansing breath and moved the blood about in her body to enhance her hearing. It was a horrible ruckus for a moment before she began to filter and sort as she had been taught to do as a child. She moved along past tent barkers, hustlers and leering faces, a dingy carnival of sweat-soaked nightmares. Tanner Row was the dark heart of the mining camp and Maude ached at the thought of being a woman here, forced to seek out the worst of the lot, helpless compared to her. She suddenly wanted to hurt Niall Devlin very badly.

There was a scream, muffled and cut short—a woman. Maude sprinted ahead, closing on the source. A hand flashed out quickly, grabbed her by the back of her shirt and another by the hair; before she could react, she was flying through the air and crashing into one of the dark alleys between the rows of tents. Maude tumbled and came up, derringer in her hand ready to fire. Black Rowan stood between her and the row. "Who are you?" Rowan said. "You're not one of the Doves and you're disguising yourself like you're one of us."

"Who's 'us'?" Maude said.

"The Sirens of the Pirate Goddess," Rowan said. "The worshipers of the Rada, the Loa Mami Wata, mother of the waves and the mysteries of the deep . . . Anne Bonny."

"What?" Maude said. "Look, I don't have time for this now, a woman is dying." She fired the derringer with intent to graze Rowan's temple, giving her a mild concussion. The pistol thundered, but Rowan was no longer there; she was twisting Maude's arm upward in a classic disarming maneuver, exactly like Gran Bonny had taught her.

"How did you learn to do that?" Maude said.

Maude was shocked, but only for a second. She drove the heel of her palm into Rowan's diaphragm and the pirate queen shifted to minimize the blow, but it still doubled her over and put her off-balance. Maude didn't let up. She snap-kicked Rowan squarely in the chin, knocking her backward.

Rowan tried to recover from the blow by staying close to the ground, on her back, twisting and trying to tangle Maude's legs; it was a style of island fighting Gran had taught her. Rowan flipped back onto her feet when she realized Maude would not fall for the entangling tricks and began to launch a series of powerful strikes. Maude countered and blocked every one and managed to counterstrike Rowan a number of times in the process. It had taken a few moments of sparring, but Maude soon realized that although Rowan knew a wide array of tricks, she hadn't had nearly the extensive training Maude had.

"Look," Maude said, blocking another punch and tumbling back away from Rowan. "This is pointless. I heard you talking to Devlin. . . ."

"I know, I heard you outside the tent," Rowan said. "I followed you, as best I could. How did you jump like that? I've never . . ."

"One of the girls out here is dying right now," Maude said, "and I'm going to help her. Try to keep up."

Maude took a step back into the darkness and was gone, racing between the shadows, toward the fading scream.

It took less than a minute, but it was already too late. Maude stepped into the filthy side alley off the row. The woman's body was torn and bleeding, the dark pool of her life spreading outward, soaking into the thirsty ground. Ten feet away she could hear drunken laughter and arguments. No one had done a damn thing to help her, even as she was screaming, pleading for her life.

Maude knelt next to her body, which had been shoved up against one of the canvas tent walls. Maude knelt and examined the wounds. They had been done with a short, sharp knife—a scalpel perhaps. There were shoe prints, not boots. Gentleman's shoes.

Something stung her arm through the canvas of the tent: a hypodermic. Maude felt herself become flushed, dizzy and hot. It was very hard to focus, to think, like gauze had been draped over her thoughts and her vision. She pulled her arm back instinctively and rubbed where the needle had stabbed her. The men's laughter out on the row was distorted and hard to hear over the thudding of the blood in her ears. She staggered back, but lost her balance and fell onto her bottom. It was hard to remember what to do or how to move.

An opiate alkaloid, some distant corridor of her mind said. *Possibly whole opium . . . Laudanum perhaps . . .* The words tumbled into each other and crashed; it was so hot and so hard to focus.

There was a ripping sound and the canvas wall next to the girl's body split as the small, very sharp knife made its incision. A man stepped through. His face was hidden in shadow by a black scarf, and distorted by the drugs affecting her eyes. The curved scalpel gleamed in the camp's torches and lanterns; it seemed too bright to Maude's eyes, like a thing made of blood-spattered light. He wore a short top hat and a fine cape; she saw spats above his gentleman's shoes.

Gentleman's shoes . . .

"Well, aren't I a saucy lucky lad this fine evening?" the stranger said, his voice booming and fading, accompanied to the symphony of Maude's blood. "You, my curious quim, you, shall be my lucky fifth. I always give my utmost attention to the last in the sacred sequence."

Maude wanted to slide into warm, numb oblivion, but a cold, strong voice—Gran's voice—barked at her, *"Focus, girl, this man is death, he will torture you and kill you and eat you and you will never see Constance again, never see Gillian or Mutt again. Focus! You know what you have to do, focus, damn you!"*

"I love my work." The killer's voice warbled and distorted as he began to drag Maude by the hair back into the torn tent. "And I want to start up again. We'll have a spot of privacy in here, my girl."

She took a deep breath and it cleared her foggy mind a tiny bit. She remembered Gran teaching her beside the ocean, part of her poison training—the first, most important part.

"If you deal in toxins, sooner or later you will get poisoned yourself," Anne Bonny had said matter-of-factly. "Then you got two choices, get the shit out of your blood and body or die a stupid git. Now, first you need to imagine the foreign substance as a different color from your blood and body and then, just as I taught you how to control your heartbeat and your breathing, you slowly, slowly begin to gather all that bad color into your stomach. Slow, lass. Keep your heartbeat down; it's the drum that summons the reaper. Calm, focus . . . you know how to keep calm, Maudie. Some poisons you may need to sweat out of you, and I'll show you that, too, but for today, it's your tummy, girl."

Maude focused on her breathing, kept her heart rate low. It was easy—the drug was making her long for stupor and sleep. The drug was darkness, swirling inside her, and she slowly drew it to her belly, more and more with each deep breath. Away from her brain, from her limbs. . . .

There was a stinging slap to her face and her eyes popped open. The killer was above her, his knife close to her.

"No sleeping, my little strumpet," the killer said. "I want you awake to enjoy this. Maybe I'll send your ears to old Boss Highfather. . . . Maybe I'll send him his new pet whore's kidney instead. I love to play with the insides so! So many filthy ladies here, so much work. This town was made just for yours truly. . . ."

"Then . . . here's a little welcoming gift for you," Maude muttered and vomited most of the poison, and a good deal of bile, into the killer's face. The man screamed and fell backward, dropping his knife. Maude caught the blade in one hand and drove a powerful finger strike into his solar plexus with the other hand. The Dove killer fell back on the ground, gasping for air and writhing in pain. Maude groaned and climbed slowly to her feet, the blade in her hand. She walked over to the killer and slowly dragged him out of the dark tent and back into the alleyway with his last victim. Maude shoved his bile-covered face into the face of the girl, her expression froze in fear. Maude placed the curved scalpel against his neck. The man's heaving and gasping stilled.

"You look at her, you pathetic little man," Maude said. She still felt the flush of the drugs in her, but she had most of her facilities back. Her voice, however, sounded like it belonged to someone other than her. The blade pressed tighter against his jowly throat. "What a mighty predator you are, you stub-dicked lick-spittle. What? No boasts now? Maybe I should give the sheriff your ears? You are nothing, you hear me, nothing!"

The killer slowly, carefully, wiped away some of the bile and vomit from his face with the black scarf and Maude realized it was Dr. Francis Tumblety she was holding at knifepoint. Tumblety looked up at her, his eyes wide with fear and hatred, glazed with madness. Maude experienced a dip of nausea, this creature, this . . . thing had been alone at her sick daughter's bedside, had touched her with these bloodstained hands. The knife began to split the skin at his throat and Tumblety laughed. It was the sound of reason dying, the sound that made cats scream in the night.

"Your inferior, little brain can't begin to comprehend my works," Tumblety hissed. "I operate within the realms of cause and effect. I am a servant of the sacred geometry, the ancient rites. Five holds power—five points on the ancient seal, the murdering star! No stupid slag can understand the clockwork of eternity."

"Let me speed you on the way to eternity, then, Doctor," Maude said. "You are an aberration, a sickness. Ending you would be a gift, a mercy, to the universe."

A pair of heavy iron cuffs thudded in the dirt by Tumblety's knees.

"Please don't do that," a woman's voice said. Maude looked up to see a slender woman dressed like a man in trousers, a bolero jacket and hat. Her long brown hair was up under the hat and to an untrained eye she would seem a man. She had a slender, delicate face and held a short-barreled revolver in her hand as she slowly advanced into the alley. "You are right, miss. He is all you said and more and he deserves to live in a cage like an animal and then dance on the end of a rope for all he's done. Don't let him drag you into his cesspool. Please cuff him and put that knife away."

"Who are you?" Maude asked.

"The law," the woman said. "My name is Kate Warne and I'm working with the sheriff. I'm sorry I wasn't in time to save your friend here, but I swear to you, he'll never hurt another girl. Please, let me do my job."

"Let her do hers," Rowan said to Kate, as she stepped out of the shadows behind Maude and Tumblety. "She's a woman, like you, like me. There's no justice for us. We're fucking property. You think any judge, any *man,* will see justice done for a bunch of slaughtered whores? This 'fine gentleman,' this right bastard will walk and keep on killing more girls."

Rowan moved to where she could see Maude's face. Tumblety struggled a bit and Maude pressed the knife deeper into his skin, slid it closer to the fat, pulsing artery that would end his existence with the slightest slip. The madman stilled.

"The only justice for us is what you hold in your hand," Rowan said. "Kill him. It's a damn sight more merciful than he'd give you, or what he gave them."

Maude looked down at the face of the squirming thing she held that aped at being human. The eyes gave it away, though. Caught here in its obscene act, its mask had fallen in the filth. Debating killing the mountain lion had been difficult; there was no difficulty here. Tumblety was far worse than any supernatural creature she had ever encountered—without a doubt, he was the worst monster she had ever seen. Monsters deserved to be slain.

"Everything your friend here just said is true," Kate said. "I've been exactly where you are, miss, and I can tell you the decision I made still haunts me to this day.

"All I can offer to convince you not to do it is that he's not human, and you are. The women he's slain deserve an accounting in front of the law. This is his justice, not ours. A knife in a dark alleyway changes nothing, but dragging him into the light, making him account for his deeds, that just might. The law isn't always fair and it's not fair at all to us, but if we ever intend to change that, we have to show we can be . . . better than him. You are better than him."

Maude looked at Tumblety. She slid the knife away from his throat and relief flooded the killer's face. It was short lived. The curved knife dropped to between his legs and there was sharp ripping sound from Tumblety's trousers. The killer screamed in pain.

"I am the Mother's justice," Maude whispered in the whimpering doctor's ear. "You will never spread the poison of your seed and you will know pain in your lust for all your remaining days, may they be mercifully short. This is my judgment, Doctor."

She released Tumblety and he fell over into the filth crying in agony. Dark stains soaked the front of his torn trousers. Maude picked up the cuffs and clamped them on him.

"He's all yours," Maude said to Kate. "Pray the law sees fit to do justice here, or I assure you I will. And you," she said, turning to Rowan, "you and I will be talking again soon, and you are going to tell me everything."

Kate reached down and dragged Tumblety by the manacles toward the edge of the alley, into the light. "I'd like to get your names as material witnesses," she said. Kate looked up and Maude and Rowan were gone. She sighed and drove a sharp kick into the whimpering Tumblety's side. "Just you and me, you charmer," she said. "Story of my life."

The Queen of Wands

The late morning sun fell across Auggie's eyes. He groaned and opened them, blinking. Gillian, his wife, rested in the crook of his arm, her head on his hairy chest.

His wife.

Auggie smiled and regarded her while she still slept. Her narrow, perfect features, the long lashes of her closed eyes and the natural blush of her full lips. Auggie held the moment—the weight of her naked body against him, her deep, even breathing. He wanted to hold this moment forever, save every nuance of it in his mind and heart, so that it would sustain him, remind him when life was hard, or fleeting, that it had all been worth it, had been more joy than it ever was pain, more beauty than horror. This moment, this memory he could wrap himself in warm and deep, and let it carry him into the darkness, happy, content.

Gillian's eyes fluttered open and she looked at him and smiled. "Good morning," she said. "What are you staring at? I must look a fright."

"You are the most beautiful sight I have ever seen," Auggie said. "And I think the morning has almost left us. We have slept the day away, like rich lords and ladies, *ja?*"

They laughed, and Gillian pulled herself closer to Auggie's chest, nuzzling into his neck.

"I never want to get out of this bed," she said. "But Auggie, we were supposed to get back to work today. We took yesterday off. The store, my boarders and customers . . . I have to find out from Maude how her date with Mutt went."

"It will keep, *meine Liebe*," Auggie said with a growl. He turned his head and kissed her softly at first, then she joined him and the kiss became more passionate, deeper.

She moaned against his lips. "Oh, I do love you so, Augustus."

"Whatever has been going on, will still be going on," Auggie said. "If the whole town gets sucked down into a pot of molasses, or the devil comes looking to arm-wrestle the sheriff, it will keep and it's not our problem, Gillian. I love you too."

"It will keep," she mumbled against his lips.

Husband and wife pulled themselves deeper and deeper into their kiss, their embrace. The world outside died to them. Nothing existed past the border of their love.

Gerta Shultz leaned against the wooden fence rail and watched with wonder as the sun climbed in the east, painting the desert in brilliant, breathtaking light. Every sunrise, every sunset was a miracle to her now, since she had been returned from the halls of the dead. It seemed her senses were much more acute than she recalled. Every detail shouted to her now. The colors seemed more vivid, everything did.

Gerta was technically in her early fifties, if you counted her life before this one, but she now looked and felt like she was in her twenties. Her pale skin had been oversensitive to the sun, but Clay's treatments with his biorestorative formula had eased her discomfort and now the morning sunlight felt like a lover's warm, familiar caress on her bare skin. Gerta raised her arms and her head skyward, almost shuddering in orgasm at the dawn's touch.

"Uh . . . Gertie? You know you're naked, darlin'?" Clay said as he approached her. "Somebody's going to see you, even out here."

Clay had given his men a few days off in preparation for the Thanksgiving holiday, which was only a few days away. Mr. Williams and most of Clay's men had kin outside of Golgotha, so Clay paid them full for the week and sent them on their way home. The livery was empty except for him and Gertie. Clay had let her have his bedroom in the main house and he had been sleeping on his cot out in the barn.

Gertie blinked and turned to regard Clay as if she were coming out of a trance. Her body was alabaster and firm, her hair was black as pitch and fell below her shoulder blades. There were faint shadows of the stitches on her pale skin, but they were fading faster every day.

The old inventor looked away. He offered her a blanket and Gertie wrapped it about herself, shuddering at the coarse sensation of the fabric against her skin.

"I'm sorry, Clay," she said. Her voice held a bit of her German accent, but less than in her old life. "It was just so . . . beautiful. I wanted to be part of it. I don't know what got into me."

"Perfectly understandable," Clay said. "You're getting used to your senses again and I'd hazard it's a big difference between old eyes and young ones."

"Almost intoxicating," she said, huddling up close to him. "Everything is so much . . . more than I remember."

"I got grub on in the house," Clay said. "Hungry?"

"Very," she said.

Clay watched in amazement as Gertie wolfed down more food. She had cleaned two plates of eggs, ham, gravy and biscuits. Still wearing only a blanket, she looked up and tilted her head, licking her lips clean of the gravy still on them.

"What?" she said.

"Nothing," Clay said. "You sure got more of an appetite than I ever recall you having. Ravenous, even."

"Is that . . . is that bad?" Gertie asked.

"Oh, hell no," Clay said. "It's a very good thing. Means that your body and your metabolism are kicking into full gallop. No, I love seeing you eat like that, Gertie. You're so . . . alive."

"I'm not a disappointment, am I?" she asked, wiping her mouth with a napkin. "I feel like I'm still me, I am just so excited by everything, Clayton! It's like I've been in prison, locked away from the sun, and now I've been set free." She took his hands in hers.

"I'm glad, Gertie," Clay said, looking down. The feeling of skin touching his was so alien to him and yet it felt very, very good. "You are free."

"Thanks to you," she said.

Clay leaned forward. "How did you feel about the wedding yesterday?"

Gerta narrowed her eyes. "You think it upset me? Seeing Augustus and Gillian together?"

"I've never been able to figure out how or why people feel the way they do," Clay said, "but I figure that had to cause you some distress."

"Clay, I was dying," Gerta said. "Augustus and I said our farewells. I told Gillian I wanted her to look after him and love him and she did. And then I was gone. The stubborn old knot hung on to me, the tattered old shreds of me, for far too long, with your help. But he finally set me free and decided to live again. And now thanks to you, I can do the same.

"No, I don't regret one moment of my old life, but this is my new life, and Auggie and Gillian have a new life too."

"Good," Clay said.

A distant look crossed Gerta's face and the joy in her eyes seemed to fade. Outside the kitchen window, a row of black crows sat on the fence, mocking with their shrill calls. "It's just . . . ," Gerta said, her voice trailing off as she watched the black birds outside. "Ravenous," Gerta said. "Do you know where the word comes from? Ravens feasting over the bodies of the slain on the battlefield. Ravens . . ."

"What, Gertie?" Clay asked.

"Clayton, is there any reason I'd be having strange dreams?" she said, looking away from the crows. "Last night, very vivid. As vivid as you and I sitting here. I don't like them, Clay."

"They wake you up?" Clay said. Gerta nodded, looking down into her coffee. "Well, it could be the nerves getting themselves adjusted. Part of the healing and the regeneration process, I reckon. Can you tell me about them, Gertie? The dreams?"

She picked up her mug and looked into the rippling black coffee. "Do I have to, Clay? They are . . . horrible."

"Please," Clay said.

Gerta sighed and looked out the window again. The crows were gone.

"I'm cold. It is very cold," she said. "I can see my breath and I'm in a hall. Part of the roof has collapsed and is exposed to the sky. It's a gray sky. Snow is drifting down into the wreckage." She swallowed hard and went on. "They are perched in the ruins, among the dead."

"The dead?" Clay said. "What dead, Gertie?"

"They look like warriors," Gerta said. "Ancient warriors, in mail and with swords, axes. Dead, bloody, scattered among the debris, slowly being covered by the snow. They are devouring the dead." She shuddered and wrapped her arms about herself.

"Who?" Clay said, leaning forward.

"They . . . I can't see their faces," Gerta says, the distant look returning to her eyes. "But they have beautiful long hair, braided, like silk or spun gold. They don't have hands, they have talons, huge, razor-sharp and caked in blood and the flesh of the dead. They rip hunks of the bodies out and then duck down like they are pecking the meat, like great, terrible birds. I can hear the sounds of their efforts . . . even though I never see their mouths. They have wings, Clay, like angels, and they wear shimmering silver-scale armor, spattered with fresh blood. They make noises like women. They make noises like birds. I don't know what they are, but they are calling to me. One instant they are these creatures, the next, ravens, then back again."

Gerta leaned over and wrapped her arms about Clay's frail form. He held her and felt her shudder, felt her new heart smashing into her ribs, like a deer, sick with terror.

"It's just a dream, Gertie," Clay said. "Your mind is adapting to your new situation is all."

"The worst part," Gerta said, looking up at him and pulling him even closer, "is the bodies they are feasting on, they change. They become . . . people . . . people I know from here in Golgotha. Others, I don't even know but in my dream I knew they were from here. Our friends . . . our neighbors . . . They are going to die, Clayton, soon. There is going to be a massacre and those . . . things, they wanted me to join them in their feast. . . ."

Gerta buried her head in Clay's chest, trying to block out the rest of the universe. Clay held her and patted her back gently.

"It's okay, Gertie," he whispered. "It's okay. Come what may I'll keep you safe. No bird-lady-things are going to hurt you."

"No, Clayton." Gerta looked up, her eyes wide with fear and something Clay couldn't begin to define or even comprehend. Desire, perhaps? "You don't understand. I wanted to join them, ached to. Whatever they are, they know me and part of me isn't dreading a slaughter, it's eager for it."

Gerta sobbed against him. Clay held her, rubbed her back and stroked her hair.

"I love you, Clay," Gerta said, looking up at him. The tears that ran down her face were black.

Clay pulled her back to him, held on like he would never let go.

"I love you, too, Gertie," he said.

The Four of Wands (Reversed)

Jon Highfather and Mutt were loading every weapon in the jail's locked cabinet and arranging them on Highfather's desk.

"Silver loads?" Mutt asked. "So Malachi Bick got his ass kicked on Main Street and I missed it. I must not be living right," the deputy added.

Highfather nodded. "One bullet in three," he said, handing another box of precious silver bullets to the deputy. "Wasn't there myself, so I don't know all the details yet, but I aim to speak with Malachi today and find out. Better safe than sorry, though. If this Zeal fella is as bad news as I've been hearing all morning, we need to be ready. Damn!"

"What?" Mutt said.

Highfather held up an empty wooden box.

"We're out of cold iron bullets. Wish we'd had time to stock back up on them, too; damn Unseelie fae."

"Hate those haughty bastards," Mutt said.

Highfather nodded.

"Yeah, I think Malachi will give it to me straight. At least as straight as he ever is. If something from Bick's past is draggin' trouble to our door again, he damn well better tell me how to help him send it on its way."

"You know, we could just let Mr. 'I Own the Town and Everybody in It' handle his own mess," Mutt said. "Take the day off."

"Well, look who takes a little vacation and all of a sudden is looking to shirk," Highfather said. "How'd it go, by the way?"

"Fine. Real fine," Mutt said, "up till Max Macomber and the village idiots decided to string me up, and then I got dragged out in the middle of nowhere to have a little chat with a fella who might be a prophet about this skull thing."

"This medicine man, Wodziwob," Highfather said. "He told you about the skull? What it is?"

Mutt nodded and jacked another round into a Winchester.

"Yep," he said. "It's bad news is what it is—the original power to murder, to unmake something, anything, really. I hid it the last place anyone would ever expect me to, after I dropped off old Snake-Man here."

"Well, I trust your judgment, least when you're not on the tarantula juice," Highfather said. "Don't tell me or anyone else where it's hid."

Highfather passed Mutt more bullets. Mutt handed Highfather back another loaded rifle.

"Wasn't planning on it," Mutt said, grinning. "Don't trust any of you crazy white people. Y'all are all catawampously teched in the head. "

"You know, Mutt, I can usually gather up about two dozen good men for a tussle, if we need them," Highfather said. "I had four men say they would stick their necks out to save Malachi Bick. Four."

"Can you blame 'em?" Mutt handed Highfather a shotgun loaded with holy-water-soaked rock salt. The sheriff added it to the table of weapons. "Bick has put most of this town over a barrel. He's about as popular as clap at a whorehouse. Not going to get too many people too eager to catch a hornet for him, Jonathan."

"I know," Highfather said. "Just thought better of people hereabouts."

"One thing you can always count on people for," Mutt said, "is to let you down. Wodziwob said Snake-Man's boss was a servant of some higher power. He may look human, but he ain't."

"And you're sure he said this being goes by Ray Zeal?" Highfather said, pausing in the reloading.

Mutt nodded.

"Hard to forget a moniker like that."

"What do you think, Kate?"

Kate Warne rocked her chair back on two legs, partly leaning against the wall. She was overseeing the cells in the back of the jail. She fed Billy, the goat kid, a handful of grass as she watched the sheriff and his deputy work. She also kept an eye on the jail's various prisoners—Francis Tumblety, the Dove killer; the Paiute Indian renegade Mutt called the Snake-Man; and the slumbering Max Macomber and his henchman. Sullen and still, Tumblety had patched up his injuries at the hand of the mysterious woman the night before as best he could and had dosed himself with pain medicine. He lay in a drugged stupor.

Most of the wounds the Snake-Man suffered fighting Mutt were already healing quickly. Occasionally the Snake-Man would look at the Secret Service agent with dark eyes and smile. Kate would make a gesture with her fingers like she was shooting him with a gun.

"I hunted enough for Nikos Vellas over the years to know a little about him, as much as anyone did," Kate said. "His father was supposedly a very dangerous and unpredictable outlaw that goes by the handle of Ray Zeal."

Mutt slapped Highfather on the back. "Of course he is," Mutt said. "You sure know how to pick 'em, Jonathan."

"So I killed Zeal's son, who sure as hell was not human," Highfather said. "I'd imagine he'll want to jaw with me a bit about that."

"Zeal has been a terror in California and Mexico," Kate said, "far back as anyone can recall. Before that, he was part of the reason Kansas was so bloody. He worked as a mercenary during the war for anyone that would pay him, or promise him and his cutthroats plenty of opportunities to rape and murder. He ended up wanted by both sides by the end of the war for atrocities. He's been behind all kinds of coach robbery, bank robbery, mass slaughters—you name it. He's bloodthirsty as they come and he's not just going to ride in with his crew to Golgotha, kill Bick and ride off. He'll eat your town alive, Jon."

"Options?" Highfather asked, looking at Kate and Mutt.

"I'd get someone to ride for Camp Bidwell and get some help," Kate said. "Could be back here in a day or two with the army. I can write a letter to send with Jim that should get you some riders here, quick."

Highfather shook his head. "I appreciate it, Kate, but we can't go running to the federals every time we have a murdering army of marauders led by some supernatural menace come riding into town."

"You get this a lot?" she asked.

"More than you might expect," Highfather said. "Remind me to tell you about Apis and his bull-god cult sometime."

Mutt whistled and shook his head "Those damn horns . . . ," he said, loading a revolver. "And then there was that time with that four-hundred-year-old Renaissance alchemist and his army of clockwork people. That reminds me, I want a raise."

"I think you are being stubborn for the sake of pride," Kate said. "You are undermanned and outgunned. Ask for help, that's why the government exists."

"Exactly," Mutt offered. "Just ask any Indian."

"Besides," Highfather said, ignoring Mutt, "when I talk to Bick we'll cypher out a plan. We have before. I don't trust Malachi—he's lied to me since the day I met him. But he's invested in Golgotha, probably for reasons I may never fully know, but he'll fight to protect her, and his own skin. Plus, I can reach out to some community leaders. We'll have backup if we need it, but I'm not sure how much or when it will be coming."

"That doesn't sound like backup, or much of a solid plan," Kate said.

"Yeah, we do tend to improvise a bit," Highfather said. "Keeps us spry. Why did you say you'd write a letter for Jim to carry? Why not ride out there yourself?"

"Because," Kate said, "the kind of madness and carnage Zeal is going to bring with him is no place for that boy. He's a sweet soul still and all of us know that you do this kind of work long enough and it . . . changes you."

"Jim's been through a lot," Mutt said. "He can handle this. He's one of the bravest and most honest people I ever met. He speaks from the heart."

"I don't question the boy's ability or courage," Kate said. "He has the makings of a great lawman, but he's seen so much horror in the last few days. . . . I just want to spare him Ray Zeal."

Mutt remembered Jim's face as they entered the alleyway and saw Molly James or what Tumblety had left of her. He knew exactly what Kate of speaking of. Sheriff, deputy and agent were all silent, lost in memory, remembering all the things that had taken the light from their eyes a piece at a time. The iron door groaned open and Jim Negrey entered.

"Morning," they young deputy said. "I hear tell you caught the Dove killer last night, Agent Warne—congratulations! Folks all over town can't believe it was Doc Tumblety, but it kind of makes sense to me now. Apparently they don't have much luck with doctors hereabouts. What are we doing about this Ray Zeal fella, Sheriff?"

Highfather looked at Kate and then Mutt, then he addressed Jim. "Jim, I need you to ride for the army command over at Camp Bidwell today. Agent Warne is going to give you a very important letter to deliver to the commander of the post. I want you to wait there for his reply and travel back with any soldiers he dispatches to us."

Jim nodded. "Yessir. Promise and me will ride as fast as we can. I'll try to be back with help 'fore Zeal gets here."

"I know you will, Jim, "Highfather said, patting the boy's shoulder. "I know."

"Well, other than writing letters, what's a girl to do in this watering hole of a town?" Kate asked. Highfather didn't miss a beat. He opened the drawer of his desk, reached inside and tossed something to Kate. She caught it and opened her palm. It was a deputy's star.

"A star?" Kate asked. "Jon, you know what you are doing? You want me to pretend to be a man while I'm wearing this?"

"Nope, you just be you," Highfather said. "That's good enough."

"You brought Tumblety in," Jim said. "It's what you do that matters, not what you look like, ma'am."

"Just Kate, Jim," she said, "and thank you. I didn't bring Tumblety in alone, I had help from this mystery lady, but thanks for the vote of confidence."

"Welcome to the club," Mutt said with a grin. "The work's dangerous as hell, but the pay's shitty. Boss is a pain in the ass too."

Kate smiled, and pinned the star on her vest. "Thank you, Mutt, and yes, he can be, can't he? This feels like real silver," she said. "Aren't these usually just tin, Jon?"

"The silver comes in handy sometimes," Highfather said. "And anyone willing to wear one of those in this town deserves a damn sight more than tin. I hereby duly deputize you as a peace officer of the town of Golgotha. Thanks again, Kate."

"No," Kate said. "Thank you."

The heavy steel door to the jail creaked again to announce Maude Stapleton's arrival.

"Mutt, Jon," she said. "I think we have a problem."

Kate stood. "Have we met?" she asked Maude. "Seems like I know you?"

"It's a small town . . . Deputy?" Maude said, looking at the star. "I do laundry for a lot of it. I'm sure we've passed each other."

"I'm sure," Kate said, but kept looking at Maude.

"What's wrong, Maude?" Highfather asked. "You look tired. You under the weather?"

"Oh, it's nothing, Jon," Maude said. "A long night, too little sleep. I've been helping Gillian with her food deliveries today," Maude said. "I wanted to give her and Auggie as much of a break as I could. They deserve it." Mutt and Constance knew what Maude was capable of, but she had worked very hard to keep her training a secret from Highfather, Jim and the rest of the town. Gran had always said that anonymity was crucial to survival.

"So what's troubling you, Maude?" Mutt said.

"Like I said, Jon, I've been taking up Gillian's route these last few days, and I think someone is trying to poison as much of the town as they can."

"Poison?" Kate said.

"I stopped at several of Gillian's customers' homes this morning and no one answered. I found the door open at Mrs. Winters' house and I found her on the floor of her parlor. There was a tray of food next to her and it had been dosed with some kind of poison. She was dead."

Maude left out the part where she deftly picked the old lady's door lock to enter and that she knew exactly the type of poison—belladonna dilute. Maude suspected the dose was designed more to sicken and weaken than kill, but the old, the young and the infirm, like Mrs. Winters, would fall to even the weakened toxin.

"Why would anyone want to do that?" Jim said.

"How did you know it was poisoned?" Kate asked Maude.

"It just seemed . . . not right," Maude said. She could feel Kate's stare. The woman was an excellent observer and detective and she was on to Maude, but there wasn't time to worry about that now. "I found a few other of Gillian's clients either sick or dead—the Raeburns, the DeWolfes. The survivors said it was two women claiming to be helping me and Gillian with her route."

"What did they say they looked like?" Highfather said.

"Older woman and her daughter. German. Said their name was Brecht," Maude said.

"I met them about a week ago," Jim said. "They're new in town."

A terrible realization settled over Highfather. He felt it was right, deep in his bones. "Got to be Zeal's people," he said. "Damn it, he's good. He sent advance scouts, infiltrators in. He's running this like a war."

"If those ladies are taking over Gillian's route, Jonathan," Mutt said, "they may have poisoned a third of the town by now."

"Maude, can you and Deputy Warne try to follow up on these Brecht women? Shut them down, Kate, and see how much damage they've done?"

Maude frowned and looked at Kate. The new deputy caught Maude's slight look of aggravation before she nodded. "Of course, Jon," Maude said.

"Lead the way, Mrs. . . . ?" Kate said.

"Stapleton," Maude said. "Please call me Maude. Let's go."

Highfather turned to Jim. "Okay, Deputy, you get to riding to Camp Bidwell, right now, you hear. We may be more outnumbered than we thought. I'm going to go see Bick and find out all I can about Zeal and this skull he wants."

"Constance is waiting for you outside," Maude said as Jim walked to the door. "She asked my permission to ride with you to the fort. I figure it's the safest place for her to be right now, till this Zeal thing blows over, if you don't mind the company, Deputy?"

"How?" Jim said. "How did she know . . . ? Okay, ma'am, I'll take good care of her."

Warne penned a hasty note at Highfather's desk for the commander of Camp Bidwell. She made sure the ink was dry, folded it and handed it to Jim.

"That should do the trick, Jim," Kate said, and patted Jim's shoulder. "Be safe."

"Don't take no risks. There and back, Jim," Highfather said. "See you in a day or two."

Jim nodded to the sheriff and then departed. Mutt took Maude's hand as Warne grabbed a gun belt and a pair of extra revolvers.

"Be careful," Mutt said.

Maude squeezed his hand. "You be careful, you hear me, Deputy?"

"Ain't I always?" Mutt said. He wanted to kiss her. Bad. But he didn't. Their eyes held each other and then they parted.

Highfather handed Kate a rifle as she loaded her pockets with spare shells.

"You trust this woman?" Kate said softly.

"I do," Highfather said. "Mutt vouches for her and that's good enough for me."

"She's hiding something," Kate said.

"I know. So are you," Highfather said. "So am I. This place is built on secrets, Kate. Watch yourself. I want you around long enough to collect a paycheck."

Kate looked at him and Highfather felt something old and full of dust and ash, crack in him, like a ray of sunlight warming ancient ice. "Don't worry," she said. "I will. You have a care, too, Jonathan."

He handed her the rifle and their fingers ran across each other, briefly.

The two women departed and Highfather and Mutt stood there for a moment looking at the battered old iron door.

"Hell of a woman," they both said, in unison, and then looked at each other. The two men laughed.

"If we survive the impending doom, maybe we can double-date," Mutt said.

"Can't," Highfather said. "You got blood all over my fancy suit."

"Fair enough," Mutt said. "Now what's our play, Jonathan?"

"You're not going to like it," Highfather said, putting his hand on Mutt's shoulder. "For starters, you're fired, Deputy."

Outside the jail, Jim found Constance, dressed for a desert ride as she had been the other day. She was stroking Promise's nose and holding the horse's reins. Maude and Kate followed him out the door. Warne handed him the folded letter.

"You knew we were going to the fort together?" Jim said. "In your dream?"

"In the one I had last night," Constance said. "It's more of the same dream, us riding in the desert. To the fort."

"Okay," Jim said, climbing up onto Promise's saddle. He reached down and pulled Constance up. She slid up onto the saddle and coiled her arms around his waist.

"I love you," Maude said to her daughter.

"I love you, too, Mother," Constance said. Then to Jim, "Ready?"

"Let's ride," Jim said. He snapped the reins, squeezed his knees into the horse's flank and Promise began a steady, powerful gallop toward the cool morning desert.

The Knight of Wands (Reversed)

Highfather rode Bright down Main Street, headed toward the Paradise Falls. It was two days until Thanksgiving, one day till Ray Zeal had promised to return. Highfather had been sheriff here at the tail end of the first boom, through the bust and now into the new boom. He knew Golgotha, felt her pulse and her breath. The feel of the town was different this morning, meaner. Highfather felt whatever it was more than he could ever define it.

"Hey, Sheriff Highfather!" Carl Hockrey shouted from the east side of Main. Highfather pulled Bright to a halt next to Hockrey and a circle of locals he was talking with.

"Carl," Highfather said with a nod. "Fellas, what can I do for you?"

"We were just wonderin' . . . well, a whole lot of folks were wonderin' if you and your deputies are actually going to get between this Zeal fella and Malachi Bick tomorrow?"

Highfather looked at Hockrey with a stare that could freeze Hell. "My job is to protect the people of this town," he said, "*all* the people of this town, from anyone lookin' to break the law or cause harm to an innocent."

"Shit," one of the men said. A near-toothless miner named Dixon, Highfather recalled. "If Malachi Bick is innocent, then the Dove's Roost is fulla virgins," Dixon said. The men laughed. Highfather didn't.

"Look, Sheriff, be reasonable," Hockrey said. "That cockchafer Bick has cheated plum near everyone in this town to line his own pockets. He put that tanner, Gaby, out of business because he couldn't pay back the money to Bick's damn bank and nobody can say he hasn't just about ruined old Auggie over at

the general store. Bick's got it comin'. Way most folks see it, Ray Zeal is just acting as kinda the hand of God here. He's gonna wipe the slate clean—balance it
all out and make it square. Nobody wants to see you hurt over a scalawag like
Bick."

"Anyone, *anyone,* comes into my town and tries to harm a citizen, I will stop
them," Highfather said. "Up to and including shooting them dead. Someone has
a legitimate beef with Malachi Bick, they can take it up with me or Circuit Judge
Mack when he comes through next month. You think I'm gonna let some shit-
house crazy gunslinger and his crew take the law into their own hands, just because you and your friends want a good show? Ain't gonna happen, Carl."

"Well, I hope you and your short britches and that damned redskin are ready
for some hate, hell and discontent." Old Dixon nearly spat. "'Cause I hear tell
this Zeal fella is a true curly wolf and he's not afraid of some old wives' tale about
you being a dead man, Sheriff, and he's coming."

Highfather locked his eyes on Dixon's laughing face. The old miner paused
and the laughter fell away as he looked into Highfather's steel gray eyes.

"He should be," Highfather said. "And I'll be waiting for him."

"I . . . I didn't mean no disrespect," Dixon stammered.

"Spread the word," Highfather said to the assembled men. "Anyone who tries
to help Ray Zeal and his men, anyone who looks on this as open season on Malachi Bick or anyone else, I will personally kill them where they stand. We clear
on this Carl, gentlemen?"

The men were sullen and silent. They nodded like scolded children and dispersed. Highfather rode on to his appointment with the most powerful and
hated man in town.

"You heal damn fast," Highfather said to Bick as the saloon owner rose from
behind his desk in his office at the Paradise Falls. "Either that, or you weren't
beat as bad as the stories going around claim you were."

"A little bit of both," Bick said. "Please, Sheriff, have a seat. Drink?"

"No, thanks. You can get me some answers before my town tears itself in two,
though."

Bick was in bloodred shirtsleeves and his black vest was unbuttoned. His eyes
looked tired and a shadow of beard marked his face. It was the most disheveled
Highfather had ever seen him.

"*Our* town," Bick corrected. "I am after all one of Golgotha's most beloved
citizens."

Highfather laughed for what it was worth and sat down in one of the chairs in front of Bick's desk. Bick finished off another drink. "That you are," Jon said. "You heard what happened up on Argent the other night? I had a little tussle with a bull by the name of Nikos Vellas. You know him?"

"Yes," Bick said. "By reputation only. I wasn't aware he was in Golgotha, or I would have dealt with him myself. He's a very dangerous man, Sheriff."

"Was," Highfather said. "Ain't no more."

"I heard," Bick said. "Very impressive. You did what a lot of men died trying to do. Someday you need to explain to me how much of your reputation is ghost story and how much is truth."

"Sure," Highfather said. "On the day you give me the truth about you. Who the hell is Ray Zeal, Malachi, and why is he gunning for you?"

"The prevailing opinion is that he is my comeuppance," Bick said with a dry chuckle. "The agency by which I will be laid low for my villainy. The justice of God."

"Lot of folks in this town figure you're long overdue for a good ass-whooping," Highfather said. "Maybe you are. Most of them haven't figured out yet that men like Zeal don't just beat down, they kill, and even fewer have sussed out he's lying about leaving the town be if they stay out of his way. Their hatred of you is blinding them."

"You believe in God, Sheriff?" Bick asked.

"After this job, several," Highfather said.

"No, no," Bick said. "I mean, is there something, some singular power that gives you comfort in the darkest parts of the night? When all seems lost, when you are in the depths of grief or you see the face of evil in this world, staring at you? Do you believe?"

"No," Highfather said. "I don't. Any true comfort I ever found in this world was in people, not higher powers."

"Perhaps that is the reason you do so well here," Bick said. "You have no horse in this race."

"My parents are very religious," Highfather continued, "and I guess I was raised that way, too, but life either sets that in you, or grinds it down."

"The war?" Bick asked, standing and refreshing his drink. "Is that what killed it in you?"

"Are you drunk?" Highfather asked Bick as he sat back down at his desk with drink in one hand and bottle in the other.

"I am having, for lack of a better term, a crisis of faith. You may not believe this, Sheriff, but even a villain like myself has faith in something . . . in God. My

God. Living here, I know there are many, but mine . . . my faith is like . . . home for me." Bick laughed and drank more. "Very much like home. And I am struck by how much evil and cruelty He allows here, especially my own.

"I was raised in a faith as well, Sheriff, and was told that God has a plan, a subtle, often shrouded one, but a plan, and the design of it was always so beautiful to me, but then I had a little talk with Ray Zeal, saw what he was capable of and how much God was willing to allow him to do, and I felt my faith shiver like glass in a strong wind. That was a long time ago, and I have fallen very far indeed from grace." He laughed and drained his glass again. "Very far indeed."

"I hear tell you had some girl with you when Zeal jumped you," Highfather said.

"My daughter," Bick said. "Newly arrived to visit from San Francisco. She hates me, only took a few days. I am nothing if not efficacious."

"Look, Bick, I'm not here to nursemaid you or be your confessor. I'm sorry for whatever happened with your girl and that you are feeling low, but in about twenty-four hours, Zeal and his men are going to tear apart Golgotha, kill a lot of people and finish by killing you. I need answers, I need you to crawl the hell out of that bottle and help me save you."

Bick blinked. "It really is that simple for you, isn't it? Whatever evil, soul-destroying thing lumbers your way, you just shoot it or punch it. Save everyone and go on your merry way. How I envy you, Sheriff."

Highfather looked at Bick for a long time. He sighed and reached into his pocket and placed a single bullet on Bick's desk. "This I save special for blowing my head off one day. It's silver, in case the bullshit people say about me is true. Most nights I have nightmares, other nights I just can't sleep at all. I stare at that bullet and try to make a list of reasons not to use it and so far the list is longer than the urge. Being sheriff of this madhouse actually helps more than you can guess. It's been a long time since I felt anything remotely like human comfort or peace. A long time.

"I saw men, fine, decent human beings, sons, brothers, fathers, torn apart in front of my eyes. Have you ever seen rivers of blood, Bick, rivers of human blood with islands of corpses between? Gettysburg, Chickamauga, Shiloh, Antietam. Then you had the horror show of trying to patch and cut and sew the ones not fortunate enough to just die, and I saw what was left of them after. The addictions, the madness, still breathing with legs and arms and souls amputated. I saw human beings act like animals to one another, worse than animals—cruelty for hatred's sake or vengeance or just plain boredom. I watched my brother, who had been a smiling, laughing, happy little boy, who I loved more than my own breath—change into someone sick at his very core, then watched him die as close to me as you are now, in the blink of an eye, and there was nothing I could do, nothing.

"So don't talk to me about evil in this world, don't talk to me about senseless cruelty. If there is some kind of a plan, we all missed the damn meeting. A man carries his faith in him, not in some god or book or manifest destiny. If those exist, fine, if not, fine—makes me no nevermind. I have a duty to myself and what I hold true. That's what keeps me going, one foot in front of the other till the end of my days. Till that bullet catches up with me."

Bick set the glass down. He seemed sober now to Highfather. The sheriff put his bullet away.

"My apologies," Bick said. "It is always horrible when brother fights brother. I know."

"Zeal," Highfather said softly.

"As you know," Bick said, "my family has been tasked with the duty of guarding these lands for a very long time. Ray Zeal was given a similar task, to stand watch over a very special artifact."

"Given a task by whom?" Highfather asked. "Who made you watchman? Who made Zeal?"

"You wouldn't believe me, even if I told you," Bick said. "After a time, Zeal grew tired of his duties and began to shirk them. Our families were well acquainted and he unburdened his charge with me, here in Golgotha, and I relieved him of his guardianship forever. His carelessness and inattention to his duty cost lives and I refused to allow that to happen again."

"He was guarding a skull?" Highfather said.

"Has it ever occurred to you, Sheriff, how things come to be? How basic human behaviors, human concepts come into existence?"

"Well, since you pointed out, I'm a pretty simple fella, no, it hasn't," Highfather said.

"For everything there is a first," Bick said. "In the dim recesses of human existence there was a man, one of the first men, and in his beautiful, terrifying palace of gray matter, he created something that had never been before that moment."

"What?" Highfather asked.

"Murder," Bick said.

Highfather shook his head, "Malachi, things have been killing other things as long as there has been anything breathing."

"No, you misunderstand, Sheriff," Bick said. "Not killing, not death—murder.

The conscious act of visualizing and ending another being, not as a basic human need, but for rage or lust or vengeance. The forbidden thrill of cannibalism: not just hunger, but the desire for alien, forbidden flesh, out of sexual need or desire to control, to play god, or merely slaying for sport—any of those other reasons you said you had witnessed. The baseless cruelty in mankind during the war, blood slaying blood."

"Like Cain and Abel," Highfather said.

"The names and the stories differ depending on the culture, the society, the part of the world. In one version of the story, the murderer and the victim are kin and they are called Kabil and Habil and the murder involves jealousy over a woman as much as jealousy over the favor of God. Not surprising, the woman ends up taking the blame of the first murder, as well as the first sin. Elsewhere, the murderer and the victim are known as Ahriman and Ahura Mazda, warring brother gods.

"The people of this land have many such stories. The Nez Perce tell of a cannibal brother catching his siblings with a rope made of intestines and eating them. The cannibal's tribe is rescued by Coyote, who tells them to shun him and flee. The Huron tell a story of the Divine Woman, creator of the universe, and her two sons. The evil one was Tawis-karong. The good one was Tijus-keha. In their version, the good son kills the evil one with a deer horn, but the evil one lives on even after his body dies, a spirit-force in the earth—a Manitou.

"The Gnostics claim Cain is the son of Lucifer, who seduced Eve and impregnated her with his breath in the Garden of Eden, so Cain was partly of the divine and hated God as much as God looked on him with disfavor."

"Which one is true?" Highfather asked.

"To a degree, they all are," Bick said. "To parse the fact from the myth is counter to the nature of myth itself, but the story of the first murder is something in the memory of the race, a dark stain—a footnote on human nature.

"I can tell you what my family knows. Long ago, a human created an idea—the thought-form of ending life—to become an anticreator. This human was the first to practice murder on another of his kind, and the act, the power derived from the act, soaked into the very soil of the earth as the blood of the first victim did. It became a compact between man and the infinite. It tainted humanity with the terrible curse of that act."

"You saying murder was invented, not in our natures to begin with?" Highfather leaned forward in the chair.

"Sadly, no. It was always there. Do you understand what a human being truly is, Jonathan? It is a wickedly smart, bloodthirsty primate with a shard of the divine, of the universe, in it. You can create such works of ephemeral beauty, beauty to match and surpass the spires of Heaven. And you can create murder, undoing with the same genius, the same soul. Your capacity for cruelty is fathomless.

"The potential was always in you, it was just fully realized, the abstract made concrete, by one human in one terrible instant, and that act gave him power—power enough to make gods take notice, to make them rage and fear."

"So," Highfather said. "What do angry, frightened gods do, exactly?"

"They punish, Sheriff," Bick said. "The First Murderer was cast out of all human society, forced to live in the fringes of it, marked with an invisible warning, a feeling of unease that made him forever seen as a predator to his own kind. Angry at God, at the universe, for rejecting him, for punishing him for simply being what he was created to be, and furious at the feminine—the representation of the generative force of life—for creating instead of destroying. The First Murderer was given a guardian to ensure he did not harm mankind and never exercised the power inside him again to slay, not even himself."

"Zeal?" Highfather said. "Was he the guardian? Because that would mean he's ancient. . . ."

"Zeal is not human," Bick said. "He guarded the man until he passed, watched most of his remains turn to dust and blow away and was given that which remained of the First Murderer to guard. Even after the Murderer's death finally claimed him, the force he conjured into the universe resided, imprisoned, in the bone of his skull, locked away and contained as much as it can be.

"Contained?" Highfather said.

"When human blood was first spilled, it soaked into the earth, tainting the future generations of man, making men susceptible to the force of what the First Murderer created. Like catching a mental cold," Bick said.

"Maybe it was helped by that worm-thing we dealt with last year? You said it hated all life everywhere and it was chained up in the earth," Highfather said.

"Perhaps," Bick nodded. "A wise assumption. At any rate, close proximity to the skull for a time can turn even the most civilized men into savages and coarse men into monsters."

Highfather rubbed his face. "Where are you keeping it? Why are the answers to so many questions I ask this week the same?"

"Here," Bick said. "In one of the old cave dwellings on the eastern face of Argent. It's been there for about seventy years or so, when Zeal originally dropped it off with my family. It escaped about twenty years ago with the unsuspecting aid of a child. It cost forty-one people their lives."

"Escaped?" Highfather said. "This skull is alive and can reason?"

"Not exactly," Bick said. "It wants free, like a caged animal. It will work with whoever it can influence to get free and rage across the world, like a wind of madness and hatred. The child, for example, helped it by pulling the teeth out of the skull and allowing them to be scattered across the world, giving the force more access to pawns susceptible to its influence."

"Well, I think it's been a damn sight busy this week," Highfather said.

"What do you mean?" Bick said.

"I mean, I have our esteemed Dr. Tumblety down in the clink for mutilating four women. I have a renegade Paiute, calls himself Snake-Man, who's working for Zeal in there with him. Snake-Man was fetching the skull for Zeal, but Mutt stopped him. Malachi, is it possible this skull pushed Tumblety to do what he did? Could it be making the people in this town eager to see your blood, any blood, run in the streets?"

"It's possible," Bick said. "But human beings don't need some supernatural impetus to commit atrocity. Sadly, it in them already."

"You said the power in the skull made a little girl pull out and scatter the teeth?" Highfather said. Bick nodded. Highfather reached under his coat and took out an envelope. "Like these? Tumblety gave Vellas' body a once-over for me. He said these were his only possessions that survived the fire. They were in his jacket pocket. Snake-Man, our renegade, had one on him as well."

He opened the envelope and dropped a large white feather and two yellowed teeth on Bick's desk blotter.

Bick slowly reached down and picked up one of the teeth as if he were reaching for a rattlesnake. He held it up and turned it before his eyes.

"These," he said, "are teeth from the skull of the First Murderer. They have a tiny portion of the power from inside the skull. If Vellas had this, then it's a safe bet Zeal's crew has the others. That just means they are more unstable and more dangerous than we imagined. Did Tumblety possess one?"

"No," Highfather said. "But we haven't had a chance to check his house yet. Why does he want this skull now, if he gave it up so long ago?"

"I truly don't know. He's insane," Bick said. "But I do know that if he destroys the skull, the mental energy, the power of that first act of all-encompassing destruction, will spread across the world like a psychic plague, overpowering the will of every man, woman and child, turning them into vicious, amoral killers. Cities will become slaughterhouses, civilizations will burn and in time, slowly, painfully, the human race will die, screaming, at its own hands."

Highfather rested his elbow on the desk and covered his face with his palm.

"Never can be easy, can it? We thought this up? We envisioned something so ugly . . . No wonder God doesn't talk to us. He's either too disappointed or too damned scared of us."

"I would have disagreed with you once," Bick said, looking at the whiskey and then dismissing it. "It's much harder for me to do so anymore. God keeps his own council. We're on our own and Zeal is coming for the skull, Sheriff, and you need to stay out of his way. He knows you killed Vellas, his son." Bick held up the pure white feather, examined it and slid it into his desk drawer along with the teeth. "He wants your blood too. I think you should leave town till this unpleasant business is over."

"I came here to suggest the same thing to you," Highfather said.

"I can't leave," Bick said. "I wish I could. I have a duty to protect Golgotha's secrets and her dark treasures. I can't let Zeal and his men gain access to them. I must do my job."

"I have a duty too," Highfather said. "Caught it the day I pinned this star on. I can't leave these people, this town, to a bunch of killers and worse, like Zeal's crew. I'm in, Malachi, same as you."

"It is very rare we agree," Bick said. "I have to admit, in this case, I like it."

"Usually only takes the end of the world for us to get along," Highfather said. "We need a plan."

"I have an inkling of one," Bick said. "But it requires a great deal from both of us and we don't have much time."

"Then let's get to it, "Highfather said. "Daylight's burning."

The Eight of Swords

Maude and Kate stood mute in the dining room of Gillian Proctor's boarding-house. All around the breakfast table were the still-warm bodies of most of Gillian's boarders, their faces contorted in shock, fear and pain as their poisoned food claimed them.

Maude closed her eyes and recalled sitting at this very table a few nights ago with Mutt. It had been so perfect, so good. *It could have been Mutt or Gillian and Auggie or Jim dead at this table, if they had made it to breakfast today.* There was Bill Caruthers and Tommy Oates, Stuart Goggins . . . others Maude didn't know, but she had seen their faces over the years. Dead.

"Damn," Kate muttered, her revolver out. She moved toward the kitchen, kicking open the door and sweeping the bright room. No one was there. Kate lowered her gun and turned to Maude, who had followed her into the kitchen, leaving the dead to their feast.

"Okay, that was a good guess they might double back to here," Kate said. "But just like everywhere else in town, we've missed them, but not by long by the condition of the bodies."

All told, about a hundred people were either dead or sick from poisoning. It appeared to Maude that the Brechts had targeted individuals and families that might stand with the law when Zeal arrived in town tomorrow.

"They hit all of Gillian's customers," Maude said. "Even ones that were of no threat to Zeal whatsoever. It's not just a mission for them, they enjoy this."

"So where does one go if one enjoys poisoning folks in Golgotha?" Kate asked as she holstered her gun and examined a used butcher knife.

Maude's eyes suddenly grew wide. "I think I know," she said.

Delmonico Hauk struggled in the straight back chair he was tied to in the dining room of his closed restaurant. His face was a swollen, bloody mass of broken bone and torn tissue from a morning of beatings from Pa and Ernst Brecht. Del had arrived before sunup to begin the preparations for the lunch crowd only to discover his restaurant had been invaded. Del was a scrapper, he had to be to survive in the boroughs and warrens of New York. He had given the odd young man, named Ernst, a run for his money when the boy had tried to jump him. But when the obese giant known as Pa Brecht had placed a meat cleaver against his neck, Del had stopped resisting and allowed himself to be tied down. After that Ernst, Pa and even the Ma and her daughter, Hilde, only recently returned from their own murderous mission, beat on Del savagely and frequently. He had lost awareness several times. It was well after dawn now and Del listened in horror as Hilde described to her brother what she'd seen on her errands.

"Und then, the little girl, she tried to claw at her throat, she didn't understand vat vas happening. The fear in her eyes, oh, Ernst, it was so pure. She watched her momma und poppa slide to the floor, the teacups crashing. It vas perfect. I vish you could have been there," Hilde said. "She died so confused, in so much fear and pain. The little ones always do! It was beautiful."

Ernst wiped a little drool from his lips and pulled his eyes away from his sister's heaving chest. The light caught his eyes and they held red pinpoints. With his pointed ears, it gave Ernst the appearance of a hungry rat. "After ve own der town, ve can have a little tea party for the kinder," he muttered gutturally. Hilde clapped her hands and nodded eagerly, her long blond tresses bouncing.

Del tried to play dead, but his heart was pounding. These people were lunatics. The monstrous mother and father were in the kitchen even now, preparing poisoned food to serve his customers in just a few hours. He wished Mutt was here, or that he could work his hands free enough to reach the straight razor he always carried in his back pocket—an old habit from his rough childhood days. But the Brechts had tied him tight. All he could do was wait and pray to St. Michael for a chance to stop these maniacs.

———

"An awful lot of windows over there," Kate said to Maude. "Even if the shades are down, no guarantee that there aren't lookouts. That's a long ways to cover in broad daylight, and they might start shooting at us or killing hostages if they were sane enough to keep any."

"There's a kitchen entrance," Maude said. "I could sneak back and try to get in that way and cause a distraction while you hit the front door."

"You are so eager to ditch me," Kate said. "I'm holding you back, aren't I?"

"I'm sure I don't know what you mean," Maude said.

"I've stayed alive a long time by trusting my hunches, Maude," Kate said. "And my intuition about you is screaming. Okay, you take the back, I'll hit the front. Want one of my guns?"

"No, thank you," Maude said quietly, her eyes locked with Kate.

"No fear of the things, no apprehension, just a mild disdain," Kate said. "I'd say be careful, but I already know you will be."

"Pay attention to what's going on in there and that front door, not me," Maude said. "Meet you in the middle."

Maude was up and moving quickly. She was hampered by her dress and re-strictive clothes, but she'd make do. Kate Warne was a very dangerous woman. She knew who Maude was, but like any good detective, she was waiting to col-lect the evidence to make her theory into a fact.

Maude doubled back up Dry Well Road and crossed over. Odd Tom's place was at the foot of Rose Hill and Hauk's restaurant had been built right next to the house he had purchased. Maude cut through Hauk's backyard and grabbed up a handful of wooden laundry pins from off his clothesline.

She reached the kitchen door and smelled the thick, greasy aroma of roasting meat, possibly pork. Maude tried the door and found it unlocked. She pushed it open and entered as silent as thought. The kitchen was large and well appor-tioned to handle a full house of hungry patrons. An enormous, corpulent man with thinning, unwashed blond hair in a filthy apron was busy chopping slabs of meat on a butcher-block table with a meat cleaver and then tossing the pieces into a steaming stew pot on the black iron cook stove. The man held up a piece of the uncooked meat and plucked an earring off the severed ear, pocketing the jewelry and tossing the ear in the pot.

Maude dashed toward the butcher, hurling the handful of wooden clothes-pins ahead of her. The tiny wooden darts thudded with great force into Pa's throat and both his eyes as he turned toward Maude. One crushed his windpipe and the other two tore through his eyes, coming to rest in the orbits of his skull.

Two things happened simultaneously that stunned Maude into inaction for a second. One, the gray, scaly mass of Ma Brecht blindsided her from a corner of the kitchen hidden to the door. Ma struck Maude with inhuman force, swatting her with the barrel of her shotgun. The blow lifted Maude off the floor and knocked her into a rack of posts and pans, raising a terrible clatter as the kitchen implements and Maude crashed to the floor. Ma leveled the double-barreled scattergun at Maude and cocked both hammers.

The other thing that froze Maude, froze the blood in her for just a moment, was that Pa Brecht, choking due to lack of air and blinded and partly brain damaged by the loss of his eyes, did not fall down. He staggered back, clutched the meat cleaver tightly and sniffed the air, turning his blind, bloody face in Maude's direction. Pa charged forward, cleaver raised.

Kate crashed through the locked doors of Delmonico Hauk's, shooting the lock off as she kicked the door in. Ernst and Hilde were both up, having heard the commotion in back. Kate heard the blast of a shotgun in the kitchen and cursed herself for letting Maude go in alone. Ernst, his sledgehammer in hand, charged at Kate, swinging the twenty-pound hammer as if it weighed nothing. He closed as the detective fired her revolver into his chest. The pistol spat fire and barked thunder, but Brecht staggered toward her, ready to crush her skull as he had done so many times before. One bullet ripped through his chest, another, another and another. Ernst fell at her feet even as the pistol clicked empty. The sledge slid across the floor and lay as still as its wielder.

Hilde had grabbed a steak knife from one of the tables. She stood behind Hauk's chair and put the blade to the restaurateur's bruised throat. Kate raised the revolver she carried in her other hand. She cocked it, aimed it at Hilde.

"Drop it," Hilde shouted, "or I vill cut his . . ."

Kate fired once. The bullet entered Hilde's perfect blue right eye, destroying it, and then her brain, before blowing out the back of her head. Hilde dropped without another sound.

"Shit!" Kate said as she raced to the kitchen.

Ma was covering Maude with the shotgun, ready to drop her if her dying husband didn't complete his last kill. Pa staggered forward, seeming to track on instinct and smell, like a shark. The cleaver was poised to split Maude's skull. Maude rose to her feet, a black cast-iron skillet in either hand. She twisted at the waist and spun like a top. The first blow to Pa's head drove the clothespins in his eyes deep enough into his brain to stop him. He lurched forward and then fell to the floor. Ma, seeing this, opened fire with both barrels of the shotgun.

Maude had trained for years under the merciless, meticulous eyes of Anne Bonny. She had been forced to memorize and practice with rock salt and then with bird shot the scatter patterns of shotguns at different ranges. She had the scars of the practice still. She knew, like she knew her next breath, where the pellets in Ma's 20-gauge were most likely to spread to and she had her cast-iron shields there ready to cover her where they might intersect with her shifting body. There was a rumble, like the world splitting, as the shotgun fired, and a thick cloud of gun smoke. One of the skillets was knocked from Maude's hand by the force of the impact, but it served its purpose. Before the smoke cleared, Maude launched the remaining skillet at Ma's neck, which ripped her head clean off, and the headless body staggered back and slid down the wall and was still.

Kate crashed into the kitchen, pistol at the ready. She found a panting, disheveled Maude and two massive, dead bodies.

"You okay?" Kate called out. Maude nodded. "You hit?"

"No," Maude said. "I'm fine. Is Del okay?"

"Yes," Kate said. "He's all right. What happened here?"

"Some kind of . . . horrible kitchen-related workplace accident," Maude said, walking past Kate out to the restaurant and Del.

Kate holstered her pistols and regarded the two bodies. She sighed.

"Bitch is good," she said, and followed Maude out.

The Hierophant

"*Hei wa!*" Ch'eng Huang said, rising fluidly as Malachi Bick was escorted into Huang's inner sanctum above the Celestial Palace by a cadre of Green Ribbon hatchet men. "This is a most delightful surprise, Malachi, and I do not receive many of those any more. *Zhēnshì fāntiān fùdì!*"

"Indeed," Bick said. "I must confess a degree of apprehension whenever I enter your domain, Huang, my old friend, I hope you can understand. *Hēng tè hé wéi liè wù.* I mean no insult."

"None taken," Huang said, smiling. He dismissed his men with a gesture. They bowed and closed the doors behind them. "I seldom go past the borders of my realm for the same reasons. Your need must be dire, indeed, to make you take the risk, Malachi. Tea?"

"Yes, thank you," Bick said. He sat on the cushions by the low teak table and Huang returned to his seat opposite him. Bick took the proffered cup. The two sipped the hot tea silently for a time. Finally, Bick spoke.

"I find myself locked in troubling thought, Huang. I am questioning the motives of my creator, my Lord. I know it may seem absurd to come to you with this, but you are the only one in this town who has an inkling of what I am experiencing."

"I disagree," Huang said. "I think any street you wander down in Golgotha, or in any other town or city on the planet, you will find many souls seeking answers of validation and proof."

"They do not possess the rather unique perspective I have," Bick said. "That we both possess. If I were to describe to you the eternal streets of gold in my home, the Pearlescent Gates, how much like your home, your heaven, would it be? Yet we both know with certainty that our heavens exist, yes?"

"I try to not be too certain of anything, until I am," Huang said, smiling. "In the fullness of time, all is revealed. I think patience is one of the major differences between your world and mine, Malachi. The West is like a youth—eager, hungry to do, to know, but unwilling to be still and accumulate the wisdom. You want it all, now."

"Be that as it may, tomorrow one of my brethren is riding into town to slay me, to do unspeakable evil to the people here. He draws his power, his commission to act, from the same source I do."

"Yes," Huang said. "And this troubles you?"

"I . . . I don't understand the God I serve anymore," Bick said. "How can He do nothing, say nothing and allow one of His own creations, His own servants to do these things unchecked?"

"You do intend to oppose him, yes? I assume the sheriff and his men will aid you in that endeavor, the little 'Golgotha Social Club' you gathered last year?" Huang said, and sipped his tea.

"Yes," Bick said. "Of course."

"Then perhaps you and they are your God's agency in thwarting the things this being intends to do."

Bick shook his head dismissively. "A quaint fiction, Huang, not a real answer."

Huang placed his cup before him. "Malachi, you and I are visitors in this strange land. We walk through it, and we swim in the waters of mortality, pretending to be of this world, but we are not. Tell me, do you recall much of your Heaven, of your time there?"

"Less with each passing year here," Bick said.

"Do you recall if you were content? Were all your questions answered there?"

"No," Bick said. "My discontent was the prime reason I was sent here, at least I think it was. I thought God was trying to show me the intricacies of His plan, but now, after Zeal, I truly don't understand any of it anymore."

"Have you ever killed, Malachi?" Huang asked.

"Yes," Bick said.

"For your mission, or for yourself, your own goals?" Huang said.

"Both," Bick said. "I killed a man, a prospector, years ago, to keep control of Argent, to keep possession of the vault, but also to make me very wealthy. I did that for me, not for my God, not for my duty. Last year I intended to kill the men who reopened the mine, but they met a different fate. "

"Did you wonder then why your God, furious and disappointed by your actions, did not come down to Earth and strike you down for your indiscretions? Your, what is the word your people like to throw about . . ." Huang snapped his finger as it came to him. "Ah, yes—your sins?"

"I didn't come to you to be mocked, Huang," Bick said.

"And I assure you, I am not," Huang said. "Did you lose your faith when your God allowed you to do as you wished, to exercise your own will, even though the actions were, as you would say, 'evil'?"

"Honestly, a little, but nothing came of it. It was the camel's nose in the tent," Bick said. "It was when I first began to doubt He was paying attention to anything going on here. Now Zeal is acting in direct defiance of Him—calling himself a god, drawing followers to himself, killers and worse than killers. He wants to drown this world in blood and God does nothing."

"One thing I like about your God," Huang said. "He's very still. Are you sure he's not Chinese?"

Bick sighed and held out his cup. Huang poured more tea.

"Not to insult or belittle," Huang said. "But we look at existence very differently than you, my friend. You see rules: rights and wrongs, good and evil. We see experience and understanding and growing from those. Behavior is neither inherently good nor evil, it simply is. Life is duality. We are good and evil, why should not our creator possess the same duality? Why only hold one image of such a vast and powerful creator as absolute? Embrace them both. Your people judge far too much, Malachi."

"And where does that leave us, exactly?" Bick said. "Wandering the desert with no map to guide us? Wander left, wander right, wherever a fickle god points?"

"If you walk the desert long enough, you will know it better than any map could ever show you," Huang said. "Inherently, our worlds have one thing in common, Biqa: All of us, immortal and man, have been given the freedom to act as we choose—to be—and then we must face the consequences of those actions, of being.

"This world is our stage. Mortals play the starring roles while you and I and our ilk are behind the curtains, doing as we see fit, wondering if the audience approves of our actions as much as the actors wonder."

"An occasional 'bravo' or catcall would be most appreciated," Bick said.

"Such actions might influence the performance," Huang said.

"Huang, you are one of the most moral beings I have ever known," Bick said. "How can you tell me there is no good or evil in creation, after all we have seen? What Raziel is about is evil. It destroys lives, disrupts the play; it is malicious harm for its own sake. How can such acts be justified, be seen as anything but evil?"

Huang sighed and stroked his beard. "It is difficult to explain to you or to anyone not inside such thought, or born to it, my friend, but I will try. The nature of mortals is wild, undisciplined—like a child or an animal. That is why it is called 'a nature.' It comes from nature, from natural forces at work upon the individual, from the individual seeking desire with no concept or care for the cost.

"Do animals commit evil? They kill without mercy or thought to fulfill a need. Some kill for sport, or acquire a taste for human flesh and blood. Are they evil in what they do? Children can be agents of chaos; they can do great harm with no true understanding of their actions and their implications. Does that make a child evil?"

"They are outside of sin," Bick said. "One must have awareness of one's own actions to commit sin."

"What you call awareness, we call teaching and enforcement. A man becomes moral through discipline and experience."

"So you think we need to educate and rein in Zeal and he will become a moral man?" Bick said. "Good luck with that."

"No," Huang said. "The closest approximation to true evil is losing control of the spirit, allowing it to run roughshod over your life and others, to rut in the self at any cost. It is the ultimate expression of selfishness and attachment.

"Raziel, like you and I, is a being more of spirit than flesh and to lose control of that spirit makes him very close to irredeemable. There is a small chance he may learn from this and change, but when the spirit runs unchecked, madness and death follow. No, Malachi, I understand why you oppose him, but do not think that your whole existence is invalid due to the actions of one misguided individual."

"God created all this," Bick said.

"Yes," Huang said, "quite a few of them."

"Yet He does nothing," Bick said. "He watches silently, and He allows sickness and death, injustice and cruelty and horrible caprice, and He does nothing."

"To act," Huang said, "would be to violate the very definition of free will. Has it ever occurred to you, my dear friend, that the carpenter built this house from the inside out, and did not give himself a key to the door, so that he could not tinker and meddle with the design? Perhaps he left his tools within, allowing the inhabitants of the home to do as they will?"

"God is omnipotent," Bick said. "He has no limits. He could act if He wished to do so."

"If He is truly all-powerful," Huang said, "then He must have the power to limit Himself."

"Leave it to you to make me feel more at ease and more confused all at the same time," Bick said.

They both laughed.

"Thank you, Huang," Bick said. "You are a good friend."

"And an excellent enemy as well," Huang said, and smiled.

"Even better," Bick said, nodding. "I have a plan for dealing with Zeal. It's dangerous and it may backfire. I need your help. If it fails there is danger for you and your people."

"If Zeal is not stopped, then my people and I are in danger anyway, so I see no choice but to help you," Huang said. "Allow me to summon us more tea and you can tell me all about your plan."

The Ace of Wands

Jim and Constance reached the end of Dry Well and Jim turned Promise east, threading through the sagebrush and the large, old homes at the base of Methuselah Hill to pick up Old Rock Road, which ran through the narrow valley between Methuselah and Rose Hills. Once they cleared the hills on either side of them, the scrubland stretched out ahead of them and the morning sun painted their view in brilliant golds, oranges and reds. Jim urged Promise on and the brown mustang began a smooth gallop across the desolate beauty that was the border of the desert. Constance's arms held him tighter and he felt her face on his back, warm, like the sun. Promise took the two youths deeper into the savage beauty of the wilderness, their hearts thudding in time to the horse's hooves.

Constance loved the feel of the sun on her face and the acceleration of the horse. Jim was an excellent rider and she loved the bond between him and his horse that she could feel easily; it was more than love, it was respect. It gave her just another reason to like and trust Jim Negrey. It was another reason to dread and hate what was coming.

"You're going to cut over to the southern road into town to save time," Constance said. It wasn't a question but more like a statement of fact, and she said it with a great deal of apprehension, almost dread in her voice.

"Yeah," Jim said. "My thought exactly, good guess."

"I was hoping I was wrong," she said. The cryptic response troubled Jim. He focused on the trail.

They rode through the edges of the 40-Mile Desert, bore northeast and picked up a dry, rutted trail that eventually became a proper road out Golgotha. It was after eleven and Promise was making excellent time. Constance was holding onto his waist and her face rested occasionally on his back. She tapped him on the shoulder and he turned his ear to listen.

"Remember I told you I dreamed about this," she said. 'Well, I was praying this part didn't happen this way, but it is. The not-so-good part is coming up, Jim, and you need to be ready. The people we are about to meet are lying to you. They want to kill us, torture us."

"What?" Jim said. "Why?"

"I don't know," Constance said, "I just saw it in the dream."

"Well, why the hell didn't you tell me sooner?" Jim said. "We could've changed it, not come this way, got help."

Constance squeezed him tight and held on.

"I don't understand what's happening to me," she said, "but I know if I try to ignore the dreams or change them, then worse things happen to everyone. All we can do is try to survive past the end of the dream, and then we can do whatever we need to."

Up ahead, the dark shapes of horsemen huddled on the road in sharp contrast to the bright desolation of the desert. Jim began to slow Promise as they neared. Four men, looking like U.S. soldiers.

"I can cut off the road, now," Jim said.

"No!" Constance said. "Not yet, please, Jim. It will be worse if you do!"

Jim reached back and patted her head as best he could. "Okay," he said. "It's all right, we'll make it through. Don't you worry."

They were closer now. Jim noticed something wasn't right. The men dressed like soldiers, sat in the saddle like soldiers and cradled their rifles like soldiers, but they had no unit or rank insignia and they flew no banner or flag. There were a few tents off the road and a civilian tent as well. From the sparse number of shelters, it looked like only this small patrol was present here. He turned his lapel over to hide his badge.

He felt Constance shift and slide behind him. Her arms slid away from his waist. She leaned forward and gave him a quick kiss on his cheek.

"Be careful," she whispered.

"Don't suppose you had any dreams with me in it since this one, have you?" Jim said.

Promise came to a halt about twenty-five feet from the four riders.

"Morning," Jim said, nodding to the grim-faced riders. "Is there a reason you're blocking the road?"

"Where you two headed, boy?" the lead rider asked.

"Virginia City," Jim said. "Our Granny lives over there. My sister and me, we live over by Golgotha. We're on our way to see her with a basket of goodies."

Constance smacked him hard in the ribs and Jim couldn't help but smile. "Is there a problem, sir?"

"Golgotha, huh?" the leader said. "You two are going to have to climb down off your horse. Now."

"What's wrong, sir?" Jim said. He patted Promise's neck, readying the horse to bolt. Constance, on the back of Promise, smiled at the soldiers, making sure to put the proper amount of vacuous fear in her look to insure they wouldn't remotely consider her of consequence. "We'll just be on our way. Thank you kindly, sir," Jim said.

"A moment," a hollow, muffled voice said. "Who have we here?"

Jim and Constance turned to see a man walking away from the tents toward them. He was slender and dressed in a vest and a well-made suit, a bit too much for the desert, even in late fall. He wore white gloves, like a servant might, and his face was covered by a long wooden mask that looked like it belonged to an Indian medicine man, or from one of the stories about the Dark Continent. The eyes of the mask were large and empty in the shadows of the ascendant sun.

"Two children from Golgotha, sir," the leader said. "We were about to send them up to you."

Jim and Constance could hear the man's labored breathing from ten feet away. It wasn't heat or poor health, it was excitement. The masked man's white hands clinched and unclenched eagerly as he regarded the two youths. Constance could feel his eyes burning into her flesh from behind the shadows and wood. Jim turned Promise, ready to bolt, but he knew the soldiers' rifles could cut them down from a quarter mile away.

The lead rider looked to the masked man and Jim knew it was all going south. He could smell the crazy off the man in the mask. Everything became silent in the desert. The wind tumbled and spun between the riders, kicking up the dust of the road. Jim took a deep breath and prepared. He saw his sister, Lottie, and told her he loved her; his throat was dry and it was hard to swallow. He wished Mutt was here, or Jon Highfather. He remembered the promise he made to Maude about Constance, and his mind calmed and cleared.

The man in the mask cocked his head and clinched his gloved hands to his chest silently. "Bring them into the tent. Restrain them. If they resist, kill the boy but please, by all means, I want the girl in as pristine a condition as possible."

Jim flipped his lapel and drew his father's revolver. He used his legs to turn

Promise and drive the little mustang to close the gap into the circle of riders, where their rifles would be a disadvantage.

"Deputy! Drop your guns!" Jim shouted.

Jim took bead on the lead rider and fired as the man was trying to aim with the rifle in the tight circle. Jim switched to the next rider and fired again; that man had already fired and the bullet buzzed past Jim's ear. Jim readied himself for the impact of the third and fourth riders' bullets. They had time, by now, to get off shots. Something flew past his face and he turned to the third rider, to see him clutching at a thin throwing knife buried deep into his throat, blood gushing from his mouth, the rifle falling from his hands. Jim glanced back to see Constance snap her hand again, like a magician summoning a card, and a second blade appeared in the eye of the fourth rider, who tumbled from his horse, instantly dead.

There was a sharp, deep ache in Jim's right leg and he saw the masked man had driven a large steel ice pick up to the handle in Jim's thigh. Blood gushed, soaking his jeans. The masked man had an ice pick in his other hand as well and was preparing to drive it into Promise's neck. Jim felt darkness closing in on him as his lifeblood gushed out. He tried to swing his pistol around to shoot the masked man in the strange empty face of the wooden mask before the madman could kill his horse, but it was hard to make his arm and hand work.

Suddenly Constance was there flying off the back of Promise and tackling the masked man. The girl and the man tumbled and rolled in the dust beside the road. Jim struggled to stay in the saddle, to stay awake; he clung to Promise's neck and tried to keep his eyes open as blood streamed down his leg.

Constance rolled up off the ground and into a hopping, aggressive stance. The masked man scrambled to his feet quickly. He was wiry and fast; he held the large ice pick like a blade and slowly worked to circle the girl.

"Well, aren't you children just full of surprises," the masked man said, his voice muffled and breathless in excitement. "I do hope the whole town is as sporting. You have something of a reputation to uphold after all."

Constance stopped and allowed the masked man to move almost behind her. As he lunged quickly at the spot between her shoulder blades, she spun and landed a powerful kick to his upper chest. The man flew back, staggered by the power of the blow. He regained his footing and, tossing the ice pick to his other hand, charged and pressed the girl, swinging the huge steel needle back and forth, attempting to slash her. Constance ducked under and around his blows, moving in to strike at one of the nerve clusters her mother taught her would drop this man, and then she could focus on helping keep Jim alive.

The masked man's knee drove into her stomach and Constance staggered forward, knocked off-balance by the force of the blow and the pain. He grabbed her by her hair and pulled hard, yanking her off-balance again, pulling her to him. The ice pick gleamed in his hand and he moved it toward her face, near her eye, which was wide with fear.

"You've had some pugilistic training to be sure, girl. But you have a lot to learn about feints and getting too focused. You telegraphed your intentions to me, and I altered the dance . . . but that was very, very invigorating. Now I'm going to slide this into your eye and you will stop having all those bad thoughts and be a good girl for me."

A gunshot rolled across the wasteland. The masked man's shoulder exploded in a spray of blood and bone that spun him and Constance to the ground. Jim dropped off Promise and fell to the ground, his father's smoking pistol dropping from his hands to fall in the dust with the boy.

"Got ya, you sumbitch," Jim muttered as he crawled toward the two. Constance rolled free of the masked man and grabbed a rock. The masked man tried to rise, and fell again. His shoulder dribbled blood on the dry desert sand.

"More fight left in you than I anticipated . . . Deputy," the masked man said, fumbling for his ice pick. "I hope you live long enough to see what Zeal does to your town, your friends and family."

Constance smashed the rock over the man's head. His mask, splintering and cracking, stopped part of the impact, but he still fell forward from the power of her blow.

"Little too focused there," Constance said as she reared back to strike again. The masked man snarled under his broken mask and twisted to drive the ice pick into the girl's chest. Jim growled and fell onto the masked man, punching him in his wounded shoulder. Jim ripped the ice pick out of his own thigh and stabbed the man in the back with it again and again. Constance grabbed the masked man's wrist and slowed the ice pick the man was slashing toward her heart. It dug into her shoulder instead and ripped down toward her chest, but she fought it with every ounce of strength, snarling like a mountain lion. With her other hand she smashed the rock into the side of the man's head again and again, with what remaining force she possessed. The man's gaze was visible to her now through the yawning portals of the mask's eyes—hatred, pure undiluted hatred.

The masked man coughed, a gurgling sound, and rich, dark blood spilled out from the narrow slit of a mouth on the mask. More poured out from below the chin of the broken wooden face.

"Damn you both to hell," the man hissed. He slumped, rattled for a moment as his whole body convulsed, and then was still.

"You . . . are a hell of a fighter," Jim said as he let go of the handle of the ice pick buried in the dead man's back. He fell facefirst onto the sand and didn't move.

"No, no, no!" Constance shouted. She scrambled across the dirt to Jim's side. She rolled him over and searched for the signs of life in his throat and wrist, as her mother had taught her. The pulse as there, weak and erratic, but there. "Please, Jim, don't leave me. This is all my fault, my damn dream! Please stay, fight for me, Jim Negrey, you hear, you fight!"

Constance tore off part of her already ripped and bloody shirt sleeve and applied it firmly to Jim's spurting wound as a bandage. She pushed firmly on the pressure point on his leg where her mother taught her she could stop bleeding. The bag about Jim's neck seemed to jump and move on its own. Constance chalked it up to a convulsion or her nerves playing tricks on her.

"Why did you lie to me back on Argent?" Jim muttered. "Two times. I counted." His eyes fluttered open while Constance worked to stop the bleeding. She looked at him as she worked.

"You sure are pretty," he said softly.

"And you are obviously delirious," she said. "I tell you what, you stay with me and I'll tell you everything. No more lies. We need to get you stabilized and then get off this road before more of these crazy people show up."

"Thank you for saving Promise," Jim said. "She's all I got left."

"She's not all you got left," Constance said, but Jim had already passed out again.

The Two of Swords

It was the night before Ray Zeal was to come to Golgotha, less than two days until Thanksgiving. The streets of Golgotha were an odd mixture of chaos and silence. Most decent folk were hunkering down for the coming storm and most of the people who were eager for Zeal and his people to sweep into town were celebrating wildly in the streets and the saloons.

Emily was packed and ready for tomorrow's stage. She had wanted to depart today, but she had been informed at the Wells Fargo Station that the coach was way behind schedule, having not shown up at all yet. She was working on a painting in her suite at the Imperial when there was a knock at the door. She sat down her brush, wiped her hands with her oilcloth, covered the canvas and opened the door. It was her father.

"May I please come in?" Bick said.

"Yes," Emily replied. "Of course." He entered and sat on the sofa, across from the chair Emily chose.

"I understand you are leaving on the next stage," Bick said. Emily nodded. "That is a very wise decision. I'd like you to be gone from Golgotha before Zeal comes back tomorrow."

"You should leave as well," Emily said. "He seemed a most brutal and unstable man on the street the other day."

"He's not a man," Bick said. "He's like me."

Emily's eyes widened.

"But he's so . . . ," Emily said. "You have to get out of here. I heard what he did to you. He'll kill you!"

"I thought you might want him to," Bick said. "I wouldn't blame you if you did."

"No," she said. "I don't want that. I'd never want that."

"I wanted to . . . apologize to you," Bick said. "I know apology is a next-to-worthless currency, but I wanted you to know about your mother.

"Your mother restored my faith in my mission, my purpose for being here. Even if angels can fall, can fail, even if God is silent, humanity deserves its time on the stage, its spotlight. I may never see Heaven again, may forget every detail of it, but I can look at your mother's paintings, remember them and be reminded of my lost home. That finite creatures of dust and mud, born to oblivion, can summon forth such beauty, such transcendent emotions and ideas . . . that is worth protecting, worth fighting for, worth dying for."

"If you loved her so much, why did you leave her alone?" Emily said. "You knew she was going to die if she had me. Her family hated her for her affair with you, treated her like trash. They hated me, too, sent me away to the orphanage when she died. I don't understand. How can you claim to love her so much and treat her like that? Let her die alone and disgraced."

"My kind experience emotions very strongly, very powerfully," Bick said. "I fell completely in love with your mother and a part of me belongs to her forever. It is the same each time we fall in love or hate, it is part of how we are made, it is how we can hold to our purposes or missions as long as we do. We, for lack of a better term, obsess.

"Your mother loved me, too, and we were very happy for a time. I was with your mother for almost a year. I wanted to be with her forever."

"Then why?" Emily said. "She deserves an answer. I do too."

"The truth," Bick said. "Our sorrow fills us up as deeply as any other emotion we experience. I couldn't bear the thought of watching her die, couldn't stand the thought of the sadness and the pain. I was a coward, an evil, weak, selfish coward, and I ran away rather than stand witness to the destruction my actions caused. I abandoned her, I abandoned you.

"I wept for your mother. Truth be told, I wept for me as well, my loss as much as her death. I wish I could say I wept for you and your loss, but I didn't. For all the tales of guardian angels, my kind makes terrible parents. I should have done for you. I didn't. I turned to building my empire here, to burying myself in the role of Malachi Bick, ruthless scoundrel, so I could ignore the pain."

"Did it work?" she asked.

"No," Bick said. "It didn't."

"When I was in the orphanage, I remember for a long time, I cried every night. I prayed to die, to be taken out of this world. One day I realized God wasn't going to kill me, he wasn't going to end my suffering. I decided that night, I could do the job myself or I could try to see what this life had for me, good and bad. I decided to stay and in time I stopped crying. I understand how you must have felt. I'm sorry. It's the worst feeling in the world to feel alone all the time."

"You forgive me?" Bick said.

Emily nodded.

"Of course I do," she said. "I love you."

Bick looked at this tiny girl, more human than divine, but her words, her words her soul touched the rocky, barren place in him. It reminded him of a place before time, a voice that he could barely recall that made all the chaos and confusion and doubt make sense.

"Are you all right?" she asked.

"Yes," Bick said, nodding, smiling. "I have a present for you."

"Really?" Emily said. Bick nodded. He opened his coat and withdrew a single black feather, straight and perfect. The color of the feather was black as coal, gently fading to a soft smoky gray at the edge of the feather.

"This is mine," Bick said. "It is part of me, a very old part. With this you can always find me and I can always find you."

Bick placed the feather in her hand.

"I freely give you this, and with it you may request anything of me, anything, Emily. You tell me to go away, I will leave; you tell me to die, and I will die. This is part of me, the core of who I am, and I share it with you, because you are my daughter and I love you with all I am."

"Are you sure you want me to have this?" she said.

"I trust you with my life," Bick said. "Just as I trusted Caleb. I have only given a few of these away in my long existence. We trust as powerfully as we distrust. It is the way of my kind. Of late, I have allowed my distrust to poison me, but you, you have shown me a grace I had forgotten existed."

"Thank you," Emily said. "I'll keep it safe, I promise. I have a present for you, now." She stood, as did Bick, and walked to the covered canvas. She pulled the cloth away.

"It's not finished, but I think you should see it."

Bick gasped and stood transfixed by the image. It was an angel high aloft with spread wings and a fluttering mane of hair like midnight that bled into the dark, threatening storm clouds that swirled about him. At the core of the storm, the rays of the sun spilled out, obscuring his face, but Bick knew exactly what that face looked like. The painting sang to him, scolded him, it was full of love and anger, joy and regret. The emotions swelled and crashed over him, like ocean waves. He was naked before this mirror. Bick's eyes welled with tears and he nodded .

"How . . . did you?" Bick tried to pull his eyes away from the painting. "It's me. All of me, even the parts I can't look at or admit."

"I've been able to do it since I was a little girl," Emily said. "When I see someone, and draw them, or paint them, I can see all of them. It's like I'm painting their soul as well, all the colors and the hues, the depths and shading."

"Emily," Bick said, "angels don't have souls."

"I disagree," she said, and covered the painting again.

Bick stood and wiped his eyes.

"That is beautiful and very flattering," he said. "Thank you."

"I paint what I see," Emily said. "Don't really have a choice in it. Look, I don't want you to die and I don't want Zeal to hurt you or anyone else. You have to get out of here, now, Daddy."

"Daddy." Bick smiled. "I like that."

"Please go," she said.

"I can't," he said. "If you painted me and saw what's inside of me, you should understand why."

"I don't," she said. "I saw you hate this place and love it too."

"True," Bick said. "I have a job to do. Zeal may not win yet. I have a plan. I'll tell you all about it. If things go very bad and you can't get away, I can tell you a secret that will lay Zeal low, but it's a dangerous gambit and only to be used if all else has failed."

"Let me stay and help," Emily said. "You'd count on Caleb, count on me!"

"Caleb is dead," Bick said. "And it was because of me. I can't bear the thought of losing you too. I want you on the next stagecoach out of here, Emily. Promise me."

"Only if you promise me I can come back and stay," she said. "You may have done things, questionable things, but you are my father and you are all I have in this world. I've seen all the colors in you, remember? There is still more light in you than darkness, Daddy. Don't let Zeal or anyone else take that away from you, or from me."

Emily hugged him tight. He held her, too, as gently as a spring rain with arms capable of ripping apart worlds. For a moment, Bick remembered this feeling from long ago before there was time or space or Earth. He remembered his home in the arms of his child.

"I promise," Bick said.

Harry Pratt answered the insistent pounding at his door in the dead of night. He had not yet been to bed. Mutt stood there. He was not wearing his star and he had a canvas bag hung over his shoulder and a Winchester rifle in his hand.

"What is it?" Harry said. "Zeal here? Jon all right?"

"I don't have much time to explain, Harry," Mutt said, "but if Zeal gets his hands on this skull"—he held up the bag—"it's real bad. He'll wreck the town and then keep going."

"What the hell is it?" Harry said.

"Trouble," Mutt said. "Golgotha-style trouble."

"Why me?" Harry said.

"Because you are the last person in the world anyone would expect me to trust with anything," Mutt said.

"True enough," Pratt said.

"No one will expect you to have it and it has to be kept safe or a lot of people are going to die, and I know you will do your best to keep that from happening, Harry."

"Give me the bag," Pratt said. Mutt handed it to him.

"Be careful," Mutt said. "Zeal's got people all over. They might come for you to get some leverage."

"Let them," Harry said. "I'll hide this and then go meet up with Jon, I can help him."

"No, Harry," Mutt said. "This isn't about a good scrap. This skull staying safe is more important than you looking good as mayor, more important than helping Jonathan. It's more important than any of us. I need you to nurse it. I know that's a lot to ask while Zeal is chewing up the town, but this is important. Please."

"I'll be damned," Harry said. "'Please'... Okay, I'll sit this one out... for now."

"If things go south and Jonathan doesn't stop Zeal tomorrow," Mutt continued, "we're going to meet up, regroup. I'll get word to you if that happens. Look for a chalk note on the back wall of the outhouse behind Elias Carol's house. Understand?"

"All right," Harry said. "Where are you going?"

"To do what Jon asked me to do and get a real good view of the show," Mutt said, and disappeared into the darkness.

Harry secured the old skull in his private safe upstairs in his bedroom, then went to bed, exhausted and only removing his boots. He had been working again all night at his office and had only been home a short time before Mutt had arrived. He hoped to get a few hours of sleep before he had to be back at town hall.

A terrible dream awaited him. He was standing in an odd room with strange electrical lamps in it. There was a tall, handsome, slender and strangely ominous man there. He was clean-cut and dressed in strange clothes of an unfamiliar fashion that almost seemed to be too new, too clean. The man was struggling with a young man of Eastern descent—he looked Chinese, perhaps. The younger boy was only partly clothed and was screaming for his life. He was pinned on a couch that also looked strangely too new, too well made. They both spoke English and Harry understood what they were saying.

"I want you to stay," the older man said in a voice that was calm and cold on the surface, yet hot with rage and madness. "I'm going to cut open your brain and make you stay with me."

Harry had felt frozen until this point of the dream, but he could suddenly move. He heard labored breathing off to his left. A strange apparition stood, unseen by any but Harry in a corner of the room. It was a fat man dressed in the costume and face paint of a clown. His breathing was labored as he watched the boy struggle and his hand was sliding down to the erection he had. The clown's thick, wet tongue slid across his lips as he watched the tableau unfold before him, mesmerized. The very existence of such a creature made Harry dizzy with anger, fear and disgust.

Harry stepped forward, feeling like he was pushing through molasses. He grabbed the arms of the older man and pulled him off the boy.

"That's enough!" Harry shouted, even though his voice sounded like a whisper to him. The older man seemed shocked at Harry's appearance, almost frightened for an instant. The boy wasted no time in running, half-naked, out the door of the room. The clown-ghost-thing shuffled after him, running as fast as his girth would allow, laughing as he ran.

Harry held the strange man's arms and watched in horror as all the emotions drained from the man's face. Something sitting on a table, behind them in the cluttered little room, caught Harry's attention. It was the skull.

"You can't save him," the man said. "You can't stop us. It's in the blood. It's always been in the blood."

The handsome man's face, his body, shifted, flowed into the screaming, raging shaggy man that had been plaguing Harry's dreams for months. The monstrous giant's cavernous, fanged mouth became the universe, devouring Harry and swallowing him into fetid darkness.

Harry awoke, wet with sweat, gasping for breath. Dawn was a threat on the horizon. He looked across the bedroom to the safe built into the wall. The painting covering it was swung aside. The locked safe door was open and the skull stared at him, mocking.

Within his sanctum inside the Celestial Palace, Ch'eng Huang stood, eyes closed, his awareness stretching out across the wastelands. He had felt Jim Negrey's life force flare and then almost flicker out. He had felt the eye surge with power to help keep the boy alive, and then nothing. He reached out, searching, calling. In this alien land, his power was focused primarily in the places his people gathered, so it took considerable effort to sift through the wasteland. He focused on the eye instead of the boy and he began to sense its presence, like a great green flame in the shadows of the world, hidden behind sorceries of concealment and obfuscation. It was only due to his close study of the artifact that he could sense its hidden power at all. The monks that had hidden it and given it to Jim's father had been very cautious and very clever.

The doors behind him opened softly and the padded footfalls of one of his men approached. It was a slight distraction, but Huang pushed it away as best he could. He was close to finding the boy and then perhaps he could get him some help.

"You may place the tea on the table," Huang said, "and then leave me."

The blade dug deep into Huang's lower back, stabbed with brutal and precise force. The blade filled him with agony the likes of which he could not recall in this world of flesh. Hot blasts of sheer rage, anger, hatred pumped into the old man like streams of venom. He lost all contact with the eye; his senses fell in on themselves, buried under indescribable pain. He staggered forward and fell to the floor.

"Don't care for the tea?" A voice like a cobra gliding across the water said in Mandarin. Huang struggled to roll over to confront his assassin. Part of the blade had snapped off in the wound and was still buried in his back. Waves of searing torment and mind-destroying aggression tore through his frail frame.

His attacker was dressed as one of his Green Ribbon Tong soldiers. His face was calm, but his eyes brimmed with insanity. "Remember me?" the assassin said.

"Chi Mo Duan," Huang said, fighting out the words, ragged darkness fluttering at the edges of this vision. "You were cast out for your cruelty and undisciplined behavior. How can this be? Why are you here, how did you get in?"

Duan held the broken blade of the knife forward so his former master could see. "Ray Zeal sends his regards, old man. When you are dead I will lead the Green Ribbons to glory and blood, as is fitting an army of assassins."

The broken blade was crystalline and a deep red in color. "Even such as you are vulnerable to red jade, old ghost. Your guards are dead. And now you will join them."

The jade knife flashed downward.

The Wheel of Fortune

The noonday sky was dark with screaming crows as Ray Zeal and his followers rode into Golgotha. Zeal rode at the fore, smiling atop his golden palomino. To his right rode Charles Cook and to his left was Colonel Whitmore. Behind them was Cook's private, fanatical army, the Praetorians, under Whitmore's bloody command. Then the wagons and support for the Praetorians, and finally Zeal's devoted worshipers, his cult, the Teeth of Cain.

A clan of gypsy murderers from South Carolina, part of the cult, played the drums and the tambourine, along with the eerie moan of the squeezebox and the panpipes, the accordion and the violin, as their garishly painted *vardo* rolled among the procession. The Romani's eyes were hooded and cold as they viewed the drunken, stupid Gaje who clapped and danced to their music but had no idea it was a funeral dirge.

Some of the cultists looked like death riding in off a long trail. They wore black dusters and wide brimmed campaign hats. Black cloth or leather masks covered their heads to hide their self-inflicted deformities. Many of the cult had hacked away their lips, ears, and eyelids over the years, and ate them in ritual sacrifice to Zeal, their bloodthirsty god.

Professor Zenith, riding his odd little cart packed with arcane-looking devices, rolled up the back of the procession, along with a small rear guard of Praetorians. All told, the force Zeal led into town was almost a hundred strong.

The sides of Main Street were filled with the less savory locals who hooted and shouted as the procession passed; many set guns off in the air in celebration. Zeal laughed and waved to the well-wishers.

Others standing on the sides of the streets were less enthusiastic; those who had tarried too long or loss track of time were now forced to watch grimly as a seeming army entered their town. These few unfortunate souls grabbed their bundles and their packages and hurried home to hide and pray for the commotion to be over, and to hope that not too many died in the latest installment of the madness that came with living in Golgotha.

The streets were emptier than usual. Many folks had decided today was a good day to stay home, while others lay sick or dead in their homes or businesses, victims of the Brechts' poisonous ministrations.

The procession moved forward, Whitmore barking orders to his men to disperse and cover key locations in the town. Troops and members of the cult peeled off from the main group as the eerie parade slowly advanced north up Main Street.

"Can you smell it?" Zeal said to Cook. "Fear and madness. It's as if this town had littered the streets with rose petals for me. I'm going to like it here."

The Paradise Falls was empty. Kerry Duell, Georgie Nance and the other employees, the bar girls, the match girl, were all no-shows today. Malachi Bick sat alone at his favorite red-felt faro table and shuffled and dealt himself a spread of tarot cards. He flipped a card, the Hanged Man, as Jon Highfather entered the mausoleum-quiet saloon.

"Malachi, still not too late to get you out of here," Highfather said. Bick said nothing. He shuffled and tossed out another card, the Queen of Cups.

"Has the stage left?" Bick asked. "Someone very dear to me is supposed to be on it."

"The stages haven't showed up in over a day," Highfather said. "Zeal's people have blockaded the roads. I sent Jim and Constance out there."

Bick frowned. He gathered the card and tossed a final one on the red table: the Magician.

"Did you pray today, Jonathan?" Bick asked.

"Nope," Highfather said. "You?"

"No," Bick said. "Come, Sheriff, let's go greet our guests."

Zeal's procession, accompanied by the town's reprobates and onlookers, stopped before town hall. Zeal climbed off his horse and pulled off his riding gloves. As he walked toward the doors of the hall, they crashed opened and two of the

Praetorians led out a disheveled and slightly bloody Colton Higbee—Mayor Pratt's assistant. Higbee was shuddering. His glasses were broken and sat on his face at an odd angle.

"Where's the mayor?" Zeal asked his two followers.

"Gone, Lord," one of the Praetorians said. "Checked his house too. This is his assistant. He will read it."

Zeal handed a rolled parchment to Higbee with a smile and leaned close to the terrified young man's ear. "Read this aloud when I tell you to, make it official, and I'll make sure you and your parents aren't dinner tonight, Mr. Higbee."

"How do you know about me and my family?" Higbee said.

"I know everything about this town and everyone in it," Zeal said. "Now be a good boy and follow my lead."

Zeal turned to address the crowd. "Good people of Golgotha, I have with me Mr. Higbee, your mayor's duly recognized agent. He has something to announce to all of you—a proclamation from Mayor Pratt. Read, Mr. Higbee."

Higbee's voice wavered as he spoke, the fear making it crack and warble. "To all citizens of Golgotha, effective immediately, I, Harry Pratt, mayor, do hereby proclaim Ray Zeal the new sheriff of Golgotha and do duly deputize his men as peace officers for the Town of Golgotha.

"Several new laws, regulations and town ordinances are listed below and will be posted at town hall and in other public places. They take effect immediately, including the imposition of town-wide curfew, and a warrant for the arrest of Malachi Bick and Jon Highfather, as well as anyone aiding or abetting these criminals. This is done by my hand this twenty-third day of November, 1870, Harrison Pratt, mayor of Golgotha."

A rumble of dissent and confusion spread through the crowd.

"What the hell?" an angry voice called out.

"Nobody said nothing about gittin' rid of Jon! This is a load of horse apples!"

"Curfew? Who the fuck said anything about a damned curfew!"

The angry voices were joined by many of the troublemakers who had welcomed Zeal to town like Caesar returning to Rome.

"Hell yeah!" a drunken voice snarled, "'Bout time that crowbait Highfather got what was coming to him! Let's string him up again! This time we'll do it right!"

"We're with ya, Ray!" another voice shouted.

"Shut the fuck up, you damn lick-fingers!" another voice called. "Have a little respect for the sheriff!"

Zeal plucked the parchment away from Higbee and handed it back to a Praetorian. "Find Pratt, check his house again. He couldn't have just crawled into a hole and hid. But first, nail this to the door."

As one of Cook's mercenaries hammered the proclamation onto the door of town hall, Zeal called out to the crowd. "Tomorrow is Thanksgiving, good people, and as your new sheriff, I promise you the best celebration you've ever had!"

A cheer came up from the crowd, not as boisterous or as heartfelt as before the reading of the proclamation, but still given voice by a large number of those gathered. Many of those who had protested the proclamation had either fled to their homes or had been beaten or bullied into silence now.

"You ain't sheriff of nothing, Zeal," a voice called out from the center of Main Street, behind the crowd and Zeal's party.

Jon Highfather and Malachi Bick strode down the center of the street, toward the assembly. "Mayor Pratt didn't write that," Highfather said, "and it has no more legitimacy than that smile of yours. You are disturbing the peace and you and your men are to disperse right now and head for the town limits, or I'm going to have to arrest the lot of you."

A rumble of nervous laughter ran through the crowd. Highfather stood his ground. One of the Teeth of Cain stepped forward, a man in his late twenties dressed like a range rider. He had a battered Stetson and a heavy pistol hanging at his hip, slung in gunfighter fashion.

"Damnation," a man in the crowd shouted. "That's Saw-Tooth McCredie!"

"Lord, let me kill him for you," McCredie said to Zeal. The gunfighter's teeth were filed to uneven, sharp points. "I've wanted to slap leather with this bastard for a long time."

"Take him," Zeal said. "For my glory."

"Step off a bit, Malachi," Highfather said. Bick stepped away, eying Zeal, who was grinning and slapping his champion on the back.

The two men walked toward each other down the middle of Main Street. The crowd grew silent.

"You know who I am?" McCredie said.

"I don't really care," Highfather said.

"I've killed eighteen men in four states and three territories," McCredie said.

"Eighteen? You are a salty dog, indeed," Highfather said, his eyes never leaving McCredie's, the humor drained from his voice and his eyes. "You keep count and everything. Go on, salty dog, bark."

Bick realized he had never been this close to Jon Highfather when he was in a gunfight. Bick tried to focus on Zeal, but he was fascinated by how calm, how aware Highfather was. The man seemed completely focused, yet at ease, perhaps more at ease than Bick had ever known the sheriff to be.

McCredie drew his gun, faster than the flutter of any eyelash, faster than an impure thought. He cleared his holster and began to level his pistol at Highfather, not really aiming, so much as shooting from instinct and experience: .44 caliber thunder rolled across Main Street. McCredie was lifted off his feet by the force of the bullet. The round shattered his sternum and then pulped the gunslinger's heart. McCredie was dead before his body hit the muck and dirt of the street, his unfired gun still clutched in his hand.

Highfather, his pistol smoking, scanned the crowd, Zeal and the other invaders. A cheer came up from the cowed townsfolk. He silenced them again with his next words.

"Clear this street and Zeal, you and your people get the hell out of Golgotha now."

"Or what, Sheriff?" Zeal said. "You intend to shoot all of us?"

There was a crack of gunfire, then another and another. Three of Zeal's men fell from their horses, dead.

"Something like that," Highfather said.

"You took out my shooters on the roof," Zeal said, nodding. "Very good, Malachi, sheriff, but you didn't think I might consider you would try something like that. Your shooters may want to hold their fire, unless you are eager to get people killed. I have something you'll want to see."

"Hold your fire!" Highfather shouted out.

On three different rooftops, Mutt, Kate and Maude waited. The dead or unconscious bodies of Zeal's snipers lay at their feet, the killers' rifles in their hands.

Zeal snapped his fingers and one of Cook's soldiers pulled out a cavalry bugle and blew it loudly. "Now wait a moment," Zeal said.

About ten minutes passed while Highfather and Bick stood alone in the street and the mob remained relatively mute, waiting to see what happened next. A lone rider, one of Cook's Praetorians, appeared, galloping off Prosperity and onto the northern side of Main, opposite Highfather and Bick. His horse halted beside Zeal and he saluted Cook. The rider held a burlap bag. He said something to Zeal, who nodded and took it from the rider. He walked alone toward Highfather and Bick. He tossed it at Bick's feet.

"Open it," Zeal said. Bick and Highfather looked at each other. Bick knelt and opened the sack. He lifted something small out of the bag by its long tangled black hair; a few tiny blue ribbons fell from the hair and dropped onto the dark cold sod of Main Street. Bick cradled the object carefully and with his other hand picked up one of the tiny ribbons. Highfather knelt as well to examine what Bick held.

"Her name was Sadie Colton," Zeal said. "At least that's what my man told me. She was eight years old. Pretty little thing, isn't she, Malachi? Suffer the little children and all that."

Highfather was up, the pistol in Zeal's smiling face. He cocked it, still as smooth and emotionless as he had been when shooting down McCredie. But Bick saw the storm burning, crashing, hidden behind his gray eyes.

"Sheriff . . . Jonathan," Bick said softly.

"Pull that trigger and they all die, the whole schoolhouse full of them," Zeal said, "and not quick like little Sadie. No, the rest will die slowly and in confused agony, like their dear schoolmaster, Mr. Worley, did. We also have the town elders. I can send you something from one of them, too, if you need proof."

"No," Highfather said; his voice was cold slate.

"That won't be necessary," Bick said. "We surrender, Ray."

"Just like the decent, honorable men I counted on you being," Zeal said.

"You are going to burn in Hell, Zeal," Highfather said as he uncocked the gun and lowered it. "You got us for now. I'll call off the shooters on the roofs."

"No need," Zeal said. "My men are killing your friends as we speak."

Maude cocked the Winchester. The smoking shell flipped free and she took aim on another of Zeal's killers.

Mutt had caught up to her and Kate yesterday after the shootout at Hauk's restaurant. He'd told them Highfather's plan to ambush Zeal's snipers. Mutt had managed to separate Maude and Kate long enough so that Maude could rush home and change into her "working clothes." Now, wearing her bandana mask over her mouth and nose and disguised as a man, Maude had silently climbed the roof and taken out one of Zeal's snipers. She knew Mutt and Kate were on other roofs, having done the same.

Now she watched as Zeal dropped the bag at Bick's feet. There was a blur before her eyes for less than a second as a pale yellow cloth slipped over her head at inhuman speed and tightened about her neck. The act had been so fast that she hadn't even had time to raise her hand to block the strangle cord. She had not heard a sound from her attacker, who even now drove his knees into her back as he tightened the cord, the coin slipped into the cloth cutting off her air and attempting to crush her windpipe. Only pure trained instinct, acting faster than her mind could comprehend, had made her lower her head and angle herself slightly to protect her larynx from being cracked like a peanut shell.

Batra muttered his prayers to Kali, begging her to accept his offering. His mind, however, drifted to his next victims, the half-breed deputy and the other woman. Once he had killed this masked man, he would move on to the next rooftop. The anticipation thrilled him and it also distracted him, so that when the masked man raised both arms straight up and spun to attempt to face him with great force, Batra flew across the flimsy roof, the hold broken by the simple leverage, speed and strength of the act.

Maude drew in air in ragged, greedy gasps. She had dropped the rifle, she didn't want it now. She sprinted, silent as thought, toward the fallen man, who she now recognized was a Thuggee assassin trained in India.

Anne Bonny's insistence on her reading about the various schools of killers and assassins had been one of Maude's favorite parts of the training as a girl. Gran said she had met and studied the Thuggee at a safe distance. She also told Maude a tale of how the ritual assassins had almost summoned their goddess, Kali, back to the world to begin an age of horrors. Gran Bonny had, of course, been instrumental in stopping them and claimed she even crossed blades with the Dark Mother herself before sending her back to Hell and saving the world. Maude always loved Gran Bonny's bedtime stories.

Maude drove a knife-hand blow down into Batra's collarbone; he tumbled and was back on his feet, but Maude's blow still cracked the bone—the full force of it would have shattered it. Batra's face was expressionless as he let his uninjured arm drop to his belt and freed his curved kukri knife.

Maude moved in again, like lightning flashing. She knew better than to assume any superiority to this man; such pride would get her killed. He had been trained as she had, for most likely as long as she had, and the Mother he swore allegiance to was one of the dark, angry faces of the Mother Maude served. Batra's blade made a soft zipping sound as it cut the air and nearly opened up Maude's midsection. Maude bent like a branch in the wind and the blade passed her.

She drove two fingers to the nerve bundle in the pectoral region of Batra's chest. The Thuggee leaned back and the blow that should have frozen his arm grazed him, doing nothing. He responded with a low, sharp kick to Maude's shin, designed to break her leg and floor her. Maude did a standing jump and the kick whooshed by under her tucked legs. She took the opportunity to drive a snap-kick to Batra's face, which connected with and shattered his nose as it drove him back, giving Maude some breathing room and the luxury of a few seconds to land, take in more air and then advance.

The only sound of the two combatants on the roof was an occasional creaking board; otherwise the battle for survival was noiseless. Batra began to dance, to spin like a top, wobbling. The fifteen-inch blade of the kukri seemed to be everywhere. Maude had been instructed in the fighting style of the dervish and this was similar, but not exactly the same. Batra's dance intensified and he pressed forward, a wall of flashing death moving Maude closer to the edge of the roof, limiting her options to move, to counterattack, breaking her cover to the streets below.

She intently studied the pattern of the dance and, to her dismay, couldn't find one. Batra was chanting now, low but audibly.

White-hot agony pushed through Maude's upper chest, a nail of sharp heat driven into her by a sledgehammer of force and sound. A bullet, fired by one of Zeal's men below, ripped through her back and out her chest. She gasped at the immediacy and scope of the pain and then her training took over and she pushed it away.

Even as the bullet was tunneling through her body, Maude shifted and spun. The exiting bullet was redirected to Batra's path and the same distorted round, steaming with her blood, caught the Thuggee in his already injured arm, knocking him to the ground. Blood gushed from his shoulder. Maude moved quickly away from the roof's edge, but not quickly enough to avoid a second bullet that bored into her upper back and departed in a spray of blood and some bone. She winced and addressed the pain. There was no time for it now. Parts of her body were numb and not responding to her demands.

She stood over the wounded Thuggee for the few seconds she could afford. The pain made her own voice, not that of a man, slip out. "We're not finished with this," she said.

Maude sprinted for the opposite side of the rooftop even as she heard the shouts of men and the thuds of boots approaching from the Main Street side. She jumped onto the roof of Gillian Proctor's boardinghouse and landed in the middle of a storm of bullets. More pain, harder now to ignore and suppress. She was getting dizzy and feeling the cold creep inside her. It was the trauma of the injuries, she told herself. She took a breath as she leapt toward the flat roof of the jail. She thought behind her she heard Mutt shouting, cursing, and more gunfire, the screams of dying men, ripped apart by lead. She calmed her mind and began the work of redirecting the blood flow. Her body responded loyally, as it was trained to, but it was sluggish. Between the struggle with Tumblety the night before, the battle with the Thuggee and now this, she was exhausted and injured and it was taking a toll on her.

She glanced to the left, down Dry Well Road. Soldiers on horseback were keeping up with her and firing at her as she ran. She hit the edge of the jail, launched upward as another bullet hit her leg and landed on the next roof . She collapsed from the injured leg, rolled and came up, moving in, away from the withering fire, only to have more bullets zing about her from shooters behind her on other roofs. Another blossom of hot pain.

She lived in her mind now, not her body. She moved by will, not muscle or sinew. Constance was out there and needed her, maybe more than she ever had; *move, move, keep moving.* There was a gunshot off to her right, several rooftops away, and she heard a man's cry of pain from behind her. She glanced over to see Kate Warne cocking her Winchester and taking bead on another of her attackers.

"Go!" Kate shouted to her. "Run!"

Maude took a moment to look down. She had run out of buildings. Below was the small circle of worn benches and the crumbling stone ring of the old dry well. She remembered sitting there with Mutt, how good and right it all felt and how much she wanted to get to do that again. The ache in her chest at the thought that she never would get to do that, to see him again, was worse than any wound, any pain could ever be.

The bullets exploded around her again. There were enemies everywhere. She breathed a good, clean breath, savored it like a wine.

"I love you," she said softly.

Maude charged, sprinting to the edge of the roof and launching herself off the building, arcing downward like a diver knifing into water. She flew down the old stone well, angry lead buzzing about her, and then was lost underground into the darkness.

Zeal's men rushed to the old well and pointed their guns down into it. They fired again, and again and again, their rounds echoing off the shadowed narrow walls. They fired until their guns were all empty, until gun smoke rose from the dark hole like a spirit seeking to escape skyward.

"Whoever that was," one of the shooters said, "they're gone."

The Five of Cups

Thanksgiving Day came to Golgotha. It was twenty-four hours since Zeal and his cult had arrived and the town was strangely silent, even for a holiday. The streets were empty, the churches and the saloons all still. The weather had turned colder and an icy rain was falling. It had started shortly after Zeal's arrival and the sky continued to weep throughout the holiday.

Word of Zeal's arrival, the proclamation, the capture of Malachi Bick and Jon Highfather, and his holding of the children and town elders spread through the town in hushed, frightened whispers. Citizens were ordered to stay home and keep off the streets. Each house was given a bottle of whiskey courtesy of Mr. Zeal in celebration of the holiday. Bands of armed soldiers—Cook's Praetorians— patrolled the streets. Those who violated Zeal's new laws were beaten and or- dered home, and those who resisted were shot dead, their bodies hung from the balcony at town hall as a warning to others. Anger simmered with the fear and it was anyone's guess which would win out in the hearts of the townsfolk.

In the cold, wet predawn hours of Thanksgiving morning, some of Zeal's fol- lowers, escorted by Praetorians, came to specific houses: seven homes, marked by Zeal himself with a blood-red handprint. They took the families' youngest children. In almost every household visited, the parents resisted, struggled, fought for their babies. Gunfire and screams followed in the early morning darkness, then there was silence again.

Many of those who had cheered Ray Zeal's arrival sobered up and saw exactly what was becoming of their town. However, few of them had the courage of their convictions, so they sat in their dark homes, drank their gifts from Mr. Zeal and brooded. It wasn't so bad, after all, was it? They weren't the ones hung up in town hall, right? They didn't have children or family held hostage, right? No, things were bad, but not bad enough to risk your life and get yourself killed. That was someone else's damn job, anyway.

Harry Pratt wished he had more tobacco while he sat in the hidden cavern below his family's mansion and crushed out the last of his cigarettes. The cave was natural, part of a maze of small, dark chambers. The main cave was filled with the treasures of the Mormon faith, including the golden plates containing the wisdom of God and Heaven and given unto Joseph Smith for a time. There were the Urim and the Thummim, the seer stones, residing in the wire-rimmed spectacle frames Smith had placed them in as he used them to interpret the angelic script of the plates. This was the point of origin for the breastplate and the Sword of Laban Harry had taken to carrying as his own.

Every manner of treasure, heavenly or earthly in nature, resided in the cave and all of it was Harry's responsibility. His father had been tasked to guard them by Joseph Smith himself before his death. It was the prophet's last commission to seek out the treasures of the faith in the desolate Nevada desert. When the caravan led by Josiah Pratt found the tiny, nameless settlement past the 40-Mile Desert, they had known they had arrived where the Lord had wanted them. They founded Golgotha and the Pratts built a fine home above these caves. When Harry's father had passed away, the task had fallen to him to guard the treasures with his life. Harry had never wanted to do this, ever, but it was his duty and for all his failings as a father, Josiah Pratt had managed to impart a sense of obligation to his son.

The lantern Harry had brought down the ladder with him guttered a bit and Harry checked his pocket watch again. It was late morning. Thanksgiving Day. He heard the thump of boots on the floorboards in the narrow corridor that led to the ladder and the secret trapdoor in the floor of his mansion. Zeal's men were still looking for him. This was their third visit since yesterday. What they lacked in effectiveness they made up for in persistence. He heard something hit the floor and smash upstairs. He shook his head.

"Another banner holiday at the Pratt Estate," he muttered.

His stomach rumbled and he wished he'd had a bit more time to prepare for his sequester down here. For the hundredth time, a thrill of terror slithered through his innards at the idea of James coming to check on him and confronting Zeal's people. But he gave Ringo more credit than that. James was a survivor, having grown up among the worst elements of the Barbary Coast. Ringo was all right, wherever he was. That certainty calmed his nerves. Being alone in this damned cave, not knowing what was happening up there to his town, his people, gnawed at him.

"And you, you're not good company at all," Harry said. "Not one damned bit."

The ancient yellowed skull that sat on a low rock did not reply, only staring with dark, empty sockets at the mayor. Harry tried to figure out why the hell he had agreed to guard the ugly thing. Harry looked at the Sword of Laban and wished he was up there fighting beside Highfather and Bick and Mutt—making some kind of damned difference. Tonight he'd sneak out and take the lay of the land. He wondered how Golgotha's other guardians were faring.

The rain kept falling and it was getting colder, just a hair above freezing. In the darkness, the fog and the overcast of downpour, no one noticed a coyote hunched low under the steps and porch leading into the Paradise Falls Saloon. The coyote had snagged, crooked yellow teeth, but his incisors were straight and sharp. There was a great deal of pain in his eyes. The coyote slowly belly-crawled deeper under the foundation of the saloon. He began to hear the thuds of boots, laughter and very bad piano playing. He waited, closed his eyes and listened, drinking in every sound, every voice.

The coyote's heart was heavy, sick with loss. The one he loved had fallen and he had been too far away to do anything, even to die with her, as she fell. Now all that was left to him was the desire to destroy, to wreck everyone who had taken her from him. He would save his friends, kill all his enemies, and then he would head out into the desert to moan and howl and weep for his lost love, his only love.

The ache in him bit deeper than the cold, and he did not care to walk on two legs anymore, to live among men and to carry a man's heart in his chest. The pain was exquisite and the most terrible he had ever experienced. His father had been right; it was foolish to want to be a man. They never knew themselves until the soul-gutting agony of clarity showed them what really, truly mattered, and then it was too late. Only a fool, or madman, would want to live that way, loving and losing over and over and over.

The coyote was silent, lost in his pain, listening, learning all he could to help him hurt those who had stolen his heart, his life.

———

The force of Praetorians, led by Col. Bradley Whitmore, smashed down the doors to the Dove's Roost Thanksgiving afternoon. The parlor was empty, the lamps all dark. The place still held the lingering scent of lilac and rose water.

"Where the hell are the whores?" Whitmore growled as he and his men entered the establishment. "We promised a mess of Mr. Zeal's people that they'd have all the whores to do with as they pleased. Where are they?"

There was a thudding sound as two figures slowly descended the grand staircase in the foyer. Black Rowan, a curled horsewhip in her hand, and the Scholar, his ever-present cudgel tapping slowly against his leg, regarded the intruders.

"I'm afraid I gave the ladies some time off," Rowan said, "after Mr. Bick, the sheriff and I had a lovely chat about your arrival. Deals were made, agreements kept and all. I'm sure we can accommodate you gentlemen, though, somehow."

"Dammit, you stupid cow," Whitmore said. "I've got men who came here to get fucked!"

"Well, then," Rowan said, smiling and readying the whip in her hand, "prepare to get fucked."

Inside the Paradise Falls Saloon, dozens of Cook's Praetorians drank, laughed and gambled. One of the cult, a scar-faced man named Muldoon, played the piano to the best of his ability, doing a horrid version of "Looking Back," while drunken soldiers tried to sing along.

Snake-Man sat sullenly at the bar, nursing a drink. He had wanted to go after Mutt, but Zeal had other plans.

"Tomorrow he'll come to us, I promise you that," Zeal had told Snake-Man. "Then you can do whatever you want with him, once he tells me where the skull is."

Ray Zeal sat alone at one of the red-felt faro tables, the one Bick normally claimed as his, a bottle of Monongahela in his fist. He took a drag on the bottle of whiskey, smiled and continued to watch the show up on the main stage.

Bick and Highfather had been stripped to the waist, each lashed tightly, spread-eagle, to a pair of crossed boards by their wrists and ankles. The two men had been beaten ruthlessly, their faces swollen and bloody. The cultists had taken turns torturing them since yesterday. Zeal's only stipulation was that they had to look good for the spectacle tomorrow, so no cutting things off.

One of the Teeth of Cain, a dead-eyed former slave named Ayot, was applying a red-hot branding iron to Highfather's chest. The sheriff hissed through clenched teeth. Ayot dabbed the sheriff's lips with a sponge of vinegar and blood in between applications of the iron. The cadaverous Haitian, who had wandered the French Quarter murdering and torturing whites for years, caressed High-father's old and new scars with wanton familiarity, while whispering gibberish in Jon's ear.

Professor Zenith, having finished applying steel-wool-covered clamp-cables to Malachi Bick's nipples, was now sending waves of stinging, numbing, bone-aching electricity through the saloon owner's body via one of the odd little wooden-box contraptions off his wagon of horrific miracles. Bick's whole frame tensed on the cross but he made no sound. Smoke rose from his chest where the clamps had burned flesh.

Zeal stood, somewhat wobbly. He had allowed the alcohol to affect him, part of his Thanksgiving/Victory Day celebration. He carefully made his way up onto the stage, nearly stumbling on the stairs, and stood before his prisoners.

"Where's your star, Sheriff?" Zeal said. "I want yours and you didn't have it with you when you surrendered."

"Gave it to a better man than me," Highfather muttered, spitting out the bitter vinegar and blood that stung his torn lips. "And a damn sight better man than you."

"I see," Zeal said. "Well then, I'll have to be sure to take it when I kill him. That was a very impressive job you did on the Brechts, by the way. You and your allies do not disappoint. Oh, that reminds me," Zeal said, slipping his hand into his pocket, "I have something for you." Zeal held one of the silver deputy stars he had taken from Jon's desk at the jail. "A small down payment for what you did to my son." Zeal extended the long, sharp pin on the back of the badge and rammed it fully into Highfather's upper chest. Highfather let out an involuntary gasp. His eyes rolled back in his head. He slumped, passing out. Zeal regarded his handiwork and then turned to his followers on stage.

"Leave us," Zeal said, and his worshipers departed, heading down into the saloon to drink and gamble with the mercenaries. Muldoon began to attempt to play "Pass Me Not, O Gentle Savior." Zeal stepped close to Bick.

"Alone at last," Zeal slurred. "Enjoying the show? Why are you putting up with this, Biqa? You could shake these humans off like fleas, lay waste to them and turn every being in a hundred miles of Golgotha into salt, present company excluded, of course. Why put up with this indignity, this pain? Still waiting for the Almighty to come save you and all his innocent flock?"

"No," Bick said through his swollen, cut mouth. "I'm not. Not anymore."

Zeal smiled. "See? There's hope for you yet, Biqa."

"Yes," Bick said. "There is. I am going to beg you, Raziel. Please . . ."

"Beg?" Zeal said. "Biqa, you are full of surprises today."

"Please," Bick repeated. "Stop this. Remember who you are and why we are here. Remember who sent us here. For your sake."

Zeal laughed and then punched Bick square in the jaw. Blood exploded from the saloonkeeper's mouth. "How noble of you, Biqa," Zeal said. "'For my sake.' I'd be more worried about yourself than trying to redeem me. The skull is out of the cave, away from the protective magics you and the Indians put on it. Its influence is whispering in the ear of anyone willing to commit atrocity, susceptible to a stronger will. It's singing to the desperate and the weak. These people already hated you, Biqa. Now they want your blood and I intend to give it to them—and you are playing right along."

Zeal clapped his hands and several carts of vegetables, breads, stuffing and gravy as well as heaping platters of steaming meat were wheeled out from the Fall's kitchen. The assembled troops and cultists on the saloon floor cheered and began to line up to the succulent Thanksgiving dinner arrayed before them.

"Care for a little meat and blood of the firstborn, Biqa?" Zeal said. "It's one of the Almighty's favorites. He does love to slaughter innocent little children, doesn't He? They're more tender when you cull them young, and tastier."

"God didn't kill those children," Bick said. "You did. You had the choice not to, and you did it anyway.

"Why do you want it back now, Raziel? The skull? You told me a long time ago you had figured out why you had been commissioned to guard it. You were happy to shirk your duties before. Why do you want it so badly now?"

Zeal took a knife from the cart of Professor Zenith's instruments. He sunk it into Bick's shoulder an inch or so and then began to slowly rip and tear the flesh, moving down toward Bick's chest. Bick shuddered and pain glazed his dark eyes. He did not make a sound.

"The skull contains the power to end a thing, to end anything, really," Zeal said, carving. "The Almighty created these divine monkeys and gave them more potential power than you or I or any of the Host could ever dream of. Why did He do that, Biqa? Why create such flawed, broken, confused little critters, with so much potential for creation . . ."

The blade sunk deep into Bick's chest, and Zeal leaned in as he twisted the blade. Bick jumped again and his skin was now waxy and pale, covered in sweat. He could feel the blood running in rivulets down his chest.

". . . and destruction?" Zeal continued. "And that was when I finally understood it, Biqa. Why God made me this way, why He allowed such a horrible creation as the skull to continue. He wanted it to be used, Biqa. He wants me to use it. To kill Him; to kill all the gods, save one, of course. I was groomed and created with this nature to rule over a cosmic slaughterhouse . A universe of cruelty and blood and rage. Forever and ever, amen."

"No," Bick muttered, fighting to hold out from the pain.

"Look what it's done to you." Zeal shook his head and made another looping cut with the knife across Bick's chest. "Living among them, living as one of them. You are so far gone you even suffer like them now. You've even tried to have families like them. You haven't asked what I've done to your pretty little daughter yet."

"You've done nothing," Bick said. "Because you don't have her. If you did, she'd be here now for me to watch you torture her. No. These mortals are full of surprises, Raziel. They are His agency here. They have the power and the will to bring even our kind low."

"Admit it, Biqa," Zeal said, still cutting. "This grand experiment of His has not gone as planned. He has created something that can imagine an end to even Him, and then gave them the power to make it happen. He wanted this. The human race is His suicide note. And I am His executioner."

Bick suddenly realized through the fog of pain that Zeal was carving the symbol of the Tetragrammaton—the name of God—into his flesh.

Zeal drove the knife deeper into Bick's abdomen and ripped upward. Bick gasped at the pain and felt his hold on awareness slipping. He shifted more of his presence away from his physical shell and discovered it was much harder now to divorce himself from his physicality than it had once been, long ago. The pain pulled him back to the flesh, unable to fully escape it.

"You are going to die tomorrow, Malachi," Zeal said. "At the hands of the creatures you put so much faith into. And I am going to enjoy every second of it."

Bick said nothing, enduring the pain of Zeal's attentions silently. Instead of praying to the Almighty, he found his succor from the agony in memories of his noble, loyal son, Caleb, and the few brief, precious treasures his daughter Emily had given him.

The Praetorians standing guard at the eastern road into Golgotha, near Rose Hill, watched as a lone rider approached in the pouring, cold rain. It was nearly dark and the sky was dead and gray, no sign of the setting sun, no hope of stars. The soldiers advanced on the odd figure: a thin man in a tattered dark suit, vest, white gloves, who wore a partly shattered oblong wooden mask. He was alone, riding a brown mustang.

"Hold!" one of the two Praetorians said. The soldier recognized the man as one of Ray Zeal's followers—the man known only as the Annihilator. "What brings you in, sir? Mr. Zeal ordered you to stay with the blockade out on the southern road."

"We had problems," the masked man said, his voice muffled by his wooden face. "The troops out on the southern blockade are dead. I was badly injured. It was two children from here in Golgotha—one of them was a sheriff's deputy. I need to speak to Mr. Zeal right away."

"What happened to the two children?" one of the Praetorians asked.

"What do you think?" the Annihilator said. "They're dead."

"Well, Mr. Zeal is over at Bick's saloon, with Mr. Cook and the others," the other Praetorian said. "They get a hot Thanksgiving meal and all the whores they can handle. We get this," he said, gesturing to the downpour.

"You sure do," the masked man said. Behind them, something flew, moved, in between the raindrops. Constance Stapleton jammed her fingers onto the sides of both of the horsemen's necks, just as her mother had taught her. One Praetorian slumped and fell from the saddle, unconscious. Constance's injured shoulder throbbed and she couldn't maintain sufficient pressure on the other one's neck to knock him out. As the mercenary began to raise his rifle, the masked man drew a pistol from beneath his coat and aimed it inches from the Praetorian's face.

"You move, you make a sound, you do anything except drop that gun and I'm going to blow your fool head off," Jim Negrey said from behind the wooden Dogon mask.

The Praetorian released his rifle and Constance took it, leveling it at the back of the man's head. Jim pulled off the mask with his free hand and stared flintily into the mercenary's frightened eyes.

"Now," Jim said. "You're going to tell us everything that's been happening here, or I swear on my pa's grave I will start shooting parts of you clean off."

Becky wondered for the thousandth time about handsome young deputy Jim. Most likely he was dead, like they were saying Sheriff Highfather was. She was so scared, but then she thought about the nice people who were looking after her, risking their own hide for her and the other girls, and she tried to push the dark thoughts away. You lived and worked at a place like the Dove's Roost long enough, it got hard to think of anything but dark stuff.

"Becky, dear, you haven't touched your supper," Mrs. Benoit said, smiling at her. The Benoits were a nice family. They had a nice home up on Rose Hill. Mr. Benoit was the finest chandler Golgotha had ever had and he made a tidy penny making candles and produced many custom candles for clients as far away as Virginia City. They had two very sweet children: Amy, who was with them at the dinner table, and Tom, who was now a hostage at the school.

"I'm sorry, I'm just scared," she said.

"We all are, dear," Mr. Benoit said. "But I've seen Sheriff Highfather do remarkable things. He's a fine man and he's never let this town down, and I don't think he will this time. We must have faith, my dear, faith that good overcomes evil."

Becky smiled and nodded. Mr. Benoit reminded Becky of the few dim memories she had of her own father, and she did feel the fear release its grip on her somewhat. When Black Rowan had told them that she and the sheriff had arranged to have all the public girls from the Roost hidden away as the children of some of the most prominent families on Rose Hill, until Zeal and his crew were gone, she had been amazed that these fine, fancy folk would take someone like her in, but they had and treated her better than she had ever been treated before.

"I am powerful thankful to you all," Becky said, tasting a small bite of dressing.

"In this world," Mrs. Benoit said, "all we have is each other to lean on when the days turn cold and the storms come, Becky. In the end, we're all in this together, come what may."

"Let us be thankful," Mr. Benoit said. "For all our bounty." Becky was. If there were people like the Benoits in the world, maybe the Ray Zeals didn't always have to win. Becky was also thankful that Mr. Benoit had never been a customer of the Roost. Some of the girls were now pretending to be the daughters to some of the well-to-do men of Rose Hill who also happened to be regular clients.

The silence of Ch'eng Huang's sanctum at the Celestial Palace was shattered by the .41 caliber bullet that ripped through Chi Mo Duan's back and exited his chest in a bloody spray. The rogue hatchet man staggered forward, vomiting black blood from his lips, and turned to face the shooter.

James Ringo leveled the derringer at Duan and fired the second barrel. It ripped through the tapestry on the far wall, missing Duan. The assassin suddenly had a slender, razor-sharp hatchet in his hand, cocking his arm back to throw as more blood drooled out of his grimacing red mouth.

"Aww, shit," Ringo muttered.

Ch'eng Huang raked the bloody, jagged hunk of red jade he had pulled from this back across Duan's throat.

"I believe this belongs to you," Huang said, coughing.

The assassin shuddered as his lifeblood gushed out of his open neck. The hatchet fell from his hand.

"He will devour this town," Duan gurgled, choking on his own blood. "He will devour you all." He made a final horrible choking sound and was silent.

"I . . . I just came by to get my pay," Ringo said. "Everyone downstairs is dead."

"Yes," Huang said, slumping forward into the arms of the Celestial Palace's piano player. "You have earned your pay, Mr. Ringo, and my eternal gratitude. Some assistance please. I must rest."

Southeast of Golgotha and sitting in the southern shadow of Rose Hill was a rise known as Methuselah Hill. Some of the oldest and finest homes in town were situated there, having been the precursor to Rose Hill, prior to the Mormon emigration. One such home belonged to old, blind Miles Press.

As the rain wept from the sky, Miles sat in the special room of his home. It had once been a grand ballroom, used by the original owners of the house back during the first silver-boom years. Now it served as the game board for his nightly duel with Golgotha. Each building, each street and home, even the camp on Argent Mountain, was reproduced with wood and chicken wire, plaster and paint. The walls of the room were covered with strange glyphs and symbols, many of Miles's own design and others that came to him in visions and dreams. He had these dreams and these gifts since he had been a young boy. His father had always believed him when he told him of the dreams.

"You got the sight, Miles," his daddy had said. "It will let you see the dead and the future, see into someone's past, even let you listen to the world's voice, its whispers and secrets. It's a great gift, Miles, but it's also a terrible responsibility. It comes with our blood, with our family, and you should always try to use it to help people."

The small wooden carvings Miles made of the people of Golgotha, all the players in the game, were arrayed where Miles saw them. Though his eyes didn't see anymore, and hadn't for many decades, he could see this room in his mind, clear as day. He moved the figures to where they needed to be. He moved the new figurine of Emily Bright out of the model of the Imperial Hotel and toward the rise of Argent, where other of his pieces were arrayed. He paused, as if listening. Then he shook his head.

"No," he muttered. "No, that ain't fair at all. Damn you, why?"

He took one of the older figures off the floor-to-ceiling shelf that composed one wall of the room. Blew the dust off the large figure and placed it where the vision showed him it should be.

"Damn you," he said to Golgotha, and then he paused and listened silently for a few moments. "Yes," he finally said, somewhat calmer. "I understand, and of course that's fair. It's just so damn sad."

Miles missed his father, Caleb—son of Malachi Bick. Missed his strong, gentle voice, his warm, loving embrace and his kind wisdom, especially at moments like these.

Outside, the wind and rain screamed off the desert and Miles understood it. He sighed as he saw the threads of causality and inevitability draw tight and he wished there were some other way for the game to play itself out. A notion crossed his mind and he made his own countermove and hoped it was the right thing to do. Sometimes pieces had to be sacrificed to save other pieces.

"Very well, let's see how you like this little surprise, hmm?"

Miles hunkered down to see his game with Golgotha through till the final turn, till the closing gambit.

Judgment (Reversed)

She was in darkness. Her body was far away and it hurt to try to be in it too much. She was pretty sure she was dead or dying. She recalled sliding across cold, damp stone, sliding through wide, iron bars, some kind of grate. Cool dampness and the smell of blood was all there was now, and the darkness. She was cold. Some part of her mind that refused to shut down reasoned that if she felt cold, smelled her blood, then she wasn't dead yet.

No, Maude thought. *No. Not yet.*

"No," a voice echoed. "Not yet, Maude."

She tried to look into the darkness, to see where the man's voice had come from.

"I am here," the voice said. "You felt me faintly at my temple in the wastes, where you fought the cougar. That blood I can sense, burning in your veins, even now sustaining your frail, broken body comes from my onetime wife, Echidna, Mother of All Monsters, who you know as Lilith. We are kin, Maude, you and I, of a sort. It must have been a glorious battle, to mark you so."

"Who are you?" Maude muttered. "Where are you?"

There was a dry chuckle; it seemed to make the floor rumble slightly. "I am the Father of Terror and Monsters, last son of the Mother and Hell itself. I have been locked away under the earth here for a very long time, ever since your predecessor and the daemon that guards these lands conspired with the Light Bringer to imprison me in this cavernous temple to alien gods. And I would show you my form, Maude Stapleton, but I am long out of practice in wrapping myself in a pleasing shape. To look upon me now would drive you mad, I'm afraid."

"I look a fright when I first get out of bed too," Maude managed to mutter, and then coughed violently. The voice laughed. The chamber shook and dust rained down on Maude.

"Even at the very precipice of death, you make a jest. You mortals are a hardy, remarkable lot. I want to give you a gift for the wonderful favor you have given me, Maude."

"What . . . what favor?" she mumbled, fighting to keep the cold from creeping into her thoughts, where this being seemed to be residing.

"When you dragged yourself across the threshold, through the grate in the sacrificial well, you destroyed part of the *pharmakis* marks that held me here for eons. You have set me free, Maude. And now I will help you to heal, to live, if you want that?"

"Yes," Maude. "I want it very much."

"Why?" the voice asked. "Tell me, Maude Stapleton, Daughter of Lilith, and do not lie, for I will know—tell me, why do you want to cling to this brief fire called life? It burns you and in the end it falters and is extinguished and you find yourself alone in dust and darkness. Why do you want this life back, Maude?"

"The truth," Maude said. "The truth is . . . selfish. The truth is I don't want to go out losing, failing. When I die I want it to have meaning, purpose, for myself, if for no one else. I have lived so much of my life in meaningless shadow, playacting for the sake of others. I want my death, at least, to be on my terms."

"Hmm," the voice said. "And what of true love lost or protecting your child?"

"That's all there as well," Maude admitted. "To have more time with the ones I love, to protect them, yes, but at the core of it, of me, to be honest, is the ache to triumph, to win. Not for anyone else but for me. For me. To know in my heart, I struggled and won."

The voice laughed again. "Spoken like a true warrior-born Daughter of Lilith. Very well, you have spoken your heart's dying truth and for that you shall be rewarded. One final warning though. . . ."

"Isn't there always," Maude said, coughing again, harder this time. Darkness fell over awareness for a moment, then she swam back up out of the cold dark water again.

"Those of your order have worked to oppose me and imprison me in the past," the voice said. "It has to do with a long-standing feud with my former wife and does not concern you. Enjoy the gift I grant you, Daughter of Lilith. We part as friends, do not seek to hunt me, or interfere with my work. Enjoy your existence, Maude Stapleton, as I enjoy my freedom. May you defeat your foes and know the warrior's peace. But you may find they are not one and the same."

Fire. Fire engulfed Maude's body, her mind. Searing, bright, pure. The fire that birthed the world and heralds its end devoured her. Then, after an eternity of bright perfect pain, it was quenched in infinite cooling darkness. Maude slept, and dreamed of being born again out of the sun, wreathed in flame.

The Ace of Swords

Thanksgiving passed and the dawn came. The rain departed, but even with the bright sunlight, it was cold. Praetorians knocked on the doors of every residence, shack and tent, spreading the word that Malachi Bick and Jon Highfather would be executed today at noon, in front of the Paradise Falls. Attendance by all citizens of Golgotha was mandatory by order of the sheriff and now mayor, Ray Zeal.

The ruins of the Reid house sat at the northern end of Argent Mountain. In the hard light of morning, they consisted of uneven, blackened walls of crumbling brick and a few charred broken bones of timber, jutting up from the frame that had been devoured by fire. The house had once been one of the finest homes in Golgotha, until fire claimed it last year. Most folks avoided the ruins, especially at night. Rumors persisted that the whole area was haunted.

Slowly, they began to arrive as had been prearranged. Kate Warne showed first, tired and cold from over a day of running, fighting and hiding from Zeal's troops. She carried a rifle and still wore her badge proudly. Next was Harry Pratt, dressed in his long heavy coat, with his breastplate and sword concealed beneath. Harry, too, carried a rifle and pistol he had liberated from some of Zeal's men who had been guarding his house.

"I don't believe we've had the pleasure," Pratt said. "I'm Harry Pratt, the mayor of Golgotha."

"Pleased to meet you," Kate said. "I'm Kate Warne, and I work for you now."

"I did tell Jon to hire more deputies," Pratt said. "I hope he's still alive."

"Me too," Kate said. "I hope that reputation of his has held; besides, I want to kill him myself for putting me in the middle of this."

Next came Black Rowan and the Scholar. The two of them carried a large carpetbag full of guns and ammunition collected from the Praetorians. "Well," Rowan said with a smile that poorly hid her exhaustion. "Isn't this quite the lovely little band we have here. Mayor Pratt, I've heard so much about you. A pleasure to finally meet you. And you," Rowan said, nodding to Kate as she dropped the bag of guns at her feet and drew out a small silver flask, took a sip and handed it to Warne, "where exactly is your grand legal system now, hmm?"

Kate raised the flask and took a drink. "I am currently reassessing my faith in the legal system," she said. "At least in relation to this damn town. Glad to see you again. We'll need all the help we can get to turn this around."

The Scholar, seemingly oblivious to the bandaged, bloody bullet wound in his leg, nodded toward a patch of dense scrub below the rise the ruins were on. "Madam, I saw some movement down there. Looked like an animal, but I'm not sure. Should I—"

Mutt walked out of the scrub, a rifle slung over his shoulder and a bloody knot of human scalps at his belt. Jon Highfather's silver star was on Mutt's vest. Harry had seen Mutt angry, giddy, falling-down drunk and taunting-mean. He had never seen the Indian like this before. Harry walked up to meet him.

"Are you all right?" he asked. Mutt looked at him with tired, red, soul-weary eyes.

"Jon asked me to be sheriff until this blows over," Mutt said, his voice a steel rasp. "He figured Zeal would take him after what happened to Vellas and he said he knew I'd come save his ass if it needed saving. If you're up to scrappin' about it . . ."

"No," Harry said. "No. Jon's right. I can't think of a better man for the job, Sheriff."

Mutt nodded and walked up to join the others. "This all we got? I was hoping for a few more."

"My people will be here," Rowan said. "I'm betting that weather yesterday threw them off a bit."

"What people?" Kate asked, but Mutt continued.

"All right," Mutt said, "we are still outgunned. I know we made a dent in them yesterday," Mutt dropped the bloody scalps on the ground next to the bag of captured guns, "and there are a damn sight fewer than there were when they rode into town, but I'd say we're still outnumbered a good six to one, at least. Jon and Bick had worked a few deals, like with Rowan here, and I picked us up some extra help as well last night."

"Who?" Harry asked.

"These people are crazy as bedbugs," Mutt said, "and sometimes you need to fight crazy with crazy. So I got us some . . . unconventional help. He'll be along. We've only got about five hours till they are going to kill Jon and Bick, so we need to figure out a way to get the hostages free and handle Zeal. He's not a normal man, at least that's what Bick told Jon. Any ideas how to deal with him?"

"I know." The girl's voice came from atop one of the crumbling, blackened brick walls. She was young, in her twenties, dressed in a simple pair of canvas work pants, boots and a shirt with a too-large barn jacket over it. Her brown hair was tied back in a ponytail.

"You are quiet as hell," Mutt said. "How'd you get up there exactly? Fly?"

"Something like that," the girl said. "I'm Emily Bright. Malachi Bick is my father. I'm here to help."

The Scholar offered the girl a hand and Emily dropped down gracefully. She looked even smaller next to Rowan's huge right-hand man.

"I know how to deal with Zeal," Emily said. "Or at least keep him distracted for a time. There is something my father told me about, it's in his desk at the Paradise Falls. If I can get in there, I can get it. It will fix Zeal."

"The Paradise Falls is Zeal's command HQ. It's thick with soldiers and Zeal's people," Kate said. "How the hell are we supposed to get you in there?"

"I'll get her in." Again, no one had heard the approach. Mutt spun around. His eyes opened wide, the light falling back into them.

Maude Stapleton, in wet, bloody, torn clothes, her bandana hanging around her neck, her hair falling down her shoulders, cleared the rise, Golgotha at her back. Mutt ran to her, laughing, whooping. Maude smiled as he scooped her up off the ground and spun her. He pulled her close, no resistance, no hesitation, no doubt, and kissed her. Maude slid her arms around his neck and returned the kiss.

"Goddamn," Kate said. "I knew it was her! Maybe we got a chance after all."

The Seven of Pentacles

The Main Street of Golgotha was choked with citizens, forced to turn out for the executions. Praetorians with rifles on horseback skirted the edge of the crowd of hundreds that ran up and down Golgotha's main thoroughfare. Even a sizable portion of Johnny Town's population had come out to watch the event, clustered together near the edges of the crowds, silent and stone-faced.

In the balcony that overlooked Main, on the second floor of the Paradise Falls, Charles Cook sat. His servant, Lazare, stood behind Cook with the ever-present parasol to give the industrial baron shade. Cook glared at the second-in-command of his private army.

"What the hell do you mean we've lost over twenty men in the last day, including Colonel Whitmore?" Cook said. "That's over a quarter of our force! These people are miners and hicks, how in the name of perdition are they taking out armed, trained and alert military personnel? What the fuck do I pay you people for?"

"Sir, I . . . ," the red-faced and frightened Praetorian stammered. "Colonel Whitmore took a group of men to acquire the whores over at the Dove's Roost last night. They just . . . vanished, along with the whores, sir."

"Shut up and get out!" Cook bellowed. "Find Whitmore and execute whoever is responsible for this, or goddamn you, I'll eat your eyeballs tonight!"

The mercenary departed. Cook sighed and took a sip from his cocktail and tried to relax by watching the massive crowd and remembering that he was in control of each and every one of them. Below, on the large porch of the saloon, more Praetorians stood guard, rifles at the ready, should the crowd suddenly develop a backbone. They had even set up a large tripod-mounted Gatling gun that could mow down civilians like wheat before a sickle, if need be. Professor Zenith was also present, fiddling with the infernal device on his wagon, readying it to terrify and suppress the crowds. The squirrelly little man had been demanding access to more children for his experiments, and Cook knew that he'd need to bring the matter to Zeal. Taking too many children of the locals too soon would cause friction. Still, they were entrenched now, with far superior firepower and the legitimacy of being in control of the government.

An elevated platform had been prepared overnight in front of the saloon, blocking a good portion of Main Street, so that everyone could see Bick and Highfather die. Yes, Cook thought, it was a beautiful, clear Friday afternoon and tonight they would celebrate and begin the process of changing Golgotha into the kind of town they wanted, culling the weak and the sentimental. Cook could feel the power of this place and its dark light, like an invisible beacon calling to those like him and Zeal. Golgotha would be the new Gomorrah. The captain of industry licked his lips just thinking about it. He was home.

Yes, a beautiful day indeed.

Below, Ray Zeal stood beside the Snake-Man on the porch to the Paradise Falls.

"I don't like this," Snake-Man said. "Have you heard anything from Chi Mo Duan? Was he successful in killing the old man in Johnny Town?"

Zeal nodded absently as he waved to passersby. The smiles on their faces were no longer genuine. They knew, finally: They understood what they had welcomed into their town and they were afraid, but it was too late now.

"Yes," Zeal said. "Two Green Ribbon Tong members showed up yesterday with a message from him. Johnny Town is secured and ours."

"I still don't like it. Pratt has disappeared, Highfather's deputies are still out there and Mutt is not to be trifled with, I can assure you."

"Part of the reason for our little show," Zeal said. "He will come rushing to Highfather's rescue and offer himself up to us in the process."

Snake-Man nodded.

"You'll get another shot at Mutt, I assure you, once he gives up the skull."

"Where were you off to so early this morning?" Snake-Man asked. "I saw you ride out without an escort."

"I was seeing to Dr. Tumblety," Zeal said. "Most remarkable man. Has a very clear vision. I helped him with something and then we said our good-byes. He is my High Priest now, my missionary in the world, and he will do truly great works."

Zeal looked up at the sun. "Well," he said, smiling at the stern-faced medicine man, "time to get this show on the road."

The Golgotha schoolhouse was a pretty whitewashed building that sat in a pastoral-looking field of grass at the northeastern base of Rose Hill. The schoolmaster's house was a small one-room cottage a few hundred feet from the school proper. The school had been built by the Mormons when they first arrived and was open to all the children of Golgotha, regardless of denomination.

The schoolhouse had seen its share of trouble, just like the rest of Golgotha—the place was rumored to be haunted. There was a weeping lady in white, her face always hidden by her long black hair, who stood in the school's yard and was often seen by travelers passing by on Old Stone Road. Then there was a horrid, hooded apparition that appeared from time to time inside the school itself, dressed in tattered shadowy raiment and carrying a hand sickle. The town had lost five schoolmasters and mistresses since the school was built and in many circles back east it was joked that being offered an appointment to teach in Golgotha was the fastest way to a very early retirement.

Inside the schoolhouse, the fourteen children had been instructed to lie on the floor and be quiet by the two people who had surprised Mr. Whorly, the last schoolmaster, a few days ago. They had laid Mr. Whorly on his desk, tied him up and then proceeded to cut him open while he was still alive. Eventually he stopped screaming and begging. The room smelled of rotting meat and rancid blood. When the children complained of having to go to the bathroom, they were dragged by the man named Elijah Barrows to the cloakroom, and told to defecate and urinate on the floor while he watched. If the children voiced their hunger, a frightening, gaunt creature who said her name was Mme. LaTour would cut off a piece of Mr. Whorly's flesh and order them to eat it. Only one child had said he was hungry after that; he had retched and sobbed after eating the flesh until he was silent, pale and still.

Barrows kept watch on the front steps of the schoolhouse during the day and then they barricaded the one door with benches, tables and chairs at night. Many of the children had begun to get ill from lack of food and water. Mme. LaTour assured them that in a few more days, Mr. Whorly's fly-covered, maggot-infested corpse would begin to look very good indeed. Then their true education could begin—they were to be the first of the new citizens of Golgotha. Each night, their two captors forced them to say prayers to something called Raziel. They did, but then many silently whispered prayers to the more gentle-seeming gods of their fathers and mothers. Others merely wept themselves to sleep, feeling more and more of their insides hollow out with each passing day.

Today was Friday and it was close to noon. Barrows was out on the steps with a pair of rifles, his knives and a few pistols. LaTour was working on another of her monstrous anatomical diagrams on the large slate board at the front of the room.

Barrows saw a Praetorian approach down Old Stone and began to cross the field toward the school. He dropped the chunk of wood he had been carving on and grabbed a rifle.

"Hey, hey! You ain't supposed to come out here unless Mr. Zeal's with you! Stop!"

The rider didn't stop. He was a slender man with brown hair and delicate features. The rider let go of the reins and suddenly had two Colt pistols in his hands.

Kate cursed as she drew the guns and spurred her horse. She had hoped to get a lot closer. The man raised the rifle, shouted for someone named LaTour and opened fire. Kate fired as well.

Inside, Mme. LaTour grabbed the gore-coated knife they had used on the schoolmaster and moved quickly toward the children. There was a crash as part of the floor exploded into broken wooden planks and nails. The Scholar had crawled under the schoolhouse hours ago and had been working to quietly loosen several of the boards so that he could push up into the room. Now that he heard the shouting and knew the Warne woman's frontal assault was underway, there was no more time to waste. He pushed on the loosened boards with all of his massive strength, roaring as he smashed up into the schoolroom. The children screamed and shouted. LaTour grabbed a young man of about twelve, Tom Benoit, pulled his hair to expose his pale neck and stuck the filthy butcher knife to his throat. The Scholar, his cudgel in hand, climbed up into the room.

Barrow's bullet whizzed by Kate as the two Colts belched fire and lead at him. One bullet ripped into his chest, the other blew a hole in the eaves of the school door. Barrows screamed, cocked the rife and fired again. Kate's horse staggered from the bullet tearing into its head. The horse tossed Kate before it stumbled off a few yards and fell over, dying.

As she fell, Kate fired two more shots at Barrows. One missed him completely, the other ripped into him again, blowing a hunk of meat out of his leg. She fell, hard, and the wind whooshed out of her chest, her guns falling into the grass. Barrows, bleeding and grunting, charged toward her, an axe in his hands.

Inside the children were silent, frozen in fear. The Scholar was unmoving, his eyes scanning the interior of the schoolhouse. The gunfire had stopped outside and it was silent now. LaTour shouted out as she maintained the knife at the boy's throat, "Barrows! Barrows, you simpleton! Attend me!"

"Even if you kill that boy," the Scholar said calmly, speaking French, "I'll snap your neck before you can reach another child." He shifted slightly to the left and LaTour countered by sliding herself and her hostage right.

"But you are a noble man," LaTour replied in her native tongue, her beautiful eyes hooded like a cobra. "You would never wish harm to come to an innocent boy, would you, monsieur?" The Scholar shifted again, moving himself to try to flank LaTour. Again the slender woman smiled like a jackal and shifted in response to the attempt.

"You have me mistaken for someone else," the Scholar said blandly. "I could care less if all these little cherubs end up under your knife. I'm here to perform a service for my employer. It's been my experience that heroics are bad for business."

LaTour frowned a little and opened her mouth to speak. The roar of two gunshots drowned out her final words. One bullet smashed through the back of her head, destroying her brain. The second zipped through the back of her throat, out the front, and buried itself in the Scholar's shoulder. He grunted but otherwise seemed nonplussed. LaTour fell, the knife tumbling from her dead hands. Tom Benoit ran as fast as he could toward the Scholar. The children screamed, a mixture of terror at what they saw and relief that the ordeal was ending.

Kate walked through the front doors of the schoolhouse, a smoking pistol in either hand. The children rushed to her and swarmed about her waist, laughing and cheering, hugging her, sobbing and begging to go home. Kate put the guns away and tried to hush the crying children. The Scholar stepped forward, the thinnest trace of a smile on his face.

"Sorry about that," Kate said nodding to the Scholar's shoulder.

He shrugged.

"It's inconsequential," he said. Two little girls were hugging his leg and he scooped them up and held them. "It's all right. You are going home." It was the most emotion Kate had heard in the man's voice since she had first come to the Dove's Roost months ago.

"Nice job, getting her set up for the shot," Kate said. "How did you know I was still alive out there?"

"I didn't," the Scholar said. "It was a calculated risk." He looked at the little girl nuzzled deeply into his wounded shoulder and chest, and smiled. "That," he said to the little girl, "hurts a great deal. Please stop."

"I'll send off the signal," Kate said. "You old softy, you."

The tabernacle was being demolished by the fury of the battle. The town elders—Brodin Chaffin, Rony Bevalier and Antrim Zezrom Slaughter—were tied and against the far wall, sitting on a long bench.

Victory Ferrell had a pair of tomahawks, one in each hand. He swung wildly at Black Rowan as she tumbled, dived and leapt, seeking a way past his slashing wall of death. She held a bell-guarded saber in one hand and a short, narrow dirk in the other, and whenever she closed in it took both her blades to keep the lightning-fast wild-eyed soldier's hand axes from striking her. Ferrell was all instinct, rage and speed, but Rowan had to admit that his sheer ferocity was more than a match for her training.

Harry was picked up off the ground and thrown into the far wall, narrowly missing the elders, who ducked as he flew past. The impact made him see stars. His spine throbbed even through his holy breastplate. The Sword of Laban clattered to the floor and Harry struggled to rise as Liver-Eatin' Douglass shambled toward him. The mountain man was well over seven feet tall and a lumbering wall of muscle and madness. Douglass grabbed Harry by the leg, intent on using the mayor like a club and smashing him against the wall again and again. Pratt snagged the sword with his fingers—it seemed to slide into his hand of its own accord. He slashed down on Douglass's wrist and the giant roared as he drew back a spurting stump of a left hand. He shuffled backward. Douglass bellowed and clutched his stump, more like an animal than a man might. Harry slid his bloody, gleaming sword gently over the bonds of Elder Slaughter and they fell away, cleanly severed. Slaughter began to untie his feet as quickly as he could.

"Get the others free and get out of here," Harry said. "Use the hidden passage, the one we came in through."

Harry's father had insisted on the tabernacle and the other formal buildings of the church having concealed entrances, secret exits and hidden passages. They hadn't been used many times over the years, but Harry was thankful today that his father had drilled him on their locations and access.

"What about you and the young lady?" Slaughter said.

Harry glanced over to see Rowan matching Ferrell blow for blow, sparks flying off the killer's axes as they clanged against Rowan's blades.

"We have this under control, I think," Harry said.

Douglass's remaining good hand suddenly smashed into Harry's side. The giant tried to grab Harry and rip his liver out; the breastplate held against

Douglass's immense, preternatural strength, but the force of Douglass's attempt threw Harry against the wall again.

"See?" Harry said to Slaughter. He spun and moved the sword to try to force room between himself and the giant. Slaughter quickly began to untie his comrades, while Harry kept Douglass busy and distracted.

Rowan had established a pattern now of strikes and parries that Ferrell was locked into it, following her dance, at least for the moment, and that was all the time she needed. Rowan snapped open the hidden compartment on her jeweled ring with a gentle squeeze of her fingers, turned the dirk into the parry of Ferrell's tomahawk and then pushed hard against it, sending a spray of finely ground glass into Ferrell's eye. The soldier gasped and involuntarily blinked, pushing more of the deadly dust into his eyeball. He started to scream, but Rowan broke his disrupted parry, knocking it aside, and ran him through with her saber. Ferrell slid off her blade and slumped to the ground, dead.

Harry felt Douglass grab him by his long coat; he turned his arm as best he could and rammed the magical blade backward, into Douglass's side. Douglass grunted as the blade sunk up to the hilt in his guts and pierced his liver. He released Harry's coat as he staggered back. Pratt spun, grabbed the hilt of the Sword of Laban with both hands and wrenched it upward with all his might. The sword opened Douglass from his prodigious gut to his throat and lodged finally in the man-monster's brain. He made a final, instinctual grab for Harry's neck as he tumbled forward. Pratt braced his boot and bended knee against Douglass's chest. The weight of the man was incredible. Harry felt the mountain man's fingers slip from him and he kicked back, knocking Douglass's lifeless mass to the floor in a widening pool of his own blood and entrails.

Covered in blood, Harry climbed to his feet, groaning. He looked over at Rowan, who was nursing a nasty hatchet wound to her leg. She waved and Harry nodded, panting. He looked over the see Slaughter freeing the last of the elders.

"Look what they've done to our tabernacle!" Bevalier shouted.

Harry shook his head.

"We need to send the signal," Harry said. "I just hope we're not too late."

The Fool

They led Bick and Highfather out into the blinding noonday sun from the cool confines of the Paradise Falls. The crowd was mostly silent; a few catcalls and boos greeted the sheriff and the saloon owner, but by now most folks in town had come to see Zeal and his crew for what they truly were and their support was sullen and at gunpoint. Those who still cheered and supported Zeal were the most callous and vicious inhabitants of Golgotha, a few hundred strong at the most. They were here to see blood and spectacle.

Both men were clothed to hide the majority of their injuries, save the evidence of beatings on their faces. Bick was marched up the stairs to the platform, where two large posts had been secured. He was lashed to a post with rope while Zeal addressed the crowd from the platform, where everyone could see him.

"Good people of Golgotha! I hope you enjoyed your day of Thanksgiving and return now reinvigorated to dedicate yourself to the great tasks that lie before us! This man, Malachi Bick, has stolen from you and from me. He has lied, swindled and cheated you and me and he has drained the very lifeblood of our town!"

The crowd murmured and more boos and shouts came from the assembled mass. Even those who feared Zeal and wanted him gone could agree that Bick was evil.

"Why ain't I up there too," Highfather mumbled from puffy, swollen lips. He was ringed by guards. Snake-Man and several mercenaries stood near him.

"Bick is the appetizer," Snake-Man explained. "You will be the main course, the sacrificial lamb. Once he gets those people riled up enough to kill Bick, once they taste blood, then it will take just a little push to get them to tear apart their beloved sheriff, and then they are ours, with us in body and soul."

Zeal continued, calling out to the crowd, a smiling beatific voice of strength and purpose. It was hard not to nod in agreement with him. "Since he has wronged you, harmed you, dear people, you shall be the instrument of his punishment, you shall lay this evil man low."

A group of Praetorians rolled a large mine cart into view. It was filled with hard, jagged rocks. They stopped it near the edge of the platform, looking up at Bick, tied and beaten.

"Those of you who feel wronged by this man, who hate this man and wish to do to him as he has done to you, step forward now and show him the true meaning of divine justice."

Zeal smiled at Bick. The crowd rumbled with debate, agreement, dissent. Gradually a small group of men and women began to step forward and walk toward the cart. "There is your answer from God, Biqa," Zeal said.

Three men and one woman lined up and were given stones by the guards and Zeal himself. "Here you go Mrs. Jackson," he said, handing the stone to the woman.

Somewhere, far across the town, three gunshots rang out. A moment later, two more gunshots rang out, also a distance away.

In the crowd of onlookers, Auggie Shultz and his bride, Gillian, held hands and watched in disbelief. They had been dragged from their honeymoon bed by the same Praetorians that had gathered their neighbors and friends to observe this nightmare.

"This can't be happening," Gillian whispered to Auggie. "I know Malachi Bick is a bad man, has done bad things, but this is barbaric!"

Auggie got an odd look on his face. He kissed Gillian, released her hand and began to push his way through the crowd.

"Augustus!" Gillian shouted. "What are you doing?"

Auggie looked back and smiled at her, then shrugged. "What is right, *ja*?"

An audible gasp rose from the whole town as Augustus Shultz walked out of the crowd and made his way to the platform. Zeal offered Auggie a rock. Auggie looked at Zeal and a little bit of the smile left Zeal's face. Auggie took the stone and walked past Zeal and the soldiers, who Zeal gestured to allow him to pass. He climbed the stairs slowly. The thump of each step echoed across the now silent Main Street.

Highfather stood as still and entranced as everyone else did. Suddenly he felt a sharp knife sawing through the bonds tying his hands behind his back. He slowly looked over his shoulder and saw a thin, lanky man in a tattered suit and long, broken wooden mask now standing slightly behind him. Zeal's men all seemed to accept him as one of their own and were too busy watching Auggie to notice that the masked man was freeing Highfather. The man behind the mask winked at Highfather and the gesture stirred a memory.

Jim! Highfather suddenly realized.

Up on the platform Auggie stood before Bick, the heavy rock in his hand. "I came to you, Mr. Bick, when I was desperate and had suffered great loss. You helped me but you were not honest in the price you would exact and you took more from me than you ever gave, yes? You have meddled in people's lives. You've hurt good people to further your own schemes and you never gave a thought for what your actions would do to others, Mr. Bick, because you thought your life was more important than ours. You were wrong, Mr. Bick."

Even the wind seemed to be holding its breath as Auggie raised the stone above his head and looked unflinching into the dark eyes of Malachi Bick. Auggie lowered his arm and dropped the stone at Ray Zeal's feet.

"And I forgive you," Auggie said.

A cheer rose up from the crowd, swept across the citizens. Auggie turned to look at the four assembled executioners. "Shame on you," he said. "This is not how we do things here, *ja?*"

One by one the four dropped their stones as Auggie's voice drifted out across the crowd. "We have law and a good man, a good sheriff, like Jon Highfather! This is not justice, and this is not right. We are good people, *ja?* We are better than this, we must be, yes?"

The gunshot cracked like the hammer of God Himself. The bullet caught Auggie in the chest and he stumbled against the other pole on the platform. Screams and shouts came up from the crowd. Gillian gasped, horrified, and began to run to her husband. Auggie looked out and caught her eye as she cleared the crowd. He smiled at her, tried to speak, but couldn't. His eyes fluttered and he fell onto the platform.

"No," Ray Zeal said, his pistol still smoking. "You're not, and this is the price you pay for mercy."

Memory is a powerful thing, memories of free candy given to children, to jokes told on the front porch of Shultz's General Store, memories of sick children given medicine when neither parent nor Auggie could afford it. A lifetime of small, decent, good deeds: the sum total of a man's life.

"That sumbitch done went and shot Mr. Shultz!" a man in the crowd called out.

"Who the hell does that bastard Zeal think he is!" Another shout from the masses.

"No one does that to Auggie!" another angry voice called out. "Let's tar and feather these dirty dogs and run them out of town!"

The crowd surged, an angry living thing. Gunshots began to ring out as Praetorians fired on the citizens who were pulling them off their horses. Shouts of the wounded and the unarmed dying were everywhere as the soldiers began to methodically pick off the locals. Those locals with irons on their hips fired back and Main Street became a battlefield .

Bick shrugged and the ropes broke around him, not that anyone noticed. He knelt by Auggie's still form. His eyes burned accusingly into Zeal's red, furious face. Gillian reached the platform. Bick put a hand on the shopkeeper's bloody chest. "Bless you and keep you, Augustus Shultz," Bick said. Gillian knelt by her husband, cradling him in her arms, and stroked his face. The tears fell in hot, heavy drops on Auggie's placid face. Bick looked for Zeal, but he was already gone.

Highfather lashed out, his hands now free at the height of the distraction. He drove a powerful uppercut to Snake-Man's chin, while Jim turned and shot two rounds, point-blank, from his pistol into a Praetorian's belly. Jim handed Highfather a pistol and the sheriff fired and dropped two of the startled Praetorians beside them, while bullets splintered the wooden posts next to Highfather's head. Snake-Man lunged at Highfather and Jon fired again but the Indian seemed to be made of smoke and lightning, and Highfather's bullet missed him as the medicine man swung himself around the opposite side of the awning posts on the saloon's porch. Snake-Man flashed down with one of his hooked finger blades to rip into Highfather's vulnerable throat. Something struck Snake-Man at the waist and tumbled the medicine man onto the dirt of Main Street. Mutt stood, his blood knife in his fist, only a few feet away from Snake-Man.

"Oh, thank God," Highfather said, nodding to Mutt. "It's the sheriff."

Snake-Man slowly got up, a smile spreading across his face. Mutt grinned, all yellowed snag and sharp, straight fang.

"Don't know what you're grinning about, lick-finger," Mutt said. "I kicked your ass in your daddy's hidey-hole. Now I'm going to kick your ass up here on my turf."

"Nuga Togu," Snake-Man said, and it began.

Both men were blurs, moving faster than the human eye could track, a storm of violence with lightning flashes from hooks and knives, sparks erupting: jumping, ducking, spinning, turning, driving fists into each other when their weapons could touch only blurring air. Coyote and Snake warred in the dirt of Main Street, their blood burning in their sons' veins.

Highfather and Jim dropped the other soldiers near the platform, grabbed their rifles and moved out. The sheriff and deputy paused, then fired back to back, clearing the street around them. Jon saw Bick run down off the platform and disappear inside the Paradise Falls.

"I was worried about you, boy," Highfather shouted over the din as he squeezed off a round from a Winchester rifle, dropping another Praetorian on horseback who had been threatening some civilians, south on Main. "Glad you made it home."

"Me, too, sir," Jim said. "Sorry I'm late." Highfather laughed.

"We'll discuss job attendance after we win the war," Highfather said. "By the way, where is Constance, before Maude skins you alive?"

"She's safe," Jim said. "Safe" was the easiest way to explain right now. Easier than telling the sheriff that a fourteen-year-old girl who could whoop a bear in a fair fight was off alone in the desert, avoiding Zeal's patrols, riding like a she-demon for Virginia City and help. "We're still seeing the Elephant here," High-father shouted. He dropped the empty rifle and blasted a Praetorian sniper off a rooftop with his six-gun as the sniper's bullet tossed up the dirt near him. "A lot of folks are going to get themselves killed, unless we get them organized." Jim suddenly saw a crew of Praetorians rolling out the Gatling gun, off at about seven o'clock from his and Highfather's position, and preparing to open fire on a wide swath of the rioting crowd that was being led into battle by Gordy Duell, the hotel dick.

"Aww, dammit!" Jim said, and ran straight toward the cluster of soldiers starting to crank up the gun. He fired Pa's pistol and whooped like a rebel, like his pa had taught him to. Three of the crew fell, dead or wounded. The other men took bead on him, dead bang, when hatchets with green ribbons attached to them materialized into the soldiers' backs and necks, dropping them where they stood.

Ch'eng Huang's Green Ribbon soldiers joined the fray, striking quickly and silently against the Praetorians from the shadows and the fringes of the crowd, where they had been waiting for the right time to strike. Jim reached the Gatling gun and Highfather fought his way over to him.

"That was the stupidest thing I ever saw," Highfather said, slapping the grinning boy on the back. "Good job. Let's get this thing spinning and pointed at the right folks."

The gun clattered like a telegraph, blasting holes in the Praetorians' crumbling lines. Highfather jumped on a riderless horse and galloped to the north end of Main, killing Zeal's men as he rode. He found a cluster of armed citizens, led by Alton Sprang, owner of Sprang's Rooms for Rent, pinned down and being squeezed by organized Praetorian fire. Highfather barked orders to the men while angry slivers of lead whined inches from him and his horse.

"You fellas, focus on that group over there behind the water troughs," Highfather shouted. He cocked and fired another rifle he had acquired from a dead Praetorian. "And you all start picking off that mounted group that keeps riding by, once their cover fire is jammed up. Focus, now breathe, and make each shot count. It's like shooting a fence post."

Even as Highfather began to secure North Main, Jim found that Zeal's troops on South Main were beginning to rally. The street was littered with bodies, but most of the noncombatants were in hiding now. The Praetorian commanders began to direct fire and whittle away at the armed citizens and Chinese hatchet men. Slowly, the momentum of the mob began to turn as the trained and well-armed soldiers cut down the rebelling townsfolk.

That was when the ropes dropped out of the sky, behind the Praetorian lines, and the pirates began sliding down them, firing and screaming as they came, many with burning fuses in their long, wild beards. They dropped from baskets beneath gray spherical orbs that hung silently in the cold, bright sky, approximately a dozen of the bizarre craft, each with a four-man crew. Some of the pirates dropped small black powder grenades into the ranks of the mercenaries from above. Explosions ripped through the Praetorian lines from the small bombs.

"And that," Highfather said, riding up, "should be Black Rowan's contribution to the shindig—some of her Barbary Coast associates. She promised me some backup and she was good to her word. I like that in a criminal mastermind."

"What are those things they're dropping from?" Jim asked.

"Hot-air balloons left over from the war," Highfather said. "Both sides used them for reconnaissance. Rowan collected a bunch of them and their pilots after the Union canceled the program. She calls them her Aerial Algerines."

"Well," Jim said as he reloaded, "don't that just beat the Dutch. They're a sight keener than cowboys, for sure."

"I'll pretend you didn't say that," Highfather said, turning his mount to dive back into the battle while Jim spun up the barking Gatling gun again.

The pirates' pistols boomed as they took the Praetorian emplacements completely by surprise, and as they hit the ground cutlasses, daggers and knives were drawn and the screaming, howling, tattooed, half-naked men cut a bloody swath through the confused and demoralized clusters of mercenaries they attacked. The Green Ribbon Tong warriors took advantage of the confusion caused by Black Rowan's pirates to strike quickly and silently as well. The bizarre assortment of troops led by Highfather and supported by Jim's withering Gatling gun fire slowly began to turn the tides of the war along Main Street in the favor of the Golgotha forces.

Inside the Paradise Falls, Maude and Emily drifted silently through the kitchen door, entering as soon as Zeal started making his initial address to the crowds. The small cluster of guards milling at the kitchen entrance never saw Maude coming, and Emily was amazed at the speed, silence and grace with which this masked woman laid low three trained soldiers.

"How, how did you do that?" the girl asked as Maude disarmed the unconscious men and tossed their weapons away.

"More practice than I care to recall," Maude said. There was a crack of distant gunfire repeated and then another series of discharges.

"The signal," Emily said. "They got the hostages free!"

"Okay, Emily," Maude said, "only move when I move and step exactly where I've stepped, yes?" Emily nodded and the two began to slowly move across the main floor of the saloon. Everyone was outside, listening to Zeal. Maude thought she heard Auggie Shultz's voice calling out to the crowd. They reached the second floor as a lone shot boomed out and Maude heard the crowd erupt in anger. A horrible image filled her imagination: Gillian weeping over a wounded or dead Auggie. *No. No, damn you, Zeal. If he brought that down on such good souls . . .*

But for now she had to stick to the plan: get Emily to the office and . . .

Batra stepped out of an impossibly small shadow to her left and blocked the hallway to Bick's office. He snapped a knuckle blow at Maude's throat, designed to crush her windpipe and kill her. Maude caught his hand and jammed a nail into his ulnar artery. He twisted and turned to get free, and as he did, Maude side-kicked him over the railing. As he plummeted toward the floor below, he caught the railing and swung back onto it, balancing on the thin plane.

"Emily! Get what you need in the office," Maude said.

She jumped after Batra onto the rail and tumbled, hands over feet, toward the assassin.

————

Mutt and Snake-Man grappled both bloody, cut and battered, raging like angry ghosts, like hot desert winds, instead of men. Mutt's blood knife tore halfway through a hitching post and stuck there, vibrating. He let go of the knife, as Snake-Man ripped an ugly gash in Mutt's stomach with one of his hook blades and followed through with a dizzying punch to the side of Mutt's head. Mutt staggered and Snake-Man pressed his advantage, trying to grab Mutt's hair and open the lawman's throat, but as he moved in for the kill, Mutt rallied and drove the heel of his palm into Snake-Man's chin, while the shaman swept his leg to knock Mutt over, but Mutt jumped clear and followed up by driving his fist into Snake-Man's face. The medicine man bellowed in pain and stumbled backward. Mutt shoved and tripped him and then dropped on top of the stunned medicine man, pinning his arms under his knees. Mutt punched him again and again, blood spraying from his face. "Give," Mutt said. Snake-Man began to open his mouth to speak. Mutt drove a fist squarely into Snake-Man's nose and the medicine man was still.

"Good choice," Mutt said, slumping.

Jagged tongues of blue-white lightning streamed down Main Street, destroying buildings, starting fires and killing and scattering troops on both sides of the conflict. Soldiers and civilians, Praetorians, tongs and pirates all were burned and killed by the electrical blasts. Several of the hot air balloons were struck and exploded, tumbling to the ground like burning party streamers.

Professor Zenith laughed as he adjusted the dials and knobs on his galvanic emitter and loosed more sky fire on hapless forces along and above Main Street. The Professor's weapon looked like a massive cylindrical rifle with a tuning fork instead of a barrel. A mass of sparking, knotted wires and cables ran from the back of the emitter to the helpless organic voltic piles that writhed mindlessly in pain in the back of his wagon. Zenith pulled the trigger and called down another electrical strike on the rabble. He was like unto a god, now, and he would wipe the street and the sky clean of the insects who dared to defy his patron, Raziel.

There was an odd rumble and a strange hum from some distance. The lightning seemed to weaken, as if its power was being diverted, drained away.

A few hundred feet farther down the northern side of Main Street, Clay Turlough's small cart had come to rest. Clay patted the horse that had drawn his wagon gently on the rump and the horse trotted away, free. Clay's wagon was covered in odd apparatus, much like Professor Zenith's, and it seemed to be drawing all the destructive electricity the professor was trying to hurl about, down into some kind of multitiered tower of steel and wires, much like a lightning rod, built into Clay's machine.

"What!" Zenith shouted, "Preposterous! How dare you trifle with the progress of science, sir!"

"How dare you pretend to call that science, sir!" Clay shouted back. "You pervert the very quintessence of science to simply slake your own bloodlust. You are no man of knowledge. I know the most probable source of your voltic batteries as well, sir and you are a madman and a blackguard!"

"You feeble bumpkin," Zenith hissed. "Your ionic grounding system couldn't stand up to a strong wind, let alone the unleashed fury of the subtle fluid!"

"Oh, and by the looks of your discharge leakage, your calculations are at fault as well," Clay called as he pulled down a heavy pair of smoked work goggles over his eyes. "Have at you, sir, may the better design win!"

"En garde!" Zenith shouted, and twisted the knob on his machine to above the safe power threshold, hurling a tunnel of lightning at Clay and his machine. Clay "parried" the blast by modulating and dispersing the harmful energy. What little of Clay's hair remained stood on end from the discharge.

He redirected part of the electricity and turned it back on Zenith, who "caught" much of it with the focusing fork on his device. The professor's wild mane of hair singed and smoked from the portion of Clay's assault that got through.

The electrical duel raged on. The sky swirled with dark clouds and alien energies while the other forces fighting along the streets recovered from the electrical barrages and began to battle once again.

Maude and Batra danced along the railing of the second floor of the saloon, trading kicks and strikes, blocking, jumping and tumbling on the four-inch wooden handrail, defying gravity with each impossible act.

"Your training is excellent," Batra said. "It is a pity you are a woman. I would enjoy facing a man as skilled as you."

"Really, now?" Maude said. "What would your Dark Mother say about that?"

Batra's cheeks darkened. "Do not mock the Dark Mother." He advanced, hurling knife strikes and sweeping kicks at Maude, angrily.

"Anger is your enemy," she said, and spun, avoiding his punch and sweeping his leg just as he began a wide kick.

Batra plummeted and smashed into the faro table. He recovered quickly and tumbled off it. He hurled a throwing iron at Maude and it struck her squarely in the chest as she flipped down onto the table. The force of it knocked her to the floor, but she backflipped and came up on her feet, hurling the odd branching weapon back at Batra. He dived toward the kitchen entrance, dodging the iron as it imbedded itself into the wall. Maude rubbed her bruised and cut chest, coughed up a little blood, raised her kerchief to spit it out and then followed the Thuggee into the Paradise Falls kitchen.

Batra had vanished. As Maude moved carefully between the wooden counters and cabinets, she took a deep breath, adjusted her perceptions and blood, and listened. He was to her left; his breathing was still, almost non-existent, but his slowed heart still thudded. She moved closer, giving him an opening to take, but he didn't.

Her hands dropped to a butcher's blade on the stained wooden table to her right. She took a step, another. Her timing would have to be perfect or he would kill her this time, but to get her shot she had to get closer, closer. Batra's muted heartbeat fluttered just a tiny bit and that was all the warning Maude needed. She hurled the knife from the table into the shadow with one fluid motion. Batra materialized, as if the darkness had vomited him forth, kukri at the ready. The blade thudded deep in his shoulder, blood blossoming from his tunic. He stepped toward her, staggered and then took another step. He blinked and then dropped to his knees only a few feet from her. He looked up at Maude with dimming eyes and muttered.

"Poison?" he said. "How did you?" He looked at his wrist where her nail had torn his flesh. "Very good."

"Better than you," Maude said.

"My apology," Batra said, his words slurring. "May Kali allow us to fight again in Hell. It would be a pleasure."

Batra fell to the floor, unmoving. His chest began to rise and fall, deeply, as the narcotic wrapped itself tightly about his blood.

"Not that kind of poison," Maude said. "You don't get to die a martyr. You get to live in disgrace." She remembered something from the fever dream when she had fallen into the well and she thought that, for a moment at least, she knew what the voice had meant about the warrior's peace.

Emily hurried to the door of her father's office and opened it. She could hear the screams and shooting going on outside through the open balcony doors. She stepped behind her father's desk and opened the top drawer. She took out the item her father had told her about and clutched it like a drowning man grabbing at a rope. She hurried out into the hallway and down the stairs. Emily stopped when she found herself face-to-face with Zeal himself, advancing up the stairs.

"Well, well," Zeal said, smiling at her. "Look what sneaked in the kitchen door while I was on the front porch. Hello, Emily. I've been looking all over for you."

Professor Zenith snarled in frustration. This hick was thwarting his every action. His organic voltic piles had mercifully, for them anyway, perished in the exchanges of energies. He was forced to rely on his backup etheric condenser to power his weapon. Suddenly the professor noticed a stabilizing of the magnetic field in regards to the orgone flow and he saw his opportunity to fry the fool's machinery and then get back to killing the other simpletons of this town.

He began to slowly increase the degree of electrical fluid through the regulator panel on the back of the cart when he felt a tap on his shoulder. It was Clay, holding a large wrench.

"You ever hear of Occam's Razor, jackass?" Clay swung the wrench with both hands and landed it successfully alongside the good professor's skull. Zenith dropped to the ground and lay still.

Clay hopped up on the cart. "I swear," he muttered to himself as he shut down Zenith's contraption, "anyone with a little copper tubing and a dynamo thinks they're a scientist these days."

The Chariot

Emily raised the white feather she clutched in her hand. "Stop," she said. "Don't move."

Zeal didn't. The smile left his face. "Now where did you get that?" he said, frozen almost like a statue.

"My father got it from the sheriff," she said. "It was from your son, Vellas. It's like the one my father gave me. It lets me command you. It can let me kill you."

"Yes," Zeal said. "It can. It is our highest expression of trust, to give a part of ourselves to another. To give them power over us. The question is, Emily, do you have it in you to kill me?"

"I . . . I don't want to," Emily said. "I don't want to kill anyone."

"Well then," Zeal said, smiling again. "That is a shame."

Charles Cook shot Emily in the back with his derringer from the top of the stairs. The girl fell forward, tumbling down the stairs, a dark flower spreading across her back. The feather, now flecked with her blood, floated down to the ground floor. It fell at Malachi Bick's feet.

"Children," Zeal said, laughing. "Gone so soon, eh, Biqa?"

"Enough," Bick said.

The Paradise Falls buckled and exploded as if a bomb had gone off within it. Every window shattered, the wall of the saloon splintered as if struck by a tornado. The carbonized remains of Charles Cook, the wealthiest man in California, floated down as hot, black ash across collapsing three-story ruins. No piece of furniture, no stick of wood, was spared being shattered to near-dust by the force that men called Malachi Bick. The form of Emily Bright lay amid the debris, untouched by the destruction. No living thing, save Cook and his master, were harmed by the town-shaking blast.

Raziel, stunned and battered by the full force of the destruction, smashed into the Dove's Roost, over a hundred yards away. Zeal crashed through the front wall of the empty house of ill repute and came to rest in the demolished parlor. He struggled to stand, the whole house creaking and groaning, threatening to collapse.

Zeal rubbed his head and turned. Biqa was there, upon him before he could even fully comprehend what had happened, looping space-time to punch Zeal a million infinites in the space of a nanosecond, converting the mass of his hand to nearly light-speed while containing, shunting, the force of each blow, to channel all the destructive force to Raziel alone, sparing the planet's atmosphere from being torn away by the energy of each punch. The Dove's Roost began to rain down around the two, but Biqa didn't care. Raziel was his universe now. Raziel crashed through one side of Scutty's boardinghouse and out the other. The building exploded, nearly atomized, from the structural damage of being hit by something roughly approximating the planet's mass. Again, Biqa calmed the angry forces of nature and minimized the destruction, while giving Zeal a taste of as much of it as the world of man could stand.

Fortunately, almost the whole town was occupied with the battle raging over on Main, so the buildings and sidewalks on Bick Street were mercifully empty.

Raziel smashed through the wall of the *Golgotha Scribe*'s office and into the newspaper's huge iron and steel printing press, converting a great deal of its dense mass into glowing molten slag. Raziel's countenance now resembled Biqa's own, torn, swollen, bruised and bleeding. The fair angel's blood hissed as it spattered on the glowing press. Raziel hefted the press with one hand and batted Biqa with it as the snarling angel launched himself at Raziel again, churning dark, primal energy in his wake like spectral wings of diluted ink. The force of the blow, as Raziel converted all the mass into pure energy, floored Biqa, especially since he had to redirect a good amount of the energy into his own personal space-time to avoid the blow shattering the planet like an egg being struck by a sledgehammer. The remainder of the newspaper building vaporized into a brilliant cascade of photons about the two of them.

Biqa, gasping and smoking, shook the charred debris off him as he lay on his hands and knees, still reeling, fighting to rise. Raziel, panting, bleeding, stayed on his feet and drew his cavalry saber. Biqa saw the blade for what it truly was— pure, divine fire from the forge of creation itself.

"'Member this little pig-sticker, Biqa?" Raziel said, staggering forward. "The old Heavenly Toothpick . . . ? 'Member wha' it can do, even to our kind? I shed a lot of angelic blood with this during the rebellion. Good times, good times. You don't have one anymore do you, Biqa? That is a pity."

Biqa struggled to his feet. He began to stagger out of the wreckage, running as best he could. The mortal form of Malachi Bick shuddered back into place as he stumbled across Prosperity Road, looking back at Raziel in all his angelic fury, flaming sword in hand. The mad angel strode after him slowly, confidently, his injuries masked by his unearthly light.

"Aw, don't run, Biqa," Raziel called out. "Have at least a little dignity. You acted like one of the Host there for a second. If you hadn't been so worried about breaking this little matchstick town, this ridiculous planet of His, you might have even had me."

Bick staggered farther down the other side of Prosperity. Off in the distance were the sounds of chaos: gunfire, explosions, the challenging shouts of the brave, the mad and the defiant, the sobs of the dying and those who loved the dying. War swaggered unchecked down Main Street. Bick fled into a small alley, running farther and deeper into the mazes of narrow corridors that made up this side of Bick Street.

Raziel followed him, picking up his pace, eager to taste Bick's blood. He advanced, ignoring everything save his weakened, battered prey stumbling up ahead. He found Bick standing, bloody but defiant, in a tiny courtyard, the nexus of half-dozen dark, twisting alleys.

"Time to finish it," Raziel said.

Bick said nothing, only glared at the gore-splattered golden angel.

"I'm going to flay you alive," Raziel said, "a molecule of perfect pain at a time."

Bick lowered his head. His eyes burned with cold, controlled anger, his mouth curled painfully into a wolf's tight grin. Raziel's sword guttered like a dying torch and the flame evaporated. Raziel's divine image shivered like a reflection in a shattering mirror and faded. Ray Zeal stood, holding mere mortal steel.

"What?" Zeal said.

Ch'eng Huang stood on a balcony overlooking the narrow crossroads of streets. The old man said nothing, merely nodded to Bick. "Welcome to Johnny Town," Bick said.

Bick charged Zeal, binding his sword arm to his side and driving a knee to Zeal's groin as he drove a thumb into the bewildered angel's eye.

The pain of the blinding forced Zeal backward, stumbling and doubled over. Bick pressed him, knocking the sword from his hand by twisting and breaking his wrist. Zeal gasped at the mortal pain flooding fully into his all-too-mortal nerves. Bick began to shuffle and snap one powerful punch after another to Zeal's stomach, then his face, then ribs. Shuffling, moving, working on Zeal like a lumberjack chopping down a massive tree.

"How does it feel to have all your power taken away?" Bick said, blood spraying from his lips with each word, each violent punch. "To have all your certainty stripped from you, and to have to fumble alone to make sense of the world? You like it, Ray? Do you?"

Bick drove an uppercut into Zeal's jaw. Blood and perfect teeth flew like confetti.

"You know what human beings know, Ray?" Bick asked as he drove a solid punch into Zeal's throat, and then followed up by grabbing the semiconscious angel by his curly blond hair and forcing Zeal down to the ground, smacking his face into the mud and muck of the street. "They find reason where they can. Even in terror and horror and death, because they have no choice in the matter. Pain is the admission price you pay for life."

Zeal was choking on his own blood, unable to breathe well due to the blow to his throat and the face full of mud. Bick held him down close to the muck of the street, occasionally smashing his head into the ground.

"And it's a fair price," Bick said. "My daughter taught me that."

Zeal was on the ground, shuddering, barely alive. Bick let Zeal go; he crawled over to the discarded sword and put it to the convulsing angel's throat, held it there for a long moment. He lowered the saber and let it drop to the dirt.

"She taught me that too," Bick said.

The Sun (Reversed)

Martin Anderton, Maude's father, rode into Golgotha with his granddaughter Constance by his side and a troop of U.S. soldiers from Camp Bidwell on Saturday morning. The federal troops helped clean up the messes, clear the debris and put out the fires. They also helped Highfather, his deputies and good number of volunteers secure the remnants of Zeal's army and cult. There was also the matter of gathering the dead and putting them to rest.

All told, the event that would go down in Golgotha history as the Ray Zeal Riot had a bloody toll. A hundred and twelve townsfolk perished, either fighting to retake their town or in the violent crossfire. Another ninety or so were reported as wounded or injured in the chaos, and the most ominous number of all were the over fifty citizens of Golgotha that simply vanished during the few days that Ray Zeal and his madmen ruled the town.

The exact casualties of Black Rowan's pirates and the Green Ribbon Tong was unknown, since these mysterious criminal fraternities recovered their own dead and kept their own councils as to their losses. Both groups were no more than whispered legend by the time the federal troops arrived.

The ladies of the Dove's Roost lost their home in what was finally described as a series of bomb blasts set off by Zeal's crew. Fortunately, the majority of the fine families of Rose Hill and the respective church denominations were happy to put the girls up, as they did the boarders and proprietors of Scutty's boardinghouse. Malachi Bick and his bank put up the money to rebuild the ruined blocks of the road that bore his family's name. There was no talk of loans, or repayment. Many suggested that after what had happened to Bick's daughter and to poor old Auggie Shultz, the infamous businessman was changed.

Black Rowan also began to channel her considerable resources into rebuilding the town as well, making sure everyone in Golgotha knew she intended to stay for a spell.

Harry Pratt stood at the window of the mayor's office, looking over the massive construction and rebuilding going on over on Main Street. It was late morning and he was waiting for his next appointment to arrive. He turned back to his desk and found Black Rowan standing there, alone.

"Rowan, this is an unexpected surprise," Harry said. "How may I be of service to you? Please understand I do have an appointment in just a few moments. I hope you understand but . . ."

Rowan smiled and waved a dismissive hand. "No, no trouble, Harry. I know you're a busy man. I just needed to speak to you about something. It won't take but a moment."

Harry gestured to a chair. Rowan sat and then he did as well. "Go on, please."

Rowan looked Harry squarely in the eye. "I know, Harry. I know about you and James Ringo. I know you two are lovers."

Harry laughed. "Really, Rowan, where did you hear such a scandalous rumor?" His guts were full of ice, and he began to taste the copper of fear in his mouth, but all of his political instincts took over.

Rowan crossed her legs and smiled. "Harry, you are an excellent liar, but I have more than accusation. I have proof. Enough proof to ensure that you lose the election next year, are banished from the church and most likely run out of Golgotha forever."

"And what do you intended to do with this so-called proof?"

"Why nothing, yet," Rowan said. "Nothing until I need to. I just want you to understand, Mayor Pratt: You work for me, now. And you and I are going to have a very long and very profitable association, which will be of mutual benefit and benefit Golgotha as well."

There was a knock at the door. Colton Higbee and Harry's eleven o'clock appointment opened the door.

"Mr. Mayor?" Higbee said, looking at Rowan as she rose from the chair.

"I was just leaving." Rowan walked to the door. "Think on it, Harry. I'm sure we'll talk again soon."

Harry nodded sternly. "Yes," he said. "We will. Count on it."

———————

Outside town hall, two men waited for Rowan. As she stepped out onto the stairs, the Scholar walked to her. "Did it go as planned, madam?"

Rowan nodded. "It did. I assume that Rony Bevalier and his son's political machine were equally amenable to our implication that we had dirt on Harry Pratt that could hand them the election?"

The Scholar nodded. "Bevalier wants to negotiate, very eagerly I might add."

"Then all our bets are covered and whoever wins the election, we win," Rowan said, walking down Main Street. Her companions followed her.

"I don't want to do this to Harry," James Ringo said, keeping up with Rowan. He grabbed her by the shoulders, stopped her and spun her to face him. "Do you hear me, Rowan? I don't want this!"

The Scholar began to reach for Ringo's hand, but Rowan dismissed him with a shake of her head. "I understand, Jimmy," she said, placing her hands on Ringo's shoulder. "But trust me, this will all work out for the best, I promise you."

"It better," Ringo said.

Rowan kissed Ringo on the cheek. "Has your big sister ever let you down before?"

"No," Ringo said sullenly. "But don't hurt him, Rowan. I swear if you hurt him . . ."

"No, trust me," Black Rowan said. "As long as we stick together, like family, Jimmy, there's no way we can lose."

Auggie awoke in his bed a few days after the riots to the stern and weary faces of Clay and Gillian looking over him. Gerta, her face still veiled, sat stiffly in her old rocking chair.

Gillian looked at Clay and then smiled. "Welcome back," she said, kissing and hugging her husband. Auggie groaned at the squeezing but also chuckled. "Sorry," Gillian said, tears welling up in her eyes.

"Aw, you ain't gonna hurt that big German moose none squeezing on him," Clay said. "You," he said, nodding to Auggie, "are a lucky man. Looks like that fat you've been haulin' about slowed the bullet down enough for me to cut it out and keep you alive. You'll be right as rain."

Auggie's throat was very dry and he coughed as he tried to speak. "You cut it out?" he said. "Where is the doctor?"

"You're looking at him," Gillian said. "After all the mess with Tumblety, the town elders decided we needed a new doctor pronto, and once they found out Clay's background they asked him to hang up a shingle."

"Dr. Turlough?" Auggie tried to laugh, but he coughed and groaned instead.

"Serves you right," Clay said. "Welcome back, Auggie. Don't try any damn fool stunts like that ever again, you hear me?"

Gillian sat on the edge of the bed, next to her husband. He took her hand and held it tightly. "Please," Gillian said. Auggie nodded, and managed to raise himself enough to kiss her. He looked over to Gerta in her chair.

"Hello, Gerta," Auggie said. "Are you all right?"

Gerta pulled back her veil. Her face was pale and perfect, her scars faded to mere shadows. "I am glad you are back, Augustus," she said, her accent an odd mixture of German and some other unknown quality. She looked at Auggie with bright eyes, but they welled with tears. "I'm glad Clay could save you."

Auggie looked into the rejuvenated face of his dead wife. He knew Gerta well enough to know, even now, in this body, that she was keeping something from him, but for right now he was happy to be alive and holding Gillian. Whatever Gerta was holding back, it could keep.

The majority of Zeal's cult was dead or in federal custody. About a dozen members of the thirty-two Teeth of Cain had managed to escape Golgotha. The prisoners, including Snake-Man, Professor Zenith and Batra, were taken away in chains with special instructions by Secret Service Agent Warne to keep them under heavy guard until they reached San Francisco by train. Zeal himself vanished and was believed to be dead, but his final fate remained a mystery.

"Well, I'd imagine that this will be a big damn feather in your cap now, won't it, Agent Warne?" Highfather said to Kate. The two of them were on horseback overseeing the federal troops loading up the prisoners onto locked wagons for the short ride to the train depot over at Hazen. "Bet they'll give you a raise and a steak diner to boot for all this."

"I'd settle for a decent bathtub and about three days of sleep," Kate said, smiling.

"I'm losing a hell of a deputy," Highfather said. "Damn good shot too. And good company to boot."

Kate looked at Highfather. He was a mess, still busted up from the torture at Zeal's hands, and exhausted, having not slept a wink since the riot a few days ago. She didn't want to look away from him, but was afraid not to. Her breath caught in her throat, but she had trained herself to hide that.

"Please stay, Kate," Highfather said. "I got nothing to offer you but more of the same. This job will kill you, or drive you crazy, but for the first time, in a long time . . ." He stopped himself and sat still.

She smiled. "When you tossed me that star, without a lick of hesitation . . . Only one other man has ever put that much faith in me, Jon. I'm riding these prisoners over to Hazen, then I got a few days in San Francisco, giving some reports no one is likely to believe, then I'm off to my new post."

Highfather set his jaw, blinked and then nodded. "Well, they are damn lucky to have you, is all I can say."

"You should know," Kate said, grinning. "It's here."

"What?" Highfather said.

Kate nodded.

"I convinced my bosses in Washington that we need someone here in Golgotha. This place is worth keeping an eye on. And I'm going to need a cover. I figure deputy will do. Unless you want that star of yours back, in which case you're going to have to wrestle me for it."

Highfather laughed. "No, thank you," he said. "You earned it." He offered her his hand in a handshake. They both held it a second too long.

"Let's get these bastards on the road, Deputy," Highfather said, pulling his hand away. Kate nodded and gestured.

"After you, Sheriff," she said.

Malachi Bick, bruised, bloody and exhausted, found Mutt on Main Street the night the U.S. troops rode in. Mutt was working with a crew of volunteers to search the debris of several burned-down buildings looking for survivors or bodies. The deputy, his face a rainbow of old and new bruises, glanced at Bick and then turned back to his work of moving aside broken wooden beams.

"What the hell you want?" Mutt said.

"I need to talk to you about the skull," Bick said.

"Talk," Mutt said. "It ain't none of your nevermind. I pulled it out of that cave so Zeal and Snake-Man couldn't git it and I don't intend to hand it over to you jist because your family owns every damn thing in sight, Bick. I don't trust you any more than I trust them with it."

Bick nodded. "You're right. . . ."

"And if we have to scrap about it . . . What?" Mutt said. "I hear you right?"

"I . . . My family was given a duty to guard these lands, to protect the terrible secrets buried here. Along the way I lost my trust in people. Started using them, like pawns. A means to an end. If anything good came out of this, it was my daughter. I need to learn to trust again. So, I'm trusting you with the skull. You kept it out of the hands of people who wanted to use its power and I'm going to trust you to keep it safe."

"Well," Mutt said, dropping the beam he had been wrestling with, and turned to face the saloon owner. "Ain't that just pretty as a picture. How goddamned magnanimous of you, Bick. You look around here. Look at all this. This is as much your doin' as it was Zeal's.

"Man like you, with all your money and power to shield, you might not know this, but us folks not quite so blessed have a little experience with this—hatred is like a shotgun. It's powerful and it rips apart everything in its path—good, bad or indifferent.

"You gave these people plenty of damn good reasons to hate you, to pull the trigger on the shotgun, and once they tend to their dying and bury their dead, they will have a few more reasons. So I'm all-overish that you decided to trust me, and I know you think you're doing good here, but from one despised son of a bitch to another, don't expect any sympathy to be coming your way. I'll keep the skull safe and I'll keep my own company on who knows about it."

Bick was silent. He and Mutt locked eyes for a long time. "See that you do, Deputy," Bick said, and walked away.

Sunday morning, two days after the riot, the survivors of Golgotha's brush with Ray Zeal's madness were mostly in their churches giving thanks for sons and daughters returned, leaders freed safely and an end to the carnage and destruction. Many mourned the passing of loved ones and friends. Songs and hymns, carried by voices raised to the clear, bright skies above, drifted across the damaged town. Songs of praise and celebration, songs of hope rising up from loss.

Jim found Constance sitting on a pile of lumber behind the ruins of the Paradise Falls. He limped over toward her, smiling.

"I heard you got back," Jim said. "Sorry I couldn't find you last night."

"Get off that leg," Constance said. She patted the plank she was sitting on. Jim joined her.

"How you feeling?" he asked. "You must be bushed after that ride?"

"I slept some," she said. "Had a bad dream, and then I didn't want to sleep anymore."

"Oh," Jim said. "One of those dreams?"

Constance nodded. She looked at the ground, and then to Jim.

"I'm sorry I lied to you when we had the picnic," she said. "You're right, it's an awful way to begin anything, and I do want to begin something with you, Jim. I didn't share with you about my mother and my training, because . . . well, because every person in my life has let me down, except my mother. My father was a selfish man; he only cared about himself and what people thought of him, of us. He tried a few times to be a good father, but he just wasn't that good a person, in general.

"My mother taught me to keep our secrets well; she said to think of the truth as a weapon that could be used to hurt us. And I know why she said that, why Gran Bonny told her that, but I don't want to keep anything between us. I like you, Jim, and I'm sorry I lied."

"It's okay." Jim put his arm around her. "Your mom is right, what you two can do, your dreams and all, it's dangerous for you. Anyway, you came clean and told me all that stuff when you were trying to keep me from dying in that tent by the side of the road. Thank you. I promise you I'll never tell a soul, ever."

"How did you know I was lying to you?" she said. "You said it right after you got stabbed."

Jim grinned. "Oh, well, y'see, my second uncle twice removed was really Blackbeard the Pirate, and he trained me in all these witchy ways, including how to tell when pretty girls are lyin' to me and how to kill folks with my earlobe. . . ."

Constance laughed and swatted him. "Stop it! How?"

"Your eyes look left for just a second when you're fibbin'," he said.

"That's a tell," Constance said. "My mother is teaching me how to not have those and how to give off false tells. How did you notice that?"

"'CauseI like paying attention to you," he said. "Every look, every little bit of you. It's all special to me."

Constance hugged him tight and he hugged her back. She pulled away and her eyes were shiny with tears.

"I have to go away, Jim, soon. Maybe today."

"What? No!" Jim said. "Why?"

"A dream," she said. "One of my dreams. I have to go. I'm sorry."

"Can . . . can I go with you?" Jim said softly, taking her hand. "'Cause I would."

Constance was crying and laughing at the same time. She pulled Jim close to her.

"I know you would," she said. "But you can't. I'll come back if I can, Jim. I promise."

Jim held her tight. "I know," he said. "And if you can't come back, I'll come find you."

Zeal awoke in darkness. He was in chains of pure silver that bound his wrists, waist and ankles. A silver collar ringed his neck and was attached to the other manacles. Malachi Bick stood before him, Zeal's saber sheathed at Bick's belt and the blood-spattered feather in his hand.

"Get up," Bick said.

Zeal struggled to his feet.

"I knew you wouldn't have the sand to kill me, Biqa. . . ."

"Shut up," Bick said, and Zeal did. "I didn't kill you, and I don't intend to. However, I can't let someone like you roam free across the Earth, can I? So that limits my options, doesn't it? You can speak."

Zeal growled but didn't try to move. "You are a fool, Biqa. There is no prison on this little shithole of a world that can hold me for long and when I do get free, I will make you and this miserable little town of yours pay for the indignity you've done to me. I serve our Lord, and I do His work. You are a rebel and a criminal to keep me from it."

Bick shrugged. "This place is below Golgotha. It's very old. There are several access points to reach this chamber, not the least of which is the old sacrificial well in town. It is an entranceway into another's realm. I allowed him to create it a long time ago when he didn't have many friends. Everyone lines up against a loser, Ray, you know that, don't you? ."

Behind Zeal the room began to brighten with light akin to a huge hearth, or perhaps a forge. He turned slowly to regard two massive bronze gates, which were swinging open. A light more bright and terrible than a million suns poured forth and a lone silhouette crossed the threshold of the gates into the cave.

"Hail Biqa!" the figure bathed in light called, raising a perfect hand.

"Lucifer." Bick nodded. "Raziel—Lucifer, Lucifer—Raziel. I think everyone knows each other."

"No," Zeal said. "No, you can't do this! You wouldn't dare!"

"Ah, yes, I remember him—Keeper of Secrets," Lucifer said, ignoring Zeal's outburst. "Yet seemed to really enjoy flapping his pie hole. Charmed."

"You can do nothing to me, Morning Star," Zeal said. "I am of the divine Host! You have no dominion over me!"

"Touchy thing, isn't he?" Lucifer said. "It appears we've lost one, Biqa." Lucifer pointed to the disturbed spell marks on the scuffed dusty floor. "I told you it would be better to just let me take them back with me."

"I'll attend to our lost charge," Bick said. He turned to regard Zeal. "As for this one, take him with you."

"You overstep, Biqa!" Raziel shouted. "I serve the Lord, God, Almighty. He will never allow this!"

Biqa looked Zeal hard in the eyes. "Then He'll stop me from doing this, won't He?"

Bick handed the blood-flecked feather to Lucifer, who took it with a smile.

"Come on, fresh meat," Lucifer said. "You have a lot of folks waiting to say hello to a pretty fellow like you. Follow me."

Zeal gave Bick a final look of horror and pleading, then began to follow the Devil back behind the burnished gates.

"Lucifer," Bick called. The Devil turned back. "Be as easy with him as you are capable. He is sick in his thoughts. One day I may ask for that feather back."

"Oh, Biqa." Lucifer sighed. "You still refuse to see, to call a thing what it truly is, to give me my due. Very well, I'll keep him safe and snug for you and very, very warm."

The two figures crossed the threshold and were swallowed in the endless light, the unfathomable heat. The bronze gates crashed closed and the cave was silent, cool and dark again. Bick stood alone. His hand rested on the hilt of Raziel's cold blade for a very long time.

The stage rolled into Golgotha, the first through after Ray Zeal's blockade had been lifted. One of the first off, helped down by Pony Bob Haslam, was a young raven-haired beauty with a stunning face and flawless body. She had a single large carpetbag with her and she was dressed in a beautiful dress of dark purple taffeta and black lace. She wore gloves and a bonnet, with a lace veil covering her face.

The lady had gotten on the coach at nearby Virginia City and told her fellow stagecoach passengers that she intended to begin a new life in Golgotha.

"I used to be a seamstress when I was a young girl," the woman said. "Before I got marr—I mean before I came to America." Her voice held a slight German accent, mixed with something else, something unknowable. "I hope to begin a business here in Golgotha. I want a new life."

Clay Turlough was waiting for the woman at the station on Main. He waved when he saw her disembark and smiled—a very uncharacteristic expression for Clay. He took the young woman's bag and they began to head south down Main, toward the new construction and the repair projects in the wake of the riot. Neither of them noticed Miles Press, watching them as they walked by him on his bench, whittling.

"How was your trip?" Clay asked.

"Dreadful, but short," she replied. "It was much nicer when you drove me over on the wagon in the night, Clayton."

"I know," Clay said, "but we must maintain the illusion. You want a fresh start, Gerta, you will need all the cover you can get."

"Not Gerta," she said. "Not anymore. According to these documents you secured for me, my name is now"—she examined the papers she had folded in her small purse—"'Shelly Wollstone' . . . Why do I think this is some kind of joke you are playing on me, Clayton?"

"It is a perfectly beautiful name," Clay said. "Besides, you'll always be my Gertie."

Her hand reached for his and Clay took it. "I found you some lodgings. I hope they will suit you, and then I hoped we might have dinner?" Clay said. "I just recently found out they have places you can go out and eat dinner."

"I would like that very much," Shelly said.

The wasteland was cold, the sky achingly crystalline blue and clear, as Mutt rode out to meet the Black Feathers. Wodziwob, Mahkah and several of the men who had first ridden into Golgotha to fetch Mutt were waiting on horseback, their mounts' foggy breaths swirling at the horses' nostrils.

"You turned Snake-Man over to the army," Mahkah said, matter-of-factly. "You know they will eventually shoot him."

Mutt shrugged. His face was a mask of bruises, cuts and the wicked crescent scar of Snake-Man's fang. "Let them waste the bullet, not me. 'Sides, that slippery nob will most likely wiggle loose. If I could, he will."

"He'll come for you, if he does manage to escape," Mahkah said.

"Let him," Mutt said. "I beat him twice. He looking for more of the same, he knows where to find me."

"You did not bring the Manitou Skull," Wodziwob said.

Mutt grinned. It looked painful.

"It's safe and sound, along with all the teeth from it we could gather back up. It's locked away and it won't do anyone any more harm."

"Back in the cave?" Wodziwob said, and Mutt shook his head.

"Nope," Mutt said. "But rest assured, it won't be troubling anyone."

Harry had agreed to hide the skull in the same place he had kept it during the crisis. Where that was, exactly, Mutt didn't know, and he didn't want to. He knew Harry had kept it safe and he figured the fewer people who knew exactly where it was, the better.

"Why didn't you bring it to me for safekeeping, as I asked you to?" Wodziwob asked.

"Because you want to use it against the white men, to wipe them out, and I can't cotton to helping with that," Mutt said. "You want to kill people, do it the old-fashioned way. Get your own damn hands dirty."

"You speak with too much disrespect to the healer!" Mahkah said, his voice rising with anger.

Wodziwob raised a hand to silence his defender and Mahkah relented.

"You are correct, Mutt," Wodziwob said. "I did consider using it to wipe the white men from our lands. Tell me, what is to keep me from sending others to fetch the skull?"

"Me," Mutt said. "Anyone—white, red, yellow—don't make no nevermind, they'll have to get through me and my friends."

Wodziwob nodded and smiled. "Very well," he said. "You are the guardian of the Manitou Skull now, Mutt, and I will trust you to its protection and to the world's protection from its terrible medicine."

"How come I get the feeling that don't disappoint you all that much?" Mutt said.

The old man laughed.

"And as for speaking to me with disrespect," Wodziwob said, "we of this council must speak plainly to one another if we are to strive for and protect the truth, as we protect these lands."

Wodziwob reached out to Mutt. He held a straight, perfect black feather in his hand. He offered it to Mutt. The battered deputy looked at it for a long time and then to the face of the old healer. He reached out with his cut and bloodied hand and took it.

"I ain't never been much of one to join anything," Mutt said. "I tend to piss people off."

"Yes." Wodziwob nodded sagely. "You certainly do."

Mutt laughed.

"But," Wodziwob continued, "you are exactly the kind of man we need in the days to come, Mutt. We shall continue to dance the circle dances. The dead will rise and call for the blood of the white man, and the white man's army will thunder across this land. War is coming, Mutt. A war of spirits and faiths. The Ghost Dance heralds it, and in the days ahead we will need a man of both worlds, red and white, and of neither, to see us through. So, welcome to the Black Feathers, Mutt, and please . . . keep 'pissing me off.'"

Mutt looked at the feather in his hand. "I'm pretty sure I can guarantee that, sir."

During the hours and days following the riot, Highfather and his people searched the town to recapture the criminals freed from the Golgotha jail during Zeal's occupation. While most were found, one never was. When Highfather and Mutt kicked in the door to Francis Tumblety's small cottage, they discovered the good doctor's final farewell to Golgotha.

The girl hadn't been a prostitute. Her name had been Rosemary Hurst, and she had been a match girl at Bick's saloon, the Paradise Falls. Tumblety had taken his time with her and the entire bedroom of his small, filthy house was a moat of blood, clumps of flesh, organs and entrails. The poor girl was barely recognizable as human anymore. Her perfect young heart lay on a silver tray, next to the bed.

"If it takes me the rest of my life I will find him," Highfather muttered. "How can a human being do this to another human being?"

"Practice, Jonathan," Mutt said. "Lots and lots of practice."

On the platter next to Rosemary's heart was a roll of parchment with a final farewell, written in the girl's cooling blood, in Tumblety's terse, formal cursive:

Dear Boss,

I want to thank you for welcoming me into your charming little town; it made me feel right at home. The stars have spoken and the numbers totaled and I have collected my five and now I must be away. There is so much work to do in this world, so many roses to pluck and prune, and my knife's so nice and sharp.

I doubt we shall meet again, but rest assured I am with you. Rest well, knowing the screams I cause will echo in eternity, my monument to the human heart.

Yours Truly,

The note was unsigned. Highfather looked around the little cottage and felt all the heat drain from the room. He felt as if a door had opened, carrying a slaughterhouse draft with it, as if a million mutilated souls, terrified, stalked, helpless, tortured and abandoned, were standing around him, mute witnesses on the shore of an age of madness, inhumanity and death.

"We put this poor girl to rest," Highfather said to Mutt, his voice cracking. "We comfort her kin. We find every scrap of evidence we can here and then we burn this evil place to the ground."

Maude came to Mutt only a few days after the riot. He was alone in the jail, looking through the lists of the missing and the dead that had been hastily compiled, reading the papers by lamplight. He stood when he heard the iron door creak and smiled at her with his already healing face.

"What are you doing about at this hour?" he said. "Laundry's been closed for a spell?" He paused when he saw the look on her face. Maude's face was bruised as well, from her battles with Batra, but there was something wrong, a deeper mark than bruises could make. "What is it?"

"Constance is gone," Maude said, and her voice quavered. "My father took her back to South Carolina with him."

"Well, let me grab Muha and we'll git saddled up and go after them," Mutt said. Moving to grab his gun belt, he headed to the door. Maude put a gentle hand on his chest and stilled him.

"No," she said. "We can't. It's not that easy."

"Why?" Mutt said.

"We fought yesterday, at great length for many hours," Maude said, her voice hardened, formalized with icy anger. "I made it abundantly clear to him that we had no intention of going back east. He accused me of parroting the cause of the suffragette, like my mother had—all her feather-brained causes—fighting for people's rights! He was more than eager to explain to me exactly how much my mother's 'little hobbies' had cost him, in peace and quiet and in business."

"Okay, so tell me what your father did exactly." Mutt took Maude's hand from his chest and placed it in his own. "Whatever happened, we can set it right."

"He took her while I was working today, under the pretense of spending the day with her prior to his departure tomorrow. He's taking her home and he said in his letter he intends to petition the South Carolina courts to make him Constance's ward due to my lack of fitness to serve as her mother."

"He can't do that!" Mutt said. "That's the biggest load of horseshit I've ever heard! You've risked your life for that girl; you break your back to make a good life for her out here!"

"He says that if the recent violence here won't convince me this is no place to raise a child, then nothing will," Maude said. "Mutt, my father is a wealthy, powerful man. He already has control of my inheritance because I'm a woman, and now he wants to control Constance too."

"I can't believe she went along with this without a fight," Mutt said.

Maude nodded.

"I know. All I can assume is that he is lying to her, or influencing her in some way."

"Maude, this is kidnapping and I can ride all the way to damn South Carolina and get her back. I'll talk to Jon and . . ."

"No," Maude said. "You won't. You think the courts there give any more of a damn about what a woman and an Indian think is right or wrong than the courts here do? And I will not steal my own daughter away in the night like some thief. No, Mutt. I'm going home, back to Charleston, and I'm going to get my daughter back and my inheritance back, and I'm going to make this right and make it fair."

Mutt was silent, holding her hands and looking down at them. Finally he said. "But I just got you back? I thought I lost you once and it damn near killed me. I was going to kill them for taking you, and then I was going to go die."

Maude squeezed his hand and leaned forward. Their lips touched, as gentle as a breeze on water, then deeper, stronger. His hands to her face, her hair; hers to his shoulders, his back, clinging with need and desire. Finally they pulled away, gasping, eyes damp and blinking.

"I'm leaving tomorrow," she said, and hurried to the door. "You trusted me before, trust me now. Please."

"I trust you," Mutt said. "I always have. Do what you have to do. If you need me, call and I'll come running. Go fight your mountain lion, Maude."

She opened the iron door. She started to say something.

"That thing you're about to tell me," Mutt said. "Save it till you git home."

She laughed, pushing back tears, and he summoned his best grin, but inside they were dying, slowly, quietly. They stared at each other in the shadows of the lantern. Emotion and meaning moved between them, unbound by the awkward shape of words. Finally, Maude spoke.

"Good-bye," she said.

"'Bye, Maude," Mutt said, his voice a dry small thing in his mouth. The iron door clanged shut and she was gone.

"I love you," Mutt said to the empty room.

The Hierophant (Reversed)

November gave way to December. The new year, 1871, was only a few weeks away. Auggie was soon well enough to get back to work. Gillian had fretted over him for a time but he seemed to make a full and speedy recovery from the gunshot wound, the scar fading with each passing day. Shultz's store saw a new boom in business as many folks looked on Auggie as a local hero—the man who stood up to Ray Zeal. Business was as good as it could be, given his limited funds and line of credit, but Auggie had never been happier. He felt like a young man again. He was wrestling the few meager crates of goods he had in the back storeroom when Gillian peaked her head through the door to the storefront.

"Auggie," Gillian said. "Someone is here to see you."

Malachi Bick stepped through the door into the storeroom. "I hope I'm not disturbing you, Mr. Shultz. I was wondering if I might have a moment of your time."

Auggie, red-faced and sweating, took a handkerchief and mopped his face. He shook his head. "No, no, please, Mr. Bick, come. It is fine."

Gillian looked at Auggie, for some cue that she should chase Bick off, but Auggie smiled and blew her a kiss. She closed the door behind her, leaving the two men alone.

"I'd offer you a chair if there was one," Auggie said.

"That's quite all right," Bick said. "I wanted to come by and see how you were doing. I heard you were up and around again. It seems you are quite fit."

"It appears Clay is a better doctor than he is a horse wrangler," Auggie said. Both men chuckled.

"Very similar jobs in many respects," Bick said. "I wanted to thank you for what you did for me, for the sacrifice you made, when you had no reason to."

"It was the right thing," Auggie said, and shrugged. "What else is one to do, *ja*?"

Bick smiled. "What indeed." He took some folded papers out of his coat pocket and handed them to Auggie. "I think you'll find everything is in order."

"Wh-what is this?" Auggie said, unfolding the documents and reading them.

"Your loans to me are paid in full," Bick said. "You are free and clear, Mr. Shultz."

Auggie looked at Bick and shook his head. "I . . . I don't understand?"

"It's the right thing," Bick said. "What else is one to do, yes?"

Auggie smiled and shook Bick's hand.

"Thank you, Mr. Bick," he said. "This is . . . Thank you!"

As Bick took Auggie's hand, a strange look crossed his dark features, almost a frown.

"Is something wrong, Mr. Bick?" Auggie asked.

Bick seemed to be looking him over.

"You are feeling fine, Mr. Shultz? No aftereffects from your injury?"

"*Nein,*" Auggie said, smiling. "I feel better than ever, *ja*?"

"Yes," Bick said, seeming to chase away his dark demeanor. "Well, good. I need you in good health. I'd like to offer you a job, several actually."

"Me? Work for you?" Auggie said, confused.

"Yes," Bick said. "I've decided that Golgotha isn't large enough yet to need two general stores, so I'm offering you the position of partner and manager of the mining company store I opened up on Argent, to be renamed—effective immediately—Shultz's General Store. I'll stay a silent partner, of course, in the venture, but you will own fifty-five percent of it and you can run it as you please, with no interference from me."

Auggie looked at Bick. "But why, Mr. Bick?"

"For the same reason I'm offering you an even more important job," Bick said, slapping Auggie on the back. "I need someone I can trust to oversee some of my business ventures here in Golgotha. I'd like that to be you, Mr. Shultz. I need someone who can tell me to my face when I've strayed from the path. I need a conscience, Mr. Shultz, and I'll pay you handsomely to be mine."

Auggie smiled. "That sounds like a full-time job, Mr. Bick."

The saloon owner laughed.

"Indeed," he said. "By half, I'd say. What do you say, Mr. Shultz?"

"Let me think on it, Mr. Bick," Auggie said, picking up his broom to dust the floor. "You'll have my answer by tomorrow."

"Very good," Bick said. "Tomorrow then, and thank you again for what you did for me, Mr. Shultz."

"My friends call me Auggie," he said.

"Auggie, then," Bick said.

Bick was about to open the door to the storefront when Auggie called out.

"Mr. Bick? Why me? Why put so much trust in someone you hardly even know?"

"Because, Auggie, you gave me something back I thought I had lost a long time ago. I'm in your debt. Good day, until tomorrow."

Bick shut the door behind him and walked to the front door of the store, pausing to tip his Stetson to Gillian. Clay was leaning against the counter and the two had been talking. They stopped as soon as Bick had opened the door. Bick gave them both a stern, almost judgmental look, as if he was looking through them, into them.

"Good day," Bick said, and exited the store.

Gillian turned back to Clay, speaking in a low, almost conspiratorial tone. "I'm worried, Clayton. Are you sure there are no side effects, no aftereffects?"

Clay shrugged. "You've seen him, Gillian, he's fine. The biorestorative is working. Just make sure you keep giving it to him."

"I am, I am," Gillian said. "He thinks I make the worst coffee in the world, but he drinks it and smiles, bless his sweet heart. Clay, did we do the right thing? Is this fair to him?"

"Would you rather visit his tombstone or have him beside you?" Clay asked. "We had to make a decision and make it quickly and we made the correct one, Gillian."

"It's just . . . You are sure there is nothing in that concoction connected to those evil worm-things, Clayton, you're sure?"

"Why do you keep asking?" he said.

"Because I've been having dreams, Clayton. Dreams about floating in that black goo, about those worm-things swimming around me. I can feel them brush against me, I feel them wrap around my legs and pull me under."

"That's just anxiety," Clay said. "You're worried about Auggie. He hasn't shown a single side effect, in fact . . ."

"Clayton," Gillian said, "I'm pregnant. I'm pregnant and I don't know if that happened before Auggie's . . . death, or afterward."

Little Roland Kinloch, age ten, kissed his mommy goodnight and knelt by his bed saying his prayers to Jesus, as he did every night, in his nice safe home on Rose Hill. Once he was tucked snug in his bed and mommy closed the door, Roland closed his eyes and said his real prayers. The ones the cold lady who had killed the schoolmaster had taught him, the ones to Raziel, the God of Murder and Torture and Pain. Roland rubbed the old yellow tooth between his fingers and it said the prayers with him, in his mind, like a secret song. He had taken it from the cold lady's body in the commotion after the rescue at the schoolhouse. Roland's was number eighteen.

Jim rode out to visit Sweet Molly and her sisters on a cold day in late December, when the sky was as gray as a Confederate's coat. He tethered Promise to the simple wooden fence that marked the edge of Boot Hill, the paupers' graveyard.

He walked out to her grave, which had only a simple little wooden cross, like most of the others. He knew it was Molly's grave because Jim had been the only one present when they put her in the hole. He had wished he knew some fancy preacher words to say. He didn't then, and he didn't now. It was cold now, almost all the time. Winter had found them in Golgotha. Molly's grave was bare dirt, cold, shifting in the frigid wind.

It all seemed so unfair to him. A sweet smile, a gentle disposition, and for that her last moments of life were filled with terror and pain most human beings could never even comprehend. It made no sense.

Jim's hand found the bag at his throat. He pulled the jade eye out as he sat cross-legged at the foot of Molly's grave. The sky darkened and the wind picked up. Jim relaxed, breathed, focused. He visualized Molly standing by her grave; her face was drawn, wet with eternal tears. Jim opened a door, pushed it open, and kicked it wide, like he was serving a warrant.

What he visualized on the other side of that door was Lottie, his little sister, running across a field of West Virginia wildflowers in a cold, bright spring. His mother singing on the porch on a June night ablaze with fireflies. His dad's hands, strong and warm and callused, ruffling his hair, picking him up to an endless blue sky, strong enough to hold him aloft forever.

"You go on now, Molly," Jim said quietly, the eye cold in his palm. "Go on through. Go on home now."

For a moment the wind across the graveyard of the faceless, the forgotten, was warm and sweet with the scent of spring. Jim tried to hold the memory of home as tight and long as he could. He visualized Molly taking Lottie's tiny hand, headed for home, for Ma's cooking and Pa's booming laugh.

The door closed, and winter returned with a frigid bluster. Jim sat for a spell at the foot of the grave. In time he stood and headed back to Promise, back to Golgotha.

The Bick ancestral home was a large but quaint farmhouse at the top of Methuselah Hill. It was a well-built house, but it was quite simple in comparison to the fine homes that stood at the pinnacle of Rose Hill.

Malachi Bick rode his black Arabian, Noche—of the same bloodline as his long departed Pecado—up the hill and to the house he had called home for almost ninety years. During almost all of that time, he had lived here alone.

He tethered Noche to the hitching post by the front door and then walked about to the back of the house. There he found Emily sitting in her sturdy high-backed wooden wheelchair, her easel set up. She was painting the distant rise of mountains, Argent at the immediate right on the easel, but most of the canvas was taken up by the western sky and the slowly fading sun, huge and orange, sinking behind the mountain, dabbing the sky with colors and hues that humans had no exact names for.

"It reminds me of the Fields of Radiance," Bick said. "I remember them; remember riding them when I see the sunset." He looked over to her and pulled her shawl closer around her shoulders. "It's getting cold; we should get you in soon. Feel like walking?"

"In a moment," Emily said. "Dr. Turlough came by; he gave me another of his treatments. He said I was very lucky, another inch or so and I wouldn't have the option to walk ever again.

"Mr. Turlough is quite an accomplished . . . physician," Bick said absently. "I hope he knows what he's doing."

Emily smiled at him and his dark musings scattered. "You are a worrywart," she said. "A huge, grumpy worrywart. It's most unbecoming."

"Am I? Is it?" Bick said, laughing. "Well, I will endeavor to be less so, then."

The sky was deepest indigo. Ribbons of dying umber, crimson and gold wavered at the jagged teeth of the horizon. The stars, bright and burning and ancient, unfurled before them from behind a gauze curtain of clouds.

"It looks like heaven," Emily said, "or what I imagine Heaven must look like." She looked up at Bick. "Is it?"

The man who was older than the stars above them put his hand on his daughter's shoulder and felt its warmth. Her hand came up and joined with his.

"This," Bick said, "is better."

Acknowledgments

These last few years have been the best and worst of times. There are so many people who have encouraged and helped me. This book exists because of their love, support, and presence in my life.

To Bob Flack, a brother and a great friend. To David and Susan Lystlund and Jim and Wendy Gilraine, for being there in my darkest hours and also for being there to celebrate the light. To Eric Branscom, for sage council and steady enduring friendship. To Tim Beason, for being as generous as he is handsome and hip. To master storyteller Mark Geary, for an invaluable book on 1800s firearms and for just being so damned cool. To Katherine Milliner, for steadfast friendship, love, and for always being in my corner. To Charles Hooper and his lovely and wise mother, Bonnie, for good advice, plenty of love and support, and the best soup in Roanoke. To Brandy S. Givens, for near-infinite patience in *finally* getting her acknowledgment.

To my wonderful children, Jon, Emily, and Stephanie, for being my strength and my solace.

To my amazing and ever-supportive agent, Lucienne Diver, and all of the fantastic folks at The Knight Agency, thank you for making me feel like family.

Thank you to my "League of Extraordinary Beta Readers": Sara Ruhlman, Susan Lystlund, Kim LaBrecque, Meg Hibbert, Leslie Barger, Steve Stanley, Patrick Crowley, and David Lystlund.

To Dan Smith, Meg Hibbert, Mike Allen, Paul Dellinger, and the incomparable Allen Wold, for friendship and for showing me what true writers are made of. I am in their debt for the generosity of their time and wisdom.

To my sister, Vickie, and brother-in-law, Tony Ayers, and all their children, grandchildren, and in-laws, for always believing in me.

To all of the terrific people at Tor Books whom I have had the honor to work with—my amazingly talented editor, Greg Cox, and Stacy Hill, Patty Garcia, Marco Palmieri, Diana Pho, Aisha Cloud, and Tom Doherty, for support, patience, and sympathy. Your kindness in my time of loss meant the world to me and I'll never forget that. Thank you. Thanks to Raymond, Swanland, for another breathtaking jacket, and to George Skoch, for his amazing cartographic skills that turned my little imaginary town into a real place.

To our sweet little cat, Wafflez, rest in peace. We miss you and love you.

To every person who read *The Six-Gun Tarot* and took the time to send me a comment or encouragement, I can never tell you how much your support means to me. "Thank you" doesn't begin to express my gratitude.

For every kind word, every gesture of love and friendship and advice. Everything counts, everything. Thank you all.